Echoes
of the
Falling Spring

A Novel by
Dody Myers

BURD STREET PRESS
SHIPPENSBURG, PENNSYLVANIA

This Burd Street Press publication
was printed by
Beidel Printing House, Inc.
63 West Burd Street
Shippensburg, PA 17257-0152 USA

The acid-free paper used in this book meets the guidelines for permanence and durability of the Committee on Production Guidelines for Book Longevity of the Council on Library Resources.

For a complete list of available publications
please write
Burd Street Press
Division of White Mane Publishing Company, Inc.
P.O. Box 152
Shippensburg, PA 17257-0152 USA

Library of Congress Cataloging-in-Publication Data

Myers, Dody, 1930-
    Echoes of the falling spring : a novel / by Dody Myers.
       p. cm.
    ISBN 1-57249-231-7 (alk. paper)
    1. Chambersburg (Pa.)--History--Civil War, 1861-1865--Fiction. 2. Free African Americans--Fiction. 3. Plantation owners--Fiction. 4. Women spies--Fiction. 5. Slaves--Fiction. I. Title.

PS3563.Y364 E25 2001
813'.6--dc21
                                                            00-068909

Introduction

During the bloody conflict known as the Civil War no other town north of the Mason-Dixon line suffered as much as Chambersburg, Pennsylvania. This beautiful little town, nestled in the Cumberland Valley, drew the attention of Confederate forces on three occasions. Chambersburg was targeted both as a major railroad junction and for its abundance of provisions and horses.

On October 10, 1862, the town was raided by General James Ewell Brown "Jeb" Stuart and approximately 1,800 Confederate cavalrymen. They destroyed the Cumberland Valley Railroad shops, took over a thousand horses, captured hostages, and relieved the town of much value, before returning to Virginia. Strangely enough, they completely eluded Union forces.

On June 26, 1863, thousands of Confederate troops camped east of town. General Robert E. Lee and General Ambrose Powell Hill met in the town square to discuss advancement towards either Gettysburg or Harrisburg. The decision made in Chambersburg to advance east toward Gettysburg was a prelude to the great Battle of Gettysburg five days later. This meeting is memorialized by a brass star on the street surface of the town square in front of the present Central Presbyterian Church.

On July 30, 1864, Confederate General John McCausland entered the town and issued an order demanding $100,000 in gold or $500,000 in Yankee currency, or the town would be burned. After experiencing the previous visits of Confederate forces, the town residents had removed or hidden all their valuables. As a result, the demands could not be met and the town was torched. Some 550 buildings burned, 2,000 people were left homeless, and hundreds of thousands of dollars in damage was done to personal property and real estate.

The period of time covered in this novel, as well as the towns and battles depicted, are accurate, but instances of military protocol may have been altered in the interest of developing the story line.

CHAPTER

– 1 –

The day that was to forever change the lives of Abigail and Sarah Kennedy began quietly enough. Certainly there had been no indication on this Friday morning that before the day ended there would be an invasion of their quiet Pennsylvania town, a rape, and a murder.

Impatiently, Abby glanced at rain beating against the window panes of Susan Chamber's parlor on Front Street, her mood as dreary as the weather outside. It was the second week of October, almost the end of 1862, marking the second dreadful year of the War Between the States. Only the muted chatter of a dozen women, the comforting tick of a grandfather clock, the settling of a log in the grate, and the steady rain pelting the tin roof broke the heavy silence. Chambersburg's Ladies Aid Society had been gathered since early morning to roll bandages, pick lint and make compresses for the numerous temporary hospitals that stretched from their Pennsylvania border town to the battlefield at Antietam Creek in nearby Sharpsburg, Maryland.

Abby grabbed another length of linen and listlessly began to scrape its surface to raise the nap. Picking lint was not her idea of a stimulating morning. She glanced sideways at her sister. Sarah did not seem to mind the tedium, but then she was always the calm, methodical one.

An hour later, Abby wiped her sore fingers on her apron, threw the length of linen into a nearby wicker basket and caught her sister's eye.

"That's that," she announced. "It's way past noon, and this is our day to help at the hospital."

"Oh, must we?" Sarah whispered. "I can't sleep at night after seeing all those poor boys with their terrible wounds."

1

"Of course we must!" Abby cut Sarah a reproachful look. "It bothers me too, but you know how important the work is."

With a groan, Sarah looked out the window at the pouring rain. "We'll be soaked before we reach Franklin Hall."

"It's only a block, you silly goose," Abby said with a chuckle. "Besides, the rain will feel good after spending all morning in this stuffy room." She pulled heavy cloaks from a peg by the door and handed one to her sister. "Pull your hood over your head, and run as fast as you can."

Together they scurried along Front Street, slipping and sliding on the muddy, leaf-strewn walkway as they darted toward Franklin Hall. The Hall had served as Chambersburg's entertainment center in happier days, then as a hospital when an epidemic of spotted fever swept through an encampment of over three thousand Union soldiers at the fairgrounds west of town. Now, together with King Street School and the Academy, it housed hundreds of men wounded at Antietam Creek. Abby had read in the newspapers that more than twenty-three thousand Union and Confederate soldiers had been killed or wounded in that terrible battle, lasting only one day. Even in her wildest imagination she couldn't comprehend that many men gathered in one place, let alone killed in a single day.

Abby and Sarah slipped into the side doorway and were soon working diligently among the rows of shattered, mutilated boys lying on makeshift litters. Abby thrust out her chin and compressed her lips. The Confederacy with their damnable "cause" had created all this senseless suffering.

She and Sarah toiled until dusk began to darken the tall windows. The rattle of pouring rain mixed with the groans, and occasional screams of the wounded so filled the room that Abby was unaware of the excitement outside until a cold hand touched her arm, and she looked up into the pale face of her best friend, Elizabeth Hartman.

"Have you heard, Abby?" Elizabeth asked.

"Heard? Heard what?"

"We've been invaded by the Confederates. Oh, Abby, Chambersburg's to be under martial law. Colonel McClure is negotiating the terms of surrender right now."

Abby gaped at her friend.

"Jeb Stuart, and thousands of Rebel cavalry, invaded us about four o'clock," Elizabeth continued, her voice edged with tension.

Sarah joined them, her face blanching at the news. "Has there been any shooting? With all the noise in here we didn't hear a thing."

"No. They've cut the telegraph lines, but they say they're only after horses and supplies," Elizabeth said, worrying the ribbons of her bonnet. "Daddy's in dire need of help at the inn, that's why I came looking for you. Every hotel in town is filled with soldiers."

"You want me to come . . . to serve Rebel soldiers?" Abby stammered in disbelief. "Never!"

"If you don't want to serve in the tavern you can help make up beds. They've commandeered every room in town. It's only for a few hours. Please!"

"But it'll be way past dark when we finish," Sarah moaned. "We can't travel back to our farm with Confederates camped all around us."

"It's almost dark, now," Elizabeth reminded her. "You can stay overnight in the hotel. Daddy will send our man to tell your papa." She pulled her cloak tight and began to move toward the door. "I must get back to help. Please come." She forced a tight smile. "General Stuart assured Colonel McClure that private property would not be harmed nor people molested. You'll be perfectly safe."

* * *

Abby and Sarah stood in the doorway of the Falling Spring Inn staring in disbelief. The murmur of voices rose and fell like ocean waves before an impending storm, washing the far corners of the crowded taproom packed with soldiers in butternut and Confederate gray.

"Abby," Sarah groaned. "Whatever can we do?"

Abby swallowed. Much as she hated the idea of serving Rebels she certainly couldn't trot off upstairs to make beds and leave her sister to cope with this room full of drunken soldiers. The poor girl was already trembling. "We must give Elizabeth a hand. She'll need the three of us to handle this crowd. I'll help here in the taproom."

"But we've never waited on tables before. We don't know how."

Abby felt herself responding to the challenge. This might actually be fun. She smiled and took Sarah's hand. "Come now, in all this noise and confusion I doubt anyone will notice that we don't know what we're doing."

* * *

Abby noticed him almost immediately as she scurried among the tables—the lone Confederate officer leaning against the wall and staring at her. Unlike most of the disreputable men crowding the room, this soldier was clean shaven and well groomed, whipcord-lean, with dark copper hair brushed back from a face of distinct, hard angles. His arresting green eyes traveled slowly down her body and then back up. He gave a half-smile of appreciation. She could feel the heat flaming her face; it was the most insulting and provocative look she had ever received. She raised her tray of drinks high in the air and flounced past him before he could summon her attention, knowing all the time that his eyes were on her, watching her.

The first hour flew by and Abby quickly became adept at moving around the crowded tables, her heavy trays bearing beef stew, warm biscuits, rye coffee, brandy, gin, whiskey, ale or foaming lager beer. Suddenly a hush fell over the taproom as three vagabond raiders banged through the front door and headed toward a table set against the log wall at the back of the taproom. They were quite drunk.

Tattered and grimy, the men wore uniforms of butternut homespun, their pants tucked into knee-high boots. Sabers and bowie knives hung from their hips, and gray or black slouch hats adorned with feathers and plumes covered long matted hair and tangled beards.

Their leader, Billy Baines, was a mite of a man who made up for his lack of size with a pair of Navy Colts. The Raiders were familiar with every mountain trail and wooded nook in Maryland and Northern Virginia, experts at striking, scattering and melting into the countryside, eluding vastly superior enemy forces.

The men sat down and were soon ignored. The din of voices resumed.

Every bench and table overflowed with boisterous Confederates, many singing "Dixie" at the top of their lungs. Around the room, conversation ebbed and flowed. Outside the rain poured and inside the drinks flowed. Curses and drunken laughter filled the room that reeked of unwashed bodies, sour whiskey, and stale tobacco. Every table was filled; soldiers lined the walls, milling around the bar. Baines and his companions were on their third round of drinks and growing noisier by the minute.

Abby had been serving food and drink for almost an hour, deliberately avoiding the far side of the room. Now, drawn by an unsettling attraction, she found herself approaching the copper-haired officer she had noticed earlier.

"Can I get you anything, sir?" she asked in a businesslike voice.

"Only your company."

"That's hardly possible, even if I had the time . . . or the inclination."

"Then a mug of ale will have to suffice." His voice was low, a slow, drawling sound.

"As soon as I can. It seems as though every Rebel soldier in this room wants to drown himself in liquor."

He gave her a sardonic smile. "War tends to do that to a man."

Unable to come up with a quick retort Abby cast him a baleful glance, and left him standing against the wall. She'd make sure he had to wait. She maneuvered her way toward the bar and served several other tables before returning with his drink. As he removed it from her tray she furtively inspected him. His eyes were green— not an ordinary green, but a deep turquoise, and when they fixed themselves on her she felt an odd lurch in her stomach.

"My name is Ford McKenzie," he said.

"I don't care to know your name."

"Oh! I thought we were becoming acquainted." He grinned. "I'd like to know yours."

With a nervous gesture she reached up to smooth her hair. "Ah . . . Abigail . . . Abigail Kennedy."

"Abigail. That's a pretty name. As pretty as the lady it belongs to."

A faint flush sped up Abby's neck, and she answered him with a coy smile. This man was having an effect on her she didn't care to analyze.

"Do they call you Abby?"

"Yes."

Just then a soldier staggered against her, knocking her off balance. Ford reached out to steady her and as his warm hand lingered on her arm she again felt that odd sensation in her stomach. Whatever was the matter with her? He was a Confederate officer, for heaven's sake—a hated Rebel—and here she was practically flirting with him.

Elizabeth hurried by and shot her a puzzled look.

Abby jerked her arm away. "I must get back to work," she said.

He nodded and let her go.

Thoughtfully Ford watched her as she retreated. He admired the way she carried herself—the proud tilt of her head and the wilful set of her chin. She moved among the throng of men with a poise few women possess, yet he suspected she was still in her teens. It was quite evident that she was not an ordinary barmaid, probably a local girl pressed into service to tend this unexpected assault on their small town. As she stopped at a nearby table to take an order, she turned so that she was facing him. He grinned, wondering if that move was intentional. Her yellow flowered dress spread its billowing material over voluminous petticoats, lovely on her trim figure. Gray eyes, framed by black lashes, were turbulent, obstinate, robust with life, and thick, ebony hair lay softly on her shoulders, the heat in the room causing tiny tendrils to curl around her face.

Ford stifled a smile as she made a great show of indifference to his scrutiny. He would like to know her better, but his stay here was only temporary. He would be back in Virginia tomorrow. "A shame," he murmured to himself, "she's a very intriguing young lady."

The evening had turned into a rowdy affair with much whooping, hollering, swearing, and thumping of boots on the wooden floor. Abby had just finished serving Baines' men another round of drinks when the tavern door flew open and her father shoved his way into the crowded room. His eyes, cold with fury, raked the smokey interior until he spotted her. With a sweep of his arm he motioned Abby to his side.

She hurried across the room, swallowing a lump in her throat. Something must be wrong back at the farm. Papa had apparently hurried in from the fields—his homespun work shirt and old fashioned broadfall trousers caked with mud. A vein pulsed in the temple of his broad face.

"They took our horses," he sputtered before she could speak. "Took them right out of the stable—Bay Hunter and Princess and Blaze. Said they'd make a fine seat for their officers." The veins in her father's neck stood out in vivid ridges and his face grew scarlet. "I've been searching the streets for hours. I swear I'll track those thieves down and kill every blasted one of them."

"Oh, Papa, I'm so sorry."

"Cannon fodder . . . that's what they'll become."

Abby's brow knotted with concern. Suddenly she saw him as old—old and tired and utterly defeated. This war was exacting a terrible toll on him. First her brother, Tom, had marched off to fight for the Union and now his favorite horses had been taken to serve the Confederacy. God, how she hated these Southerners; it was their fault the country was at war.

"Come, sit down," she said.

He exhaled heavily. "They gave me a worthless receipt, mind you. How in the world will we farm without horses?"

Abby looked away, shaking her head in commiseration, but a shout from the bar drew her attention to the filled trays waiting to be served. "I'll talk to you later, Papa. I must go now; Sarah and Elizabeth can't handle these tables alone."

"I plan to stay the night. I was worried about you two girls. It's not safe to travel, the roads are swarming with scavengers."

"What about Brandon?"

"Ila is with him. He's thirteen, old enough to stay at home as long as our servant is there. The damage to our farm is already done. . . .

the wretched Rebels stole everything they could lay their rotten hands on." He glanced sourly around the room. "This is no place for you and Sarah."

"Elizabeth and Mr. Hartman need our help."

"Well, I'll wait here until you are finished."

More tankards of dark ale were served to the table against the wall. Abby's father, a narrow line etched between his brows, sat quietly, his pale eyes flickering over the crowd, pausing, then settling on Baines. He cocked his head and watched him intently.

Abby and her sister shuttled between tables with confidence now.

Billy Baines watched the girls while swigging lustily at his mug. The one called Sarah captured his imagination as she moved about the tables sedately, vulnerable to the jibes of the noisy soldiers. Blond and pretty, with a heart-shaped face now flushed with color, she was rounded in all the right places, yet not heavy in arms or hips. Only her bodice showed the maturity of full breasts that made a hot wave sweep into his belly.

"Girl!" Baines yelled, waving his pewter mug in the air to attract Sarah's attention. "What must a thirsty warrior do to get another drink in this god-forsaken watering hole?"

"Shut up, Baines," one of his companions muttered, casting an embarrassed glance around the suddenly quiet room.

"Yeah, Billy. You want these Northern folks to think we Southerners are uncivilized?" the other man asked, color flushing his bearded face.

Baines banged his fist on the table with a hollow laugh. "Don't give a particular damn what the citizens of Chambersburg, Pennsylvania think of us. Long as they hand over their fat horses and keep my belly filled." He wiped spittle from his mouth with the sleeve of his filthy jacket, his gaze traveling up and down the lush figure of Sarah, as she approached with full mugs of ale. "And maybe furnish a little poo-tang for a man far from home."

When Sarah leaned over to place the drink before him he ran his hand up her arm. She jerked away so violently the ale slopped over the table and onto his lap.

"Slut! You'll pay for that," he bellowed, clutching her arm in a viselike grip.

She gave a little squeal of alarm, and in seconds Abby and her father were at her side.

"Take your hand off my daughter," Mr. Kennedy growled, his eyes blazing.

"Your daughter, huh? Pretty little thing. That other gal yours, too?"

"Indeed she is. Now . . ."

At this moment, the red-haired officer Abby had been talking with earlier strode toward the table with an air of command. "Baines, I believe you and your companions have had enough to drink tonight. It's time you leave," he ordered. There was no doubting his authority.

Baines wiped away a small mustache of ale foam with his sleeve and jumped to his feet, knocking his chair against the wall, his face flushed with indignation. One of his companions grabbed his arm. "Come, Captain Baines. You know General Lee will have your ass if he hears about any Southerner mistreating a woman."

Baines swayed on his feet and opened his mouth to protest, then snapped it shut. His gaze roamed up and down Sarah's body, coming to rest on her full bosom, lust plain on his flushed face. His companions snickered and took his arm, steering him toward the door of the hotel, and within minutes they splashed from the shelter of the tavern into the blowing rain.

Baines had set up camp along Falling Spring Creek, not more than a mile east of the center of town, and he fell onto his cot fully clothed, seething with drunken resentment and unrequited desire. The more he thought about the shapely girl the more intense his desire became. He cast a look about the darkened tent at his loudly snoring companions. He wanted the barmaid from the hotel, but any girl would do. He sat up, his blood aflame, tucked his colt.44 into his belt and crept outside. It had stopped raining and a heavy fog enveloped the camping area, swirling about the tents like clumps of wool awaiting the spinning wheel.

He followed the creek and within half an hour heard the roar of tumbling water. It was the sound of the waterfall he had heard earlier—the hotel must be close by.

He rested, breathing hard. The inn was dark except for one tiny window where a lantern flickered behind flimsy curtains billowing in the gentle breeze. Billy moved closer. The window was set into a slight protrusion from the rear wall, probably not much more than a sleeping alcove. He drew closer, chuckling with drunken delight as a shadowy figure moved to stand in front of the open window. It was the shapely girl from the tavern who had been serving him. Sarah, the one with the big tits. Luck was with him tonight.

The girl doused the lantern and moved to close the open window, then hesitated as though savoring the sharp cold air.

Billy held his breath. She lowered the window, then moved away. Quiet descended and Billy sank to the ground to wait.

He gave her half an hour to get to sleep, then crept to the window, worked it open slowly, and pulled aside the fluttering curtain. Moonlight illuminated the sleeping girl, her full figure outlined beneath a thin sheet.

Hot blood rushed to his groin. Silently he squeezed himself through the narrow opening, for once thankful for his small stature, and carefully lowered himself to the floor.

He was on her in seconds, covering her mouth with his hand as she frantically tossed her head in terror. The force of her resistance caused him to lose his grip on her mouth, and she bit one of his fingers. With an oath he pulled his revolver from its holster and pushed it into the side of her throat.

"Lay still if you want to keep your pretty neck," he growled. He gathered her face between cruel hands and covered her lips with his, a hard brutal kiss not intended to give pleasure. She writhed beneath him, her eyes transfixed with horror. "Now let me see those globes of yours," he said, tearing at the fabric covering her breasts.

Her lips formed a mute plea and she gave a terrified scream. Then her eyes rolled back in her head and she seemed to lose consciousness. Her nightdress rode high on her legs, her breasts spilled from the torn fabric. He almost lost control. He was hard as a stick.

It was over in seconds and his spent body collapsed on hers. He lay motionless for a moment, then as he heaved himself from the bed the door flew open and the girl's father and her sister, clad only in their nightclothes, entered the room.

In the throes of his climax he had carelessly allowed the revolver to slip from his fingers onto the floor, and now his eyes searched frantically for its whereabouts. Abby, seeing her ravaged sister spread-eagle on the bloody sheet, threw herself at Billy like a rabid dog. She hit him with such force he fell backwards against her advancing father, and they both fell to the floor. Both sets of hands scrambled for the revolver, but only one found it in time to take aim and fire.

"Oh, my God," Abby screamed. "You've killed him!"

CHAPTER
– 2 –

Captain Ford McKenzie struggled from the depths of a deep sleep. He had been dreaming that he and his servant, Esau, were anchored behind his St. Simons, Georgia home, laboring to pull a large fish into their unstable skiff. The sky roiled with black thunderclouds, the sea churned, and Ford felt terror, knowing that the fish would surely swamp their tiny craft, hurling them into the churning water.

His eyes flew open as someone vigorously shook his shoulder. He was covered with sweat from the horror of the nightmare and, bewildered, opened his eyes to squint upon the face of General "Jeb" Stuart's black servant.

"Marse McKenzie, de General he wants you. Dey's been a killing at one of de taverns in town. He waitin' there fer you."

With an oath, Ford swung his legs over the side of the cot and shook his head to clear it. It was pitch dark in the tent, and very cold. He shivered and folded his arms against his chest. After a lifetime of mild Georgia winters he couldn't believe the numbing cold of a fall night in Pennsylvania.

"Light the candle and fetch my clothes," he commanded. "It's freezing in here."

"Yes'r."

"What time is it?"

"Way pas' midnight," the servant answered as he teased the lamp wick with a taper until it glowed. He placed the lamp next to the bed and handed Ford his trousers.

"Where am I to go?"

"De tavern . . . Dat one beside dat waterfall. It be called Fallin' Spring."

Ford felt a sudden chill of apprehension. Could it involve the riffraff he had ordered from the inn, or even Abigail, the girl he had been talking to? Why else would General Stuart summon him over a simple barroom dispute? He wasn't a regular member of Stuart's cavalry, was only on a temporary assignment, and would be returning to his own regiment bivouacked in Virginia come daybreak.

The servant began to heat water on a little camp stove and assemble Ford's shaving gear.

"Let that go," Ford said, his voice softer now that he was fully awake and saw the man shaking with cold. "I won't take time to shave. Make us some coffee quickly while I dress."

"Coffee'll hep," the servant agreed as he busied himself at the tiny oil stove. "After it boils I go out and saddle y'ur horse."

"Have some coffee yourself before you go out. The night air is damp and cold."

The servant's face bore a look of surprise, then a huge grin spread over his ebony features as he placed coffee beans in a tin bucket and started to mash them with the butt of a musket. The servant reminded Ford of Esau, his own body servant, whom he'd had to leave behind in camp. He had been one of the fortunate officers, allowed to bring his manservant with him when he left his plantation on St. Simons Island. He admitted he was lost without Esau, who made the hardships of camp life much easier to bear, but the message Ford carried required a clandestine ride into Pennsylvania and a quick return to Virginia.

After hurriedly gulping a cup of black coffee, he mounted Ruffian, his dappled gray gelding, and turned him toward Chambersburg and the inn where he had dined earlier. Again, Abby intruded into his thoughts. He remembered her quizzical gray eyes as she tried to hide her interest in him. Hopefully tonight's fracas didn't involve her.

Tallow candles illuminated every room on the ground floor of the Falling Spring Inn, and a small knot of horses were tethered beside the doors leading into the tavern. Ford threw Ruffian's rein over a hitching post and hurried up the steps.

A fire-blackened fireplace blazing with fresh logs occupied the back wall of the small room. To the right of the fireplace, close to the heat of the fire, sat a warming closet and from it the fragrant scent of coffee filled the air. In the center of the room a small group of uniformed officers formed a semicircle around the seated figure of a weeping girl. When she lifted her face to observe his arrival he noted with raised eyebrows that it was indeed Abby.

For some reason the young lady had had a disturbing effect on him the night before as she moved from table to table in the crowded tavern. He had watched her all evening, admiring her poise and the determined thrust of her chin as she performed her clearly distasteful tasks. Abby had a shapely, feminine figure that had filled him with sweet longing. He hadn't felt that kind of reaction to a girl since he left Georgia, and Cerise, at the beginning of the war.

Now, he found the face turned up to him extraordinary. Her dark hair was unbound and lay in wild disarray, her eyes the angry gray of clouds on the leading edge of a thunderstorm. It was not that she was beautiful in the conventional sense, but she had a way about her that was unique, and left a lasting sense of self-possession.

Clad only in a nightdress and robe, her bare feet planted squarely on the floor, she gave the impression that in normal circumstances she would smile easily. Now she was very grave and kept her composure only with difficulty.

Major General J.E.B. Stuart, the flamboyant chief of the cavalry corps, stood watching the girl, his face pinched with anger. He looked up and Ford saluted smartly.

Stuart returned the salute, then ran his fingers through his brigandlike whiskers. "At ease, Captain McKenzie," he said. He cleared his throat. "I'm afraid this young lady has just suffered a terrible loss. Her father was shot and killed by an intruder." Stuart lowered his voice. "Her sister was assaulted and the attacker reacted violently to the sudden appearance of the father. From what I can determine he may have been a renegade guerrilla raider, following the army, hoping to pick up a few stray horses. He most certainly was not a Confederate soldier." Stuart's mouth tightened. "I have made it clear that I hate guerrillas, except perhaps for Mosby's Raiders. This man was certainly not a part of my force on this expedition, but unfortunately, the townspeople will assume he is a Confederate. It reflects poorly on us and our troops."

"The identification is positive, General?"

"Yes, unfortunately. This girl was with her father when the shooting occurred. She remembers the Raider as a patron in the tavern where there had been an unpleasant altercation earlier in the evening. She tells me that you ordered the man, called Baines, from the tavern when he made unwelcome remarks to her sister. This was proper action on your part and I commend you for it. Now I want you to organize a search party at once." Stuart stroked his long, flowing beard and looked Ford square in the eye. "I needn't remind you of the gravity of this crime. General Lee's orders are that anyone harming a civilian, especially a member of the female sex, is to be hanged. This man, while not a part of the regular army, is a Southerner and a murderer."

Ford felt a quickening in his stomach. He glanced at Abby's white face, a study of desolation, then looked quickly away. He didn't really want this assignment, was on a volunteer mission, and could probably demand to be allowed to return to his unit. But he would do anything to erase the pain from those stormy gray eyes.

General Stuart removed his gaze from the girl and moved away. "Take a few men from Colonel Butler's regiment. He's been ordered to remain in Chambersburg as rear guard when I move out in the morning." He hesitated. "I'm under orders to turn south before daybreak. The Yankees know of our whereabouts. I understand you are quite familiar with this area."

"Yes, sir, my family has roots in nearby Perry County and I have relatives in Carlisle. I studied law at Dickinson College. When the war broke out I returned to Georgia and soon after joined the Confederacy."

Stuart nodded. "Then you are well qualified to lead a search party. I want it known that the murderer was pursued and captured by Confederates. You are not under my direct command and I hate to delay your departure, but I am asking you take on the mission."

Ford snapped to attention. "Glad to be of service, sir. Baines will guess that your plans are to head south. He'll probably try to circumvent the army and head west towards the mountains. We'll find him, rest assured."

He saluted the general and strode from the room.

Abby watched Ford go, her emotions ricocheting like hailstones. She was numb with shock, unable to comprehend what had happened to her. The Rebel . . . this man with whom she had heedlessly flirted in the taproom only hours ago . . . was setting off on a mission to apprehend her father's murderer. What irony! He seemed reluctant to go at first, but she observed an interest in his eyes that had nothing to do with the mission he had been assigned. Would he make a thorough search for Baines, or was he only trying to impress her? Well, she would know soon enough.

* * *

Stars began to fade and the sky lighten as Ford directed his hastily assembled search party west in the cold fog of the autumn morning, turning at the town brick yard and heading up a steep hill towards the distant outline of the mountains.

There was little to break up the scenery for the first few miles other than an occasional house with its barn and outbuildings. Names like Welsh Valley, Zion, and Lemasters appeared on sign posts and barns, speaking of the Welsh and Scots-Irish settlers of the valley. Then a cluster of homes and small businesses appeared at the summit of a mighty hill: a lumberyard, a harness maker, a general store and a post office bearing the name "St.Thomas." The houses had

cared-for lawns bordered by great clumps of lavender chrysanthe-
mums, the arid smell of burning leaves lingering in the fall air. Ford
remembered passing this way only days before as he followed close
on the heels of General Stuart heading north from Mercersburg to
Chambersburg.

Hawks dipped and soared in the lightening sky over fallow pastures, and across the valley the Blue Ridge Mountains rose in undulating curves like the backs of large dolphins, their peaks wrapped in
gauzy veils of cloud as they faded off into the southwest horizon.

The road followed a ridge, the grades more gradual now, and
Ford's artist's eye appreciated the magnificent vista before him. The
valley was like a huge bowl sculpted by hazy blue mountains. Pump-
kins lay in piles on stubble fields between marching rows of wigwam
corn shocks, whole acres covered with goldenrod and crimson honeysuckle. Smoke curled from farmhouse chimneys; lanterns glowed
in barns where morning chores were already well under way; a dog
barked driving cattle out to pasture. Overhead a golden eagle circled
and thunder rumbled in the distance, while far up the ridge a wild
turkey yelped.

Different, he mused, *from my island plantation, yet there is a
sameness to the gentle peace of land under cultivation whether it be
Northern corn or Southern cotton.* He felt a surge of homesickness
and swallowed hard, then shook his head angrily. He was an officer,
fighting for a cause, and he had a grim duty ahead of him. He spurred
Ruffian onward.

It was a good five miles across the valley floor, and as he rode
toward the hills he thought briefly of the events that had brought
him to this place. After the devastating losses suffered in the battle
at Antietam Creek, General Lee had moved his army back to the
Shenandoah Valley to regroup and refurbish. To do this, Lee needed
time, and he desperately needed horses. Jeb Stuart's carefully cho-
sen cavalry force of close to two thousand men was ordered into the
Cumberland Valley to disable the railroad, gather information, and
secure as many horses as necessary. When Lee needed to get a message to Stuart he was informed that Captain Ford McKenzie, of the
31st Georgia, was familiar with the local area, and Ford, bored by the
inactivity of camp life, agreed to take on the mission. Now, his message delivered, he should have been on his way back to Virginia.
Instead, here he was on what he strongly suspected might be a fruit-
less search for a renegade murderer and a ridiculous need to prove
himself to a girl he barely knew.

I suppose, he thought wryly, *since I am not a member of Jeb
Stuart's elite cavalry I am expendable.*

The tiny village of Fort Loudon loomed ahead, cradled in the arms of the enfolding mountains. The sky was growing dark, and Ford sniffed the air. Rain was definitely on the way. Just what they needed to make the hunt more impossible. He ordered a halt beside a lazy stream on the edge of town to water the horses before beginning the ascent into the imposing forest rising from the valley floor. An old man sat on a mossy bank with a fishing pole in his hands. He scrambled to his feet when he saw their gray uniforms, his eyes widened in alarm.

Ford strode toward him. "Have you seen a man this morning riding fast towards the mountains?" he asked tersely.

"Yep."

"How long ago?"

"Got 'bout an hour on you. Headed toward Mt. Parnell, thet knob over yonder." The old man waved his arm southward, his eyes gleaming with satisfaction. "You'll never ketch 'im in them mountains."

"Mount up," Ford yelled to his men as he dashed toward Ruffian. "We've not time to finish watering."

Within minutes they were pounding across fields covered with frost toward the mountain rising straight out of the valley floor, its peak wrapped in blankets of fog.

At the base of the mountain Ford halted, threw up his hand, and addressed his men.

"Baines is probably holed up in a cave somewhere; he'll be the devil to find. Our only hope is to spot his horse. We'll keep together as best we can but traveling in these dense mountains is difficult. If you find him, fire your musket into the air. Be careful. Remember he's a desperate man wanted for murder."

Ford chose the trail to his left. As he rode, his gaze swept the ground for recently trampled underbrush or horse droppings. Mountain laurel and thorny berry vines grew in profusion, providing a dense barrier to his progress and tearing at his uniform and hat. Riding soon became impossible. He dropped to the ground, tied Ruffian's reins to his belt, and began to walk. Through the trees he could see that the other men in the search party were doing the same. Using his sword, Ford hacked through the heavy underbrush, swearing under his breath. The trail, overgrown with brambles, was no longer visible, but he felt a troughlike depression, probably an old Indian path, in the earth beneath his boots. He'd follow it.

The mountain laurel was taller now, the tree tops thicker, the air scented with pine. Small animals scampered from the underbrush all around them, and Ford smiled as the horse kicked out a covey of quail that exploded into the air with a flurry of wings like popcorn over a hot fire. The only noise was that of the other searchers. A pine

grove of Eastern Hemlock and white pine soared to the sky like
straight brown colonnades, their tops a dark lacy fringe against gray
clouds like a great green cathedral. Pine needles and bark shards
softened the thud of hooves, and Ford had the sense that his commands to Ruffian should be whispered, not spoken.

The undergrowth became thinner, the walking easier, and Ford
and his men swung themselves into saddles, picking their way up
the steep ascent, across fallen trees, over mist-covered streams and
across ravines strewn with boulders. The Pennsylvania woodland was
cleaner, easier to traverse than Southern forests where jungle-thick
vegetation swarmed with sand-fleas and mosquitos.

Ford's eyes raked the woods, searching, searching, searching,
finding nothing.

Following a small stream, they came upon a secluded clearing
where what had once been a small cabin was now little more than a
fallen-down pile of logs barely managing to support a tar roof. Ford
drew up sharply and motioned his men to stay in the woods and
cover him. He jumped to the ground, threw Ruffian's bridle rein over
a nearby sapling, and unbuckled his rifle. His heart began to pound.
This would be a perfect hiding place for Baines. Holding his rifle at
the ready he cautiously approached the cabin. Birds flapped in panic,
and black, wispy wasps buzzed in and out of the openings. But the
cabin appeared to have been undisturbed for many years. Baines
wasn't here.

He motioned for his men to fan out and moved on, intent on
finding his quarry, ignoring the fat drops of rain that had begun to
pelt his shoulders.

* * *

Only minutes before, Billy Baines had squeezed himself out of
the narrow opening of a cave just wide enough for his small frame,
blinking against the sudden sunlight, fumbling with buttons in the
urgent need to relieve himself. As he watched his warm stream soak
the mossy undergrowth at his feet, he eyed a nearby oak with low-
spreading branches. It was a perfect lookout from which to observe
the mountain behind him.

Billy hurriedly buttoned his trousers and ran to the tree, hoist-
ing himself into its protective coverage. About halfway up he found
an opening through the branches that afforded a clear panorama of
the mountains and valley below. *Perfect*, he thought. He straddled a
thick limb and leaned back against the rough bark, his eyes sweeping the scene before him as he removed his Colt from its holster and
laid it on his lap. His stomach growled. God, he was hungry. He hauled

a piece of hardtack from his pocket and began to chew. His head throbbed and a wave of bile burned his throat. Damn liquor! Made a man get himself into all kinds of trouble.

The sky had grown dark as night, thunder grumbled a warning, and rain began to fall. Suddenly he heard a sharp ring as a horse's hoof struck a rock. He swung his head toward the sound, all senses alert. A clearing several hundred feet in front of him swarmed with men and horses. Realizing that he was cut off from the protection of the cave he scrambled down the tree and headed for a clump of deep underbrush that would offer better protection. His fingers tightened on his revolver.

Commands could be heard, and a man on horseback moved across a small clearing from behind a fallen-down cabin. As Billy watched, the horse began to pick its way along the trail leading directly towards his cover. He licked his dry lips and drew his second Colt. The man's approach was quite audible now. Fool, he thought bitterly. No sense how to track a mountain man. Horses were a dead giveaway in mountain pursuit. He had tethered his own mount away from the cave where he had taken cover the night before.

Rain began to fall heavily and lightning flashed close by, but his thoughts were only on the form moving toward him.

Billy reached up to wipe rain from his face. He could see him clearly now. He was a Confederate—an officer—the lightning revealing gold buttons on a gray tunic. Billy's heart pounded as he raised his Colt and fixed his quarry in its sights.

At that instant a bolt of lightning rent the sky; the tree in which he had perched only minutes before split in half and exploded into flames. The officer's horse reared frantically, pitching him to the ground. He landed only feet from the bush where Baines crouched. Their eyes met—staring in astonishment. Recognition was instant.

Baines sprang forward, leveled his revolver, shot and missed. Before he could get another shot off, the officer fired. Baines hit the ground with a thud.

He sprawled in the mud of the rain-soaked trail—dying. Above the red sumac bushes at the roadside lingered the telltale smoke of the shots just fired, fast melting into the grayer blue haze of the storm.

Baines tried to focus on the man bending over him, and for an instant remembrance flared as he gazed into the green eyes of the red-haired officer.

"You caught me," he mumbled in surprise.

The officer nodded. Supporting him in his arms he held a canteen of water to his lips.

"I'm going to die," Baines said simply. "I know that." In the near distance a horse whinnied, to be answered by another. Baines turned his head toward the sound. "Take care of my horse, he served me well. I . . ."

The officer waited for him to speak again, but the effort had drained him and he closed his eyes, slumped lower in the officer's arms, and lay quite still.

* * *

Ford had a bitter taste in his mouth. The killing had not been a pleasant one, but then neither was the crime that precipitated it.

As the search party worked their way down the mountain Ford's thoughts drifted to the girl waiting for word about the fugitive. He was eager to give her the news.

Once in Chambersburg, he turned the search party over to Colonel Butler and headed up the main street of the town toward the center square and the Falling Spring Inn. But the doors were tightly locked, windows shuttered. He stopped a man hurrying by, a bucket of water swinging from his hands.

"Have you seen the occupants of the inn?" he asked.

The man gave him a look of pure hatred. "I think Miss Elizabeth and Mr. Hartman are inside with the Kennedy girls."

Ford sat for a moment, thinking, uncertain of his duty. He remembered Abby's look of anger and appeal. He wanted to be the one to tell her Baines was dead. Still, to tarry here was unwise, even dangerous. Another major campaign was forthcoming and his own company, the 31st Georgia, needed him.

He grinned ruefully and shook his head. Who was he kidding? There was no way he was going to delegate delivery of that message to someone else. He wanted to see the appreciation in Abby's eyes.

He moved back to the locked door of the inn and knocked firmly.

A gray-haired gentleman opened the door. Ford recognized him as the harried man who had dispensed drinks from behind the small bar the night before—a square, massive man, his bulk and bulbous nose evidence of his enthusiasm for his own beer. His eyes swept Ford's uniform with icy contempt.

"And what might you want?" he asked sourly.

"I understand Miss Abigail Kennedy and her sister are here."

"Yes."

"I am Captain Ford McKenzie. I would like to see them, sir. I have news about the search for the perpetrator of a crime committed here last night."

The man's eyes narrowed and a muscle twitched in his jaw. "Those are mighty fancy words. You mean the Southern bastard who raped Sarah and murdered her father, don't you?" With a flick of his wrist he motioned Ford inside. "Abby and Sarah just finished talking with Reverend Isner . . . makin' arrangements for their father's burial. I'll see if they want to talk with you."

With that he left Ford just inside the front door and disappeared down the dark hallway.

Ford looked around him. At the end of the hall a stairway ascended to the upstairs rooms, probably those maintained by the inn for travelers. To the left of the hallway were three closed doors while on his right an open archway opened into the dining room and bar of the empty tavern. From somewhere at the end of the hall the aroma of roasting meat, spices, and onions permeated the air. Ford's mouth watered; he was suddenly ravenous.

The door through which the man had disappeared opened and Abby stood in the opening looking at him. His breathing quickened. Even distraught she was lovely.

"Come in, Captain," she said, turning back into the room. He followed her inside and closed the door.

Abby looked in surprise at the disheveled captain striding toward her. His tunic was torn, his hat had been discarded, and his trousers were mud-smeared. He smelled of horse, smoke, and blood. Self-consciously he ran his hand through his rumpled hair and gave her a tentative smile.

Abby did not return the smile. "I hear you have news for us," she said coldly. "I hope it's that the criminal was caught."

Ford nodded.

Abby felt a shiver of surprise. She had not really believed that the Confederates would make much of an effort to find the criminal. Yet Captain McKenzie looked like he had gone through a lot to capture him. But then from the very beginning she had felt that something about this Confederate, who said his name was Ford, was different.

After a brief introduction to Sarah and Elizabeth, Abby directed Ford to a wing-back chair beside the fireplace and took a straight, wooden chair facing him.

Silence filled the room as everyone looked at him.

He cleared his throat. "The felon was captured and is dead," he said simply.

Sarah gasped and began to weep. Elizabeth gathered her into her arms while Mr. Hartman moved to Abby's side and placed a beefy hand on her shoulder.

"How . . . how did he die?" Abby asked, her voice wavering.

Ford hesitated, then slowly he described his part in ending Baines' life.

Silence again descended on the room, broken only by Sarah's quiet weeping and the hiss of the small fire in the grate.

Ford rose and looked down at Abby. "You and your sister have my heartfelt apology. I speak for all of us in the Confederacy. War brings all nature of men together; please don't judge us by the actions of one."

Abby rose also. "I'll show you out," she said, her voice a lifeless monotone. She walked him out into the hall, closing the door behind her. At the front door he turned and looked directly at her. A long ten seconds passed during which Abby watched the green eyes across from her darken with compassion. She dropped her gaze.

"I can only imagine your pain, Abby. Again, I'm sorry," he said softly.

"I know," she said and, for one abandoned moment, felt the need to rest her forehead against his broad shoulder. Abby pressed her hands together. She was startled to realize that she had almost reached out to touch him. Then her voice turned to ice. "But being sorry doesn't alter the fact that our lives have been changed forever. You are a Rebel, our enemy, I hate all of you."

Ford's face set in hard, bitter lines. "I have tried to make an apology, but I see it is falling on deaf ears."

"I don't need your excuses, I . . ."

"Sshh! Let me say this and then I'll leave you to nurse your anger. Hatred can only poison the life you must rebuild. This war was the fault of neither one of us, but we must live with it and its consequences. I will not now, or ever, apologize for being a Southerner. I am proud of my state and have a duty to defend her." He reached out and touched Abby's cheek, a light exploratory whisper of the fingertips that got her full attention. He looked as though he wanted to do more.

Abby stepped forward, fighting the urge to press her fingers against that hard thin mouth, then she stuck out her chin defiantly. "Go, Rebel," she stammered, turning away.

She watched Ford close the door and walk out into the watery October dusk.

That evening, as the Rebels moved south, Ford put his spurs to Ruffian and rode out of Chambersburg toward the Potomac and Virginia.

CHAPTER

– 3 –

The golden October sun rose slowly in the east, its scarlet and silver rays casting a buttery sheen on the Kennedy's brown field-stone home nestled under the protection of a dozen magnificent elm trees. Passengers in carriages traveling the dusty road often turned to look admiringly at the august home, known as "Brookside," its meadow and orchard near the curve of a tumbling stream bordered by sweeping blue-gray hemlocks and surrounded by green paddocks with gleaming white fences. At first glance, one would believe it had been untouched by the ravages of war, unless one noticed the empty paddocks, the plundered fields, and the dark shuttered windows.

Given time, these physical scars would heal, but the emotional scars that haunted the occupants of the house would not be so easily erased.

Abby stretched her long limbs, yawned, and pulled the eider-down comforter to her chin before she reluctantly opened her eyes to sunlight struggling through the slats of the wooden shutters. Why did she feel so heavy and sad—she who always bounced out of bed eager for each new day? Why was she feeling so tense? Instantly she remembered.

Her father would be buried today.

The door opened and Ila, the Kennedy's free black servant, walked to the bedroom window and pushed the shutters open.

"It be late, Miss Abby. That pill the doctor give you make you sleep like a baby. You need some of that good sunlight to brighten up you' day."

"I don't want the shutters open, Ila," Abby mumbled, sadness and tension straining her voice. "The house should be kept in darkness 'til after the funeral."

Ila said nothing.

"Besides, I want to lie a few more minutes; this day will be long enough."

"It be past eight. Yore little brother and yore poor sister be up this long time."

The mention of Sarah brought a fresh stab of pain, and Abby felt a cold fist close over her heart. "Close those shutters again, do you hear?" she commanded, her voice as cold as death, "then pull the drapes and leave me alone."

"Yore daddy turn over in his grave if he hear how you talk to me," Ila said with a deep frown. She knelt by the hearth, fixed fresh kindling, deposited two fresh logs, and coaxed the infant flame with the bellows until it began to blaze. "It be cold out. There was a pane of ice on the rain barrel this mornin'."

Abby yanked the comforter up to her nose and rolled onto her side, blocking the view of the slender, chocolate-brown servant who had moved to the foot of her bed and watched her with tight lips. Abby felt a flush of remorse; it was unlike her to speak harshly to Ila. True, Ila was a servant, but Abby had always struggled with the urge to treat this beautiful girl more like a friend than hired help.

"The funeral be at noon," Ila reminded her. "If you don' get up soon, I can't dress y'ur hair proper."

Abby sighed as she pushed the covers aside. She swung her legs over the side of the bed, pulling a cotton robe over her night-dress. As usual, Ila was right. This day, with its sorrow-filled finality, couldn't be put off much longer.

"Lots a folks be comin' here for supper an' the Rebels done cleaned out the smokehouse. Don't rightly know what we gonna feed 'em," Ila said, shaking her head.

Abby stroked her chin in thought and the memory that had brought them to this day began to fade as she contemplated the immediate problem of providing a funeral meal without meat. The raiding soldiers had not only cleaned out the smokehouse, but they had taken most of the chickens and wild fowl. She gritted her teeth, angry heat flushing her cheeks. Beneath her breath she uttered a most unlady-like oath.

Abby began to dress while Ila moved to the wardrobe to retrieve the long black gown Abby had worn to her mother's funeral only a year ago. She settled the somber wool over Abby's head and fastened the tiny buttons stretching from waist to neck. Abby sat down at her dressing table where Ila began to fix her hair, parting it in the middle, easing the natural waves over each ear, smoothing it down with a bandoline and a small comb, then winding the remaining shoulder-length strands into a thick bun which she secured at the nape of Abby's neck with tortoise shell pins. "Did you hear me, Miss Abby? What we gonna do?"

Abby stood and walked across the room with a determined stride. She would do what she always did when she was upset. She would solve the dilemma. Papa had always said "you can feel sorry for yourself or you can meet the problem head on."

"I'll think of something. Mr. Jamison might be able to help us. I understand the Rebels somehow missed his farm."

"If you took Miss Sarah along it might help get her mind away from her trouble."

Abby frowned. Would her sister be up to riding? Still, getting out of the house on a useful errand might help get her mind off her terrible ordeal. She smiled and patted Ila on the shoulder. "That's a good idea. Go help her get ready, and tell Brandon to hitch up the pony cart."

"Yesum."

As Ila softly closed the bedroom door, Abby walked to the window, pushing the shutters open to gaze across the way at the orchard of apple trees covered with an early October frost. Brandon walked dejectedly across the lawn carrying a pail of milk. Only one pail. The hated Rebs had taken all but one cow. A dull, empty ache gnawed at her stomach as, for a moment, she allowed herself to think about her losses. Her father . . . her sister's lost virginity . . . her own once carefree laughter. She wondered if she would ever laugh again. Could this terrible war possibly be worth all it was costing? In the distance a train whistle sounded its mournful wail as it moved through the Pennsylvania countryside carrying the victims of Antietam to their final resting places in the North, and, in memory, she heard the sad strains of martial music, as daily the hearses passed through town, their coffins draped with flags.

Abby drew a deep, shuddering breath constricted with anguish. Enough despair! She must be strong for Sarah and Brandon. The funeral was set for noon.

She had been putting off going into her father's bedroom since the night of the murder, but she had to retrieve his wallet if she were to pay Mr. Jamison for some beef. She walked into the room and stopped. Her father's work-worn boots, covered with a film of mud and manure from the barn, sat neatly beside his chair waiting for feet that would never wear them again. Abby's eyes filled with tears and a sob clogged her throat. She would never hear Papa grunt as he tugged the boots off or see him wiggle his toes in relief. He really was not coming home. She would never, ever, see him again.

She turned and ran from the room, slamming the door with all her might. Someone would pay for this!

* * *

That afternoon the mournful procession wound down a leaf-strewn footpath beneath the shade of ancient oaks, maples, and sycamores, blazing crimson and gold in the fall sun.

The curving path led from the Presbyterian Church of the Falling Spring to the nearby creek, its water glimmering like tarnished copper, muddy from recent rains. Granite obelisks, headstones, and angels of grief marked the graves of the Scots-Irish and other God-fearing families who had worshiped here for years. Riffles of water purled over the rocks of the shallow creek as it whispered past the tree-shrouded cemetery; mist rose and hung in the clear cold air, and yellow leaves scurried about the feet of the mourners.

The grave-site was open. Waiting. Abby held her weeping sister in one arm and her young, white-faced brother in the other. I must be the strong one, she reminded herself. Inside she wept, but outwardly she presented a brave front. When the final prayers were said and the casket lowered into the earth, Abby looked up into the heavens. A verse, heard long ago, flashed through her mind. "Vengeance is mine—I will repay, saith the Lord." Silently, she clenched her fist. "And so saith I," she mouthed. "So, by God, saith I!"

* * *

A week had passed since the funeral, and Abby, with a bleak, wintery feeling, trudged from the barn toward the house. The evening sky was colored with streaks of scarlet and orange as the sun sank behind the ridge of brooding mountains. The red sky reminded her of the tall, copper-haired soldier she had found herself so strongly attracted to the night of her father's murder. There was no denying she had been drawn to him. For one crazy moment she had been on the verge of throwing herself into his arms. Only in gratitude, she reminded herself. Still the thought brought a warm flush to her skin. But thoughts like this were foolish; surely she would never see Ford McKenzie again.

I apologize on behalf of the entire Confederacy, he had said.

What a laugh that was.

Memories of her father's death shot through her like a quiver of arrows.

Abby's eyes brimmed with tears. She entered the spring-house and placed a bucket of milk into its cooling waters, remembering General Stuart as he looked her straight in the eye and promised retribution. Her chin jutted up as it always did when she was warding off a hurt, and she straightened her spine in vexation. Retribution would never erase her sister's disgrace or her father's death, but Baines' death certainly helped.

Meanwhile, there were endless chores to be done. The only moments of rest came after supper. Then she could take one of her precious books to the rocker by the fireplace and lose herself in a world of fiction and happy endings.

* * *

December was unseasonably cold. Abby pulled the curtains aside and peered into the gloom. In a sheltered corner of the yard, under a dark green holly bush, the Christmas rose was in full bloom. Gray, lowering clouds promised snow by morning, and Abby pulled her shawl tighter around her shoulders as she moved to the stove to pour herself a mug of hot coffee. The smell of this morning's holiday baking filled the air: a fruit cake, lebkuchen, sandtarts, hickory-nut macaroons, and soft sugar cookies. A cooling mince pie sat proudly on the window-sill awaiting the table on Christmas morning, and a fragrant pine tree from the back wood lot stood in the corner. Thanks to her father's thriftiness and foresight in hiding their money behind a loose stone in the cellar wall they were not destitute, and a few presents had been placed beneath the tree's branches. Yet despite the bustle of holiday activities she felt a heavy weight in the pit of her stomach. She had always loved Christmas, but despite all their efforts to put on a happy face for Brandon's sake, the house was full of bitterness and grief.

That night she stayed downstairs late, reading her favorite book for the third time. Finally she snapped it shut and, holding her candle high, wearily made her way down the hall toward her bedroom. At Sarah's door she paused, suddenly aware of the sound of muted sobbing.

Abby stood uncertainly, the sobs tearing at her heart. Should she intrude? She knew the reason for her sister's grief and had been concerned about Sarah's withdrawal, her apparent inability to express the anger that must be devastating her. They had always been close, exchanging girlish confidences about boys, sharing their dreams for the future. But this time Sarah had shut Abby out, hugging her sorrow to herself as in a dream.

Well, it was time to act. Resolutely Abby pursed her lips, set her chin, marched into the room, placed her candle on the bedstand, and reached out to gather the figure huddled beneath the blanket into her arms.

Her touch seemed to loosen the dam of restrained torment and Sarah sobbed uncontrollably. Abby stroked her hair and crooned softly, rocking her back and forth.

Eventually the heaving sobs quieted and Sarah sat up. Abby plumped a pillow behind her back and waited.

"I can't live with this," Sarah sobbed. "Why couldn't I just die along with Papa?"

"Sshh. Don't say such things. I know it's hard now, but we'll all survive this."

"Yes, of course we will. But we could bury Papa . . . we can't bury my shame." Her face twisted in anguish. "Oh, Abby, whatever am I going to do? My life is ruined, no man will want to marry me now."

"That isn't true. The right man . . ."

"You know it's true," Sarah blazed. "Maybe you don't see the upturned eyes when people pass me on the street. Or hear the whispers that stop when I enter a room." She began to cry again. "I just can't bear the shame."

"It wasn't your fault!"

"Of course it wasn't. But people choose to forget that. They see only a soiled woman."

Abby bit her lip, searching frantically for words of comfort. Fairly, or unfairly, society would look upon Sarah as a fallen woman. She too had heard the whispers—that perhaps Sarah had encouraged Baines while serving him at the inn. After all, no townspeople had been present to witness the truth.

Abby felt crushed by the weight of responsibility. And what about Brandon? How could she explain to a fourteen year old the tragedy that had befallen Sarah? She swallowed, willing the tears away from her own eyes. Somehow she would have to provide a home for Sarah and Brandon. Her brother Tom might never return and if, please God, he did, he would want to marry Elizabeth, to start a family of his own, to peruse his dream of opening a woodworking business in Chambersburg. Tom was entitled to his dream. But how in the world could two girls and a young boy work a one hundred-acre farm without their father?

Rage against the Confederacy knotted Abby's stomach.

She fought to keep her voice neutral. "People forget, dear. Give it time. It will soon be Christmas and every woman in the county is frantically busy, with no time for gossip. And sometime the right man *will* come along and pay no heed to your unfortunate accident. He'll see only the sweet, good-hearted person you truly are." She smiled and added, "the Sarah we all love."

Sarah turned her head and stared silently at the candle sputtering softly on the bedstand. The glowing light showed such anguish Abby felt tears well in her own eyes.

"A man will certainly have to take heed," Sarah said angrily. "There will be no chance for him to forget my disgrace." She turned to stare into Abby's eyes. "I'm pregnant!"

* * *

To Abby, the end of 1862 and the first months of 1863 were a kaleidoscope of resentment and fear.

Winter passed with no major battles, but April announced the opening of another season when the thunder of cannon would once more roll across the land, and the casualty lists would stretch out endlessly. Tom wrote that he had seen action at Fredericksburg and "was mighty sick of war." She did not know how much longer the conflict would last, but she felt it had been with her forever and might go on forever.

Then late in June she decided to take matters into her own hands.

Colonel A. K. McClure, owner and editor of the local newspaper, state legislator and vehement opposer of slavery, settled back in his leather arm chair, crossed his elegantly clad legs, and lit a cigar. He studied Abby, perched on the edge of her chair, watching him intently, her eyes flashing an inner anger she tried hard to conceal.

"Why have you come to me?" he asked.

"I heard, through the grapevine, that you control a loosely knit group of amateur spies . . . couriers who have been quite successful in keeping Governor Curtin informed of the Confederate activity on Pennsylvania's border."

A smile crossed McClure's lips, not quite reaching his eyes. "You're right, of course, but Abby, all of my couriers are men. I've never considered women, especially not girls."

"I'm nineteen years old. Hardly a girl anymore."

"Are you certain you want to do this, Abby?" he asked softly. "You know serving as a secret agent can be dangerous, often life-threatening. It's a job usually reserved for men."

"Revenge is worth any danger," she answered, sticking her chin out defiantly. A coy smile crossed her face and she looked at him through lowered lashes. "Besides, the Southerners' chivalrous attitude toward women presents a perfect opportunity for female operatives. No Confederate would dare take the life of a lady."

McClure cleared his throat. "Is revenge for your father's death your only incentive to take on such a task?"

Abby hesitated. How to tell this man of the disgrace she and her family would suffer upon the birth of Sarah's illegitimate baby? Better not to bring that subject up; he would not understand. Instead she answered, "No, not my only reason. I'll admit revenge and anger for what the Rebels did make me so angry I could spit, but, Colonel McClure, I believe in the Union and I hate slavery. Do you know the history of our servant girl?"

"I believe I heard that she was the child of runaway slaves."

"Yes. Papa sympathized deeply with the cause of the Negro, and our home, Brookside, served as a stop on the Underground Railroad for many years. A cutout of a running man on the barn served notice that it was a safe haven. Ila's parents were captured running from Brookside."

"Were they killed?"

"They were either killed or returned to the South. We took Ila in and raised her as a free servant. She was only ten at the time. Since the beginning of the war I've searched for some way to help the Union. I . . . you know my brother serves with the Pennsylvania Reserves. . . . I can't shoulder a musket and serve in the army, but here, so close to the border, there's surely something I can do to help."

McClure stroked his mustache and spoke slowly. "We've had reports that General Lee is moving his troops north toward Pennsylvania. Governor Curtin is quite alarmed. More specific information would be helpful. I believe your family was originally from Maryland. Do you still have relatives there?"

"My aunt lives just across the Potomac from Shepherdstown; near Sharpsburg."

"Do her sympathies rest with the North or the South?"

"The North. She owns a large estate . . . Roselawn . . . bordering Antietam Creek. My uncle was a Southerner, but when he died of scarlet fever, Aunt Isobel freed all her Negro slaves."

The colonel puffed on his cigar and studied her. She chewed on her lip, her thoughts racing. Handled right, no Confederate would suspect her of being a spy. She had not thought of her Aunt Isobel's strategic location, but a contact near the Potomac would indeed be valuable to the Union. Maryland had not seceded, but it was considered a hostile state, its loyalties deeply divided, a constant threat to all those north of the Mason-Dixon border.

Colonel McClure nodded his head and thoughtfully pulled at his lip. Then he smiled. "As I said, I've just received reports that Lee's entire army is on the move, headed north toward Pennsylvania. They'll be fording the Potomac at various places and I imagine Shepherdstown will be one. Would you be interested in paying your Aunt Isobel a visit and, while there, observe anything you can about Confederate troop movements in the area?"

"Oh, yes. Yes, I would."

"Then pull your chair closer and listen carefully," he said, and as afternoon traveled toward dusk he explained the duties of couriers and information gatherers. Abby listened attentively, her face alive with interest. What a wonderful adventure awaited her!

After leaving Norland, Colonel McClure's magnificent estate a mile north of Chambersburg, Abby walked resolutely along the

Harrisburg Pike with a surge of elation. At last she would be doing something worthwhile instead of simply rolling bandages and picking that dreadful lint for the Ladies' Aid Society. She couldn't wait to tell Elizabeth. She stopped suddenly, her face wrinkled in thought. Elizabeth was her best friend, and practically engaged to her brother; but might it somehow harm her if she were exposed to Abby's intentions? She continued walking toward the Falling Spring Inn, but more slowly now, as she considered her dilemma. She was bursting with excitement and she just had to tell someone. Telling her sister was out of the question. The baby was due next month and Sarah's depression was already so great, Abby feared for her sanity. She needed to talk to her friend, someone who could really understand, if only to dispel her own keyed-up emotion.

She finally gave up trying to devise a specific plan. Things always had a way of working out. She would see how the conversation went before she confided her news. News that she was going to be a Union spy!

As she ambled through the soft afternoon, Ford McKenzie kept invading her thoughts. There was something about him that had fascinated her, something magnetic, and, of course, he was handsome. But there was something else. The day after her father's death she had seen a sadness in those green eyes that were more than compassion for her loss. She suspected that something had gone awry in his life. Someone had hurt Ford McKenzie very badly. But why in heaven's name was she wasting time thinking of him? He was a Southerner—a Rebel—her sworn enemy.

She picked up her steps, eager, now, to see Elizabeth. The scent of honeysuckle and freshly mowed grass wafted heavy in the spring air. Spring had come early that year, and along the banks of the snaking Conococheague Creek pink peach blossoms vied with starry white dogwood for the attention of the passer-by. The town of Chambersburg, home to two generations of Abby's family, snuggled in the bosom of a narrow valley bounded on the east by the South Mountain Range of the Appalachians and on the west by the steeply rising Tuscarora Mountains. It was a prosperous town, founded in 1792 by Benjamin Chambers at the confluence of Falling Spring Creek and the Conococheague Creek, and it now served as the Franklin County seat, crossroads of two major turnpikes, and the western terminus of the Cumberland Valley Railroad.

Abby left Falling Spring Creek and turned west past the T.B. Woods Foundry on Third Street, where they were at this very moment doing their duty by working day and night to forge cannon for the army, past Mrs. Ritner's Boarding House where John Brown had stayed while planning the raid on the arsenal at Harpers Ferry, past the county jail, toward the waterfall and the inn, a secretive smile playing on her lips. She couldn't wait to share the tale of her first spying assignment.

Elizabeth's home, a moderate sized two-story brick residence, had been converted to a tavern in the early 1800s, where wagons crossing the Cumberland Valley made a last-minute stop before traveling west to Pittsburgh or south to Baltimore. In those days the yard was often filled to overflowing and wagoners slept on the barroom floor. When Elizabeth's father bought the tavern, he added a sleeping wing and dining room. The inn perched on the west bank of Falling Spring Creek, its eastern foundation almost touching the rushing water of the falls from whence it got its name.

Abby slipped up the alley, bypassing the stable and wash-house, to enter by the rear door. The hallway, crowded with barrels of whiskey, crates of produce, sacks of flour, sugar, rice, and coffee beans, wafted a heady aroma into the close air. Bundles of onions hanging from the rafters sent off a distinct aroma of their own. Abby wrinkled her nose with pleasure and mounted the steps to the second floor.

She found Elizabeth making a bed in one of the guest rooms. After greeting each other with hugs, Abby pitched in to help, pulling the sheets taut until they were smooth as a baby's bottom.

"There," Elizabeth said with a flourish, sweeping her hand over the finished bed, "now we must go to my room where we can really talk."

Seated in plain Shaker rocking chairs near the window of Elizabeth's bedroom, the two friends, alone at last, looked at each other with real affection. Elizabeth was a pretty girl, diminutive and full-figured with eyes sweetly expressive, dimpled cheeks, and nut-brown hair that she wore braided and wound around her head.

"How is Sarah?" she asked softly.

"She's good physically, but . . ."

"But?"

"I worry about her mental state." Sudden tears filled Abby's eyes and Elizabeth leaned forward in alarm. "I . . . I'm sorry," Abby said, swiping at her eyes in a futile gesture. "I'm as surprised at the tears as you are. But I *do* worry about how she will receive the child once it arrives; in fact I worry how I will accept it. And I *do* miss Mama and Papa so much. And Tom. Sometimes everything comes crashing in on me, like now, and I simply give in to despair."

"No. I'm the one who should be sorry. If I hadn't asked for your help that terrible night you wouldn't have been at the inn and none of this would have happened."

"Nonsense. I don't blame you. It's this stupid war, being fought because the arrogant South insists on continuing its inhuman institution of slavery, and that beastly man who raped Sarah . . . that's what killed my father."

"But, what if . . ."

"We can spend our entire lifetime saying 'what if.' Now let's talk no more about that. Have you heard from Tom? The last letter we had was from Chancellorsville in May."

Elizabeth pulled a crumpled letter from the pocket of her apron. "This came several days ago. Here, read it."

Abby eagerly took the outstretched envelope from her friend and began to unfold it. She hesitated, her eyes seeking Elizabeth's. "Isn't this personal?"

"Yes, but I want to share it with you. After all, he's your brother and I know you love him too. Read it." She rose and moved to stand in front of the window.

Abby placed the letter on her lap and began to read: *"While in line of battle the shot fell thick and fast around us. Then, smack dab in the middle of the fight, the words of Papa sounded in my ears— pray to God and you will go through the battle safe. I felt the need of prayer something awful. Now, I prayed as hard as ever any sinner did. I prayed the last prayer of Sampson, 'Oh Lord, help me this one time.' And suddenly, Elizabeth, some still, small voice seemed to say to me—'Fear no evil. I am with you.' Elizabeth, I tell you when the hour of real prayer comes, all the memorized prayers you learned by heart as a child take wings and fly away. You utter words that pour from your heart. And God answers—he really does. I don't know the reason, but I was no more afraid during the fight than I am this minute.*

Then, I was struck slightly on the head by a rifle shot and fell to the ground. I crawled into a small ditch which was within a few feet of me. This did not give me much protection; the grape shot plowed up the ground around me like a parcel of hogs had been rooting. I looked up in a few minutes and I saw some fifteen or twenty Rebs. That was the only time I felt afraid during the fight. I was sure to be a prisoner. But, behold, they were our prisoners, being led back to our lines. In a few minutes I saw several of my company going back. I got up and went with them."

Abby turned the page to read on, finding assurances that he had not been severely wounded and that he believed they had been victorious in the battle. Then the letter turned personal as he began to tell Elizabeth how much he missed her. Abby folded it without reading further, and laid it aside. She went to stand by her friend at the window, looking at the bright waters of the falls, frothing and tumbling their way to the placid Conococheague. It was a view that always brought a lump to Abby's throat, and she reached out and took Elizabeth's hand.

"I'm sorry, dear," she said. "Your heartache is different from mine, but no less deep."

Elizabeth sighed. "Still, I've only one person to worry about, and you have the weight of your entire family on your shoulders. It must be terrible to look at Sarah in her condition and be constantly reminded of what happened."

"Worse, though, Elizabeth, is the lack of sympathy from the townspeople. I doubt Sarah will ever find a husband."

"I know how you must feel . . . to be faced with the burden of providing for a baby who is not wanted. With Tom away in the war you're in charge of everything. I admire you so. How do you handle everything? How do you manage to face life with such grim determination?"

Abby squeezed her hand. "Life's funny, you know. When you think you're facing a blank wall and you can't see ahead, a door suddenly opens, and God guides you through. I believe that has happened to me." She did not add that the open door appeared to be a career as a Union spy.

"I guess you're right. If only this war were over and Tom could come home, everything would be so much better for all of us."

"I'm afraid that's wishful thinking, dear friend. I was just talking to Colonel McClure and he confided to me that a large mass of Lee's Confederates are moving north. He's afraid the next big battle could be right here in Pennsylvania."

Elizabeth's brow wrinkled in bewilderment. "Why would he tell you that? I didn't know you were that well acquainted."

The two friends looked at each other, and Abby resolved not to look away from Elizabeth's troubled eyes until she'd made up her mind how honest she dared be. They were best friends. She must be truthful with her. Friendship demanded that.

"I went to him and volunteered to work as a courier," she finally said.

"A what?"

"A courier. A person to carry messages when needed. A woman is much less likely to be questioned than a man. He . . . Colonel McClure . . . has asked me to visit Aunt Isobel in Maryland and gather what information I can about the Rebel troop movements."

"But good heavens, Abby, that's spying! That could be dangerous. A lot of Marylanders have strong sympathies for the South. Doesn't your aunt own slaves?"

"No, not anymore. I believe I can ask for her help. This information about the intended actions and strength of the Confederates could be terribly important to our government. Who knows, Elizabeth, if the North is prepared it could save Tom's life."

"What about Sarah? How can you leave her when the baby is due so soon?"

"I'll only be away for a few days and the baby isn't due until next month. Besides, Ila will be with her." Abby cocked her head, her chin thrust out. "I intend to do this, Elizabeth."

"Suppose you're discovered. Wouldn't they treat you as a criminal?"

"I'm simply paying my recently bereaved aunt a short visit. If I happen to observe some unusual happenings while I'm there who's to be the wiser?"

"If the Rebels are in the area, they might detain you."

"I know. I must be careful they don't discover my true identity." She hesitated. "I'll admit Sarah is a concern. I'd take her with me if she were in any condition to travel."

Without hesitation Elizabeth replied gently, "I'll go out and stay with her. I don't approve of what you're doing, I think it's dangerous and foolhardy, but I've always known how impetuous and willful you are, quite unlike me."

Impulsively, Abby reached out to hug her. "And I often wish I was as even-tempered as you. I'll feel so much better knowing you're with her. You're like family to us, you know."

"Someday, I hope to be family."

Abby's eyes widened in delight. "Does that mean that Tom has asked for your hand?"

Elizabeth's face turned scarlet. "Before he left, we spoke of it."

"Oh, how wonderful. My best friend married to my brother. I can't believe it." They hugged once more and Abby felt the wetness of her friend's cheek. "Elizabeth, he'll come home, I just know he will. The war can't last much longer and anything I can do to help end it will be for the both of us. This country has a terrible problem to solve. It needs brave men *and women* to work it out and I want to do my little part." Seeing the amusement in her friend's eyes she felt her lips twitch. Then she threw back her head and laughed, "I know . . . I know. You think I'm making excuses to justify my little adventure into the murky world of spydom. But our history books tell us the outcome of many a battle has been influenced by someone forewarning the opposing army. Maybe in some small way I can be the one to do this."

"And for avenging your father's death and Sarah's child," Elizabeth commented wryly.

"That too."

"But, what if . . ."

"What if . . . what if!" Abby interrupted, aware of the sharpness in her voice. "Instead of *what if* I prefer to think *why not?*"

They fixed each other with level stares. Then Elizabeth dimpled and Abby erupted into full rich laughter. She rose, placing her shawl around her shoulders. "I must be going. I have a long walk ahead of me and it'll be dark soon."

"Don't you have the carriage?"

"The Rebels have taken every horse we have, except for one splayed work horse, and Brandon is using him today to work the north field."

In the downstairs hall of the inn, Abby put a hand on her friend's arm, looking at her intently. "You mustn't tell anyone of our conversation. It could be dangerous for you and for Colonel McClure and his entire operation. I'm sorry to burden you, but I really needed someone to talk to, and I trust you."

"That's what best friends are for. Just be careful."

Abby smiled a little. "I will, Elizabeth. I know how much the family needs me." Her smile widened as she headed for the front door. "Just think. Someday you might be able to tell the whole world you knew the famous spy, Abigail Kennedy."

She walked to the door, firmly pulled it open, and without a backward glance, passed through the narrow storage area, out of the hotel into the dusk of early evening.

CHAPTER

– 4 –

Spring announced a new campaign in this second year of the mighty War Between the States. Through the Shenandoah Valley, in the shadow of the Blue Ridge Mountains, they marched north toward Pennsylvania, Robert E. Lee's army of approximately seventy-five thousand men—the victorious army of Fredericksburg and Chancellorsville—the Army of Northern Virginia.

Lee's plans were apparent now—Harrisburg, Philadelphia, then Washington.

They marched with colors flying, bugle calls echoing and re-echoing through the mountain passes, drums beating, songs of Dixie on their lips. Some were hatless and without shoes; some were hungry. But they were veterans now, brave men, determined to strike a final blow to end the war.

Just where the armies would engage in battle was still a mystery. The commanding officers did not know. Lee did not know. But clash they would.

And here, too, was Captain Ford McKenzie of the 31st Georgia Volunteer Infantry, twenty-six years old, trekking north once again in the early summer of '63. The campaign had begun early in June when they left their encampment at Hamilton's Crossing in Virginia. At first they marched at night to avoid detection by Union spy balloons, proceeding at two-mile intervals before resting for ten minutes, striving to cover twenty or twenty-five miles a night. Ford did not like the night marches. Campfires were prohibited, and he longed for his pipe, hot coffee, and an understanding of the country they were passing through. He was almost relieved when Yankees discovered them camped at Culpeper. With the need for secrecy gone, they were able to proceed in the daylight across the Blue Ridge Mountains and into the beautiful Shenandoah Valley.

The spectacle before him was truly exhilarating. The towering tops of the Blue Ridge seemed to mingle with the skies, the turnpike road winding like a serpent as the immense mass of men could be seen for many miles creeping along in the shadow of the mountain. A tide of pride washed over Ford at the sight. He was proud of his division, a part of "Stonewall" Jackson's old corps, now under the command of General Richard Ewell and led by General John B. Gordon, a commanding figure highly respected by his men, who rode his horse well, had a booming voice and a tender heart.

Ford and his company of men had been ordered to stay about a mile in the rear to keep a sharp outlook for Yankees. He turned in alarm as he saw a small group of cavalry approaching, then sighed in relief as he recognized his younger brother Joshua.

Josh reined in beside him, rubbing his hands together briskly, his blond hair tousled from the rising wind. "Ran into Yankee pickets outside Ranson," he announced, "but they ran like a covey of sandpipers on the beach when they caught sight of us." Josh's Southern drawl was more pronounced than Ford's and "beach" sounded like "baaach." He removed his cap and brushed dust from its crown. "Man, but I'd give five dollars for a drink of cold water. More important, I'd give all I have for a clean shirt and a bath. My girl, Polly, should see me now. I'm blacker and raggeder than a parcel of nigras."

"And I'd give all I have for a breakfast of Mamma's sausage gravy and biscuits," Ford said.

Josh laughed. "Always thinking of food, big brother."

"Well, I hear those Pennsylvania farmers have hefty beef and even fatter hogs." Ford rubbed his stomach and grinned. "That should provide us with some hams and sausage. But stop talking about food, will you? We're all half-starved. I've had nothing but a ration of cornmeal and hardtack for days."

"I'll admit a mess of Esau's beans would taste mighty fine," Josh said. "At times I'm sorry I didn't bring a servant with me."

Ford looked at Josh with affection. Ragged or not, he was a handsome devil—square-cut jaw, thick blond hair, slanting eyebrows, and an instinctive appreciation for beautiful women, mint juleps, and fine horses.

The McKenzies were a small family; a sister died in infancy of scarlet fever and their father of a heart attack just before Fort Sumter. When Georgia seceded, Josh was one of the first from St. Simons Island to volunteer, joining a cavalry regiment mustered in Savannah. The cavalry suited him; it was the service of choice for most Southern gentlemen. Ford smiled wryly. It would have been his own choice had his enlistment not been so impulsive, propelled by personal reasons that still tore at his heart.

He and Josh rode together a little ways, then Josh turned to the right, away from the main road, to rejoin his company. Ford kept pushing his men forward toward Shepherdstown, where they planned to join the rest of the brigade and camp for the night. The road followed a small creek, meandering among oaks and hemlocks—the June sun warm on honeysuckle and wild roses clinging to stone fences. As an amateur artist he always observed the beauty of the land with a practiced eye. The farms were old Virginia, stately columned houses with fenced paddocks, empty now, as were most of the fields. Ford knew it would be his last contact with his Southern roots for quite some time, maybe forever. He pulled himself erect in the saddle, swallowing hard, and ordered his foot-weary soldiers to rest for ten minutes. He led Ruffian to the shade of a wide-branched maple, and holding the reins lightly while the horse nibbled on a patch of tender grass, slid wearily to the ground and rubbed his back against the rough bark of the tree. In the distance he could see the gray-clad line moving north through an undulating countryside, interspersed with woods and fields of ripening wheat. They were drawing close to Pennsylvania. Would he get back to Chambersburg? Would he see the black-haired girl that kept invading his thoughts? Would the next battle truly end the conflict he had somehow gotten caught up in? He sighed and placed a blade of grass between his teeth. What was he doing here? He didn't approve of this war. What was it that bound him to fight for the "cause"? Was it patriotism? He was uncomfortable with the word. It was a woman's word, a word not often spoken aloud by men, an emotion buried deep inside their conscience. He was a Southerner, considered himself a gentleman—most of the time—well educated and heir to a prosperous St. Simons Island plantation. But life had taken him into a rushing tide that surged over the land and men, leaving only death, ruin, and desolation.

Sometimes he wondered what any individual man could accomplish in such a gigantic conflict. But there was inspiration in the air; he felt it from his men, and he felt himself drawn to the coming battle as the waters of a river run to the sea. He was anxious for the fray, and anxious to prove himself once more.

In the warm sunlight he relaxed, drowsy as the hum of a bagpipe. A vision of Abby's face floated into his thoughts, and he remembered that night when he told her of Baines' death. He had felt certain she was about to move into his arms before she realized that he was the enemy. Had she been drawn to him by the need for comfort or something more?

After a moment he got up, walked over to the old stone wall and ran his fingers along its rough surface. He wondered what she was really like, this girl called Abby, but he doubted he would ever get to know her well enough to find out.

He pulled out his late father's pocket watch, a gift from his mother before he left for the war, and ran his thumb over its finely etched surface. Seven P.M., time to move on. Ford swung himself back into the saddle. "Fall in," he barked. "Shepherdstown is dead ahead." He swept his sword toward the twinkling lights in the village at the bottom of the valley. "Make camp there. We'll cross the Potomac into Maryland before dawn."

Ford was stretched out on his cot when Esau opened the flap of the tent and entered bearing a pie with the unmistakable tart aroma of sour cherries.

"Smells wonderful," Ford murmured, his voice raspy with fatigue. "Where in heaven's name did you find cherries?"

A huge grin spread over the wide features of his servant, and he chuckled as he placed the pie on a small folding stand next to the cot. "Some of dah boys done paid a little return visit t' that farm we passed. That orchard be hangin' full'a ripe cherries jest askin' to be picked an' put in some pies."

"I hope they didn't take more than cherries."

"Maybe a ham or two and some sausages from the smokehouse. If'n I was you, I'd not say nothin'. They tol' me they paid for everthin'."

"I certainly hope so. That poor farmer probably lost all his cattle to the Yankees, and you know Lee's orders are to pay for everything we take, either with currency or a receipt."

Esau lifted a slab of pie onto a tin plate and handed it to Ford. "Dat farmer didn't want no Confederate money, so they give him a receipt."

"You seem to know a lot about what happened, Esau. Are you sure it was soldiers that paid the farmer a visit?"

"Yes'r." Esau busied himself with the pie.

Ford's face softened as he looked at the ebony servant who had been with him since childhood. Esau was taller than he, strapping, and big-boned, with broad protruding brow ridges, flaring nostrils, and a heavy jaw. They had grown up together, playing, sharing adventures, but ever mindful of their role in the relationship. To Northerners it was master and slave, but to Ford and Esau it was a relationship neither could define.

"Those men of you'rn sure daft with whiskey tonight," Esau said with a frown.

Ford knew it to be true. They had raided a Federal wagon train just north of Winchester and plundered a considerable amount of whiskey and rations. He took a big bite of pie, smacking his lips and nodding his head. "Their spirits are indeed high. They know that this coming battle could well be the victory that decides the war, or at least brings us the support of England or France. If all goes well, we might be home by fall." Esau bustled around the tent, laying out fresh linen for the morning and arranging Ford's toilet articles beside a basin. No answer was needed or expected.

"Besides," Ford continued as he finished off his pie and yanked at his boots, "They're all eager to show the North the reality of war on its own soil. Poor Virginia has been plundered and raped till it can stand no more."

"Yas, Marse Ford. That sure 'nough be true."

Ford removed his tunic, handing it to Esau before collapsing on the cot. "God, I'm tired," he groaned.

"If'n you'd allow me t' march alongside you I'd see t' you better."

"I know you would, but you know the rule. All servants must stay to the rear during a march. I can't make an exception."

He looked at Esau, who stood like a rock, head down, refusing to meet his eyes. As always in moments such as this Esau gave him the feeling that inside the intelligent, handsome head were thoughts that he would never know or understand. Ford smiled now, looking at him with real affection. "You know how important you are to me, Esau. There's no reason for you to feel inferior, but you know the rules as well as I do."

Esau looked up at him, his ebony face alight with satisfaction. "I knows my place, Marse Ford. But ain' nobody eber gonna look after you but me. Nobody as smart as me."

Ford winced. Therein lay the problem. Despite his mother's reluctance, Esau had been allowed to attend him during his years at Dickinson, and since then his smattering of education made him feel and act superior to the other slaves. Ford sighed and closed his eyes. "The pie was delicious, now let's get some rest. . . . we've a long march ahead of us."

But Ford found himself unable to sleep and, after tossing and turning on his cot for over an hour, he rose, lit a candle and pulled out his map to study it in the flickering light. His leg throbbed from a wound received early in the war at Cold Harbor. God, he hoped that didn't portend rain tomorrow. Camp life, and a climate foreign to the volunteers from Georgia, ravaged their ranks; fevers, dysentery, and rheumatism claimed as many lives as enemy bullets. He grimaced. *Twenty-six years old and aching like Methuselah,* he thought with disgust.

Ford put the map aside and withdrew a daguerreotype from his pocket. The sepia tones of the photograph did nothing to reveal the soft beauty of the young girl it pictured, but his mind supplied the details. In the mellow candlelight he studied her likeness, finally giving in to homesickness as memories crowded in and he remembered the first time he had seen Cerise at St. Simons.

He had just packed up his charcoal and drawing paper, about to depart the widow's walk atop his home when he heard the door squeak open behind him. A young girl emerged and stood outlined against the azure blue sky, her eyes blinking in surprise at his presence.

He sucked in his breath and gulped. She was quite the loveliest thing he had ever seen, with hair the color of a raven's wing, full, well-defined lips, and eyes that perfectly mirrored the deep violet blue of her calico dress billowing in the soft breeze. He took her to be about seventeen.

"Hello," he said.

"Hello." She stepped toward him. "I'm sorry if I'm intruding. I didn't know anyone was up here."

"I was just about to leave. I've been sketching." He turned and swept his arm to indicate the beach and ocean behind him.

"Are you an artist?" she asked.

He laughed. "I'm afraid it's only a hobby." His eyes swept her lush figure. "Ah . . . my name is Ford McKenzie."

"Ford McKenzie? Of McKenzie Grove?"

"The same. This is my father's plantation. And you? . . . I don't recall seeing you on the island before."

"Oh, I don't live here. My mother and I are from Savannah. She's a seamstress, here to make the dresses for Lydia Catton's wedding." She took a step forward and tilted her head to look up at him through thick eyelashes. He felt a wave of heat—he had never seen eyes so intensely blue.

"My name is Cerise. Cerise Descartes."

They turned toward the railing enclosing the widow's walk and stood silently gazing at the breathtaking sight before them. Huge oaks trailing whiskers of blue-gray spanish moss shaded the house, while before them the undulating marsh grass ended on a sand bar before giving way to blue skies and the gentle swell of the Atlantic. Ford finally found his tongue. "I paint mostly landscapes, but I do some portraits. I would love to paint you here, leaning on this rail, framed against the sky and ocean."

Cerise blushed. "How gallant. I'm flattered . . . really flattered. Do you mean now, this very instant? I'd want to wear a better frock."

"No. The light is fading. Tomorrow morning when the sun is directly overhead. And your dress is perfect. It brings out the blue of your eyes." He didn't add that it also showed her full breasts, narrow waist, and rounded hips to perfection.

"All right. I'd love to," she said with a demure smile.

"Would nine o'clock work for you? Or do you have duties with your mother in the sewing room?"

"Lordy, no. I can't sew a stitch. Nor do I want to." She hesitated and her fingers worried a pleat in her skirt. "I don't know why Mamma insisted on my coming with her." Her eyes narrowed and her voice trembled with an emotion Ford couldn't place. Ford felt a sudden chill, then he smiled and turned to pick up his paints and supplies. "Tomorrow then, if it's a clear day."

He left her on the roof and descended the narrow stairway, filled with anticipation, a barely concealed sexual appetite, and an inexplicable apprehension.

Over the next week they met every morning. Ford purposely drew out the sessions, sketching her first, then using his watercolors to fill in the colors of sky, sea, and woman. Cerise was a woman in every sense of the word, and as the painting moved to completion so did his conviction that she was a woman he had to possess.

He was putting the final touches to the painting when gray clouds scudded across the sky, obscuring the sun and kicking up a gusting wind.

"I guess that's it," he said, dipping his brushes into a jar of water before wiping them on a paint-spattered cloth. "A storm's on its way and I can easily finish the portrait in my room."

"I'm sorry to have it end," Cerise answered coyly. "I've enjoyed our mornings together."

"Will you be leaving McKenzie Grove soon?"

"In a few days, but Mamma has agreed to come back next month to prepare some summer frocks for Mrs. Cater. I may come with her."

"A month is a long time." Ford moved next to her and they both leaned on the railing peering out at the wild and beautiful Southern sea. Her full breasts swelled above the low-cut bodice of her dress, and the wind lifted her skirt to reveal slim ankles. He was aware of the smell of her, a warm clean smell of jasmine and some feminine brand of soap. The sides of their arms touched and neither moved away. A hawk fought the buffeting wind and red-winged blackbirds darted among sea oats on the sand-swirled dunes. He put his arm around her.

She turned slightly to face him. A gust of wind tugged at her hair and droplets of rain wet her cheeks. He lowered his mouth to hers, tasting the sharp tang of ocean spray as she melted against *him. He nuzzled her soft neck, his hands twining in her ebony hair, wanting to feel every sweet contour of her. Cerise moved closer, uttering a small sound deep in her throat. She stood on tiptoe to kiss him again and this time it was different, filled with warmth and passion. She radiated a sultry beauty that ignited a raging flame of passion within him. He looked into her smoldering eyes and saw her answer there. They kissed once more, then together they moved to the privacy of the small room at the top of the house.*

Ford re-placed the picture in his pocket and placed his hand behind the flame to blow out the candle. He noticed his fingers were trembling. How could anything that had started out so beautifully have ended with such heartache?

Before sunrise the next morning the 31st Georgia forded the sparkling Potomac. Ford, astride Ruffian, waited on the Maryland shore watching the progress of the men wading the swirling river. A smile began to tug at his lips; it was an amusing sight. To the taller men in the army the passage was comparatively easy, but the short-legged soldiers were a source of anxiety to the officers and provided constant entertainment to their long-legged comrades. With their knapsacks high up on their shoulders, their cartridge-boxes above the knapsacks, and their guns lifted higher still to keep them dry, they battled the current from shore to shore, slipping, sliding in the mud and slime, stumbling over the boulders at the bottom of the river. Ford marveled that no one drowned.

The regimental band was the first across, and they struck up the friendly "Maryland, My Maryland" as the last of the regiment struggled ashore, laughing and swearing.

They milled around in dripping butternuts—uniforms dyed brown from walnut shells, faded and torn. Ford stood up in stirrups and waved his hat in the air. "Move out," he shouted, struggling to maintain a straight face at the sight of his wet, bedraggled troops.

Later that morning their laughter ceased as they resumed their march which sadly led them past Sharpsburg and Antietam Creek. Not a man among them could forget the terrible battle they had fought there such a short time ago, nor the friends they had lost. Ford's body slumped in the saddle. It did no good to dwell on such sorry thoughts. It was a shame they had to pass this way, but such was war. Bitterly, he snapped Ruffian's reins and pulled himself upright.

"Pick up your pace if you want to reach Hagerstown by nightfall," he shouted, waving his men forward. "We'll stop at Sharpsburg for rest and lunch."

Lunch was barely over when a scout rode up, jumped to the ground and bounded over to Ford. "General Early wants you to hold up, sir," he said. "He's five miles to your rear, just now crossing the Potomac, and needs to confer with your General Gordon."

Several soldiers standing nearby heard the message and gave a whoop of joy. Ford grinned. The unscheduled rest was welcome.

An hour later General Early, together with General Gordon and two other officers, rode into camp. After a hurried consultation Gordon walked back to where Ford awaited orders and pointed to a gracious mansion on the crest of a distant hill, gleaming white in the morning sun.

"General Early wishes to commandeer that farm for the balance of the day. It's important that we have a meeting and discuss our strategy before we enter Pennsylvania."

Jubal Early walked up to Ford and received his salute with a slight smile. "I'm sure the men won't mind a day of rest," Early said. "We've a long march ahead of us and I want our troops alert for the coming battle. Moreover I need to have a meeting with all my officers. I'll call on the occupants of that home ahead of us personally." He looked Ford hard in the eye. "You will accompany me, Captain McKenzie. Have the 31st move into fields surrounding the home and make camp. A show of strength never hurts."

"Yes, sir." He glanced at the home in the distance. "It looks mighty gracious; just like one of our Virginia plantations."

"I hope the inhabitants are as hospitable," Early said with a twinkle in his eyes.

CHAPTER
– 5 –

Isobel Wallace sat ramrod stiff in her side chair listening to Abby's account of her father's death, Sarah's rape, and the plunder of their farm and town. Except for several sympathetic clicks of her false teeth Isobel made no comment until Abby finished her story.

"You know, my dear, I sympathize with the plight of the slaves, but I always thought Southern men extremely chivalrous toward the female sex. I find it hard to believe General Lee would tolerate such behavior from one of his soldiers."

"This man, Billy Baines, had no sanction from the Confederacy. General Stuart called on me, personally, to apologize." Abby's face hardened. "That still doesn't excuse the Confederates for this war or what they stand for."

"Have they caught the scoundrel? This Billy Baines?"

"Yes. A Southern officer tracked him into the mountains and shot him." A sudden vision of Ford, copper hair disheveled, face grimy with soot, invaded her mind and a smile tugged the corner of her mouth. "It's rather a long story, Aunt Isobel, but whether Baines is dead or not, I'll find some way to get revenge for what he and the Rebels did to us."

Isobel rose and walked toward the window. She was tall and big-boned, with wide shoulders, no waistline, and an angular face displaying high cheekbones. She was really rather homely, but her face was softened by full-bodied gray hair, with deep waves, fashioned into a bun at the nape of her neck. Abby always thought that somehow God had gotten mixed up when he handed out gender and Isobel should have been a man. But first impressions rapidly fell away when she spoke. Born and raised in rural Virginia, she had a decided Southern accent, her voice reflecting a kind, caring person with a sense of humor. Combined with her Southern twang it created an instant liking.

44

Now, she turned and looked at Abby with a soft smile. "And this search for revenge . . . does it somehow explain your sudden visit?"

"I . . . ," Abby stuttered and looked away. How much should she admit? She did not mistrust her aunt, but instinctively she sensed the perils inherent in alerting too many people to any spying mission. Still, this was her father's sister and part of her family. Abby decided to be honest. She lifted her chin and smiled very slightly, holding Isobel's eye. "Yes . . . yes it does. We've heard rumors that General Lee is planning a major invasion of Pennsylvania. The army will certainly move through Maryland, and Governor Curtin needs to know specific information about their strength and route. I need a place to stay while I gather what information I can."

Isobel hesitated, her lips pursed, then she nodded. "Take the carriage tomorrow morning and go to Frankford's Mill for my flour. A gristmill is the best place I know of to hear the latest war news and gossip. Oh . . . and dear . . . you might talk to the servants. They have an unbelievable grapevine going."

"I'll go first thing in the morning." Abby jumped up to plant a kiss on the weathered cheek. "Thank you, Aunt Isobel."

But the next morning it was not necessary to go anywhere. She and her aunt had just finished a leisurely breakfast when a frightened servant ran into the room to announce that a large band of Rebel soldiers were gathering on the front lawn. Abby's spoon clattered to the table as a loud knock sounded on the front door. Isobel jumped to her feet.

Within minutes the butler appeared. "Two officers be at de door. They wants t' talk t' the master."

"Tell them the mistress will see them in the library," Isobel instructed the servant firmly. "And make certain they wipe their muddy boots before they walk on the carpet."

They waited for five minutes, then with long purposeful strides and a determined frown, Isobel led Abby to an open door at the end of the hall.

Two officers rose to greet them as they entered the library. Abby gave a startled gasp. One of the officers was Ford McKenzie.

He seemed as startled as she. "Miss Kennedy," he drawled, sweeping his plumed hat across his chest with a sardonic grin, "I'm surprised that we should meet again."

"You shouldn't be surprised since you Southerners seem to be quite determined to invade our homes," she replied tartly.

"This is your home, then? I thought you lived in Pennsylvania . . . in Chambersburg."

"I do. This is my aunt's home. I'm here for a short visit, and, I might add, we resent your intrusion."

Isobel was listening to the exchange with a look of bewilderment.

"You know this man?" she asked.

"I'll explain later, Aunt Isobel."

The other officer cleared his throat and Ford immediately snapped to attention. After exchanging names, Ford's superior got right to the point: "We need to commandeer your farm for a short time. The house will serve as headquarters for Major General Jubal Early while our forces assemble and set up camp. We have forded the Potomac at Shepherdstown and the men need dry clothing and a hot meal."

Isobel cut her eyes to Abby and quickly back to the officer. "How long do you plan to stay?" she asked.

"Only till daybreak."

"And where are you headed?" Abby interjected, struggling to keep the eagerness out of her voice.

"North," he said with a slight smile and a wave of his hand. "And that's all you need to know, Miss."

Later that morning, while Abby was arranging fresh-cut flowers in the dining room, Ford sought her out. As she watched him enter the room with long, sinuous strides, her heart began to thump. *He moves like a cat,* she thought. It was unbelievably sensuous.

"Abby," he murmured, "you look lovely. The color in your cheeks is most becoming."

She fought to keep a smile from her lips. "And you, sir, look considerably more presentable than the last time I saw you."

His thin lips curved in a crooked grin. "I imagine I do."

"Your fellow officer said you are headed north once more. Will you enter Pennsylvania, do you know?"

"I don't know our plans." Ford frowned and looked at her intently.

"Ah . . . I don't believe I ever thanked you properly for apprehending Mr. Baines," she stammered.

"It was only my duty," he said. "I've thought of you and your family many times . . . wondering how you were coping with the loss of your father."

She stood very still, biting her lip. Yes, she had lost her father, but suddenly a vision of Sarah, swollen with child, came to mind and tears welled in Abby's eyes.

"Are you all right?" Ford asked quietly, his eyebrows puckering together in a frown. "I'm sorry if I opened old wounds."

"I'll be fine in a minute. . . . I was just thinking of my sister. She . . . is carrying Baines' child."

She watched the hard planes of his face soften and recognized the mysterious sadness in his eyes—and wondered.

"Oh, my God," he said. "That must be every bit as painful as the death of your father. Is there anything I can do?"

"No, thanks anyway." Her voice began to tremble and she looked at him helplessly. "I really don't want to talk about it."

"Abby, I'm so sorry." He moved toward her, and, unnerved, she jammed more flowers into the already overfull vase, causing it to tip dangerously. They both reached to steady it and his warm hand covered hers. As it did she swayed towards him.

He reached for her, drew her to him, wrapped her in his arms. Unable to stop the bitter tears, she wept on his broad shoulder. With her father dead and Tom away in the army there had been no masculine presence to offer her the solace of enfolding arms; no one had been available to help her deal with her own anger and confusion.

He stroked her hair and kissed the top of her head. "Please don't cry. I'd like to help if I can."

She did not know how it happened, but suddenly his lips were pressing hers. She kissed him back, melting against him, savoring the warmth of his body. When the kiss ended, she pulled away, and he spoke her name. All at once she heard the distinctive Southern drawl, saw the gray uniform, saw what she perceived as arrogance in his eyes, and she almost choked as all of her hurt and humiliation rose like acid in her throat. He was taking advantage of her vulnerability; and she had let him. Angrily she pushed him away. He made a move to draw her to him once more, and seething with anger she slapped his face.

"How dare you?" she hissed. "Everything you stand for has caused anguish to me and my family."

"You forget the anguish your soldiers have caused my homeland," he retorted hotly. "Do you think my loved ones have escaped unharmed? All the battles have been fought on *our* soil, destroying *our* farms and *our* crops. Virginia has been devastated. This is war, little lady, in case you've forgotten."

"Then take yourself off to fight for your so called 'cause' and leave me alone. You had no right to kiss me."

"You're right—I had no right to kiss you; for many reasons which you don't know. I was only trying to comfort you." Ford fingered the red welts slowly appearing on his cheek where she had slapped him and his green eyes glinted like frozen ice. Without a backward glance he stalked from the room.

Abby tried to pass the afternoon knitting, but kept fidgeting in her seat until finally she threw the afghan she was working on aside and walked out onto the lawn. Tents covered every inch of grass as far as she could see; cloying wood smoke filled the air; men in dirty gray uniforms lay everywhere. She walked toward a garden bench where she settled herself to watch the unbelievable scene. Ford walked across the lawn, his intention to join her unmistakable. She rose, averted her face and, gathering her full skirts in her hands, hurried back across the lawn toward the house.

Shortly after the evening meal General Early turned and fixed her and her aunt with a level stare. "You might want to retire early this evening, ladies. We wish to use the library later tonight . . . free of interruption."

Abby's heart began to thud. A meeting meant that details of their mission would be disclosed. Somehow she had to overhear those plans.

Isobel glared at General Early, her mouth drawn as tight as the drapes. "It is not my habit to intrude on gentlemen who wish to retire for cigars and conversation," she replied sharply, "however, my niece and I will go upstairs to our bedrooms, if that is what you desire."

"Please."

Abby bridled at the man's presumption. She stuck out her chin. "Come, Aunt Isobel, we will give these *gentlemen* the privacy they demand." With a flounce of her skirts she took her aunt by the elbow and they walked regally into the hall.

Together they went up to their rooms; however, as soon as Isobel's door closed, Abby removed her shoes and tiptoed, barefooted, out of her bedroom into the hall and down the darkening stairway, grimacing at each squeaking floorboard.

She gained the door to the library and held her ear to the key-hole. No voices broke the silence. Gingerly she turned the knob and went inside. After a quick, cursory glance around the empty room she ran to the heavy velvet drapes drawn across french doors opening onto a veranda. Carefully, she concealed herself behind the drapes.

The room was oak-paneled and very formal. The left wall was lined with bookcases; to the right, beside the fireplace, sat a large oak library table. The windows ahead stretched almost from floor to ceiling and were curtained in heavy velvet. All of the drapes were drawn, the room illuminated by several oil lamps resting on small tables beside comfortable leather armchairs.

Minutes ticked by. She dared not sit down for fear the bulk of her body would be discernable. Instead, she pressed her back against the cold glass of the french doors and tried to slow her breathing.

Within the hour, Ford, the general, and five other officers entered and settled themselves into comfortable chairs. They lit cigars and exchanged quiet conversation while one of the men unfolded a large map on the library table.

General Early began to outline their plans. "Ewell's plan is to make a raid into Pennsylvania, as far as Harrisburg if possible, and encircle General Hooker. If successful, it will be a brilliant achievement. But we must exercise great secrecy—success depends upon that. Our troops must have no idea where they are going."

"I suggest we hug the mountains closely," a young officer suggested. "Go north through Hagerstown."

The general smiled. "Yes, and we will continue to march parallel to the mountains as we head north." He then went on to disclose his plans in great detail.

Abby listened in stunned silence. Generals Longstreet and Hill, with the full contingent of the First and Third Corps, would converge on Chambersburg, and from there would decide where to initiate battle.

Chambersburg! Why Chambersburg? Sweat formed on Abby's brow.

Voices rose and fell as the officers discussed plans and troop strengths. The room grew warm, as it filled with choking cigar smoke. Ford rose to open a window. She watched him in mute terror. Suppose he moved to open the french doors behind her. She almost gagged on the smoke and her fright.

"We'll leave before daybreak," the general said as he began to roll up the map. "McKenzie, please go up and advise Mrs. Kennedy that our meeting is over. She is free to lock up if she desires."

Ford turned from the window with only a cursory glance at the french doors, and the men filed out of the room. Abby heard the thump-thump up the stairs, then a knock on her aunt's door. All was silent, then another round of knocks, louder this time. Faintly, she could hear a voice raspy with sleep.

"What's all the ruckus about? My niece and I were sleeping."

"Sorry, ma'am," Ford's masculine voice answered. "Our meeting has concluded. The general thought you might want to lock up and assure yourself that all lamps are extinguished."

"Thank you. That will not be necessary. I do not wish to disturb my niece."

The door closed and Abby waited until receding footsteps faded along the short corridor, then into silence. He had not discovered her absence, had believed her sleeping. Relieved, she sucked in her breath and crept up the stairs to her room, pondering her situation. There was no doubt in her mind that this information had to reach

Governor Curtin quickly, but Confederate picket lines must extend for miles in advance of this invading force. Time was short—she must carry the information north. But how?

She pushed open her bedroom window, taking deep gulps of fresh air to clear her head. Ghostly branches of trees traced shadows against the silvery moon and a soft breeze kissed her cheek. Slowly, a plan began to form in her mind. She had noticed several pine coffins in the wagon shed, presumably kept on hand for servant burials. She would powder her face white, dress in her aunt's mourning clothes, and leave in the morning as soon as the soldiers vacated the house. She knew that often widows, whose husbands had been killed in the service of their country, made the trip north to claim the bodies for Christian burial. Colonel McClure had given her the name of a courier at Greencastle who could telegraph her message to the governor. But first she had to record the information and think of a way to conceal it on her person, in the event she was stopped and questioned.

She moved to the desk and found a sheet of tissue-thin foolscap and a quill pen. It was almost dawn before she finished her task. With trembling fingers she carefully secreted the tissue in the coil of hair wound around her head. Now, the only thing remaining to be done was to dress in Aunt Isobel's widow's weeds and secure her blessing.

Daylight streaked the heavens when Abby, convinced that all the Rebels had departed, dressed in poke bonnet and ankle-length black dress, stole from the house, hitched one of Isobel's horses to a ramshackle wagon and, with a great deal of pushing and shoving, managed to heft an empty coffin onto its bed.

Guided by fading stars, she took the National Road to Hagerstown, then traveled north, over hills and valleys, through streams and forests. She was to the Pennsylvania border before she spotted a sentinel. Was he Union or Confederate? As she drew closer she saw the gray. Fear clutched her throat. But after peering at her intently the Rebel's gaze faltered on the coffin and he waved her on.

Once beyond the border she relaxed, stopping at a farmhouse to ask the owners for a light meal and oats for her horse. Fearing to travel at night she pulled into a grove of trees and slept fitfully in the bed of the wagon. Early the next morning she found the telegrapher, who was sitting in his Greencastle office with a worried expression on his young face.

"I've just come from Maryland," Abby said, clasping and unclasping her hands, "and I've information that discloses what the government needs to hear—the plans of General Lee to invade the North with all of his forces. You must wire this information to Governor Curtin at once."

"Can't. Some dang Rebel pickets went past here an hour ago. Cut all the telegraph lines."

"How about Chambersburg? Maybe you could ride there and send the message."

"More'n likely those lines are cut too. An' I can't leave here. Gotta try and fix things."

"Oh, bother!" She sighed in complete exasperation. "Then there's nothing for me to do except ride on to the capital with the message, myself. The governor must notify Lincoln of the Confederate plans."

She was exhausted, reluctant to climb aboard the hard seat in the wagon again; yet she knew it was the expedient thing to do.

Lee's army could not be far behind.

* * *

Finally, in a small village just north of Chambersburg Abby found a telegraph office with lines intact. She breathed a sigh of relief. She could end her journey and have the telegrapher relay her message to Governor Curtin. Once that was done she turned her horse toward home, smug with satisfaction.

Despite her euphoria, Abby was dead tired. Her body slumped on the bouncing seat, her eyes blinking furiously to stay awake.

It was afternoon, the twenty-fourth of June, when she turned the decrepit old wagon with its empty coffin into the lane leading to home. Suddenly she jerked upright in the seat reining the horse to a stop and gaped in stunned silence at the unexpected sight before her. A dozen horses were tethered in her yard; soldiers in butternut or gray lounged on the steps and front porch of her house and in the fields behind the barn tents stretched as far as the eye could see.

Cold fear gripped her, then anger. It was obvious that they were Confederates and had commandeered her home much as they had done her aunt's. What should she do? When the soldiers realized she was the mistress of the house, surely they would question her disheveled appearance, her mourning costume, and the empty coffin. Her mind raced as the horse snorted and shook his head impatiently, sensing oats and a comfortable stall nearby. As she turned to calm both the horse and her racing heart, she saw a woman's plump figure emerge from the front door and walk to the edge of the porch.

Elizabeth!

Her friend shaded her eyes, and her gaze searched the driveway, pausing when they reached the horse and wagon. Slowly, she descended the front steps and began a leisurely stroll in Abby's direction.

Abby pulled the horse and wagon behind a tall clump of mountain laurel to block her view from the house and waited.

"Abby, oh Abby, is it you?" Elizabeth cried as Abby jumped to the ground. They threw their arms around one another. "I thought you'd never come!"

Her eyes widened when she realized that Abby was dressed in black, and her gaze flew to the coffin resting in the back of the wagon. "Wha . . . is it Tom?" Her faced turned deadly white and Abby grabbed her before she fell.

"No . . . no, Elizabeth! It's all right. No one is dead; this is only a disguise."

Elizabeth took a deep shuddering breath before she wrenched herself free of Abby's grasp, her blue eyes blazing.

"What a terrible thing to do!" She ground out the words between clenched teeth.

Just then Brandon came tearing down the lane and skidded to a stop, his chest heaving, his face gleaming with excitement.

"Ila says to come quick. Sarah is having her baby."

* * *

Sarah screamed for the doctor, writhing and throwing her body about the bed in agony.

"He's coming, fast as he can," Ila said soothingly, turning Sarah on her side with gentle hands. "We hafta check and see how ready this little one is. I've helped bring out many a baby, so you jest relax and let Ila he'p you."

She began massaging Sarah's distended stomach with warm oil, her knowing fingers moving quietly as she checked and rechecked. Abby didn't care for the troubled look on her face.

Sarah was clutching Abby's hand between spasms of pain when all heads turned toward the window. "Carriage coming. Doctor Suesserott, most likely," Ila commented, relief clearly audible in her voice.

The doctor burst into the room and pushed past both women as he rushed to Sarah's side.

Within minutes he turned to Ila. "The baby has not turned," he said in a low voice. "I believe it is in distress. I'd like you to stay and help me."

Ila merely nodded.

He turned to Abby. "You'd better leave. It will be some time until your sister gives birth. Your servant and I can handle things."

Abby shook her head. "I'm staying!"

"Then stay out of the way."

Abby moved back to her chair beside the bed and took Sarah's hand. "Relax dear. I'm here with you."

Tears streaked Sarah's cheeks. "I'm so afraid," she said, gritting her teeth as another pain struck.

"It'll be all right. The pain will soon be over." Abby caressed her sister's damp forehead. She was as frightened as Sarah. She had seen many animals born on the farm, but her mother had shielded her from seeing the actual birth of a child. And what kind of a creature would it be, this baby conceived in such a terrible way? She clutched Sarah's hand, her lips pursed with suppressed fury.

The doctor was talking quietly to Ila, and Abby strained to listen. " . . . a breach birth, I'm afraid. I can't get the baby turned and it may be in trouble."

Against her will, Abby hoped it would die. It would solve a lot of problems for all of them.

Morning sun was beginning to stream through the bedroom window when the doctor's deep voice jolted her from a drugged vigil.

The doctor was bending over the bed. "The feet have presented themselves, Sarah. When you feel my hand pressing on your belly, push with everything you've got. Now, Sarah! Now!"

She screamed. "I can't. I'm tearing apart." She thrashed on the bed, heaving her back into the air, panting and gasping, her hand clutching Abby's so hard her nails tore into Abby's palms, bringing blood. "I can't!" she screamed one more time.

Abby felt herself grow faint. Was her sister dying? she wondered frantically. Images swirled and a thick velvet fog washed over her. She couldn't faint, for heaven's sake. It was Sarah having the baby, not her. She raised her hand to her mouth and bit her knuckles.

"Your baby's coming. Help me now," the doctor implored Sarah, his voice loud and urgent. With one final scream her sister arched her back in a spasm of pain, her eyes rolled, and she sank back against the pillow unconscious.

Abby jumped to her feet. An excited voice broke the sudden quiet and she heard Ila's voice cry the word "girl."

"Cut the cord with these scissors and tie it off," the doctor ordered Abby, handing her a piece of Manila twine. At her dumbfounded look he added, "in two places." He turned to Ila. "Help me with the baby. She is not breathing." He was holding the infant upside down, vigorously smacking it on its bottom. Its face was blue and it made no sound. The doctor looked at Ila. "Help me clear the mucus from her mouth and nose." He put a finger in the baby's mouth and pulled out a long string of mucus while Ila did the same with its nose. Abby shuddered. It was downright disgusting. Suddenly the infant began to whimper, and the doctor once more smacked her on her bottom. She began to cry lustily.

Abby had completed the distasteful task of tying off the cord and wiped blood-stained fingers on her apron. The sheet beneath Sarah was soaked with blood. Suddenly she felt faint again. If this is what it was like to give birth, then, by God, she would never have a child.

Slowly Sarah opened her eyes. Her gaze flew around the room, uncertain and fearful, coming to rest on Ila swabbing the whimpering infant with a towel. Abby placed a cool cloth on her sister's forehead, pushing sweat-soaked hair from her face. Roughly the doctor pushed her away. "Take care of the infant," he ordered. "Sarah needs my attention. The afterbirth is presenting, the perineum has torn, and she is bleeding heavily."

Ila, busy with the doctor, motioned to a strip of cloth hanging on the side of the cradle. "Put that belly band 'round the chile's middle, then wrap her up so's she don' catch cold."

Abby did as she was told, handling the infant with distaste. It felt slightly sticky, its hair streaked with blood, its face scrunched and red, its eyes squeezed shut. She wrapped it in a small blanket and placed it in the cradle sitting at the foot of the bed.

Activity around Sarah's bed seemed to have ceased, and the doctor began to pack his instruments in his black bag. Ila picked up the crying baby and brought her to Sarah. As she moved to place it at her breast, Sarah pushed her away with amazing strength.

"No . . . no . . . no," Sarah sobbed. "I want no part of that *thing*. Take it away."

"Now, now, honey," Ila crooned. "You gonna feel much better once the milk come."

"No!"

Ila and the doctor exchanged glances. "Give her time," he said gently. "Do you have someone to send for a wet nurse?"

Ila nodded. "Elizabeth be downstairs. Miss Yoder willing to come."

"I'll tell her to go for her on my way out. I must leave; I have other patients to tend to. If Sarah starts to bleed again, send for me at once."

Abby had been standing silently beside the bed observing this exchange. They had all feared Sarah's rejection of the baby and Abby herself felt a powerful revulsion. She shook her head. It was un-Christian to have such thoughts and she felt ashamed. Still, the thoughts were there. She began to busy herself, washing the blood from Sarah's torso, talking to her quietly. Ila slipped a clean gown over her head and began to comb her hair. In the cradle the baby cried to be fed.

With Sarah comfortable, Ila picked the little girl up and began to rock her back and forth. Still she cried. Finally Ila walked over to the bed where Sarah was watching with wary eyes.

"Please, Sarah baby . . . this li'l chil' be hungry. It won't hurt you none to nurse her this one time. It will be a good hour afore Miss Yoder gets here."

"No . . . I don't want to touch it."

"Come now, Sarah honey. This not like you."

Sarah did not answer.

Slowly, Ila lowered the baby to Sarah's swollen nipple and held it there. The baby instantly began to suckle. Sarah grimaced with pain, but as the infant's face became calm and it waved its tiny fists against her breast, she reached out with a finger and wonderingly touched the soft down covering the infant's head.

Abby watched in disbelief as a slow, beatific smile softened her sister's features. Sarah enfolded the baby in her arms holding it gently against her breast.

Minutes passed until the sated baby fell asleep. Ila removed her from her mother, looking at Abby coyly. "Put her in her cradle, will you? I needs to tend to Sarah."

With a start of surprise Abby looked at the warm little bundle placed in her arms. She peered at it intently. Did it look like the man who had fathered it? Impossible to tell this soon. As she gazed at the tiny face she was ashamed. It was wrong to harbor such feelings, she knew it was wrong.

Bubbles of milk lay on the baby's rosebud mouth and Abby gently wiped them with the edge of the blanket. The baby seemed to smile and unconsciously Abby placed her finger on the unbelievably tiny fist. The infant's little fingers wrapped themselves around it and Abby's maternal instincts flared. Tenderly she placed her in the cradle and drew the blanket tight.

Ila moved back from the bed with a triumphant grin. She propelled Abby toward the door. "I believes you can send that Miss Yoder home when she gets here. Mama and chile gonna get along just fine."

* * *

With the wet nurse dismissed, Abby sat in the kitchen nursing a cup of hot coffee, relating the details of the past night to Elizabeth. "I just don't understand. She looked at it with love."

"And why shouldn't she? She's a mother."

"A mother to what?" Abby said bitterly. "To a rapist's child?"

"To her child. And I don't understand you. You keep referring to the baby as *it*. *It* is an innocent child who did not ask to be conceived or thrust into this unwelcoming world. A little girl who will need understanding and compassion all her life—not condemnation."

Abby lowered her head and fingered a pleat in her skirt. She knew she shouldn't feel the way she did. It was unfair, un-Christian. Her anger and inability to forgive had always been her personal demon. She remembered the tiny fist curling around her finger. So warm—so trusting. *It . . . the baby . . .* did deserve a chance. She would always bear the stigma of being an illegitimate child, a burden great enough without her family adding to it. Besides, since Abby already had the responsibility of caring for Sarah and the baby, it would be easier on everyone if she could grow fond of *it . . .* the little girl.

She looked up at Elizabeth with a watery smile. "I'll try, honest I will, but for now all I want is to crawl into my bed and sleep for at least twelve hours."

"Good—and when you get up the Confederates will have left and you can tell me all about your adventure in Maryland."

Ah, yes, Abby thought wearily. *Maryland.* It seemed like weeks ago, instead of just days.

CHAPTER

– 6 –

Starting from Sharpsburg before dawn on June twenty-fourth, General Early took a route north, hugging the western face of South Mountain. With a spring in their step and high spirits Ford's regiment entered Pennsylvania, determined to show the North what war was all about. Through Cavetown, Smithsburg, Ringgold, Waynesboro, Quincy, Altondale, they came, marching in the shadow of the mountain through a land of long, rolling hills, acres of swaying wheat, and waist-high corn. Mountain laurel, hanging thick with pink and white blossoms, crowded both sides of the trail, and the woods were thick with oak, elm, and hemlock. Ford sucked in his breath. It was an artist's paradise, and for the first time since the war began he longed for his paint and brushes. He was only a dabbler, but he had always enjoyed painting.

The scent of cooking, pine, and wood smoke from an occasional cabin wafted in the early morning air. Fog still lingered in the belly of the valley, but to his right Ford could see the hump of another mountain range rising out of the mist.

They reached the hamlet of Greenwood, situated on the turnpike between Chambersburg and Gettysburg, just as a full moon appeared on the horizon. Ford rode back along his line shouting orders.

"We'll make camp here and wait for orders from Generals Gordon and Early."

Supper that night was a feast—bully soup, a hot gruel made of cornmeal and army crackers, mashed in boiling water, ginger, and confiscated wine. With bellies full for the first time in a week the foot soldiers slept on their arms beside a tumbling creek.

But sleep would not come to Ford, and that night he rode over to Josh's camping area and sought out his presence. Josh sat by a flickering campfire roasting a potato impaled on his bayonet and seemed glad for the company.

"Feel like taking a short walk?" Ford suggested.

Josh rested his potato in the glowing coals, and they strolled to the edge of the encampment where they settled on a large rock. Ford relaxed in the thick silence, breathing deep the pungent smell of smoke and leaf mold, the war for the moment forgotten.

Josh finally spoke. "Darn if I think much of the Pennsylvanians I've seen so far. Bunch of fat farmers with fatter wives. They've seen nothing of the real war, and most have never even seen a cannon."

Ford's face crooked in a half smile. "What surprises me is the rough, profane language many of the women use. I've never heard a lady swear before. Except for prostitutes, and they're not supposed to be ladies."

"And I dare say you've seen your fair share of them, big brother," Josh said with a laugh winking at Ford. "But, I do agree. These Northern gals have no class at all. Not like our gracious Southern women."

Ford sighed. A vision of his lovely, serene mother sitting on the wide veranda of their island home flashed before his eyes. He lit a cigar, the lucifer match flaring in the darkness, and inhaled deeply. "Sometimes, Josh, I despair of ever hearing the soft Southern drawl of our people or see the marsh grass wave its welcome as I row across St. Simons Sound. If only this coming battle decides the war once and for all and we can return to our own way of life."

"It'll never be the same, Ford, regardless of what the South wants or who wins the war. The end of slavery is in the wind, and if the slaves are set free we'll be forced to plant far less acreage. We may have to find a crop other than cotton."

"Maybe that's God's plan. I've never felt easy with the issue of slavery, anyway." Ford stubbed his cigar viciously against the rock. "And I sure as hell wouldn't fight in this bloody war if that were the only issue."

His brother did not answer, and Ford sat quietly, lost in thought. Night once more spread its protective cloak about his shoulders. He leaned his head against the cold rock, looking up at the stars overhead. Once more a memory of his mother invaded his thoughts as she said with that sweet smile of hers: "The heavens declare the glory of God." He swallowed past a lump in his throat. A man needed that assurance when he was facing the horror of battle. It was at times like this, in the quiet of the night before the coming fight, that he felt cold fear clutch his gut. Ford knew that for every fighting soldier fear is the most faithful of companions, for it remains with the soldier through thick and thin, usually whispering softly when engaged in the heat of battle; saving its most powerful voice for those moments of uncertainty just before the fight is joined. And each soldier had to deal with fear in his own way. Some days he could ignore it; some days he could face and overcome it; one day he might fall victim to it; but if he were to survive he would never be without it.

Josh nudged him in the ribs. "That ole potato should be 'bout done and I could use a cup of coffee. Let's go."

They rose and walked slowly back to camp. A bank of clouds and evening mist obscured the moon; only the glow of a hundred campfires penetrated the night sky. As they neared the camp he could hear the boys singing:

>We are tenting to-night on the old campground
>Give us a song to cheer. . . .

Outside his tent, Ford turned to Josh with a sardonic grin. "I'm going to turn in. Hopefully, we'll still be alive tomorrow night to share that tin of coffee."

Josh slapped his cap on blond curls at a jaunty angle. "Hell, yes. God is on our side!"

* * *

The next morning Ford set off with his men to garner food and horses from farmers in the area, and that afternoon, General Early rode into Chambersburg to visit General Ewell, the Second Corps commander, and get his orders. Upon his return he gathered his officers around him and began to speak.

"Men, I've been directed by General Ewell to head out tomorrow for York, by way of Gettysburg. . . . "

Ford shut his eyes as Ewell droned on, a surprising surge of disappointment shooting through him. He had been hoping for some excuse that would allow him to call on Abby Kennedy.

". . . cut the Northern Central Railway that connects Baltimore with Harrisburg and destroy the Wrightsville-Columbia bridge across the Susquehanna," Early was saying. The general stroked his beard, his fiery black eyes snapping. "Sounds like fun, doesn't it, boys? Now, to get ready for this little expedition I want to strip our column of all unnecessary burdens that'll slow us down; so this afternoon I'm going to send most of our wagons to Chambersburg until we return. Captain McKenzie, I'll need every available servant to drive the wagons into town." He fixed Ford with a baleful glare. "Including your personal man."

"Yes, sir. I'll find him and have him report to you immediately."

"Good. We should have the drivers back to camp in time to prepare supper. Tomorrow we'll take at least five empty wagons for whatever supplies we can lay up along the way. The pickings should be good. I count on the hospitality of these well-fed Dutch farmers.

Ford saluted smartly and went in search of Esau.

* * *

Esau was among the first to pull his utility wagon into one of General Ewell's camps southeast of town.

After unloading his cargo his eyes swept the road before him, settling on a brownstone farm house in the distance. *It'll be a couple hours afore we be ready t' return to camp,* he thought. *More than 'nough time t' take a little jaunt over to dat farm an' get Marse Ford a fat ole chicken t' boil in the pot fo' supper.*

Esau began to amble along a small creek teeming with brown trout. He wished he had his fishing pole with him. Still, Marse Ford had said he favored some chicken and dumplings. "Bound t' be some chickens at t' farm up ahead," he muttered to himself.

Determinedly, he turned his footsteps up the dirt lane that led to a brownstone farmhouse surrounded by shady elm trees.

The red barn had a funny looking sign attached to its side, like a man running. The lane led past the barn, and his eyes sought the hen house. He'd see what there was before he'd offer money. Marse Ford told him time and time again they had to pay for what they took, although he couldn't see any harm in taking one little chicken.

Just as he was turning from the barnyard, a plump hen flew across his path and landed on a pile of cut oak stacked against the side of the barn. "That be a Rhode Island Red, sure 'nough," he muttered to himself. "Tasty 'nough to make a fine stew." Quietly, he sidled up to the woodpile. The chicken was busy pecking bugs from the firewood and did not notice him at first, but just as Esau shot his hand out to grab it by the neck it took flight directly into his face. Startled, he fell against the woodpile, his arms flailing and his legs buckling beneath him.

Too late, he saw a copperhead hit the ground and coil to strike. He had fallen almost on top of it. The snake's neck curled back and the hinged jaws sprang open, fangs glistening with venom. Esau watched it as though in slow motion.

Then it struck, a copper flash of lightning, and the fangs buried deep into his leg. He staggered from the impact and screamed in terror.

Pain streaked up his leg and he could feel the venom burn deep in his body.

"Lawd have mercy," he cried, as he sank to the ground.

* * *

Abby was never sure which she had heard first—the furious squawking of the chickens or the agonized scream of the Negro.

She dropped an armload of fresh linens onto the bed and raced from the room, down the stairs, out the door, across the yard, past the woodshed to the chicken house. A Negro was lying on the ground, clutching his leg, moaning and rocking back and forth. Ila squatted on the ground beside him, trying ineffectively to calm the obviously frightened young man.

Abby dropped to the ground and yanked up his trousers to reveal two small bloody punctures on the calf of his right leg. She began to rip the fabric open while Ila groaned in dismay.

"Was it a copperhead? Did you see it?" Abby asked him.

"Yessum. It were brownish-red with a broad head, a copperhead, right enough. I'm a gonner, fer sure!"

"Ride for the doctor, Ila. Take the carriage."

"We got no horses left to pull the carriage," Ila reminded her.

"Then fetch me some whiskey and a knife. Hurry!"

Ila ran.

The Negro closed his eyes and sank into Abby's arms. "I kin feel the death comin' on me. Don't let me die alone, Miz. Send for my Massa."

So he was a slave, Abby thought bitterly. Probably with the Confederates who had set up camp near Greenwood. She sighed and tightened her grip on his writhing leg. "You're not going to die, young man, but you must lie absolutely still to keep the poison from moving through your blood." She tore a strip of ruffle from her petticoat and began to twist it in a tight tourniquet above the wound. "What's your name?" she asked, trying to distract him.

"Esau."

"Well, Esau, we've no time to get your master here. Or a doctor. You'll just have to trust me."

The young man slumped against her, his eyes white against his ebony skin. Abby rubbed his sweating forehead and squeezed his hand.

Ila rushed across the barnyard clutching a long slender kitchen knife, a bottle of whiskey, and a pail of turpentine.

Abby raised an eyebrow.

"Turpentine works best," Ila said.

Abby grabbed the knife and knelt to her task. She knew what she had to do, and she held the leg tightly, hoping that he would not wrench from her grasp when she cut into the wound.

"Hold him for me, Ila," she instructed the trembling girl. "Tight."

Esau screamed when the blade sliced into his flesh, diagonally across the punctures. Abby put her mouth to the bleeding wound and sucked as deeply as she could to draw the venom into her mouth. She spat it onto the ground and repeated the action three more times before she picked up the pail of turpentine and splashed it into the open cut.

He screamed once more and Ila hung on to him as tightly as she could. When his screams had settled into a low moan she held the whiskey bottle to his lips while Abby applied a makeshift tourniquet.

Abby gritted her teeth and winced as she rinsed her mouth with whiskey. She rinsed and spit and rinsed and spit yet again.

"Get me some water," she finally gasped.

Ila sprinted across the barnyard to the horse trough for the water, bringing it back in a heavy gourd. Abby took it and rinsed her mouth with the cooling liquid. She offered the dipper to Esau, who was sweating profusely, and he drank deep, the water dribbling down his chin.

"Now, you must stay perfectly still," she said firmly. "I'll loosen the tourniquet from time to time, but we must keep what venom might still be in your leg from reaching your heart." She laid him back on the ground and gave him what she hoped was a reassuring smile.

After instructing Ila to fix Esau a pallet of straw, she hurried to the kitchen for clean cloths, hot water, a blanket, and a box of Epsom salts. Within the hour they had him bandaged and as comfortable as possible.

"I'll stay with him tonight," Ila offered.

Abby nodded her approval. "He shouldn't be moved until tomorrow, then we'll bring him to the house." She didn't add—"if the poor soul is still alive."

* * *

When supper time came and went and Esau did not return, Ford felt a knot of concern growing in his belly. Something was not right. Though they had not seen Yankees in the area the locals seemed friendly enough, none of them bearing arms or offering resistance to the occupation. It didn't occur to him that Esau was now in the free North and might decide to escape; his only thought was that his servant might be hurt somewhere, and with growing concern he walked to the cluster of tents housing the Negroes.

"Have any of you seen Esau?" he asked a strapping black man lounging on the ground.

"Las' time I laid eyes on him he be headin' for a big farm 'long dat little creek close t' the field where we took the wagons." He chuckled. "De barn have a pitcher o' a running man on it." His brow narrowed into a deep furrow as he pointed heavy fingers toward

Chambersburg. "Sayed he were goin' to ask fer a chicken for his Massa's supper."

"How long ago was that?"

"Dat be afer'noon."

Ford pursed his lips and turned back towards camp. Maybe he had somehow missed him; probably right now Esau was cooking up a fine meal of stewed chicken.

But he had not returned; so after securing permission from General Gordon, Ford saddled Ruffian and headed back into town to find the farm house where his servant had last been seen. He felt a stab of anxiety in his gut. Something had gone wrong—way wrong.

In the gathering twilight he rode north along a dusty road labeled "Falling Spring." The road had been cut into deep ruts from the passage of hundreds of wagons and artillery, and Confederate tents stretched as far as the eye could see where camp fires glimmered and battle flags waved.

Ford saw the distinctive red barn, which did indeed bear a wooden cutout of a running man. He raised one eyebrow in a questioning slant, wondering about the curious symbol. An impressive two-story home of rough brownstone, fronted by a long white porch, stood perpendicular to the main road facing the farm buildings, and behind the barn a hill rose with extensive apple orchards marching up its steep slope, thick with maturing fruit. Geese and ducks swam in a brook that cut through the meadow land where Jersey cows stood ankle deep in its cooling water, and ahead of him the light brown home blushed pink in the setting sun.

He mounted the steps, raised the knocker, and waited.

The door was opened by Abby Kennedy—he recognized her at once. What in heaven's name was going on here? Was it fate that their paths continually crossed?

From the startled look on her face it was obvious that she was as astonished as he. She made an obvious effort to regain her composure, and her eyes glinted with cold anger as she stared at him.

He cleared his throat. "I'm searching for my man-servant. His companions say he was last seen here."

"You mean slave, don't you?" Her voice dripped sarcasm.

Ford ignored her comment. "Have you seen him?"

"Oh, yes. Yes indeed. He's out in my woodshed."

"Your woodshed?"

"He was trying to steal my chickens and a copperhead got him."

CHAPTER

– 7 –

Abby watched the blood drain from the heavily tanned face of the captain whose slave lay in her woodshed.

"Is he . . . is he?. . ."

"Dead? No! But he well may be before morning."

A spasm crossed Ford's face and Abby felt almost sorry for him.

Almost.

In spite of herself her voice softened as she continued. "I heard his cry . . . above the clamor of the few chickens I have left . . . and gave him what aid I could. Our hired girl is with him now." She stressed the word "hired," hoping he would catch the difference.

"Take me to him, at once!" he commanded. She thrust out her chin, glaring at him. He moved his hands in a placating gesture before adding, "please."

They picked their way across the farm yard, a three quarter moon washing the landscape with pale lemon light, neither one speaking until they reached the little woodshed at the rear of the house. A wooden door tilted crazily from one hinge and inside a lantern glowed against the deepening dusk.

Ford hurried to the side of his servant lying on a pallet of straw. Tears began to run down Esau's face. He spoke in a weak, pinched voice. "Oh, Marse Ford, I be on fire. Somthin' a'squeezin' mah heart."

Ford dropped to his knee and took Esau's hand in his own as his glance took in the bandaged leg. He fixed Abby with a questioning look. "Did you bleed it?"

She nodded and moved to wring out a towel in the pan of salt water. "The water is cold again, Ila. Run up to the house and bring down another bucket of hot water. I'll watch him."

Esau began to convulse, his breathing erratic and labored, his body shaking with fever, his leg flailing. "Grab him," she yelled. "He mustn't move . . . the poison will travel."

Ford reacted quickly, stretching himself over Esau's writhing body to control the shaking. For the next few minutes he held him tight until the jerking stopped. Esau groaned, his muscular body twitching with pain. Foam bubbled from the corner of his mouth, as Ford cradled him in his arms. Gradually Esau quieted, half asleep, half awake, his eyes soft and trusting as they rested on Ford's face.

"I'm sorry, Esau, but I'm afraid I must leave you here with these fine ladies," Ford said gently. Tears formed in Esau's eyes. "We've orders to leave at first light. General Early has learned that Union forces are nearby, and the 31st has been ordered to leave at dawn for York." He stopped, aware of Abby listening intently. "I can't wait for you," he finished carefully.

"Who gonna take care o' yuh?"

"Hush now." A half smile lifted one corner of Ford's thin lips. "It'll be a struggle, but I believe I can care for myself." His arm tightened on Esau's shoulder. "It's you who needs the care. I feel certain these ladies will tend to you until I can come back."

Esau nodded weakly.

Abby watched in wonder. The feeling between the two men was something she had not expected to see.

Ila returned with hot water, and hastily wrung out another towel to place over the swollen skin. "He be quiet now," she said. "I'm gonna stay with him tonight." Her gaze never left the face of the handsome Negro.

His eyes were closed and Ford slowly lowered his head to the straw. Esau began to mumble, his words running together. Garbled words, strange words.

"He's speaking Gullah, a dialect from his past," Ford commented.

Abby frowned, her eyes questioning.

"Gullah is the language of the low-country slave . . . a consolidation of several African dialects and English. The language of his parents."

"Slaves!" Abby spat the word and turned her back to wring out another towel.

A deep growl rumbled from Ford's gut and he raised his brows in embarrassment. "Sorry, I haven't eaten since morning," he mumbled.

Abby hesitated, brushing straw from her long apron, pushing back a tendril of hair that had escaped its pins. Almost against her will, she heard herself say, "Come to the kitchen with me then, I need to boil fresh rags to apply to Esau's leg. We've some left over stew from supper and a loaf of fresh bread you can have."

Once more they crossed the moon-washed yard, distant trees and hills gray-black silhouettes in the charcoal sky. "I see you made the trip from Aunt Isobel's without further mishap," she finally said, her words clipped and brittle.

"And through some of the most beautiful countryside I have ever seen." His tone was deceptively soft, almost lazy in its inflection.

"I'm glad you had time to notice." Abby did not give him an opportunity to answer as she flounced through the screen door into the kitchen. He was several steps behind her, and she smiled as the screen closed with a sharp snap. With a deep scowl he pushed it open and followed her.

A round-eyed youth looked up in surprise from the corner where he sat in a chair, pushing a cradle back and forth with his foot. The boy's face flushed as his gaze traveled over Ford's uniform.

"Ladle some stew into a bowl for the soldier while I put some water on to boil," Abby said to her brother.

"Let the all-fired Rebel git it for his own self," he grumbled, running his hand through cow-licked hair that stood up in spikes. "He's the *Enemy*, in case you didn't notice."

"I noticed. Now, do what you're told. And mind your English, Brandon. The phrase is 'get it for himself.'"

"That's what I said. And I'll never serve the likes of him." With a baleful look in Ford's direction he stomped from the kitchen.

With a deep sigh Abby watched him go. She really couldn't blame him; why on earth was she feeding this Confederate? Glumly, she motioned Ford to a walnut plank kitchen table, filled a crockery bowl with hot stew, and plopped it down before him. She heard his stomach grumble once more as he dipped his spoon into the simmering contents and began to eat voraciously. Abby moved back to the stove. She knew that Jesus commanded, "If your enemy is hungry, feed him," but she wondered if He realized just how hard that sometimes was.

Abby saw the captain's look of appreciation as he glanced around the cozy kitchen. Several rockers topped with colorful afghans sat close to the walk-in brick fireplace, oil lamps flickered, and the air was heavy with aromatic stew. She saw his eyes linger on a shelf containing her books, then back to her with a sardonic smile. He tore off a hunk of bread and dipped it into the rich, red broth.

"Umm. Not as spicy as our low-country Brunswick Stew, but every bit as good."

"Brunswick Stew? I never heard of it."

"It's a local dish. Named after a town on the Mainland. They make it with chicken and pork, and dozens of different vegetables and spices simmered all day."

"Are you from an island, then?"

"St. Simons Island, Georgia. Separated from Brunswick by rivers and a wide salt water marsh." His voice with its soft Southern drawl grew pensive as he spoke. He mopped up the remaining stew with another hunk of bread, averting his face as though aware of the homesickness it reflected.

Abby, after placing a steaming mug of coffee on the table, moved back, watching him, a stir of vague emotion rippling over her being, and which for some reason, she did not care to analyze.

A soft mewling sound came from the cradle in the corner, and Ford glanced toward it with a strange look on his lean face. He pushed his chair back from the table and strode toward the infant, his boots tapping on the wooden floor. He stood for a moment gazing at the baby, now crying lustily, before speaking.

"Looks like a newborn. How old is it?"

"Only a few days."

His eyes traveled over Abby's slim form and he frowned.

"But you don't look . . . "

Her lips began to twitch. He thought the baby hers. Maybe she should just let him think that.

"Boy or girl?"

"A little girl," she said, busying herself at the stove.

"Do you mind if I pick her up?"

His request surprised her, but she nodded her head in assent.

He bent over the cradle and lifted the little girl into his arms.

He looks at home with a baby in his arms, Abby thought, watching him covertly. She flushed at the sudden warmth that rushed to her face.

He cradled the baby and tenderly placed a finger on her soft hair, a touch of sensitivity on his manly face. "I've had some practice." His face sobered as he looked into the tiny face.

Again, Abby felt the stir of that strange emotion. His presence was forceful, self-contained; yet his face indicated a character of gentle feeling.

Ford walked over to the table and sat down, still rocking the now quiet infant back and forth in his arms.

"What's her name?" he asked.

"Amanda."

"She has your black hair."

Still, Abby said nothing.

"I've a son, only two years old, whom I haven't seen for over a year."

So, he's married, she thought, feeling a strange quiver of disappointment. Of what she was not certain—envy?—jealousy? Or a bit of both. "Is your wife?. . ."

He turned abruptly from her questioning look. "She's in Savannah. She . . ."

"I see."

"No, you don't," he retorted sharply.

The baby started to fuss once more, and Abby lifted her from his arms. "She needs to be fed," she said, turning to look toward a shadowy form entering the room. He watched as the girl they called Sarah took the baby and settled into a rocking chair. The infant quieted and they sat huddled together as close as eggs in a nest. Ford's smile turned into a look of bewilderment as Sarah opened her blouse and offered her breast to the searching mouth.

Rattled, his eyes raked the room for Abby. She saw his surprise and gave him a sassy smile before turning her back. His face hardened at the deception, but then he should be used to female deception. He recalled their conversation, realizing with a jolt that Abby had never really said the child was hers. It was an assumption on his part. But damn the girl. She had not denied it either.

"I must go," he said coldly. "Ah, about my servant . . . I'll return early tomorrow morning to check on him. I'd appreciate it if you could care for him until he's well enough to travel."

"Servant? You mean your property, don't you?" she retorted scornfully. "The man most certainly must be watched carefully. We've a lot of copperheads in this area and their bites are often fatal, but Ila will take good care of him." A slight smile tugged at Abby's lips as she remembered the tender look on Ila's face as she ministered to the man in her woodshed.

Ford opened the kitchen door and turned back to tip his hat. "Thank you for your kindness, Madam," he said with a wry smile. "I don't know what lies ahead, but rest assured I'll be back to claim Esau . . . or my property, if that's how you wish to think of him."

"That's exactly how I wish to think of him," she said, tilting her head proudly with a flashing challenge in her eyes.

* * *

The next morning when the baby began to cry, Abby lifted her from her cradle and handed her to Sarah, who stood with outstretched arms. "Amanda has your eyes," she remarked.

"And your chin," her sister answered with a hearty chuckle.

"Poor thing."

Sarah unbuttoned her dress and exposed a full breast, already leaking milk, which she offered to the squirming baby who waved her tiny fists in anticipation. She smiled at Abby. "Your determination, too. Just listen to her nurse."

Abby pulled a rocker close to Sarah and sat quite still, watching her sister through half-closed eyes, feeling a trace of envy as she took in Sarah's motherly form. Although two years younger than Abby, at seventeen Sarah had filled out quickly and already had wide hips and an ample bosom. They were so different . . . she and her sister . . . different in physical appearance as well as personality. Sarah resembled their father's kin, blond and blue-eyed as were both her brothers. Only Abby resembled her mother, with the tall, athletic body and darker coloring of the Welsh. But it was more than Sarah's physical maturity that brought a smarting of tears to Abby's eyes. There was an unusual serenity about Sarah. She was a born mother, quiet and nurturing, a look of peace on her face as she caressed the soft down covering Amanda's head, whereas Abby possessed a restless energy that had led her into unchartered waters since she was a small child.

Abby pulled a basket of paper toward her and set to work, twisting tapers to be used to light the fireplaces that warmed every room. The parlor mantle clock chimed the hour and morning sun streamed through the muslin curtains framing the tall kitchen window. Seven o'clock already, she mused. I wonder what today will bring?

Sarah lifted the sated baby to her shoulder and rubbed her hand in a circular motion around the infant's back. "Ila tells me that red-headed officer stopped before dawn to check on his servant," she said.

"His slave, you mean," Abby snapped.

"Whatever. They do seem to have a real affection for one another, though. The Negro is quite a comely man, don't you think? Ila seems quite taken with him. She never left his side last night."

"Just what we need! A budding romance between our one remaining servant and a devoted slave. And don't forget, dear sister, his so-called master is a Rebel, an arrogant Southerner, the likes of which seem bent on robbing us and raping our women."

Sarah raised her eyebrows. "Such bitterness, Abby. It's not becoming to you." She looked away. "I gave the officer what strawberries we had left and some hot biscuits to take with him."

"You mean," Abby sputtered, "you're passing out our precious food to the Rebels? For God's sake, girl, one of them killed our father."

"Yes, one of them . . . only one. You can't hold the entire South accountable for our personal tragedy. These soldiers trudging through our fields are fighting for *their* home and *their* cause the same as we are for ours. They're hungry and footsore and I for one intend to share what we have." The baby gave a hearty burp, dampening Sarah's collar with curdled milk. She paused to wipe liquid from both her neck and the baby's mouth before she lowered Amanda to her arms.

"And hard as it is for you to understand, Abby, I forgive the man who brought such grief to us. It's up to God to pass judgement, not me. Besides," she added, cradling the sleeping infant against her chest, her blue eyes glowing with love, "for the life he took he gave another."

Abby shook her head in disbelief. Although she had grown to love Amanda she simply could not understand her sister's forgiveness to the rapist.

Ila shuffled into the kitchen, her thin shoulders sagging with weariness. She approached Sarah with arms outstretched to take the little girl and place her in her cradle.

"You've been up all night," Abby said gently. "Go to your room and lie down for an hour. We can manage."

"After I fix your breakfas', I'll go."

"Please do, Ila." She hesitated. "How is . . . what's his name . . . Isah?"

"Esau. He be much better this mornin'. The fever down. He be mighty worried about his master, though."

"Soon that man will no longer be his master," Abby said with a scowl. "Doesn't he know that after this war Lincoln will declare all the slaves free?"

"Sure he know. But he say he and Marse Ford be friends."

"You seem to have become quite well acquainted with Esau," Sarah commented. "Maybe you can convince him to stay here. We could certainly use a good hired hand and the man looks to be honest."

Ila's eyes sparkled and a shy smile pulled at her lips as she moved to the stove. "I tell him you asked when he be himself. He be strong as a draft horse—took all I could do to hold him still while he fightin' that devil fever. Now, what you girls want for breakfas'? I got enough cornmeal left for some fried mush or we could have fresh eggs."

"Eggs," Abby said. "Save our cornmeal. At least the Rebels left us a few chickens."

By mid-morning Abby could no longer contain her eagerness to relay her information to Colonel McClure about General Early's movements toward York. She gave Sarah the excuse that she wanted to fetch Doctor Suesserott to look in on Esau, who once more lay in a stupor, burning with fever. Abby doubted the Negro would last the day.

The sweet smell of spring wafted heavy in the air as she walked slowly, humming to herself, the swish of her skirts mingling with the soft whisper of Falling Spring Creek as it meandered north on its way to the Conococheague. She turned east, following its shallow bank. Here, corn grew tall, orchards wore ripening apples—Winesaps, Rambo, McIntosh—barnyards housed chattering guineas and chickens. She smiled, hugging herself, thinking of her first spying adventure, anxious for her next assignment.

She took a shortcut across the north pasture, continuing to follow the creek as it twisted and turned toward town. The day was warm, the sun already high in the sky, and she paused for a moment to focus her eyes on the rippling water. Branches of trees, blue sky and white clouds were mirrored on its gleaming surface, a sight that always gave her a feeling of peace.

After making a quick detour to Doctor Suesserott's apothecary and receiving his assurance that he would call at the farm to check on Esau, she retraced her steps and hurried along King Street.

The street was wet from a recent shower, the humid air heavy with the odor of horse droppings, damp grass, and the nearby paper mill. She lifted her skirts high and hopped over a large mud puddle, grinning to herself at her unladylike conduct, before turning north on the Harrisburg Pike toward Norland, impatient to tell Colonel McClure of troop movements toward York.

Matilda McClure answered her knock on the door. She was a handsome woman who appeared to be in her thirties, her smile warm, her eyes curious.

"Abby. So good to see you. Are you here to speak to the colonel?"

"Yes, if I could."

"I'm sorry, dear, he isn't here," she said. "He left on business yesterday and I don't expect him home for several days."

Abby felt a sudden stab of anxiety in her stomach. "But, I have . . ." She pondered what to say next. Did Matilda know of the loose ring of couriers and scouts that the colonel directed? She must. Abby had heard rumors that she had actually devised a plot to free Captain Johnson from the town jail after he was arrested during John Brown's raid on Harper's Ferry.

Mrs. McClure apparently sensed Abby's consternation and smiled reassuringly. "If you've important information I suggest you contact Judge Kimmel. He's been appointed by Governor Curtin to supervise affairs here and has much the same interests and contacts as my husband."

Abby thanked her and hurried back to town.

Her message finally delivered to Judge Kimmel, Abby walked briskly toward the inn. She hesitated briefly and cocked her head to listen to a disturbing rumble. She knew that sound; the sound of a distant cavalry column, the low grumble and jar of thousands of hoof-falls. She had heard it before.

It was market day and local farmers had brought their goods into Chambersburg to swap or sell at the large Market House on the corner of Queen and Second Streets. The Diamond was packed with shoppers, buckboards, and carriages, horses standing rump to rump at the hitching posts beside their buggies.

A crowd of curious onlookers lined both sides of Front Street, looking with awe at the advancing column of Confederates. Men watched in solemn curiosity, children scampered about waving tiny flags and calling out to the soldiers, and women wore small Union flags pinned to the bosom of their dresses. Onward the advancing Southern troops marched, bands playing, the air throbbing with the sounds of "Dixie." Abby felt almost faint at the size of this invading army, and it was soon apparent that these men were well groomed, alert, and ready for battle.

She pushed her way through the crowd to join Jacob Hoke, owner of the town's most prosperous dry-goods store. He stood framed in the doorway of his shop watching the scene with heavy lidded eyes. Jacob was in his mid-forties, slight, with straight brown hair parted on the side and trimmed neatly around his ears. He wore glasses with large lenses and thin metal frames. His suit was close-fitting, well pressed, and the dress shirt heavily starched. Altogether, he presented an air of intelligence and lively interest, a solid man, a man who, by nature, was precise and methodical about everything he did.

He greeted Abby with a pleasant smile and gestured at the invading army. "It's been like this since Tuesday; the streets have never been clear of soldiers. Regiment after regiment and brigade after brigade with immense trains of wagons pass the store all day long. Abby, I swear there are at least ten thousand men—infantry, artillery, and cavalry—camped nearby."

And more to come, Abby thought bitterly. If the plans she had overheard at Aunt Isobel's were true, four times that many men would descend on Chambersburg during the next few days.

"I guess you heard they commandeered our house for several days?" she asked.

"I did. And that you have a wounded slave on your hands."

"That we do. A mighty sick one, too. He and a copperhead tangled in our backyard. But what about you, Jacob . . . and your wife? Has anyone in town been harmed?"

"I assume you heard about Isaac Strite."

"No . . . what happened?"

"Rebels became drunk after raiding a farmer's wine cellar. They went to the Strite farm and demanded money. Poor fellow gave them all he had. When another group came by with the same demands he had no more to give them, so they killed him. Put his body in a manure pile and left."

Abby wrinkled her nose. "How terrible for his family. Have they caught the murderers?"

"No, not yet. By the way, Abby, I'd keep Ila close to home. You know the Confederates are rounding up all the blacks they can find and shipping them south, regardless of whether or not they were born on free soil. They claim any nigra to be a contraband."

Abby swallowed dryly. Ila was, after all, the daughter of escaped slaves.

Mr. Hoke continued, "Only last week from thirty to forty Negro women and children, made captive here in Chambersburg, were taken to Greencastle in wagons bound for Virginia. A chaplain and four soldiers were in charge of them, and when the Confederates rode into Greencastle they found a crowd of angry citizens gathered in the square, probably inspired by Tom Pauling, proprietor of the Antrim House."

"I know Tom. We sell produce to the Antrim House. Everyone knows how hot-tempered he is," Abby commented.

Mr. Hoke smiled thinly. "Well, the citizens disarmed the guards and traces were cut—allowing the horses to run into the country, and the Negroes set free."

"Thank heavens for that. But these are terrible times we are living in, Mr. Hoke."

"Indeed they are. War seems to bring out the worst in all of us—North and South alike. Just yesterday our very own citizens raided the storage warehouse over on King Street."

"I knew the King Street school house had been commandeered for a hospital, but I didn't hear of a raid. Our people, did you say?"

Jacob ran his hands through thinning hair and shook his head sadly. "A large amount of government supplies . . . crackers, beans and bacon . . . were stored in the railway freight office. The Rebels hadn't found them, and some of our people had no scruples whatever about taking from the government everything they could carry, rather than leave it for the Southerners. They raided the warehouse and, before you knew it, had cleaned out every single cracker and bean in the place." He smiled thinly. "It was a disgraceful scene, Abby, and I saw it with my own eyes. Men, women, even children scrambling to roll barrels of crackers and beans down the street, scolding one another and fighting among themselves. I saw one lady—I won't mention her name—kick another lady for a side of bacon. That stirred up a real ruckus, I want to tell you." Jacob pursed his thin lips. "Honestly Abby, I don't know what gets into people at a time like this. Imagine looting your own neighborhood when our nation is fighting for its life."

Abby laughed in spite of herself, visualizing the scramble. "I know it's wrong, Mr. Hoke, but it rather tickles me to know that the arrogant Rebels won't be filling their bellies on our beans. And speaking of beans, I need a few things before I go home."

He nodded and opened the door of the shop for her. It was a typical country store, stacked and hung full of all sorts of interesting items: buggy whips, oatmeal, bolts of calico, Lebanon bologna, thread, tar, coffee, tobacco, nail kegs, and penny candy. The molasses barrel with its crank handle stood in the corner on a crust of sticky syrup, and a potbellied stove occupied a prominent space in the center of the wooden floor. She took a deep breath, savoring the distinct aroma of the large shop, staring in surprise at shelves still displaying merchandise.

Jacob saw the look. "The Rebels took a few barrels of molasses and salt. They assured me that they were not vandals come to burn and plunder, but to wage an honorable war. I must admit they were honorable—full payment was made in Confederate script."

"Worthless paper," Abby snorted. "Just like their worthless honor."

Jacob gave her an odd look. "Maybe," he said. He pointed across the street. "See that horse hitched in front of the Franklin Hotel and the officer standing out near the middle of the Diamond as if watching for someone to come up Front Street?"

"A splendid looking man."

"Indeed he is. That's General A.P. Hill, commander of the Confederate Third Corps."

Just then a young boy came barrelling up the street, his face radiating excitement, crying out to all who could hear, "General Lee is coming! General Lee is coming!"

Abby ran into the street, with Mr. Hoke on her heels. A slow procession of about twenty or thirty finely mounted officers were coming toward them. "That's Lee's staff," Jacob whispered.

Abby's stomach fluttered as she watched the entrance of the men into the Diamond. They stopped immediately in front of her. General Lee, as he sat upon his horse in the public square, looked every inch a soldier. He was in his fifties, stout built, of medium height, hair strongly mixed with gray, and a rough gray beard. He wore the Confederate uniform without ornamentation except for an insignia on his collar designating his rank. His hat was of soft black felt without trimming other than the cord around the crown. The

men comprising his staff were a splendid looking group. Finely
mounted, neatly dressed, and excellent in horsemanship, they presented an appearance that filled Abby with reluctant admiration. A
vision of Ford, tall and handsome in his gray uniform, standing in
her Aunt Isobel's parlor, skittered across her mind like autumn leaves.

Across the street A.P. Hill mounted his horse and moved slowly
toward Lee, holding his hat gracefully above his head. Lee rode to
meet him and they held a short, whispered consultation.

"That, Abby, is perhaps the most important council in the history of this war," Jacob murmured. "It may very well decide the fate
of our government. If Lee goes on down the valley, then Harrisburg
and Philadelphia are threatened; if he turns east, Baltimore and Washington are in danger." He clasped and unclasped his thin hands. "Our
government must be told which way he turns as soon as possible."

Abby chewed on her lip. Colonel McClure was not in town. But
someone had to carry the message of Lee's movements to Harrisburg. The generals were still talking—the council taking place only a
few feet from where she stood—but she couldn't hear what they
were saying. Suddenly, General Hill raised his hand and pointed his
finger east, in the direction of Gettysburg, and Lee nodded his head.

Throwing discretion to the wind, Abby turned to face Jacob. "As
soon as I see for sure which way he goes, I'll set off for Harrisburg."

Jacob's eyes blinked with incredulity. "You? But you're only a
girl!"

"Don't be foolish, Mr. Hoke," she retorted scornfully. "We've no
time to secure a scout, and the telegraph lines have all been cut.
Someone should go at once."

"But . . . well then, if you must. Wait until I get the notes from
the journals I've been keeping. Margaretta and I have kept track of
the numbers of troops and cannon passing through Chambersburg
from the upstairs window of our shop. It's information Governor
Curtin should have."

Just then the council between the two generals ended, and Hill
fell back, allowing Lee to go in advance. Reaching nearly the middle
of the Diamond, Lee turned his horse's head eastward toward
Gettysburg.

After securing Jacob's journals, Abby, giddy with excitement,
gathered her skirts in her hand and began to run toward the livery
stable behind the Falling Spring Inn. She would take Elizabeth's horse
and start for the capital at once. Her next mission was about to start!
Time later for explanations to a bewildered Jacob Hoke.

CHAPTER

— 8 —

Abby, flushed with excitement and eager to inform Governor Curtin of what she had observed between A.P. Hill and Robert E. Lee in the Diamond, stopped briefly at Brookside to inform Sarah of her mission, don a somber black bonnet, and grab several apples. To avoid occupied Chambersburg she turned Elizabeth's horse north, keeping to the bank of the creek.

Just beyond Norland a cloud of dust, and the cadence of drums and marching feet, alerted her to an approaching column of Rebel soldiers. A picket, astride a large black stallion, accosted her gruffly.

"Where are you going at such a pace, madam?"

Abby's arms blossomed with goosebumps as her mind searched frantically for an answer.

"To serve as midwife for the mistress of that farm house in the distance," she replied, the words seemingly coming from out of nowhere.

The picket looked at her keenly and then tipped his cap. He turned to his men. "Let her go to perform her womanly duties." He smiled at Abby. "Wait by that rail fence until the soldiers pass. You'll not be harmed."

With heart pounding, Abby waited for them to march by before resuming her journey. At noon she halted by a village pump to quench her thirst and water her horse, but within minutes she was on her way again. She passed through woods and open fields, forced to ford streams several times, getting her long skirts and boots wet and her temper even wetter.

An hour later, she was again stopped by a Rebel scout and once more she told the same story. Confederate troops seemed to be everywhere. Her situation was perilous; she should feel fear, yet instead she was puffed up with self-confidence and exhilaration. She chuckled to herself. This business of spying was actually fun. She would have to ask the colonel about another, more important, mission—become a really important spy.

But, as her horse churned up a cloud of dust from the dry road, her mood sobered. Memories of her father had a way of invading her thoughts at the oddest times. She missed him with a desperation she would not have thought possible. It was not fair that Brandon had to grow up without a father, that Amanda would have no grandfather to tell her stories. At times like this Abby felt overwhelmed by the crushing weight of farm work and responsibility.

Before the war she had been courted by her neighbor, Jimmy Meyers, and for a time had actually thought she was in love with him. Marriage, after the war, might be a solution to all her problems. Yet, when they kissed she never felt the wild boiling flame of desire the books, hidden in her bureau drawer, hinted at. She chuckled. She had sure felt a boiling flame when Ford McKenzie kissed her.

Abby closed her eyes and tried to focus her mind on the soothing sounds of approaching evening—to rest, to forget the task ahead and to stop yearning for what was not to be.

Just as she reached the summit of a long hill her lips formed a mute "O" and she reined her horse to a stop. Ahead were hundreds of tents lining both sides of the road. A flag was flying. Was it Union or Confederate? She strained to see, but she was too far away and smoke from suppertime campfires obstructed her view. She sat twisting the reins in her hand, her stomach churning. There was no way around the camp, and if she turned back she would lose valuable time. Dare she try her midwife tale again if these were Rebels? After all, this was a major encampment, not a lone sentry. What if?. . .

Resolutely, she lifted her chin and yanked the reins. She could not sit here like a ninny and ponder *what ifs*. She hated *what ifs*. The message must get through.

As she descended the hill a flag snapping in the wind became much clearer. It was Confederate. Her breath quickened as she urged her horse forward. If her midwife story were to be believed she must appear to be in a hurry.

A guard sat astride a large horse blocking the road, rifle drawn. "Halt," he barked.

She reined her horse and quickly related her story.

"Sorry, Madam, I cannot let you pass. Come with me."

Now, the adventure was no longer fun. Fear came crashing in on her, swallowing her whole. Abby gulped, her throat parched and dry.

The guard rode beside her until they came to a tent where a group of officers were huddled around a map. "Dismount and wait," he ordered. He approached a slight man sitting at the far end of the table and spoke, gesturing at Abby. Abby could see by his insignia that the man was a general. Thank God not the one she had encountered at Isobel's.

The general rolled up his map and nodded to the sentry who returned and took Abby firmly by the elbow. "The general will talk with you," he said. He never let go of her elbow.

Abby noted with surprise that this general had only one leg. He was of sallow complexion and looked quite ill. Still he presented a commanding appearance and she fought to keep her voice steady as she addressed him.

"Please, sir, I am a midwife on my way to deliver a baby at that farm just ahead." Vaguely, she waved her arm up the road, praying that there was indeed a house in the direction she pointed. "The young husband says the baby is a month early and it is their first. I must get there quickly or the poor woman may die."

"You seem mighty young to be a midwife."

"It's my mother's profession. I've assisted her since I was a child. Mother is sickly now and I am attending her calls. Please, sir—I must hurry!"

The general stroked his beard thoughtfully. "I suppose," he said, "I could send Peterson with you."

Abby felt her knees quake, but managed to maintain eye contact. She did not reply, certain that her voice would betray her. She could smell her fear. She had to hide it. No matter what, she couldn't let the general see it.

"Still . . . my men have had a very long march today and are dead tired," he said. He studied her face for what seemed an eternity, then nodded bruskly.

"Proceed on your mission."

Clear of the encampment, Abby pulled off to the side of the road and headed for the nearest bush, her gut knotted with an ominous cramp.

* * *

A dog yipped in excitement, loping alongside her horse in the pink dawn as she pulled into an awakening village. Harrisburg was still miles ahead and she was so tired she could barely stay awake. She had slept for only a few hours, mainly to rest and water the horse, and she felt a stab of anxiety. The trip was taking too long . . . maybe this town would have an operating telegraph.

She almost collapsed with relief when she found the telegraph office intact, the telegrapher eager to transmit both her message and a condensed version of Mr. Hoke's notes.

Her duty done, she headed for the nearest inn to secure oats for the horse and a hearty breakfast for herself. Then she turned south, toward Chambersburg and home.

* * *

General Lee, after turning east in Chambersburg, set up camp a short distance from town along the Gettysburg Pike in a grove of trees, known locally as Messersmith's Woods. It was a beautiful location, shaded and quiet, and he and his staff where still there when Abby rode into town to return the horse to Elizabeth.

She found her friend in the kitchen of the inn, kneading dough. "When you put that bread to rest let's go down to the Falls where we can talk," Abby said. "I don't want anyone to overhear our conversation."

They settled themselves on the bank overlooking Falling Spring creek as it frothed and tumbled over huge rocks to fall into the placid Conococheague. The falls were a popular spot for boys to spark their girls, but only their echoes remained—the young boys were gone to war now and the spot deserted.

Abby gave Elizabeth a detailed account of her successful mission to the state capital, adding a few embellishments on her encounters with Confederate pickets.

"Weren't you scared out of your wits?" an impressed Elizabeth finally asked.

"Never! Not that I wasn't in mortal danger every minute."

She couldn't keep a smile from dimpling her cheek as she added with a laugh, "Well, maybe I was a little bit scared."

Elizabeth laughed. "You're something else, Abigail Kennedy. I could never do that. I must tell you, though, that the inn has been crowded with Rebel officers and I've kept my ears open, but learned nothing new. I don't think they know more than that they're headed over the mountains toward Gettysburg."

Abby's face sobered. "I passed General Lee's headquarters on my way into town. I wonder that he still tarries in Chambersburg. Do you think the great battle might be fought here?"

"Papa says A.P. Hill has advanced all the way to Cashtown and there are signs that Lee is about to follow." She hesitated. "General Lee has earned the admiration of quite a few here in town. The first thing he did was order that all barrels of whiskey in the warehouses be emptied into the gutter and set on fire, then he gave strict orders that no one was to be harmed and made it known that any citizen could approach him with any complaints. Mrs. McLeaf, brave soul, went to his headquarters and told him of the hardships many of the families were experiencing because of the plunder to their farms.

Lee sent an order to the guard at Stouffer's mill for ten or fifteen barrels of flour for the poor of the town."

"That doesn't excuse the fact that he is the leader of the Army of Northern Virginia and responsible for the plunder in the first place."

"No, of course it doesn't. But he does seem to be a gentleman and very humane. He gets an exceptional amount of love and respect from his men. People can't help noticing it. I wish he were on our side. Papa says he graduated from West Point and was asked by Lincoln to lead the Northern armies, but he declined, saying he had to defend the honor of his home state of Virginia. Don't you think that noble of him?"

"Yes, but . . ."

"There was another incident too, involving Dr. Suesserott. He also visited the general and asked to have a blind mare exempted from capture because it was needed to plow his corn. While Lee was having the exemption papers prepared, Dr. Suesserott says he watched Lee carefully and that he never saw so much emotion depicted on a human countenance. He came away mighty impressed with the general."

"I don't want to hear any more of your hero worship of our enemy," Abby snapped. She rose and brushed a few leaves from her skirts. "You had best get back to your bread; it has surely risen by now."

In silence they walked back to the inn.

* * *

Ila knelt beside a sleeping Esau and felt his forehead. His brow was cool, the fever gone. He opened his eyes and looked at her, his face breaking into a weak smile.

"Your face be a beautiful thing for a sick man to see bending over him," he said.

Ila flashed him a coy smile. "Come now, you been so sick anybody look good to you."

Esau's eyes ranged freely up and down her body. He shook his head. "Not as good as you."

Ila felt heat rise in her throat. "Let me prop you up and see if you can feed yourself," she stammered. "I got some soup for you."

"Not *chicken* soup?" he said with a twinkle in his eye.

Ila laughed. "Not the one you were after. This be one o' them scrawny hens Miss Abby been keeping for soup and such. Now sit up and mind your manners. Today I think we can move you out o' this here wood-house and into a room at the back of the house."

"I don't know whether this ole leg carry me that far."

"You sure enough be too big for me to carry. We'll get Miss Sarah and Brandon to he'p."

"An' Miz Abby? I haven't seen her for a day or two."

Ila averted her eyes. "She gone up to Newville to visit a sick friend. I expect her back come mornin'.'"

That night, with Esau settled in an empty room next to hers, Ila changed the dressing on his leg and found him watching her intently. He nodded toward a small stool beside the bed. "Can you sit a spell?" he asked. "I miss havin' someone to talk to."

"I s'pose so. Everbody done tucked in for the night." She settled herself on the stool and folded her hands on her lap.

They were quiet, each one appraising the other. Finally, Esau broke the silence.

"You're not a slave, are you?"

"I surely not. Mr. and Mrs. Kennedy took me in when I were only ten years old, and they always pay me a decent wage. I worked in the kitchen till I old enough to be a personal maid to Miss Abby and Miss Sarah."

"You say *took you in*. You an orphan girl?"

Ila felt a cold fist close over her heart. "I don't know," she mumbled. "Probably."

Esau's brow knotted in question.

"My mammy an' pappy were runaway slaves," she confessed. "We was on our way to Canada when the Kennedys hid us in this very house. They was a tiny little cubby hole 'hind the fireplace and we was there two days. Slave catchers was looking in all the houses for runaways, so we had to leave. A slaver picked up our trail when we was barely out o' the north field. Mammy hid me in a shock of corn before she and Pappy run to get away." Ila's face twisted in anguish at the terrible memory. "Soon after that I heard shots and screams. Don't know if they were killed or taken captive an' returned to our owner in Georgia. I sat out most of th' night, wishing someone would help me. Or some voice would . . . explain why such things happen to our people." She sighed. "Someday, maybe I go to Georgia and hunt for them."

"That be my home, you know."

"Georgia?"

"Yes. But I never knew no slave who run away. All the masters, 'cept maybe Butler King, treat his people right."

Ila gave him a scorching look. "How can anything 'bout bein' a slave be right?"

Esau grinned. "You mighty pretty when you mad."

"Don't try to soft talk me. I don' understand you, Esau. You seem perfectly content to belong to someone else."

"Not jest somebody. I belong to Marse Ford an' I be mighty proud to be a McKenzie nigra. My massa the best in the whole worl'; he give me his name, even take me off to school wif him." His eyes shone with pride. "I can read and write."

"An' didn't you ever look at that big plantation house an' think you should be sitting up there runnin' things?"

"That plain foolish, girl. Sure I had some readin' and writin' but I know I ain't smart 'nough to keep books and run a plantation. Sometime, when all us slaves be free, my children or my grandchildren can learn how, but not me, Ila."

Ila yanked at her apron and looked at him bleakly. "If they hadn't made us slaves in the first place and kept us down for so many years maybe you and I could do those things now."

"I knows that, but it ain't Marse Ford's fault. I be given to him when I was a child, to honor and serve him, same as a woman be given to a man. Maybe that change someday but for now that the way it be with me."

"You're touched in the head, that what you be." She rose and tenderly pulled a light sheet over him. "We talk on this later. Get you some sleep, now. We don' want that ole fever comin' back."

Perfect white teeth gleamed in his ebony face, and he shot her a knowing wink. "We talk more, that fer sure. An' maybe more than that."

Ila felt an odd sensation in the pit of her stomach.

God, but he was one handsome nigra.

CHAPTER

– 9 –

Meanwhile, Ford and the 31st Georgia were on the move, trudging along a winding road through the hazy South Mountains, shirts sticking to their backs, the heat already palpable. Yet, despite the misery, beauty abounded. Gray-green hemlocks of enormous girth formed a canopy over their heads; lush rhododendron grew in profusion along the rutted trail; and a mountain stream gurgled and whispered to the sound of marching feet. The heady smell of pine and crumpled leaves filled Ford with an irrepressible longing. He was tired of war, tired of roads that led only to battle and bloodshed. For some of his men, this road would become an end, an end to life and dreams. Yet onward they plodded, down the dusty road, toward tomorrow and whatever lay ahead.

Ford's reverie stopped suddenly, every sense alert to danger. His brows wrinkled in concern as he peered through the ground-hugging mist to a billow of black smoke and shooting flames. There was trouble ahead.

"Halt," he barked, reining in his startled horse. He waved his hand in the air, motioning the men to take cover in a fringe of woods. The smoke cleared momentarily and he could distinguish the butternut-uniformed men of Jube Early's advance unit running with torches, firing a group of buildings. What the hell was going on? Torching private property was a direct violation of General Lee's occupational policy. There'd be the very devil to pay for this.

With an oath, he directed his men to take their ten-minute break beside the road while he rode forward to investigate the fire, reining Ruffian in a long, loping canter down the Chambersburg Pike. He reached the first of the burning buildings and stopped a grimy, unshaven soldier waving a torch overhead.

"What are you doing?" Ford demanded.

"This here's the Caledonia ironworks of ol' Congressman Thaddeus Stevens, one of them damned radical abolitionists what's caused all this trouble. We been tol' to put the bastard out of business," the man replied with a fanatical gleam in his eye. "Ol' Jube ordered the whole damn thing burned to the ground."

Ford shook his head in disbelief. Jubal Early's conduct in burning the ironworks was rank insubordination. The general could be court-martialed for deliberately disobeying Lee's orders. But then, Early was a headstrong, independent cuss, and every one in his command knew it.

Ford returned to his own company and ordered them to move on, leading the column of weary men, hands light on the reins, his saber swaying to the motion of the horse. In the village ahead glimmers of light pierced the haze of near-morning as wives, alone and lonely in their farmhouse or barn, lit the lamps and prepared for another day of man's work. Ford felt a pang of guilt and swore beneath his breath.

The 31st spent the afternoon in Gettysburg garnering much needed hats and shoes, most of them from shops, but quite a few from reluctant citizens. Then at five o'clock on Saturday morning, as the rising drift of eastern light turned a cloudy sky into an opaque, pale red, they began a march of twenty-seven miles to the city of York. It had rained the night before, and for once the fates were with him. Ford offered a small prayer of thanks that his regiment was privileged to march on the Pike while the other poor devils were relegated to traveling through the mud. *Funny*, he thought, *the small things we learn to be grateful for.*

The country they were passing through was magnificent with rolling farmland, dwelling houses of stone and brick and immense barns that looked like castles. Wheat had been cut and clusters of conical ricks stood among the stubble. But as they trudged along they were met with stony stares and sour countenances. "Not very hospitable to their Southern visitors," Ford muttered to himself.

Suddenly, Josh appeared at his side and reined up beside him with a wide smile.

"Do you see that fool up ahead?" he asked with a chuckle.
Ford blinked in surprise at a farmer, dressed all in black with a long flowing beard, standing before his house making weird, ritualistic motions.

"What the devil is he doing?"

"I believe he's one of those Amish men we've been told have farms in this area."

"Probably thinks he's protecting his home against plunder with those hex signs and mumbo-jumbo." Ford, grinning sardonically, raised his hand, and waved to the poor fellow, who faltered momentarily and then proceeded with his gyrations in a frenzy.

They bivouacked that night four miles west of York, throwing tired bodies down in fields full of piping insects and the agreeable smell of ripe wheat. As Ford prepared his meager supper, he keenly felt the absence of Esau. He looked with dismay at the hardtack in his hand. Made of flour and water into a flat cracker about three inches square, it was anything but palatable and had the consistency of concrete. How should he prepare it? He remembered Esau often fried it with salt pork, but Ford was tired and that seemed like too much trouble. He'd just dunk it in his coffee and hope for the best.

He wondered how Esau was faring and realized with surprise how much he missed, not just the man's ministrations, but his *presence.*

Thoughts of Esau brought thoughts of Abby—Abby with the jet-black hair and snapping gray eyes. After the battle, wherever that was to be, the troops would undoubtedly return this way on their way back to Virginia. Then, when he stopped at the Kennedy farm to retrieve Esau he would see her again. He shook his head in disgust. Why in the world was he fantasizing about this girl? To pursue her for mere sexual gratification was wrong. If he had any sense he would stay away from the farm and send an aide to pick up Esau.

That night, lonely and somehow apprehensive, he sought out his brother. They sat together sharing a tin of hot coffee, the campfire dying to a dull red heap of embers. Josh made a face. "This coffee's strong enough to float an iron wedge. Wish old Esau were here to boil us a decent pot."

Ford chuckled. "I miss him, too. The hardtack biscuits I downed for supper had weevils in them. I much prefer my 'meat' cooked."

Josh grinned. "Do you know where we're headed?"

"York."

"Seems odd to me that old Baldy Ewell is splitting his force like this. He's streaming north toward Carlisle and we're going east toward York. If a major battle is being planned you'd think they'd keep us all together."

"I don't pretend to understand strategy, I just obey orders," Ford said. He decided that sounded a little pompous, so he added, "I trust General Lee to have a handle on all of this."

"Well, since I'm the pan whose handle they're playing with, I like to know how the minds of our so-called leaders work. God only knows what direction Hill and Longstreet's Corps will take. Guess we'll find out soon enough; I feel major trouble in my bones."

Ford nodded. "I feel it too; the sense of a gathering storm." He swirled the coffee in his cup and fell silent.

In a tree overhead an owl hooted and in the distance a dog kept up an insistent bark. Fireflies sprinkled the night with light. Josh drew deep on his pungent cigar, the red tip glowing in the dark. "Do you ever think of Cerise?" he asked softly.

The question surprised Ford and for a moment he did not answer, then he swallowed past a lump in his throat, and spoke. "Not any more than I have to." He grimaced. "I loved her, you know. Her betrayal cut deep, like a vulture stripping flesh from a helpless critter. I'll never let myself love another woman and be hurt like that again. Never!"

"Yes, you will, Ford. I don't mean get hurt again, but you'll love again. Not all women are like Cerise."

Ford shook his head violently. "All any woman wants is a husband to take care of her. Now, let's speak of something more pleasant."

"Yeah, like the coming battle, maybe?"

"Or whether tomorrow's march will be through mud or clouds of swirling dust. I don't know what trick of the devil led me to enlist in the damn infantry. At least the cavalry doesn't get sore feet."

"No, they just get sore behinds."

"Ford?"

"Yes?"

"I'm sorry if I opened an old wound when I talked of Cerise. I feel so lucky to have found my Polly. I've asked her to marry me when this sorry war is over. I just want the same happiness for you. Can't you forgive her?"

"No, I can't. Sometimes I wish I could for the boy's sake, but I can't, Josh. Come now, we'd better turn in. We move out before daybreak."

Ford walked slowly back to his unit, Josh's words about Cerise swirling in his head. He fingered an unopened letter in his pocket and gave a deep sigh. Time enough later to read it.

Before striking his tent for the night he stirred up his campfire, crushed some coffee beans with a rock, and put the beans into a small copper boiler to brew over the coals. When the coffee had boiled for several minutes he filled his tin, hooked it over his little finger, and carried it to a nearby clearing. The night air was hot and muggy, the trees around him motionless in the still air. Ford ran sweat-slicked hands through his long red hair. He'd have to see Sergeant McCleary tomorrow—the sergeant had the only pair of scissors in the company sharp enough to cut hair.

He reached into his haversack and withdrew the letter delivered to him at morning mail call. It was from Cerise and he had ignored it all day. Now he tore open the envelope with an odd mixture of reluctance and anticipation. Surely it would contain news of Michael, whom he hadn't seen since his first leave over a year ago. In the fading light of evening he began to read:

"Dearest Ford,

Today's post brought a most welcome letter from you, dated early in April. The Confederate Postal system seems to be somewhat lacking in efficiency and I suspect that by the time you receive this note you will have left your winter quarters, and, if the Savannah papers are correct, your regiment is with General Lee as he pushes north into Pennsylvania.

Your mother is in good health and seems to be accepting her exile here in Savannah quite well. Of course, she mourns your father and misses her island home. The news from St. Simons is not good, but I will not burden you with that now.

Michael is growing like a weed and gets into everything. He is a very intelligent little boy, jabbers from morning till night, and says 'no' to every request.

I miss you, Ford. Our time together before Michael's birth was short, but very sweet. Someday I hope you will find it in your heart to forgive me for the hurt I brought you. Love is . . ."

He could read no more. He tore her letter to shreds, his fists convulsed with suppressed rage. Love—how dare she speak that word! How could she have used him like she did and speak of love? He threw the letter into the fire and watched it curl into ash.

His anger slowly ebbed as he thought of Michael. He longed for the touch of that trusting little hand clutching his. The poor tyke was growing up in a house full of women, with no masculine influence in his life. Would Michael even remember him when he returned from the war? He doubted it.

But the letter had evoked unwelcome memories of a passion once shared, and despite himself, he remembered a night shortly after their wedding when they had sought the beach and took each other on the warm sand, the cool incoming tide washing over their feverish bodies. He felt a stirring in his groin and hurriedly rose to douse the flames of his small campfire.

"Unfortunately, the flame in my belly can not be as easily extinguished," he muttered to himself.

Well, he could fix that.

A goodly number of women followed the army providing for the sexual needs of the men. Tonight, by God, he would avail himself of their favors.

But on this night the camp follower who offered herself reminded him so strongly of his wife that all of the pent-up frustration at his disastrous marriage came boiling to the surface when he looked into the woman's blue eyes. In disgust, he left the tent, his need unrequited.

A young aide was waiting for him outside his tent when he returned to camp late that night.

"Sir, I've been instructed to tell you that a deputation from York, led by the Burgess, appeared here several hours ago and surrendered the town in the hopes that private property be protected." His lips twitched as he tried to hide a smile. "General Gordon called a meeting of all the officers, but we couldn't locate you, . . . sir."

"Thank you, private. That is most welcome news. It will make our occupation that much easier." His hand moved to pick up his still folded tent. "Good night, and thank you for waiting."

"Good night, sir."

Over the next two days they skirmished with the Pennsylvania militia, seized the Wrightsville bridge which spanned the broad Susquehanna, then were forced to retreat. The wooden bridge, recaptured by the Yankees, was torched and completely destroyed, and Early's advance to the Pennsylvania state capital halted.

Then on the morning of July 1, 1863, everything changed. Just before daybreak Ford received surprising orders. They were to break camp at once and retrace their steps westward, their destination the vital mountain pass at Cashtown, between Chambersburg and Gettysburg. With aching limbs and a great deal of cussing the men shouldered their muskets, slung their knapsacks over their shoulders, and trudged off into the darkness.

Robert E. Lee's Confederates and the men of the Union, now under the new command of Maj. General George G. Meade, were assembling in the vicinity of Gettysburg. The 31st was ordered to head back to the small crossroads town they had passed through only days before.

Gettysburg, then, might be the scene of the great battle.

* * *

Ford could hear the roar of cannon, muffled and toned down, coasting on the wind, long before they reached the edge of Gettysburg. The battle was on and he felt his pulse quicken.

"Double-quick, now!" he shouted to his men.

Down the Heidlersburg Road they ran, screaming the wild Rebel yell at the top of their lungs. This was the battle they thought would end the war, and not a man among them felt reluctant to be a part of the important fray.

Ford cocked his head and listened to the sharp startling crash of musket fire bursting through the morning air. There was no mistaking that fierce fighting loomed ahead.

General Gordon suddenly appeared beside Ford. "Halt," he shouted. "Take up positions on the left side of the Pike and wait for orders."

Just then a courier galloped in with the news that Federals bearing the flag of the 1st Division of the 11th Corps, commanded by Brigadier General Francis Barlow, were contesting the advance of a line of Alabamians and had extended his line so that his right flank rested on a small knoll near Rock Creek. Along with support infantry, a battery of four Napoleons rested on this elevation, and the Yankees were giving a good account of themselves.

Gordon stood up in his stirrups and waved to his brigade. "The Alabamians are in trouble. Form a line of battle."

It had grown quite warm and humid, the temperature climbing into the mid-seventies under a cloudy sky. Ford bounded to the ground, throwing Ruffian's reins to a waiting servant. He always fought on foot, side by side with his men.

Muskets were lowered, powder and lead slugs tamped down long barrels, men removed their caps and wiped sweaty brows and contemplated the coming ordeal.

Edging forward with the rest of his company on hands and knees, Ford led them into a wheat field shimmering like golden silk in the sun. Glistening bayonets moved through the wheat like a silver wave across the field of gold, bullets snapped and buzzed among the swaying shafts of grain, and Ford heard a mighty *whoosh* as a bullet whizzed past his head. He could feel his heart pound in his ears. He rose to his feet, waved to his men to follow and bolted across the field, jumping fences, wading across the shallow creek, charging the enemy with the fury of a man possessed. The feel of his musket was reassuring, but it didn't offer much defense against the enemy, who seemed to have the wheat field zeroed as a prime target.

They covered the last mile at a run. Ford caught sight of the Union position atop a small knob directly in front of him. "Take cover," he screamed, "in the woods." He halted his regiment in a wooded area directly in front of the enemy's line, his eyes studying the field before him.

Beyond a small creek blue uniforms swarmed over the crest of the knoll, forming themselves into a formidable line. He pulled his pocket watch from his trousers to observe the time; it was four o'clock. The earth shook beneath his feet from the furious cannonading and a sudden stab of anxiety clutched his gut. Sweat trickled down his armpits. No matter how often one was exposed to it, no man ever got used to battle.

The Alabamians were still throwing plenty of lead at Buford's horse soldiers, ramming Minie balls into their muzzle-loaders, the staccato *Pop—pop—pop—pop* piling into the morning air, mixing with the rhythmical *bang,bang,bang*, of Yankee carbines.

Ford almost gagged on the acrid smell of sweating horses and men, amid pungent whiffs of blue-white powder made of saltpeter, sulphur, and carbon, smelling for all the world like rotten eggs.

Suddenly, above the clamor, he saw Gordon, pistol in hand, leaning down the neck of his horse as he urged it forward. When they were within a few hundred yards of the Union line he boomed, "Forward, Georgians."

Out of the woods the 31st charged, battering and slugging their way past Rock Creek, yelling and whooping, pouring volley after volley of deadly Minie balls into the front and flank of the knoll. The Yankees returned the fire, and the woods sounded to the snarl and snap of lead slugs whacking trees and the peculiar *whoosh-c-thump* of bullets breaking into flesh. All anxiety was gone now; Ford felt only the heady power of battle. He bit off paper cartridges and rammed lead Minie balls home in the long barrel of his musket, firing a hail of hissing lead into the face of the Yankees. Beside him a Confederate battery of cannon swerved into position, horses foam-flecked and wide-eyed.

From the moment the 31st came charging out of the woods the contest was over. Exploding shells smothered the Union position. Ford trained his field glasses on General Barlow, who was screaming orders to rally his Yankees, and saw him fall to the ground, apparently wounded.

In the midst of smoke roiling up in a thick cloud and an unending bedlam of earsplitting noise, Ford and his infantry smashed forward, and section by section the enemy yielded. They were engaged in hand-to-hand combat now. Suddenly Ford caught a glimpse of Josh in the erie light of the hazy battlefield. He was in a fierce fight with a blue-clad soldier. Sabers flashed and then there was only one man standing.

He wore blue.

Ford threw caution to the wind and rushed to the spot where his brother had fallen.

Josh looked up with an apologetic grimace. "I'll be all right," he muttered hoarsely. "Got me in the shoulder, but I don't think it's bad." Suddenly he yelled. "Watch out behind you."

Ford turned and in a sudden lifting of the smoke saw his opponent, saber upraised, eyes wild. It was too late to use the musket.

He leaped forward and both fell to the ground under the impact. Ford was caught underneath, but with his wiry strength soon rolled to the top position. Suddenly, the soldier gave a mighty push, hurling Ford to the ground, whacking his head against an abandoned caisson.

Everything dissolved into blackness.

Slowly Ford's wits returned. Through pain-glazed eyes he saw a shadowy form bent over him. It must be the enemy. He started to struggle against the weight of a heavy arm.

"It's all right," Josh said, fighting to break Ford's hold. "I finished him off."

Within minutes, they were back in the fray—Josh with blood staining the shoulder of his uniform and Ford with a throbbing headache. The Yankees formed a new line, a few hundred yards to the rear, but the Rebels roared in and rattled it loose, and the Yankees fell into full and final retreat, running pell-mell across the ravaged fields toward the protection of the town streets.

Ford swept his hat from his head and gave a brief yell of victory. This part of the battle had been won. He bowed his head and worded a silent prayer of thanks, then waved to his men and set off in pursuit of the fleeing Yankees. They tumbled and floundered into the streets of Gettysburg, a sorry sight, groups of panicky, demoralized men darting down blind alleys and side streets with Ford's Georgians in hot pursuit, grins of victory on their powder-blackened faces.

Swarming through the streets of Gettysburg, horses and men were caught in a jumble of colliding, disorganized regiments. The Yankees were hopelessly snarled. Confederate shells whined and burst between the houses; bricks and debris fell to mix with abandoned canteens, shattered wagons, and dead bodies. Adding to the confusion, a few panic-stricken citizens rushed into the streets, begging the Yankees not to abandon them to the onrushing Confederates.

Eager to get back to Gordon for orders, Ford commandeered a horse, turned the pursuit over to one of his young officers, and galloped towards the low knob of land where the Union line had cracked. As he approached the field he saw General Gordon, with Josh beside him, kneeling over a downed officer, offering aid. He rode up to them with a sick feeling and jumped to the ground fearful that the wounded officer might be their own Jubal Early. Surprisingly, the officer on the ground had a handsome, boyish face and wore a uniform of blue. Gordon, speaking earnestly to Josh, pressed a white handkerchief into his hand. Dumfounded, Ford watched as Josh fixed it to his bayonet.

"What in the hell?. . ."

Josh grinned, his exhausted face traced with little rills of grimy sweat, punctuated by blackened teeth and lips where gunpowder had spilled over from bitten paper cartridges. "Don't worry, big brother, we aren't surrendering. That's the Yankees' General Barlow on the ground and he's badly hurt. His wife is a nurse with the Army of the Potomac and Gordon has asked me to fetch her."

Ford turned back to General Gordon who was holding the head of the fallen enemy officer, offering him a drink from his canteen. Ford's heart soared with pride. Even in the heat of battle Gordon acted like a true Southern gentleman.

In the meantime the retreating Yankees had formed a defense line on a ridge of ground containing the town cemetery. Gordon now moved his regiment into the long, low fold of ground that lay at its base, between the cemetery and a high hill on the Culp farm. Looking through his field glasses, in the pink glow of sunset, Ford could easily discern Yankee cannon lined up beside gray tombstones.

But the battle for that day was over. Attempts to attack the high hill behind them were abandoned and Ford and his men dug in for the night. Then, as the sun sank in a blood-red glow, weary men in the woods and fields began to lay away their dead.

Ford stood mutely looking up at the night sky. There were low, scattered clouds and an eerie brightening and dimming of the land as the moonlight modulated from clear to muted halftones. Triumphant Southerners were everywhere amid the debris of the recent fight—canteens, cartridge cases, muskets, and dead soldiers. Long gray lines of victorious Rebels stretched as far as he could see on both sides of the conquered knoll and tattered smoke clouds hung over the ridge.

The next morning, Thursday, July 2, came in hot, the air thick and sultry after a windless night. As the first streaks of light prodded the morning skies, Ford moved his men into position between the creek and a stretch of railroad tracks to wait for orders. General Ewell had ordered Early to resume his attack on the now heavily fortified Culp's Hill, but he held the 31st in reserve. All day, as the Confederates vainly tried to attack the hill; Ford was forced to listen to the whine and din of exploding shells as they shattered branches and ricocheted off rocks, the lofty oak trees literally shot to death.

That evening they supported Early's assault on East Cemetery Hill, but fell back when it was determined that the crest could not be taken without further reinforcements.

Uneasy brushfire erupted throughout the night and Ford could get no sleep. Nervous pickets, hearing any kind of noise in the darkness—the wind turning a leaf, a jumpy rabbit, a branch falling to the ground—would shoulder their muskets and fire, then somebody would fire at the man who took the pot shot, until muskets were going off all around, bright, quick streams of light whipping out in the darkness. It would all die down almost as soon as it happened, only to start up again somewhere else along the line.

July 3 dawned hot and humid. Except for the distant rumble of horses and caissons being moved about, not a sound of guns or muskets could be heard on all the field. Ford gravely placed his cartridge cases on a rock affording easy access to load, and leaned back to wait.

The day dragged on and by noontime the sun had burned off any haze left from early morning. With the sky bright and clear, the temperature rose into the high eighties. Sweat ran down Ford's forehead, dripping into his eyes, and created half moons of darkness under the arms of his woolen uniform. All across the battlefield the tenuous quiet persisted.

Somebody had scrounged up a few chickens, some butter, and a loaf of bread. Ford tried his hand at stewing the chickens along with some potatoes and brewed a large pot of coffee.

Josh appeared at his side. "Mind if I join you?" he asked.

Ford smiled. "Only if you'll help me eat this pot of stewed chicken. Lord, I miss Esau's cooking."

Josh pulled up an empty cracker barrel and a quick end was put to the stew while they discussed the previous day's action. Josh had found General Barlow's wife and brought her to him. With her nursing care he should recover.

"I should get back to my regiment," Josh remarked. "We're being held in reserve, same as you, but I don't know when we'll be called up."

Ford pulled out his watch. "12:45", he muttered, "and no action, yet. Stay awhile and share a smoke with me."

Cigars were lit, and Ford and Josh lolled upon the warm ground with half open eyes.

Within seconds after closing his eyes, Ford was jolted wide awake by a tremendous roar. He jumped to his feet.

"Great God almighty," Josh gasped. "What was that?"

There was no mistaking the distinct sharp sound of cannon—hundreds of cannon!

Ford ran for Ruffian and began to saddle him. Bless his heart, the horse had become so used to the sounds of war he was still docilely munching grass.

Josh had disappeared and all around him men were moving in frenetic activity. The earth shook beneath Ford's feet. It sounded like every fieldpiece of both armies were booming away at each other, and the flash and the thunder, like a hundred summer storms, centered on the thin ridges south of Gettysburg. Great banks of foul smoke rose in the heavy air to blot out entire sections of the landscape as effectively as fog rolling in from the sea, and it seemed the sky must surely cave in from the tornado of staggering crashes. Ford held his ears. Luminous flashes of light, muted to a deep orange color behind a layer of smoke, spoke to him of the terrible battle. Through the haze he saw Gordon approach and dismount.

"Captain McKenzie, General Ewell has requested a courier be sent to General Lee to inform him of our position." A slight smile pulled at Gordon's lips as he added, "Lee's south of town—where all the noise is coming from." He held out a gauntleted hand with a folded slip of paper. "Will you send someone to deliver his message?"

"I'll take it myself, sir."

"Good—then I know it will get to General Lee without mishap."

Ford set off at once. It was a good six miles, circling around the Federal lines, to reach Robert E. Lee. The cannonading had ceased and Ford could hear the beat of drums and the rising tide of marching feet. He spotted the general a slight distance ahead and spurred Ruffian in his direction. Lee sat astride his horse, Traveler, watching the action in front of him through field glasses. Ford had seen him many times and each time he was struck anew by the dignity and presence of the man. The general thanked Ford and took the proffered note from Ewell, reading it carefully.

Ford retreated to a nearby stone wall to watch the unbelievable scene before him. Long columns of soldiers were moving forward, regimental flags and guidons fluttering. As far as his eyes could see, the massed forces of the Confederacy were moving forward across an open field toward the waiting Yankees. The guns were silent as rank upon rank of men marched to their drums. Ford closed his eyes. He had never seen anything so glorious . . . so glorious and so appalling.

Advance Rebels stormed over a rail fence, muskets barking, both sides catching unmitigated hell. Men and horses fell, caught by shell splinters, bowled over by the ghastly crunch of cannon balls; every now and then a wild blast consumed an entire group of men and animals in one swift carnage as a shell connected with a limber or caisson, blowing up the ammunition box in a geyser of splintered oak spokes and axles and metal fittings.

The Rebels were moving fast, beginning to run now, driving in with everything they had—musket fire, artillery, bayonets, and the raw courage that allows men to wade into pointed guns. They streamed across the Emmitsburg Road toward a clump of trees amid a wild confusion of sulphurous smoke and yelling and shooting and cursing and dying. In the peculiar rising ecstasy of battle, which can transform men into brutal killers, they battered and shot the future out of each other.

In battle, time is an elastic sort of thing. For some it stretches out to great length; but for Ford it was short and concentrated. His hand trembled as he trained his field glasses on the long stone wall and the clump of trees behind which thousands of Yankees were raining lead and canister on his yelling countrymen.

He saw it happen. Saw the tide of battle turn. Saw his fellow soldiers fail to make the stone wall under the unbelievable hail of bullets. Saw them begin to retreat, slowly at first, then at a full run. Men fell over dead comrades without a word, staggered past men screaming their dying lungs out; others, the living, kept up a running babble of profanity as they streamed across the pocked field.

Suddenly, his spy glass picked out the young standard bearer of Wright's Georgians. He saw him stumble and fall, the flag disappearing into the churned mud beneath him. Ford swore. He knew that boy—had gone to school with his brother. A killing rage swelled in him. He flung his glass to the ground and spurred his horse over the wall, storming across the field toward his fallen comrade and the proud flag of his regiment.

He heard the whine of the shell, felt the thump of the bullet as it slammed into his flesh, felt Ruffian begin to fall, but he never felt the wet grass as his head hit the ground.

CHAPTER
– 10 –

All night and early the next morning, throughout the valley, the rumble, like distant thunder, of retreating infantry, cavalry, and artillery reverberated above the angry rain.

Abby laid her book aside and tugged the kitchen curtains open to peer though gray drizzle, looking for the source of the ominous din. "Does anyone know who won the battle?" she asked.

Ila shook her head. "Must'a been us. One o' Mr. Chambers men come by, headed to Gettysburg with food, an' he says the Rebels are retreatin'. Thousands an' thousands of them."

Abby sighed. She felt no sense of satisfaction at the sorry sound of trudging men. Men were hurting—regardless of the color of their uniform. Impatiently, she fastened the shutters to deaden the noise.

At the stove Ila prepared johnnycakes, and the rich smell of corn and boiling coffee soon dispelled Abby's gloom. Amanda made small mewling sounds in her cradle and Abby moved to pick her up.

"You're going to spoil that child if you pick her up every time she asks for attention," Sarah commented.

Abby laughed. "Look who's talking."

Ila fixed Abby with a glum look. "I'm sure they be no laughing among those poor boys passin' nearby, headin' south. All mornin' long they's been wagon after wagon of hurt boys, bleeding and moaning and calling for their women."

Sarah took Amanda from Abby's arms and sat down to nurse. "Round up every piece of cloth you can find," she said. "We'll tear it into bandages. And gather any blankets we can spare." Sarah saw the surprise on Ila's face. "I know . . . I know, these soldiers are our enemy, but they're torn and wet and it's our Christian duty to help them."

Abby's eyes misted over. How like her sister that was. Sarah's faith was earth-simple and rock-hard. Abby felt a profound ache of pure envy. She, herself, felt a secret joy that the North had apparently won. She forced herself to turn to Ila. "Send the bread you baked yesterday, Ila, and take some preserves from the cellar. I imagine they're hungry, too. And get Brandon. He can load the wagon."

"That little boy go with Chamber's man to Gettysburg. He's worried about his brother."

"That snip!" Abby exclaimed. "He should have asked permission." Ila rolled her eyes.

"Brandon's right," Sarah cried. "We should search for him in Gettysburg, too. He may have been wounded in the battle."

"You have the baby to look after," Abby asserted emphatically. "I'll get Elizabeth and we'll look for Tom together. She must be frantic with worry." Abby swallowed dryly, wondering if her brother's unit had been in the fighting. And more than once she had thought of Ford.

With a determined tilt of her head she eyed everyone in the room. "We'll find Tom, if indeed he is at Gettysburg."

She didn't mention Ford.

* * *

It was in the sanctuary of the German Reformed church, on the corner of Stratton and High Streets, that Abby found her brother.

Despite the fact that the roads between Greenwood and Gettysburg were choked with wagons she and Elizabeth had arrived in Gettysburg just as the sun was beginning to sink on the horizon. They soon learned that Tom's unit had been engaged in the heaviest fighting south of town. And that Tom was missing.

With mounting dread they entered the small church, identified as a hospital by a hastily fashioned white flag. Never in Abby's wildest dreams could she have imagined the sight that assaulted her eyes. Bleeding, torn bodies, some sitting, some lying, covered every inch of space the little church could provide. Stretched end-to-end along the pews were wounded and dying soldiers, some clutching at gaping wounds that spilled puddles of blood on the wooden floor, some screaming in pain, while others cussed in anger, and others cried in agony. Doctors worked feverishly at three tables made of doors ripped from the Sunday School rooms, barking orders to trembling aides. Scalpels flashed and saws sighed in the fetid air. Abby felt bile rise in her throat as she spied a large wicker clothesbasket, in front of the pulpit, filled with amputated limbs. Blood was everywhere and moans and screams filled the church which until now had been witness only to the quiet prayers of its parishioners.

Elizabeth cried out and covered her face with trembling hands. Abby drew her friend into her arms, hugging her tightly against her own shaking body.

A gray-haired woman, holding a cup of water to the lips of a pale youth, gave them a quizzical look.

"I'm looking for my brother," Abby stammered. "He's with the Pennsylvania Reserves, missing from camp. We're searching all the hospitals."

Without waiting for a reply, Elizabeth pulled away from Abby and ran down the aisle immediately in front of them, anxiously searching the faces of the wounded men.

The gray-haired woman hurried to the stretcher of a young Confederate soldier crying pitifully. "Look for your brother if you must, but we sorely need any help you can spare," she said wearily.

Half an hour later, after searching both sides of the center aisle and giving what help she could, Abby saw Elizabeth gesture frantically from the far side of the sanctuary. She hurriedly finished tying a bandage on a torn leg and ran to Elizabeth who was bent over a blue-clad soldier lying on a cot crammed into the corner. By the time she reached their side Elizabeth was cradling him in her arms. It was Tom.

She felt as though a trapdoor had suddenly opened in her stomach. A bloody bandage bound his head, his uniform was covered with mud, his face smeared with black powder. She dropped to her knees beside him and grabbed his hand. Tom opened his eyes and a slow smile of recognition lit their depths.

"It isn't as bad as it looks, Sis," he said. "The Doc says a ball just grazed my skull and I should be back in action within a few weeks." A smile pulled at his lips. "You know how hard-headed I am."

Elizabeth raised a tin of water to his mouth. "Lie still, dearest. Don't try to talk. I'll see if I can secure a clean bandage and wash your face. We . . ."

"We must get him out of here," Abby interrupted. "As overworked and crowded as they are they'll surely allow him to be nursed at home."

"I'd like that." His voice grew weak and he closed his eyes.
Abby jumped to her feet. "Let him sleep, Elizabeth. I'll find a doctor or an officer and see what we must do to take him home. We can clean him up there."

"Hurry, Abby. I can't stand this dreadful place a minute longer." Tears streaked Elizabeth's face as she cradled Tom's head in her lap.

Just then Abby heard a familiar yell and looked up to see Brandon running down the aisle. His face turned white at the sight of his brother's closed eyes and, sobbing, he dropped to the floor beside him.

Tom opened his eyes and focused on the grief-stricken boy with a reassuring smile.

"What'd the bastards do to you?" Brandon cried.

For once Abby did not correct his speech. Instead, she placed her hand on Brandon's shaking shoulder. "Tom's wound is not serious. Come with me, we'll see what we need to do to get him released."

She soon found that the removal of a wounded soldier from the sanctuary was met with relief instead of concern. "Take as many as you can, lady," a doctor in a blood-soaked smock said with a weary sigh. "More are being brought in from the field every minute and we've no space or medicine."

Abby sped outside and moved the wagon closer to the church doors. A husky lad of about sixteen leaned against the church wall, watching the dismal scene with anxious eyes. Abby ran up to him. "I need help," she cried. "Follow me inside. My brother's been wounded and we need help to carry him to the wagon."

The boy followed her eagerly, apparently glad to be needed. With Brandon's help they placed Tom on a litter and had begun to maneuver him through the crowded aisles when Abby's glance happened to fall on a soldier lying on a nearby litter, his eyes closed, his face white as death, the left leg of his gray uniform ripped off, his thigh torn and bloody. But what made Abby stop was copper-colored hair, wildly out of place.

She placed a hand on Elizabeth's arm and nodded in the soldier's direction. "We know that man," she said quietly. "He's the same one who tracked Baines into the mountains and then killed him. It's his manservant that is recovering at Brookside from a snake bite."

"Is the Rebel dead?" Brandon asked, staring at the officer's ashen face.

"No, but he appears to be seriously wounded," Abby said.

At the sound of their voices Ford opened pain-clouded eyes. They flickered with recognition when they finally focused on Abby. "Please," he moaned. "Please, help me. They want to take off my leg."

"How can I help?"

"Take me out of this hellhole. Esau can save my leg, I know he can. Please!"

Abby hesitated, considering her options. The wound gaped open, disclosing bone and muscle. The leg probably should come off. If not, he would need extensive care. Esau was not fully recovered himself. Still . . .

She looked into the wounded eyes staring at her with angry appeal.

"Brandon, you boys take Tom out to the wagon and lay him in the back. I want to check on this officer. Since his servant is already recuperating at our home, perhaps we should take him with us."

"But . . . but he's a Confederate,"Brandon sputtered.

"He's wounded," Abby snapped. "Now do as I say."

* * *

Low clouds obscured the moon and a soft drizzle fell as both men were carried from the wagon to an upstairs bedroom. To make caring for them easier a cot was installed beside Tom's bed. Brandon fidgeted, uncertain what to do. Elizabeth bathed Tom's face while Esau, though still weak, began to work on Ford's leg.

Esau let out a loud gasp when he unbound the blood-stiffened bandage covering Ford's wound. Blackened flesh and splintered bone protruded from its depths. Esau knelt on the floor beside him, his face haggard with worry.

"Eberthing gonna be fine, Marse Ford. You gots ole Esau t' tend t' you, now," he crooned, tucking a blanket around Ford's shoulders.

Ford opened his eyes. Abby saw them soften as he placed a pale hand in the outstretched brown palm.

It's almost like they're friends, she thought in surprise. *How can that be when one is Master and one is Slave?*

The room was stifling in the humid July heat and Abby moved to open a window, pushing back the shutters to leave in what little breeze might be moving. She stood for a moment, head tilted, chin high, as she listened to the labored breathing of the wounded man.

"Brandon, you ride into town and see if Doctor Suesserott can come by. I know he's busy—at least three of the churches in Chambersburg are being used as hospitals—but tell him we need help for Tom."

As Esau tenderly ministered to the wounded Rebel, Tom watched them through narrowed eyes. "He's a prisoner, you know," he said, looking Abby full in the eyes. "When . . . or if . . . he recovers he must be turned over to our army."

"Of course!"

CHAPTER
– 11 –

Esau's anxious face bending over him brought a degree of comfort to Ford during the next few days as he slipped in and out of consciousness. From time to time a voice penetrated the deep fog, assuring him that "Esau take good care of you, Marse Ford," and that, too, brought a degree of solace.

One morning he awoke to a strange, stringent sound. Was that metal clattering on metal? Why? Panic overwhelmed him; were they cutting off his leg? His eyes struggled open, every muscle tense. Before him stood a tall, slim girl, dropping silverware on a tray, her face enveloped in a cloud of black hair. A groan escaped his lips and she looked in his direction. With a murmur to someone in another bed she set the tray on a stand and moved to his side.

"I see that your eyes are clear this morning," she said. "Do you recognize me?"

"Abby?"

"Uh-huh."

"Where am I?"

"Our farm. We found you in Gettysburg . . . at a church serving as a hospital. We were looking for my brother."

His stomach tightened as memories came surging back. With dread he reached to feel for his leg. It was swathed in bandages, but, thank God, it was still there.

Someone moved in the nearby bed and Ford's brows drew together as he turned his head to stare into another man's eyes.

"Who? . . ."

"Tom Kennedy, Abby's brother," the man said. His eyes reflected some emotion Ford couldn't fathom. "Lieutenant Tom Kennedy, Pennsylvania Reserves."

Ford closed his eyes. Adversaries in war, now bedfellows in the same house. He lay thinking about it. *Could they have exchanged*

*bullets in the battle just finished? Could this man's bullet be the one
that shattered his leg? Could his own bullet be the one that wounded
Tom? How had either of them gotten involved in this awful war? And
who had won the battle just finished?* He opened his eyes again to
see the other watching him intently. "Captain Ford McKenzie, 31st
Georgia Volunteers," he croaked in a voice ragged from inactivity.
He tried to rise, but Esau placed a firm hand on his chest and pressed
his head back against the pillow.

"'Nuff talk, Marse Ford. You still be mighty sick, but thank the
Lawd that ole devil fever done leave you."

"How's my leg? It hurts like hell."

"An' it gonna hurt t' it be all healed up."

Abby approached and sat a tray on the table beside his cot. "Eat
some oatmeal," she commanded, avoiding his eyes.

My, she is a forceful one, he thought. As steam from hot por-
ridge, and what smelled like fresh biscuits, reached his nostrils, he
realized he was famished. How long had it been since he'd eaten?

"I'll be glad for some oatmeal," he said. "But not lying flat on
my back. Can I sit up?"

Esau and Abby exchanged looks, then he saw her nod and beckon
to someone.

A young girl with skin like creamed coffee, whom he recognized as the Kennedys' servant, approached the bed. Esau raised
him to a sitting position while she placed several pillows behind his
head. Esau smiled at her and stood back, beaming at Ford.

"My, my. Yuh sure 'nough look good sittin' there all proud and
straight." He picked up the bowl and began to ladle oatmeal onto a
spoon. Ford eyed him angrily, then took it firmly from him. "I can
darn well feed myself," he grumbled. "It's my leg that's been torn up,
not my arm."

But after several trips from the bowl to his mouth his arm began
to tremble and perspiration beaded his lip. The weakness humiliated him. He glanced to see if the women had noticed, but they were
fussing over the man in the other bed. Meekly, he allowed Esau to
take over.

Ford suddenly thought of his brother. *Had Josh survived the
battle? If so, had he searched for Ford and, unable to find him, assumed
him dead? And what of Ruffian?* Ford had felt the horse fall. *Was he
crippled? Dead?*

His heart ached with the not knowing.

He watched while Abby and the colored servant they called Ila
helped Tom cross the bedroom to a rocking chair sitting before an
open window. The room was small and plainly furnished, but light
streamed into the room from three deep-set windows. Ford's cot sat

beside a single bed with iron posts; the only other furnishings, an oak washstand with a basin and pitcher, stood beneath an east-facing window that was open to the light. No curtains covered it nor did pictures adorn the walls. A smile lifted one corner of Ford's mouth. A good indication of the nature of the man who occupied it, he thought ruefully.

His eyes locked with those of the lieutenant watching him— steel-blue eyes that offered no sympathy. He had moved ably, so his wounds could not be that serious. Vaguely, Ford sensed danger.

When he finished off the oatmeal and two hot biscuits, Esau eased him down to plump pillows. The bedlinens smelled of the sun and triggered memories of home and sun and sea. Someone had placed a vase of roses on the bedside table, and he remembered the last time he had savored the enticing smell of Matilda Page's extraordinary rose garden on Retreat Plantation. He closed his eyes and let the memory bob to the surface of his mind like a cork.

It was Ford's twenty-first birthday, late afternoon on a September day, free of the tropical humidity that smothers the barrier islands during the hot summer. Eager to share the day with his best friend, Henry Lord King, he turned his horse south on Frederica Road, savoring the enticing smells of St. Simons: sun, salt marsh, and jasmine. He skirted a dark swamp, before emerging into brilliant sunlight. A vast marsh stretched before him, golden-green, candid and simple, teeming with unseen sea-life from the flooding tide, silent except for the occasional call of a marsh hen.

The heavy scent of roses hung in the July air as Ford cantered through the mile-long tunnel of towering oaks that led to Retreat. Spanish moss hung from the live-oaks like a chinaman's chin whiskers. Ruffian's hoofs crunched on the shell carriage path, the fragrance of hundreds of flowers and herbs: beebalm, chives, dill, sweet marjoram, roses, hydrangea, azalea and jasmine wafted on the breeze. Mrs. King, it was said, would not tolerate any plant without a scent, and sailors had reported that a freshening breeze often told of landfall at the barrier island long before they entered St. Simons Sound.

He left the protection of the oaks and turned Ruffian towards the manor house. Lordy hailed him from the cotton barn and came loping down the path with his body servant, Neptune, close on his heels. Ford reined Ruffian beside a tabby building that had been built to serve as a slave hospital and waited.

Short, slightly overweight, with brick-red hair, he was Ford's senior by three years. Because they both had red hair people often mistook them for brothers.

"Whew, its hot today," Ford said, pulling his damp shirt away from his chest.

"An' the gnats are fierce," Lordy answered with a grimace, slapping his arm and squashing half a dozen of the tiny, biting, black fleas.

"Tide's in. Let's go swimming."

"Good idea. There's some decent wave action."

Ford squinted and shifted in the saddle. "Ah . . . where are the girls?"

Lordy grinned. "Mamma took them to the village. No gals here to see us naked—'cept maybe a few slaves and they don't count." He looked down at his servant. "Want to go swimming, Neptune?"

"Sho do!"

Lordy swatted at another gnat. "Let's go. Last one in's a coward," he called over his shoulder, throwing his shirt toward Neptune as he ran toward the beach.

Ford quickly shed his own clothes and dropped them on the sand. Within minutes he was chasing Lordy through the breakwater to the smoother waters of St. Simons Sound.

He turned onto his back and floated, looking overhead at the snowy wings of sea gulls, dipping and gliding in the warm ocean currents. Before long Lordy headed for the deeper waters of the channel separating St. Simons from Jekyll Island. Ford was content to catch the waves closer to shore, and not far away Neptune swam with strong strokes, his black body glistening like the fins of a dolphin breaking water.

Later that afternoon Ford and Lordy stretched out on the beach, the hard-packed sand cool with the receding tide, the sun bathing their nakedness in golden light.

Neptune approached wearing a worried frown. "You best cover yourself, Marse Lord. This sun burn that white skin of your'n like a lobster."

Ford laughed. "The curse of red-heads. How we do yearn for a tan to rival our dark people."

Neptune handed both of them sweet-smelling huck towels. Ford haphazardly draped his across his lower torso.

Lordy gave him a wicked grin. "That's right. You don't want to burn the family jewels. . . . half the girls on the island would be devastated."

"Especially the one I'm pursuing now."

"Not Cerise Descartes?"

"Yep." He noticed an odd expression on Lordy's face. "You know her?"

"I've heard of her." He grew silent.

"And?"

"Well, when my sister, Margaret, visited Savannah to have some dresses fitted by Mrs. Descartes the talk was that the seamstress was quite upset because her daughter was involved with a married man. A red-skinned Cherokee Indian to make matters worse. That's why Mrs. Descartes brought Cerise to St. Simons . . . she wanted to put an end to their affair. I'd be careful if I were you."

"Idle gossip," Ford retorted hotly. "She's the picture of innocence— the most naive girl I've met in a long time."

Lordy raised one eyebrow, started to say something, then closed his lips in a tight line.

Ford rolled over on his stomach. He had no wish to pursue that conversation further. He nestled his head on one arm and with the other worked a handful of gritty sand into a small mound. A covey of gulls settled on the beach, white breasts facing the sun.

"I missed you while you were at Yale," he finally said. "Somehow I don't see you taking up the law. Is it what you really want, Lordy?"

"No, it's what Papa wants. I'd rather take over management of Retreat, but he says Tip is older and better suited. What about you?"

"I really don't care that much for the law either—Pa has me enrolled at Dickinson, in Carlisle, Pennsylvania—but the life of a planter suits me just fine. Maybe I'll dabble in painting and women in my spare time. No stuffy old office for me." His face grew pensive and he knocked the mound of sand apart. "Nice dream, isn't it? But it's all immaterial now. If Lincoln's elected there will be war."

"Then you and I can don fancy uniforms and march off together," Lordy said, jumping to his feet and brushing sand in Ford's face. "An' just remember, gals are mighty impressed by men in uniform."

With a groan Ford turned his head toward the wall. The memories hurt as deeply as his wound. He cut his eyes to Tom still sitting by the window. If he had to share a room with his enemy he might as well talk to him.

"When did you catch the bullet?" he asked.

"Second day of fighting. We were south of town. How about you?"

"The last day, I guess, south of town, too." Ford's eyes misted. "I guess my horse is dead."

Tom's face softened somewhat. "I know what a horse can mean to a man. What was his name?"

"Ruffian."

"We had a horse named 'Bay Hunter' that was like a member of our family. He's now in the service of the Southern army, thanks to Jenkins' raid last year."

Ford started to reply, then stopped. Pursuit of that topic would only lead to harsh words. He closed his eyes, memories of St. Simons still and whole in his head. He tossed and turned on his cot, finally falling into a drugged sleep—mere memories replaced now by a bottomless dream.

Fog veiled the marsh bordering McKenzie Groves, and Ford was climbing the steps of the three-story plantation house surrounded on three sides by a broad piazza. The front porch faced the marsh, but the back opened to four miles of sandy beach, and it was there he headed. A gentle breeze swirled the fog around him like steam, blocking his view of the Atlantic. The silence and tranquillity were palpable as he leaned his elbows on the rail circling the porch. He heard something give a wild cry and cocked his head. Probably a gull, lost in the fog.

Esau appeared at his side. "You mama say for you t' hurry an' dress for dinner."

"In just a minute." He took a deep breath. "What a beautiful picture this would make, Esau. Nothing but shapes and shadows in the eerie light created by the fog."

"Well, you got no time t' be painting pictures. You mama want you now."

"Go get my bath ready. I'll be up in a minute."

Esau left and Ford turned his head toward the sound of waves lapping the shore. Something was moving out there. What was it? He squinted in an attempt to pierce the fog. It was headed across the beach. It was . . . it was Cerise walking out of the fog like a ghostly apparition, her arms outstretched toward him, naked, her body swollen with child. Then she turned with a secret smile on her lovely face and stepped into the ocean and dissolved into the swirling fog.

"Cerise," he screamed. "Cerise!"

Someone was vigorously shaking his shoulder and he struggled up from the depths of the dream, his heart threatening to break through his chest.

Tom stood beside his cot with a somber face. "I tried to wake you. You were having a nightmare." He raised his eyebrows. "Who's Cerise?"

Ford drew a deep breath. "My wife."

"Ah, yes. Abby mentioned that you're married; we must see that you get some writing materials. You'll want to tell her that you've been wounded and are a prisoner of war." Tom smiled, but not much of a smile because it tended only to stretch his lips.

Ford felt the blood drain from his face. Of course! He should have realized it sooner. Wounded or not, he was in the home of a

Union officer. A prisoner? Never! He would never allow himself to be a prisoner. Just as soon as he was fit to travel he and Esau would see about that. His mind scrambled to form escape plans, then, feeling Tom's eyes still fixed on him, he strained to hide his thoughts as his eyes searched the room. "Where are the others?" he asked.

"Sarah is putting the baby down for her afternoon nap; Esau and Ila are preparing a fresh dressing for your leg. The other members of my family, Abby and Brandon, are shopping in Chambersburg. Afraid it's just you and me, comrade."

Ford looked him straight in the eye. "Who won the battle?"

"Why, we did, of course. Your precious Robert E. Lee is well on his way back to Virginia with his tail between his legs."

Ford turned his head. Defeated? After their glorious victories the first two days and their gallant charge on the third! How could that be? Gall stung his throat.

He turned away from Tom's mocking smile. Sun motes danced in a shaft of light from the tall window. He fought tears of weariness and pain, then he cleared his throat and once more looked up at the tall, blond lieutenant.

"You look strong and well enough. Your wound must not have been serious."

"Just a flesh wound, it grazed my skull. Looks worse than it is. I'll be rejoining my unit by the end of the week. I've instructed Abby to turn you over to the authorities when you're well enough to leave your bed, but who knows, after Lee's trouncing in Gettysburg the war may well be over by then."

Ford closed his eyes.

Tom continued. "I see the news doesn't sit well with you. Well, that's the way of war." He turned toward his bed. "I also feel the need for a little nap. Pleasant dreams, Captain McKenzie."

Sleep, of course, would not come. Ford lay watching a fly beat itself against the window, his mind tumbling back to his disturbing dream, until Esau opened the bedroom door and entered quietly. He was carrying a tub of steaming water, and behind him Ila's arms were full of towels and bandages.

"Glad t' see you be awake, Marse Ford," Esau said. "It be time to bathe you and change the dressing on you' leg." He and Ila worked together, neither speaking, but Ford could not fail to see the tender looks that passed between them.

Well now, he wondered, what is this?

* * *

That night, Esau met Ila at her small cabin behind the main house, as had become their habit after everyone was bedded down for the night. Ila glided into his waiting arms and after a deep satisfying kiss rested her head against his big chest. He could feel her heart thump against his ribs. Tenderly, he reached down and kissed the top of her head.

They kissed once more before Ila pulled away and settled herself on the top step. She felt for his hand and tugged him down beside her.

They sat holding hands, the blanket of night wrapping them in a warm cocoon of quiet. All around them fireflies twinkled their beacon of love, and crickets chirped their courting song. Esau looked at Ila's profile silhouetted in the moonlight—fine features with high cheekbones and a long slender nose. Her hair glimmered, soft as butter in the sun. There had to have been a white man in this girl's not too distant past, he thought with an inward chuckle, but he would never voice his suspicions to her.

He pulled her closer, his heart swelling with love. She gave a deep sigh of contentment. "I love the feel of your big arms 'round me," she said. "I'm gonna miss you when you go."

"Don' have t' end, you know. You could come south with me—Marse Ford wouldn't care."

Ila gave a mirthless laugh. "Don't you realize Captain McKenzie ain't goin' nowhere 'cept a Northern prison?"

"I knows. I heard Miz Abby and her brother talkin'."

"What you do then?"

"Maybe get work somewhere nearby and wait for him t' get out. Then we go home t' our island."

Ila's eyes blazed. "You don't owe that man nothin'. Don' you know you no longer a slave. That Mr. Lincoln man signed a paper makin' you free. You can stay here and work for a wage on this very farm. Miss Sarah tole me to ask you."

"Never! I'll never work for the family what sends Marse Ford t' prison. An' Georgia slaves not free 'cause Georgia 'ceded. Marse Ford explained that paper of Mr. Lincoln's to me." Esau's broad brows drew together in deep furrows. "'Sides, you just don' understand 'bout me and him. 'Bout how we played and fished together and how he took me off to college wit' him and let me get some learnin'. I don' know as how I wants t' be free. What would I do? I don' know no other way."

"An you just bein' too stubborn to try. Do you always want to be a servant, dependent on them McKenzies even for a pair of shoes? You' smart, Esau, you have reading and writing. If you don't want to work on the farm you could get a good job somewhere's here in the North . . . maybe in one of the city factories."

"Lawd have mercy, woman. You call that better? Workin' in one o' your cold, dirty factories for pennies a day? Not t' be on my warm island? Never t' see the tide wash over the bar on a clear night or run barefoot on the warm sand? Woman, I never wants t' live in the cold North. Besides, the McKenzies always been good to mah family. They give me their name an' when they had to 'vacuate St. Simons an' go to Savannah, they take my mammy and pappy an' ever one o' my brothers and sisters with 'em. On the island we had us a nice piece of land for a garden and they built all our people nice tabby cabins."

"What's tabby?"

"They burns a big pile o' sea shells to get lime, den they mix the lime with sand and shells an' it get hard just like a rock. Most all the houses on the island be made o' tabby." Esau sighed and tipped her face up to his. "I love you, Ila. You knows that. I want you t' be my wife . . . t' have my babies. But don' ask me to leave my island. Or leave Marse Ford now when he need me so bad. You think on comin' wit' me when this war be over." He kissed her again, aware of the wetness of her tears.

"I love you too, Esau. I just don' see no solution for us. You never gonna catch me in the South where the only name a white person know for a black person be slave." She buried her head on his shoulder and sobbed. "You always gonna be bound to the McKenzies, free or not, an' much as I love you, I couldn't live like that."

"Hush now. Don't fret—we work out a way. Let's not talk on it anymore. If the Lawd want us t' be together He'll show the way."

In the barnyard a dog barked and soon several others joined in the chorus. Esau's heart was heavy as he sat waiting for quiet. Was there a solution to their problem? Was their love enough to cover the loss of the place each held most dear? Just now he couldn't see any answer unless one of them made a mighty sacrifice.

The dogs quieted and he pulled her into his arms and kissed her once more, hard and urgent, all questions forgotten. With a grunt, he pulled her to her feet and led her to the door. "I believes we got us some serious lovin' t' do," he said with a wink.

"You some kind of devil, Esau McKenzie."

CHAPTER

– 12 –

Abby and Sarah sat side by side on the edge of the porch snapping beans to be canned later that day. It was a hot, humid afternoon and perspiration beaded Abby's upper lip. She blew a sigh of weariness. Plow, plant, hoe, cut, can—the endless summer of trying to farm without her father. She had hoed and pulled weeds among the rows of vegetables until her hands and nails were chafed and worn, and now with two sick men to care for, she and Sarah were near exhaustion.

The swing squeaked in a far corner of the porch as Elizabeth and Tom talked quietly together. After a brief period of silence they heard Elizabeth groan in despair.

"Tom must have told her he's leaving in the morning," Sarah commented sadly.

Abby nodded. "She'll be devastated. She's spent every free moment she could spare from the inn tending to him."

"I heard him talking to you a while ago. He looked angry. Is anything wrong?"

"I disputed his wish to immediately deliver Captain McKenzie to the authorities. I . . . well, I did promise to turn him over to Colonel McClure the moment he's well enough to travel."

"What about Esau?"

"I'll try to get him to stay. We can certainly use an extra hand with Papa gone." Abby chuckled. "It shouldn't be too hard. Have you seen the way he looks at Ila?"

"And the way she looks at him. Unless I'm very much mistaken there's something going on between those two."

Abby emptied her beans into a large crock and scooped another pan-full from a brimming canvas sack. The sun was unbearably hot and she was beginning to develop a headache.

"Esau tells me the captain's leg is infected now," Sarah said.

"Yes. That man goes from one crisis to another. I almost wonder if it isn't all put on." Her eyes narrowed and her mouth tightened. "Oh, I almost wish he would die," she said in a ragged burst of anger. "He's a tremendous burden on us. I don't want him here. He's insolent and demanding. I hate him."

"Abigail Kennedy," Sarah's shocked voice interrupted her denunciation. "That is a terrible thing to say. I think he exhibits excellent manners, he seems to be a true Southern gentleman."

"How can you defend a . . . a *Rebel* after all they've done to you—after killing our father, ravaging our farm, stealing our horse, wounding our brother." She did not mention leaving Sarah with a shattered life and an illegitimate child. Bitter tears burned at the corner of her eyes. She brushed them aside impatiently, determined not to yield to the emotion, summoning her anger, denying her disturbing attraction for Ford.

Sarah's brow wrinkled in vexation. "That *Rebel* is a human being and a mighty sick one at the present. He's destined to go to prison. If you want him out of here so badly then a little human compassion might speed his recovery." Her voice softened. "Abby, do you remember that time we found an injured cat in the woods? It was wild and when you picked it up to try to tend to its broken leg it scratched and clawed your arm, yet you didn't push it away. You wrapped it in your apron and carried it home and nursed it back to health." She smiled and placed a hand on Abby's arm. "Captain McKenzie deserves the same kindness. After all you're the one who brought him here. You don't have to like him, just extend him the same compassion you gave to that little animal."

Abby's shoulders slumped, then she lifted her chin. Sarah was right, yet the man was her enemy, and she was determined to turn him in. "Well, if . . ."

A sudden shout interrupted her retort.

"Hey, Sis. Come look at all the peaches I picked," Brandon called from the backyard.

"Praise the Lord," Sarah exclaimed. "Look at what that boy has in his baskets."

Their brother proudly pulled his wagon to the stoop, laden with two bushels of lush, ripe fruit. Abby sighed with relief at the bounty. Thank heavens the peaches and apples were still green when the Rebels passed through, otherwise they would have plundered the trees like they did everything else.

She hurried to join Brandon in the yard, glad to end the disturbing conversation with Sarah. "Oh, these are lovely," she said, lifting a peach to rub its warm fuzzy skin across her cheek. She took a big bite and sweet juice dribbled down her chin.

"They's lots more gonna be ripe in a few days," Brandon said with a grin.

"*A lot more*," she corrected.

"Huh?"

"*A lot more* will be ripe in a few days."

"That's what I said."

Abby laughed and reached down to tousle the top of his head, causing the cowlick to spring to life and his face to flush.

Brandon ducked from her hand and began to lift a heavy basket from the wagon, his young muscles straining under the load. She took hold of one of the wire bails and helped him carry it to the porch. "Guess you'll be doin' your ole canning now," he said, wrinkling his nose. "Think they's enough to make a pie or two?"

"I think we could manage that. Why don't you see if you can find us enough corn for supper, then Ila can boil it and fry us a piece of ham with fresh peach pie for dessert. How does that sound?"

Brandon scowled. "You know the garden corn's been trampled flat by those stinkin' Rebels! I already searched every stalk for enough to can."

"But I'll bet if you looked again you could find just a few more."

For a moment Brandon looked like he might cry. "Geez, but I miss Papa, sometimes."

"We all do. I know it's hard."

"Might be a few I missed," he mumbled. "I'll look. I wanna get that alfalfa cut afor it rains, but if they's any corn left I'll find it."

Abby was on the verge of correcting his English one more time, but instead she squeezed his thin shoulder contritely. "What ever would we do without you, Brandon? You've been forced to be the man of the family long before your time."

Embarrassed, he hitched up his trousers and grinned. "Guess someday I'll make a right smart farmer."

And a man, she thought to herself as he loped across the yard toward the kitchen garden.

* * *

While Ila washed the dishes from a scrumptious supper of country ham, fried potatoes, corn on the cob, fresh lima beans, and peach pie, Sarah settled down to nurse the baby while Brandon and Esau went out to do evening chores. Abby picked up a book by Elizabeth Wetherall, but for some reason she could not get interested in the trials and tribulations of its pretty heroine. Instead her glance kept traveling to the pan sitting on the kitchen table containing one last slab of peach pie. *Ford would enjoy it*, her mind said. *He's had nothing but soup for days. Still, it's Esau's job to take the pastry up to him.*

But Esau is busy and I'm just sitting here reading a silly book. She pursed her lips, sauntered over to the kitchen table, and placed the pie on a tray. Sarah looked puzzled, but said nothing as Abby lifted the coffee pot from the stove and added a mug of hot coffee to the tray.

"I'll take this up to the officer," she mumbled as she walked to the staircase rising from the kitchen to the sickroom above.

Sarah smiled.

The room was stifling hot and, after placing the tray on a bedside stand, Abby moved to open a window to the evening breeze. Ford's eyes were closed, his breathing deep and regular. Abby stood looking down at him—at the lean torso, at the broad shoulders tapering to slim hips, at the tousled copper hair, at the ruggedly handsome face. A thin sheet covered long legs stretched nearly the full length of the cot and did little to conceal the outline of his maleness. Abby felt a hot wave sweep into her belly.

What was happening to her? She wanted to rest her head against those broad shoulders and run her hands through the rich waves of his hair. She thrust her fists into her apron pocket. This was all wrong. She was shocked at her feelings. You should be ashamed, she told herself; look away, don't think those things.

But she couldn't look away. Abby had never before felt real desire. Many boys had courted her, their kisses sweet, their embraces gentle, almost as though she were made of spun sugar. This man's arms would be strong, his kisses demanding. She was unprepared for the yearning that confused and worried her now.

She caught her breath when she found Ford McKenzie peering at her intently. Slowly, his eyes took on a knowing look and his mouth twisted in a mocking smile. She felt heat flush her face.

"I've been awake," he said with a salacious wink.

She could have slapped him.

He reached up and caught her hand. "Come sit on the bed. It seems like years since I've felt the soft presence of a woman beside me and . . ."

"Forgive me, Captain," Abby interrupted hotly, "I would sooner sit on a bed of vipers. You cannot possibly imagine the hatred I feel towards you and the entire Confederacy. I came only to bring you some pie and coffee while your servant is engaged in meaningful labor. The sooner you are out of my house the better."

"Now, just a minute." Ford returned her harsh glare in full. "I've suffered just about enough of your vicious tongue. May I remind you that my presence in your home was not of my choosing. On the contrary, I want nothing more than to leave this god-forsaken place and return to my outfit."

"And I played no part in the events that brought about your present dilemma," Abby spat.

"It was your damn Blue-coats that placed me in this dilemma," the captain bellowed. "You brought me here. You . . . you . . ."

Abby fixed him with a level stare. "This conversation will get us nowhere. In my eyes you are the enemy. I trust you will remember that." She watched his tight lips twist from anger to a mocking smile. His smile shook her, slow and unstinting and a bit crooked, gaining much of its appeal from the surrounding austerity of his sharp, thin face.

"Will nothing serve to soften your heart and coax a smile from your lips?" he asked with a seductive drawl. "Lips that I remember to be warm and sweet."

Abby quickly averted her gaze from the twinkling green eyes that regarded her provocatively. "I assure you, Captain, I wish to forget that moment of weakness," she answered sharply. "I wanted only comfort . . . and I have little reason to be joyful."

"Yes, I know your losses. But, Abby, both sides in this conflict have suffered tremendous misfortune and will suffer more. Forgiveness to one another is the only way we'll ever heal our wounds. And speaking of wounds, your cool hand on my injured leg could do a lot to mend it." He reached once more for her hand which she jerked away as though she touched the lid of a boiling pot.

"Don't, Rebel!" she cried self-righteously. "*Don't touch me!* I cannot stand to have Confederate hands paw me." Tears began to slide freely down her cheeks. "You are a married man, *Captain*, in case you've forgotten and I will not abide your unwanted advances."

"My marital status is of no concern to you," he said bluntly, fixing her with cold speculation. "Someday, I'll explain."

"Believe me, I won't be around to hear your explanation."

His smile continued to make light of her words, but there was a darkening sadness in his eyes as he watched her.

Abby was aware of the virile timbre of his voice; she still felt the touch of his warm hand on hers. *I am angry*, she reminded herself. She thrust her chin in the air. "The pie and coffee are on the table. I trust you can reach it without my help."

She flounced out of the room.

* * *

Unable to sleep, Abby watched the bright circle of a full moon from her bed. The moon was perfectly framed by the window, like the charcoal drawings in one of her books, and her mind supplied the hidden details: trees like smoky silhouettes, dark fields of wheat, the distant bulge of the mountains. Bull frogs croaked beside the swift-moving waters of Falling Spring Creek, a whippoorwill called from the stand of locust trees, and an owl answered from the old oak tree standing guard beside her window. Peaceful sounds that paid no mind to war or human sorrow.

A sudden unexpected memory of Ford lying upstairs in Tom's bedroom invaded her mind. The strong angle of his jaw, the mocking twist of his lips when he spoke to her, the knowing light in his eyes. No! No! She didn't want to think of him. It frightened her. He made her uneasy in a strange and different and exciting way. She would put all thought of him out of her mind. He held no promise for a future.

At that moment she believed it.

The next morning a grim-faced Esau entered the kitchen by the side door. "You bettah come quick, Miz Abby. It be the captain. He be done take a turn for the worst. He have a real bad fevah an' . . ."

Forgetting her previous admonitions to herself to treat the Rebel like the enemy he was, she pushed her plate aside and jumped to her feet. Ila hurried to Esau's side and Sarah joined Abby with a look of dismay. "We must see what we can do," Sarah said in a hushed voice.

The four of them entered the sick-room to find the captain writhing on his sodden cot. The room reeked of festering flesh and carbolic acid. Ila pulled the wet sheet aside and held a basin of warm water while Esau cut away the stained bandage. Abby felt slightly nauseous at the sight of the repulsive red, swollen area around the wound. "It looks highly inflamed," she commented, placing her hand on the fevered skin. "It is certainly infected."

Ford opened his eyes.

"Tell me, ma'am, what makes you an expert on the subject?" he grunted sourly, jerking the sheet to better hide his privates from her examination. She almost smiled at his modesty. He attempted a feeble grin, but from the pinched look on his face, Abby determined that the man was suffering excruciating pain.

Esau lathered a washcloth with soap and meticulously cleansed the ugly gash. "Yuh jest be quiet now, Marse Ford. Esau take care o' yuh, same as he always done."

That's right, Abby's mind screamed. Your slave has always tended to your every need. To the surprise of everyone in the room she picked up her skirts and stomped out.

Let his blasted slave take care of him.

Chapter

– 13 –

Later that night, at a scarred, wooden table in the summer-kitchen, Esau ladled another dipper of vegetable soup into his bowl and smacked his lips.

"Glad you like my cookin' so much," Ila said with a smile.

"You'd make a man some wife."

"Oh, is it only my cookin' you like?"

"Woman, don' you go puttin' words in my mouth. You know better'n that."

Ila laughed and sashayed over to the stove with an exaggerated sway of her hips. Esau's spoon stopped halfway to his mouth. She wore a long-sleeved red print bodice over a long, dark skirt, and a perky red turban was wound around her head. Although he preferred to see her silky hair bouncing on her shoulders, the turban did show off her high cheekbones and warm coloring. She was the prettiest thing he'd ever laid eyes on, and a flush of desire washed over him like an incoming tide.

"You behave yourself or you be in that bed afore you have a chance t' clear that table," he said with an evil leer.

"Shush you mouth, man." She sat down beside him with a mug of hot coffee. They ate in silence for several minutes and then Ila cocked her head and looked up at him. "Miss Sarah tole me the captain be married and have a little chile. You never tol' me that."

"Well, he do and he don't."

"What you mean?"

"If'n I tell you, promise you won't run t' Miz Sarah or Miz Abby with what I say."

"Promise."

"Marse Ford up an' married a gal name o' Cerise just afor the war come. It be quick 'cause Miz Cerise be expecting a baby an' Marse Ford's mother be real upset about it."

116

"Why?"

"She say Miz Cerise a common woman from Savannah an' she want Marse Ford t' marry a plantation girl."

"Tain't no good reason. I don't know as how I like his mama."

Esau shook his head. "Miz McKenzie the fines' woman I ever knowed. She guessed somethin' not right." He chuckled. "Our women 'spected Miz Cerise got fat awful fast. They wise in the way of birthin' an' they be right, 'cause she had that baby only six months after they be married. I never knowed a man so crazy for his wife, but things change mighty fas' after that baby come. It were a little boy, dark like us, looked just like an Indian. No way it could be Marse Ford's baby."

"Lawd, have mercy!"

"I heared 'em fight terrible in their bedroom and Miz Cerise she tell him the chile belong to a Cherokee Indian, name o' Grayhorse. She said she didn't marry the Indian 'cause he already married."

"What'd the captain do?"

"He come stormin' outa that room, cussing her somethin' awful, his face all purple. Then he get roarin' drunk an' stay that way for three days. Weren't long after that he sign up for the war. Marse Ford never did share his bed with her after that night, but he promise t' support her and the baby. Say he be honorable even if she weren't." Esau's throat constricted, memory of his master's grief still heavy. "He be mighty good t' that little boy, though. Say it weren't the chile's fault. They name him Michael an' when Marse Ford go home on leave las' year he tote that little boy ever' where he go."

"My, my!" Ila got up and poured Esau some coffee. She tilted her head and looked at him coyly. "Tomorrow Sunday. I be thinkin' it nice for you to go to church with me."

Esau sipped the hot coffee. Did he want to commit himself to this woman? Because that's what going to church together meant. A lot of differences stood between them. He studied her anxious face.

"I be mighty proud t' go wif' you," he said with a tenuous smile.

* * *

Ford leaned heavily on a makeshift crutch, staring from his open bedroom window at the crystal clear creek they called Falling Spring, glinting like a thousand stars as it meandered through the nearby meadow. He longed for paints and canvas, but the scene also invoked homesick memories of the sea as it lapped the shore behind McKenzie Groves, sun-dappled and serene.

Home! Barrier Islands called Tybee, Katherine's, Sapella, St. Simons, Jekyll, Cumberland, Amelia. Beautiful, gentle, golden isles lying serenely along Georgia's Atlantic east coast; plantation country. A place of gracious living and lavish beauty, of hospitality, of sailing and swimming and fishing and lounging in the sun. *Gracious* living that is, until war brought that life to a sudden, bloody conclusion. Now, sadness lay over the islands. Robert E. Lee had ordered St. Simons evacuated early in '62, and despair filled the hearts of his mother and other plantation owners. His island was a life in limbo, a world of memories. Would it—could it—ever be the same?

But he would not allow himself to be ruled by self-pity. He eyed the bedroom door. He had grown to hate this room, this austere, cheerless room, this imprisonment. Despite the open windows it smelled of sickness. He assumed that the spiral stairway, just outside the only door in his bedroom, led to the kitchen, where the delicious smell of boiled coffee wafted on the air. Could he manage the steps without Esau's help? Well, he'd most certainly give it a try!

Hanging on to his crutch with one hand, and the banister with the other, he descended the stairwell one painful step at a time, sweating profusely. He halted on the landing to stop the trembling in his leg, before hobbling down the balance of the steps to a small entry hall. He was right. The kitchen was immediately on his right, the smell of cooking strong and welcoming. Leaning heavily against the wall, he peered unobserved into the room, watching the two sisters and their servant prepare supper.

The spacious kitchen with its huge fireplace was cozy; a cat slept under an open window, and the grandfather clock in the sitting room behind him bonged as it struck seven. *A room of extraordinary warmth*, Ford thought. *But it is Abby's presence that gives the room life.*

A book lay open on a little table where an oil lamp burned against the fading afternoon sun, and a slight breeze pushed at muslin curtains framing tall windows where red geraniums paraded along the deep sills like ducks in a row.

An infant cried and he heard the rocking of a cradle in a shadowy corner of the room. He watched as Sarah picked up the baby and settled into a Boston rocker, turning to shield her body as she offered the baby her breast. They looked so right together—mother and baby. The sight evoked memories of Michael at his mother's breast; so innocent, so untouched by the tragedy around him.

Ford's eyes turned to Abby as she and Ila handled steaming kettles of food which hung in the flames. A long iron rod about two inches in diameter, supported by a post in the fireplace, permitted them to swing the pots away from the fire and ladle servings into crockery bowls. The tantalizing aroma of onion, tomato, and some unidentifiable herb filled the room. Abby walked to the plank table sitting in the middle of the room and placed a metal plate at one of the three table settings.

She looked up and saw Ford standing in the doorway. He watched her expression change from one of annoyance to . . . what? It was inscrutable.

"Ila, I see we have company," she said. "Fix the officer a place at the table." Her lips compressed into a tight line. "At least tonight you won't have to carry his food up to his bed."

Sarah placed the baby in her cradle and walked to where Ford still leaned against the wall. "I'm glad to see you recovered from the fever and downstairs, Captain." She moved to help him, but he placed a restraining hand on her arm.

"I can manage," he said bruskly, hobbling across the room to gently ease himself onto a ladder-back chair which Ila had pulled up to the table.

Abby said something that sounded like "harumpt."

Ford leaned back and examined her. She wore a dark gown, and her eyes were the same gray color, the color of a pewter sky. They returned his look in a most appraising way while a warm flush crept up her neck.

Quickly, she wiped her hand across her forehead in an attempt to disguise her discomfort. "It's terribly hot in front of that fire, but Brandon was hungry for vegetable soup, and it's best simmered all day."

"I'm surprised you still use a fireplace for cooking."

She looked offended, then smiled. "We do use a summer kitchen most of the time, but the house is damp from the recent rains, and we thought a fire might take the chill away." She moved back to the fireplace to help Ila, and Ford watched her retiring back with keen interest. She was really quite appealing when she smiled, and it was one of the few times he had seen her with her guard down.

Sarah joined him at the table just as Brandon came clumping into the kitchen. A spasm of irritation crossed the boy's face when he saw Ford sitting at the table.

"I ain't sitting at a table with any ole Rebel," he said fiercely.

"Don't say 'ain't,'" Abby corrected.

He glared at her.

Sarah reached out with a placatory gesture. "Mind your manners, Brandon. The Bible tells us to feed our enemy."

Brandon gave her a "you-don't-really-expect-me-to-believe-that" frown, then sank into the chair at the far end of the table.

Abby sat down beside Ford. Her eyes narrowed speculatively as she avoided looking at him.

"Now that the good captain can maneuver the stairs on his own, I assume he is well enough to be handed over to the authorities and leave us in peace," she said.

Ford bristled at her terse words and it took a great deal of self-control to keep his rising temper in check.

Brandon directed a sneer in his direction.

After Sarah said grace, everyone concentrated on eating. The only sound in the room was the rattle of cutlery on plates, the subtle sound of chewing, and the hiss of a log settling in the grate.

As Ford ate, he surreptitiously observed the two women. Like most men of his generation and culture he divided women into two categories—ordinary females and ladies. These two women confused him. Watching them, he perceived that their demeanor had, by necessity, been altered by the war.

They weren't ladies in the true sense of the word, but neither were they ordinary. Southern men thought of ladies as fragile, delicate creatures needing protection from harsh reality, including frank language and knowledge of the seamier aspects of life. They were placed on pedestals, worshiped and protected, because they knew nothing about the real world and its ugliness. At least that is what he had been raised to believe.

He concentrated on his soup, listening carefully to the snippets of conversation exchanged by the family gathered around the table. Brandon, Sarah, and Abby chattered away while he alternated between sips of coffee and secretive glances at Abby. Once or twice he looked up to find her eyes on him, but she quickly looked away. Brandon was relating a funny story and Abby began to laugh—a rich, deep laugh that seemed to bubble from her throat like a bottle of champagne when the cork is pulled. Ford was startled by it; he had never heard her laugh and he watched her expression in fascination. He had always thought her pretty, but the animation on her face made her almost beautiful. She had a look of fire in her unusual gray eyes, a look of interest, of intelligence, of curiosity.

Suddenly he felt a return of the longing she had first kindled in him. It had been a long time since he had experienced a loving relationship with a woman, and he did not doubt that Abby was a woman in every sense of the word. Something in his gut warned him to go slow. He sensed that for the first time since Cerise this girl had the power to hurt him. He wasn't ready to love again.

Well, he would solve that problem. He would seduce her—reinforce his disdain of all women and move on. There was an excited stirring below his waist. Ford shifted in his seat, dropped his napkin on his lap, and launched into a tense conversation with Sarah, hoping to prolong the meal and give himself time to recover.

Sarah gave him a puzzled look.

* * *

By mid-August, Ford walked farther each day, took all of his meals downstairs, played with Amanda, and watched the love between Esau and Ila blossom. He had been an invalid, and, he reminded himself, a captive, for more than six weeks. He detected a look of speculation on Abby's face when she looked at him, but there was also another look that he saw when she did not know he was watching her. Was it regret?

He dared to hope.

On this evening he found himself alone with her on the big porch that spanned the front of the house. Sarah had taken a fussy Amanda upstairs, Brandon was visiting a friend, and Esau was in the kitchen with Ila.

Abby was absorbed in one of her interminable books, while he eagerly scanned the past week's paper for news of the war. There had been no battles since Gettysburg, the armies sitting on opposite sides of the Rapidan River in Virginia, keeping an eye on one another as they rebuilt their forces.

Carefully, he folded the paper, rose and stretched. He saw Abby glance up from her book. Their eyes locked and held for a moment. She looked away first, a faint flush on her cheeks.

"Do you have a beau?" he asked.

"Before the war I was keeping company with Jimmy Meyers, a neighbor whose farm adjoins ours."

"Is it serious?"

"Not really. He's serving with the 126th Pennsylvania; he didn't see action at Gettysburg because he was recovering from a wound received at Chancellorsville." She gave Ford a sour look. "Maybe even from a gun fired by you."

He shifted in his chair. "What are you reading?" he asked to change the subject.

"A story about James the First and his wife Elizabeth and the English persecution of the Scots." Her eyes twinkled. "But no one, absolutely no one, could defeat the Scots. Not anything the English could do to them could make them surrender." She laid the book aside. "You're a Scot, aren't you?"

"Half. My mother is English."

"And do they fight a lot?"

"My father is dead. But to answer your question, no, they did not fight. They were extremely happy with each other. . . . not at all like the English and Scots in your book."

She fixed him with a demure smile. "And do you wear a Scottish kilt when you are home?"

"No, again. But my grandfather served with the Scottish Highlanders and as a lad I longed to learn to play the pipes and march alongside him in the parades."

"Why didn't you?"

"College . . . then the war."

"And marriage?"

"My unfortunate marriage makes you very curious, doesn't it?" he retorted sarcastically.

"Don't be cynical. It doesn't become you. For a moment there, when you were talking about your family, you were almost human."

"I'm sorry. . . . Cerise and my little boy are a very personal matter."

Abby cocked her head and gave him a tight smile. "I see the way you handle little Amanda. You must miss your little boy very much."

"I do." He looked out at the star-studded sky and suddenly he felt an overwhelming need to tell this girl of his hurt. He cleared his throat. "Michael was born six months after Cerise and I married. The boy was not mine."

"How do you know?"

"He was fathered by an Indian, his heritage quite evident in his features. When I confronted Cerise, she admitted that she had an affair before we were married. The father's name is Grayhorse, and he is a Cherokee." Ford grimaced, his white knuckles gripping the arm of the chair. "And he was married to a princess, daughter of the chief of his tribe, and not at all inclined to leave his wife and disrupt his political aspirations in Savannah. He represents his tribe before the Department of Indian Affairs."

Abby groaned. "But, just an affair, Ford. Can't you forgive her that? You admit you're fond of the boy even though he's not biologically yours."

"If it were only that, I might. But she knew she was pregnant and deliberately tricked me into marriage . . . into making me believe she loved me. Betrayal I can't forgive."

"Have you considered divorce?"

"Many times. But I want Michael to stay with me and I'm not sure Cerise would go along with that."

Abby's face looked incurably sad. "Then you do plan to stay with her?"

"I gave her my name. . . . I'll not take that away. That's all she has of me, though. I doubt we will continue to live in the same house when the war is over. We'll see." Ford sighed. "I do miss the little fellow. None of this was his fault. And . . . ," Ford swallowed, "and I did love Cerise very much. He's a part of her."

His eyes grew cold. "Now ask me anything else you want—about the battles I've been in, the horrors I've seen, the death, the senseless loss of friends and comrades. I'm an expert on all of that."

Abby's eyes softened with compassion. "Your eyes show so much pain, Ford. It helps to talk, as you've just done, and I'm a good listener."

He settled back into his chair, staring absently across the road at the moon-washed orchard rising still and silent in the night. It would help to unload all the anger. But where could he begin? Cold Harbor—Manassas—Fredericksburg—Gettysburg. Bitter memories all, but only at Fredericksburg had he felt the gut-wrenching grief of a personal loss.

Something about the soft glow of the stars, or the smell of night coming on, made him think of his friend Lord King. He began to recount the story to Abby, and as he talked, the memory of that night seemed to expand and glow till he lived it in the present—and made Abby live it also.

On a wintry night in December 1862, General Jubal Early began to move forward in support of the Confederate lines positioned on a ridge just west of the besieged town of Fredericksburg. Cold, hungry, without coats, many without shoes, men left bloody foot trails in the snow as they trudged along the narrow, rough roads.

They camped that night near a railway crossing, but Ford could not sleep. The Georgia Sharpshooters were bivouacked nearby and he sought out the company of his friend, Lord King, whose lamp still glowed in his tent. They talked quietly of home and loved ones. Then, about midnight, they left the tent and strolled to the banks of the Rappahannock to gaze at the enemy campfires across the river.

"Many of those fires will not burn tomorrow night," Lordy commented, his voice so soft, Ford had to strain to hear.

"And many of ours, I'm afraid. I expect it to be some fight."

Lordy stared at the river a long time without speaking. Finally he said, "Earlier tonight as Neptune and I watched the moon rise above that hillside, he made a comment that made my heart break. He said, 'Looks like high water on the bar, Marse King.'" Lordy sighed. "I wonder if I'll ever see moonlight shimmering on the sandbars of St. Simons Sound again."

Something in those words chilled Ford's heart.

In the morning, as the sun's rays began to penetrate the shroud of damp fog, Ford's brigade moved into position along the crest of a high bluff. Following the gentle sweep of the river below Fredericksburg, the Union line, numbering more than a hundred thousand men, extended as far southward as he could see. Confronting them were the Confederate troops, occupying impregnable positions on Marye's Hill and the adjoining heights.

All day the battle raged, the Federals marching by the thousands across the open field toward the woods and the waiting Confederates. Wave after wave of blue falling in heaps on the open field from the withering shot of the men behind the wall. Ford felt tears well in his eyes. Why did the fools keep coming against such odds? They seemed to be walking into the very arms of the Confederates. The thrill of battle had long since faded, and he felt nothing but hot anger at the dogged determination of General Burnside to send thousands of brave Union soldiers across open ground to die in such sickening numbers. But that is war, Ford thought grimly. Those that command don't fight.

Late in the afternoon the shooting tapered off. Thousands of men lay in piles, dead and dying on the frozen, sloping field beyond the woods.

Ford was squatting beside a campfire eating a meal of cold beef and biscuits when he heard his name called. He looked up into the diminutive face of Neptune Small, Lordy's manservant.

"Oh, Marse McKenzie," Neptune sobbed, "I know my po Massa fall. He out der somewheres in dat cold field."

"How do you know?"

"He done up and offered to ride across that awful field wif a note from the general."

"Sounds just like Lordy," Ford groaned.

Neptune nodded his head and Ford saw a tear run down his cheek. "He nevah come back. He daid—I know he daid. I feel it in mah bones."

Ford jumped to his feet with a bleak, wintry feeling. He placed a hand on Neptune's thin shoulder and squeezed it gently. "Have you checked the hospitals?"

"No suh. I needs your help. Dem doctors don't take kindly to us slaves bothering 'em."

"We'll check there first. Get Esau. He's in my tent."

When they were all assembled, Ford led the way to the division hospital. Grimly he and the two servants walked among hundreds of mangled men, some with arms off, some with legs off, all groaning and crying out for help.

But Lordy was not among them.

They left the hospital and set off across the field of battle at the base of Marye's Hill. Ford hailed a cavalry officer approaching on horseback.

"We're searching for Lord King. Have you seen him?"

"Not since early afternoon. Have you checked the hospital?"

"Just came from there."

"Then look out in the field," he said, waving a weary arm toward the scorched earth before them. "Doubt you'll find him in the dark, though. Best wait till morning light."

"Not if there's a chance of finding him alive."

"Well then, good luck."

Ford looked at the determined look on the slaves' faces and did not need to ask their commitment. Together they crawled down the dark hill, oblivious to the occasional musket fire still barking from both sides, and headed for the open field. Bodies were thick on the ground, lying in bloody heaps, disassembled in every haphazard and grotesque position the mind could imagine. Ford's stomach lurched with spasms of nausea.

"Esau, I'll take the middle of the field. You start from the right side and, Neptune, you start from the left. Work your way toward me. Fortunately there's a moon giving some light. Keep down, crawl if you must, and don't use your lanterns—they'll attract musket fire."

Ford began to crawl over the bodies, searching vainly for Lordy's face. Bits of leather, belts, and canteens littered the ground. Many of the dead were lying face down in the freezing mud, and he had to lift them to look for the features he searched. Many faces were completely gone, or shattered beyond recognition. A shell whistled across the field and he threw himself to the ground, landing on top of a still warm body. He rolled the blue-clad figure over and felt for a pulse. None. Apparently the boy had been severely wounded and left to die, alone on the frozen ground. The same could be true of Lordy—he might still be alive. Ford struggled to his knees and continued his search.

Suddenly, Ford heard a keening wail from the area Neptune was searching. The cry cut through him like a knife. Oblivious to the danger, he rose and began to run across the field. Neptune was also standing, cradling a blood-soaked soldier in his arms.

"I find him," Neptune cried, his thin body shaking with sobs. "I seed dat red hair o' his in dah moonlight. He be daid."

Ford wept as the first light of dawn came up on the dead face of his best friend.

Silence fell; Ford stared unseeing across the porch into the darkness. Abby had sat wordlessly throughout Ford's tale, and when he looked up, he saw a tear glisten on her cheek. "And your friend," she whispered, "was he buried there at Fredericksburg?"

"No. Neptune vowed to take his body home to St. Simons for burial in the family plot at Christ Church. I don't know if, or how, he managed it. He would have had to walk the entire way." Ford was unable to keep the trembling anger from his voice. "I found out later that Lordy had completed the mission he was sent on, but on his way back he sustained seventeen bullet wounds and died before he could reach his unit."

Abby kept her eyes steadily upon him, her face etched with sorrow. "You must put it behind you, you know. The anger, I mean."

"And have you been able to manage that, Abby?" He saw her lips quiver and her eyes cloud, as though just now remembering who and what he was.

"You'll be well enough to report to the authorities soon," she said. "My brother keeps writing, questioning my seeming reluctance to turn you in."

Ford stared hard at her before replying softly. "I believe you've become fond of me—that you'll miss me when I'm gone."

She bit her lower lip. "Yes," she said.

"You don't have to report me, you know. You can help me to leave and rejoin my unit."

She rose and wheeled about to face him. "I believe it's time we retired," she said, her face pinched and tight. He rose and moved toward her, then thought better of it, and with a heavy chest, he entered the house and limped up the stairs to his room.

CHAPTER
– 14 –

It was hot. The August sky colorless and still, no clouds visible, the thermometer sitting at 98 degrees. Abby pushed damp tendrils of hair from her face as she placed the last mason jar of freshly canned peaches on a shelf in the earthen basement. A trickle of perspiration ran between her breasts.

She, Sarah, and Ila had been canning since before dawn, and as Abby climbed the cellar steps back to the kitchen she promised herself a respite. Ila was cleaning the mess from the canning session and Sarah was rocking Amanda. After pouring herself a drink from the sweating water pitcher, she walked across the kitchen to the small shelf where she kept her precious horde of books. Reaching behind the novels she extracted one hidden from view. Carefully, she placed it in the pocket of her full skirt and headed out the back door. A few minutes by the creek under the shade of the willow would do wonders to restore her spirits before the afternoon task of working the garden where fat red tomatoes hung from the vine and the last of the green beans were ready for harvest. She groaned. Harvest meant still more canning. Still, she should be glad the vegetables had not been mature enough for plunder by the invading Rebels.

Queen Anne lace bloomed in the fallow field that reached from house to creek, and Abby trod a well-worn path that led straight to the shallow bank of the Falling Spring Creek.

She settled in her favorite spot where an ancient gnarled willow dipped its trailing branches to cast dappled shadows on the glinting water. Across the creek a buggy rattled across the stone hump-backed bridge, and a frog jumped into the water with a noise so sudden it startled her. With a laugh she spread her long skirts and lowered herself to the grass, so close to the stream that she could reach out and let her fingers trail in the cold water. She sat quietly, watching three ducks float round and round, going nowhere.

A large lump formed in her throat. She could never be happy any place on this earth other than right here. She should put all thoughts of Ford McKenzie from her thoughts, marry Jimmy and settle right here. Falling Spring Creek divided the Kennedy farm from that of the Meyers, and in the hazy distance stood the stone farmhouse where Jimmy's parents waited for the return of their son.

From the pocket of her skirt she pulled a slim romance novel and leaned back against the rough bark of the tree. A grin lifted the corners of her mouth as she remembered the shared laughter when Elizabeth presented it to her at Christmas. Her friend had spotted the book at a stationer's in Gettysburg and amid much blushing and stammering purchased it from the leering clerk. According to Elizabeth she would never venture into that particular store again.

Soon Abby was deeply engrossed in the story, already read many times. Lulled by the sun and trickle of the little creek chuckling over round river stones, she closed her eyes, letting her imagination fill in the details the author had tantalizingly omitted. So engrossed was she in her fantasies that she did not hear the approaching footfalls on the soft grass until a twig snapped nearby. Her eyes flew open to gaze upon the tall figure of Captain McKenzie.

Flustered, she secreted the novel beneath her skirts.

Ford placed his makeshift crutch against the tree and leaned his broad shoulder against its trunk. He looked down at her with a sardonic smile.

"Reading, I see," he commented, his soft Southern drawl one with the shimmering heat.

"Yes."

"Can I ask the title?"

"No, you cannot." She pushed the book further beneath her skirts.

Ford's thin lips lifted in a half smile, and Abby had the uncomfortable feeling that he knew the nature of the book she was hiding. He continued to lean against the tree, not speaking, watching her with those striking green eyes. When he looked at her like that she felt the impact of him clean in the pit of her stomach.

Sunlight ignited the copper fire of his shoulder-length hair and played across the narrow planes of his rugged face. Now she could understand the pathos of the heroine of her novel as she yearned for the forbidden stable boy.

She bit her lip. For heaven's sake, this was Ford, her sworn enemy, her prisoner, not some romantic figment of her imagination.

His eyes never left her. She felt heat begin to engulf her, her stomach fluttered as with a thousand butterflies, and in consternation she began to rise to her feet.

He reached out a hand to help her.

"I am perfectly capable of rising to my feet without assistance," she said tartly.

"I've no doubt you are, but my Southern manners demand that I offer assistance to a lady." He took her hand in his and gently pulled her off the ground and onto her feet. He didn't let go.

"Ford," she said matter-of-factly. "It's getting late, I must get back."

He did not answer but began to pull her toward him. Abby felt her legs weaken but Ford's strong arms were around her, holding her tight against his chest. He smelled of tobacco and sweat, with a faint hint of the rum he used to wash his hair—a deep masculine scent. He was going to kiss her and she was powerless to stop him. Ford lowered his head and cupped Abby's face in his strong hands. The touch of his lips was light, soft and warm, but Abby felt a hot wave sweep her from her head to her toes.

He stepped back, his eyes dark and smoldering. "I've been wanting to do that since the night I first saw you."

Abby could not speak. Her body ached with an inner longing, her mouth was dry, and she ran her tongue slowly over her lips. Beside her the creek whispered and gurgled; one of the ducks flapped its wings and took flight.

Ford leaned forward, his finger moved gently over her lips, and he tucked a lock of hair behind her ear. He kissed her again, his thumb caressing her neck, his lips more demanding. His hand moved to the back of her head, stroking her hair, his lips moving against hers. She thought she would die. Their lips lingered, then he stood back to look at her, his hand once more reaching for hers.

Abby moved then, away from him, struggling for control. She reached down to retrieve the book still lying on the ground and stuffed it into her pocket.

"I think we should forget that happened," she said softly. Ford kept his eyes on her, waited. "It's almost dinner time and everyone will wonder where I am." She moved resolutely away but Ford paid no attention to this. Instead, he stepped around her with amazing agility for one with an injured leg, blocking her way, and again put his hands on her arms. Abby felt paralyzed.

"This is impossible," she said. But in her heart she knew it wasn't impossible. She had wanted his kiss. She had wanted to feel his arms around her.

"Abby," he whispered. She could feel his warm hands on her arms, pulling her toward him, his breath hot against her face.

"There's something very wrong with this," she said.

"What's wrong with it? Don't tell me you don't feel the same attraction I do. And don't tell me it's about my being a Southern soldier because it isn't. I know how I feel and I suspect I know how you feel." He reached out and touched her cheek.

"You're still married," she said simply.

"There is nothing I can do about that until the war is over."

"But . . . "

He tugged her hand. "Come, let's talk."

Abby felt a kind of terror rising up in her, the knowledge that this was a fast-moving storm with unforgiving winds, this moment in time with Ford McKenzie. And yet, part of her wanted this moment, this chance to taste the forbidden. She felt the earth tilt, wanted nothing more than to melt once more into this man's arms.

"It's much more than your marriage," she stammered. "You don't know me, don't know my responsibilities." Up at the house a door slammed and Sarah's voice called her name. "Ford," she said. "I must go. I think it's best we keep a distance, at least until we have time to really talk."

He moved away from her, retrieving his crutch from against the tree, his face dark with emotion. She nearly reached out and touched him, then. Nearly. After all, this was the truth she had been hiding from—that she cared for him more than she hated him.

His eyes still on her, he backed away. "Tonight. After everyone is asleep. I'll meet you on the porch and we'll talk."

Abby nodded and without another word ran toward the house.

That afternoon the post delivered a letter from Tom reprimanding her for not having turned the Rebel over to the authorities. She had to make a decision—Ford had already stayed longer than she should have allowed. And her growing feeling for him must stop at once.

Yet, somehow, in Abby's thinking, fighting and killing the enemy on the battlefield was *honorable*, but sending him to a dank prison was *less than honorable*. She shook her head. She simply could not let herself feel this way—her duty was clear. She tried to summon up her old anger, visualizing the face of her father, the face of Sarah's rapist, the terrified faces of fleeing slaves, the despairing faces of mutilated Union soldiers lying in hospitals, and once more hatred erupted from her soul like lava from a volcano.

She laid the letter aside. She would see Judge Kimmel this very day and tell him of Ford's presence in her home. The sooner the job was done, the better.

* * *

Exhausted, Ford lay across the bed. A walk shouldn't take this much out of him. At this rate he would never have the strength to escape Brookside and find his way back to his regiment.

Gradually his breathing slowed and he left his mind wander back to the encounter with Abby. What had started out as a simple flirtation had turned into a need that was gathering steam like a fast-moving locomotive.

He groaned and flopped over on his stomach. He had no right to compromise Abby's virtue. She deserved more from him. Despite the humiliation that Cerise had inflicted on him, he was still bound to his marriage vows. His life was unsettled, his emotions still raw. "Abby spells trouble," he said to himself. "Trouble I don't need, complications I don't want."

Thoughts of Cerise always stirred up memories of his little boy. And he always thought of Michael as *his* little boy. He thought of Michael with a deep unreasoning yearning, made more acute each time he held Sarah's infant in his arms. He wondered if he would survive the war—survive to teach his son to swim, to ride his pony across the sandy beach, to fish the salt water marches surrounding McKenzie Groves. Would there even be a plantation for Michael to inherit? Ford's heart ached as he thought of home.

He was sprawled across the bed, lying in a state between sleep and wakefulness, when Esau entered the sickroom with Sarah at his side. She pulled up a chair and smiled down at him.

"I think it's time we talk," she said.

He looked at her with apprehension. "Talk?"

"Of a way to help you escape. Esau and I have come up with a simple plan that we think will work."

Esau shifted from one foot to the other and gave Ford a forced smile.

"Let me hear it," Ford said bruskly.

"We'll dress you as a woman in one of my frocks, give you one of our farm wagons and a mule and set you on your way."

Ford fingered his beard and thought about the complications. It was foolhardy and dangerous.

"I'd never pass as a woman," he said.

"Yes, you would. If you shave and keep your face shielded with a large bonnet and don't speak."

"What about Esau? I won't leave without him."

"He'll go with you and drive the wagon. We've already talked it over. He'll load the wagon with sacks of grain and, if stopped, he can say you are on your way to the gristmill."

"Suppose I'm questioned, forced to speak."

"Let Esau do the talking. If that doesn't work, pretend you are very shy and don't speak above a whisper."

It might work, Ford mused. It just might work. It was a long shot—a very long shot, but better than the alternative of prison. "Can you spare the grain? And the mule?"

Sarah's cheek dimpled. "No, of course we can't. But I honestly can't think of any other way to get you away."

"You could be in danger yourself. Held for treason if they find out you aided my escape."

"Make no mistake, Captain. I will swear you stole the clothing and the wagon. You must be aware, however, that, if caught, your punishment will undoubtedly be harsher than if you were simply a prisoner of war. The choice is yours to make."

Esau had been listening intently, his dark eyes flashing from Ford to Sarah and back again.

Ford grinned broadly. "There's really no choice, is there? It's a risk worth taking. When?"

"Tomorrow morning under cover of darkness. You can be in Maryland by nightfall. According to Tom's letter, Lee's army is south of the Rapidan River, near Mine Run."

Ford raised his eyebrow.

"I'm afraid you must act quickly. We received a letter from Tom this afternoon urging us not to delay turning you over to the authorities."

Ford reached over and took Sarah's hand. "Odd that you should be the one to show forgiveness."

"I've no quarrel with you, Captain. Have you ever read the teaching of Micah in the Bible?"

Ford shook his head.

"Micah said, 'You do not delight to stay angry forever but delight to show mercy.' I think soldiers on both sides are fighting for what they believe. It's not up to me to judge who is right and who is wrong."

She rose. "I'll give Esau a dress and bonnet for you, as well as a map, but he must wait until everyone is abed to ready the wagon."

"You would make a good spy," he said in a teasing voice.

Was it his imagination or did she get a queer look on her face?

"Ah . . . one must do what one can do," she answered, obviously flustered.

What was going on here?

Sarah turned her attention to his servant. "Come, Esau, I'll show you where everything is. Captain, you should get as much rest as you can. Tomorrow will be a grueling day."

Indeed it would be. He would either get shot, imprisoned, or make his getaway to Maryland, a hostile state.

Outside the door, Abby leaned against the wall. She had heard it all. Her thoughts swirled and she almost cried out. She should notify the authorities before Ford had a chance to escape. But could she? Oh God, what should she do? Her first duty was to her country, wasn't it?—to Tom and to all of the Union soldiers fighting in this terrible war. Her stomach contracted like a fist, the memory of Ford's kiss a burning coal.

Still, Ford had mentioned taking Esau with him. What would that do to Ila? Any fool could see that she was in love with him.

Still . . .

With a feeling of navigating through swirling waters she gathered her skirts and fled down the hall.

* * *

Tears swam in Esau's eyes. There was no doubt in his mind where his duty lay. He must help Marse Ford get back to his regiment. But what about Ila? How could he make her understand? What could he say to ease her pain? With hesitant feet he entered the summer kitchen where she was stirring a bowl of yellow batter. Trays of warm cookies rested on the table and the delicious aroma of molasses and ginger made his mouth water. He crept up behind her and slipped his arms around her slender waist.

"Mercy, you 'bout scared me to death," she said, half turning to look up at him, her face flushed with pleasure.

He brushed the top of her head with a kiss, the knot in his stomach drawing tighter. "Ummm. You smell 'most as good as those cookies you bakin'." His arms tightened, pulling her closer.

"Now you behave yourself an' let me get this batter spooned out. What you doin' in my kitchen this time o' day, anyhow? Don't you have chores to do?"

"I needs t' talk t' you, Ila. Finish up your baking and set with me a minute." He moved away from her, grabbed a warm cookie, and pulled a chair up to the table.

Within minutes Ila had the last tray in the oven. She wiped her hands on her apron and wrinkled her brow. "What ever so 'portant it can't wait till tonight?"

There wasn't an easy way to say it. He'd just have to tell her.

In a rush he told her of Sarah's plan to help Marse Ford escape. "An' so," he finished, "I be leavin' early mornin'."

Ila sobbed. "Why, Esau? Why must you go? You soon be a free man. That Mr. Lincoln say so."

Thoughts swirled in Esau's mind like waves in a thunderstorm. Ila insisted he was free. Did he want to be free? What did free really mean? Free to marry Ila and stay in the North, or free to leave his beloved island and the only home he had ever known? He shook his head. His heart ached with love for Ila, but loyalty to Ford would not let him abandon the master he had always served. At least not until the war was over.

"No, I not be free. Not free like you mean." He slammed his fist on the table, his face contorted with anguish. "Lawd, woman, I loves you, you knows that. Remember how kind the Kennedys be t' you all your life. Now that they need you so with their Pappy gone, would you just pack up and move on? No! Same with me and Marse Ford. When the war be over I come back t' you and we work things out."

"An' you think I still be here waitin' for you?" she asked bitterly.

He rose and took her in his arms once more, tilting her face up to his. "If you loves me like you say, you will be."

With a sob she wrested herself from his grip. "You leave now, I never forgive you! Never! Now get out o' here. Go take care of your *Master*—you think he need you more'n I do."

The smell of burning cookies filled the small room as Esau slunk away.

* * *

Late afternoon sun propelled waves of heat into the small bedroom above the kitchen, and Ford tossed and turned on the sweat-soaked sheets in an uneasy sleep. Then, just as shadows began to fall, he awakened with a start and sat bolt upright in bed. Loud voices reverberated from the room below. His heart pounded in his chest as heavy boots clattered on the wooden steps and the door of the bedroom flew open.

Two *blue*-uniformed officers strode to the foot of his bed. "You, sir, are a prisoner of war," one of them barked. "Get dressed."

Abby, Esau, and Sarah crowded into the room behind the soldiers and Ford's gaze flew to Abby's face. She looked away. *Bitch!* Ford's mind screamed. *Compassionate and caring one minute and betrayer the next.* He had once mistaken a woman's honor and later suffered the abject humiliation of that mistake. It was an error he would never make again. This very thing was only one of the reasons he had vowed never to lose his heart to anyone. He still felt the raw pain of betrayal. He had felt the signals pushing against him like ripples in a pond. But he had ignored them.

"I . . . I need help to dress. My man . . ."

"Your *man*?" one of the officers, a balding, sour-faced man, sneered. "This darky no longer belongs to you or anyone else."

"But I can't. . . ."

"He'll not be in prison to help you dress, so you better learn now. Out of the room, everyone." He looked at Ford. "I'll be downstairs."

Ford crossed to the door that had been left open a few inches. He closed it with a dungeonlike bang.

Painfully, he hobbled around the room gathering up his few possessions: a razor, a comb, a small Bible, and a few pictures. His tunic was intact and he still had his slouch hat, but his shredded uniform trousers had been replaced with a pair of Tom's castoffs. As he dressed he seethed with rage. One more day and he would have been away.

He grabbed his crutch and lurched down the steps. Everyone stood silently, watching him. He stood with his feet wide apart, his shoulders square, like the officer he was. With teeth clenched, he strode over to Esau and grabbed his big hand, imploring him with his eyes to understand that he could speak no words of farewell. To Sarah, standing with Amanda in her arms, he directed a slow smile of thanks. Then he turned to Abby and swept his hat low with a mocking salute.

The sour-faced officer moved to his side and ushered him toward the door.

"Where will you take him?" Abby asked in a strained voice.

"The jail in town, until we can arrange passage to one of the Union prison camps."

"Which prison camp, do you know?"

"Probably Fort Delaware," he said with obvious mirth. "One of our *finer* prisons."

As the men disappeared down the lane, Abby sank to the porch step, a bundle of misery. *This is what I wanted, isn't it?* she thought wildly. *He is the enemy that brought war to our doorsteps. This is only one segment of the circle of war—fighting, killing, wounding, being captured. It was part of HIS bargain when he donned a Confederate uniform, part of MY bargain when I vowed vengeance for my father's death.*

Yet, she got no pleasure out of his capture, did not want to see him go.

Sarah sank to the step beside her and placed a comforting hand on her arm. "We all liked him," she said. "I know it must have been hard for you to turn him in."

"Turn him in? But I didn't! Tom did."

Sarah frowned. "What do you mean?"

"When the officer first identified himself he said that they had received word from Lieutenant Thomas Kennedy that a Confederate soldier was recovering on his farm from wounds received at Gettysburg."

"You realize that Captain McKenzie thinks it was you."

"What difference does it make?" Abby retorted, her voice quivering. "He hates me now. He's gone. He thinks I betrayed him. We'll never see him again."

On a golden September morning, only a week after Ford's capture, Esau approached Abby, his face haggard with worry.

"I jest come from the jail in town where they holdin' Marse Ford," he said. "He be awful sick, Miz Abby. Say he got the runs. The army men keepin' him there till he be well 'nough t' take to the prison."

"I'm sorry to hear that, Esau, but I'm afraid there's nothing we can do."

"Yesum." He stood for a moment in silence, his broad brows wrinkled, his dark eyes pleading. "Some o' Ila's chicken soup maybe help."

Abby looked away, her face a deepening hue of shame and guilt. By bringing Ford home with Tom, she had brought this whole disaster upon him. Had she left him to be taken with Lee's retreating army he might not now be a prisoner of war. After all, the man had tracked and killed her father's murderer—had shown genuine compassion for her family. She knew that he, himself, could never be guilty of such a barbaric act as that perpetrated by the raider. And if she were to be honest with herself she had begun to care deeply for him.

She looked back to Esau who still watched her, his face impassive and still. She had to say something . . . do something. "Tell Ila to kill one of the chickens and make some soup, with extra for the captain."

A look of relief flooded Esau's face, and then, white teeth gleaming in his ebony face, he gave her a speculative smile. "Does you want me t' take it t' him or does you want t' go?"

Was it her imagination or did those intelligent eyes watch her knowingly?

Abby felt the heat rise in her throat. "I'll take it. . . . I feel I should apologize to the captain."

With a nod of his wooly head, Esau hurried off to find Ila.

Swinging a tin pail of hot soup by its bail, Abby walked resolutely along the dirt road that led to town and the jail where Ford was temporarily detained. The countryside showed a sharp beauty; goldenrod and blue asters filled the barren fields, Virginia creeper and sumac, already orange and crimson, portended the magnificent fall colors soon to come. The heavy fragrance of ripe grapes hung in the air, and chattering blackbirds feasted on sunflower seeds, filling their bellies before beginning their journey south.

All along the meandering stream grist-mills labored, their wooden water wheels splashing in the noonday sun. She skirted an orchard where the boughs hung heavy with red winesaps, while under the trees cows munched on the windfalls, the air sweet with the smell of rotting fruit. Stacks of wooden crates sat waiting for the fall harvest. But where would farmers get pickers this year? Where would she get pickers? The answer was simple—she wouldn't. The job would fall on them—two women, a young boy, and Esau, if he were still with them.

Hard to believe that not too many miles distant this beautiful land was ravaged by smoke and gunfire; that men faced and killed one another in bitter battle, many not knowing the reason why they fought. Tears filled her eyes. Right now Tom might be lying under some Virginia apple tree, his blood seeping into the fertile soil.

She followed the bank of Falling Spring Creek, swinging her pail, mulling over her predicament. In her heart she forgave Ford, no longer held him accountable for the offense to her family. She still could not accept the fact that he owned a slave, or that his loyalty lay with the South, but she suspected that was a matter of culture more than choice. Besides, what difference did it really make? He was married, would return to the South after the war, and she would never see him again. Still, she wanted him to know of her forgiveness. For some reason that was important to her.

With quickening footsteps she turned down King Street to where the jail sat on the northwest corner of Second Street. It was said to be the strongest in the state, built in 1818 with three-foot-thick walls of bricks baked of red clay from the banks of the Falling Spring and Conococheague Creeks. A twenty-foot-high limestone wall hid the gallows and the exercise yard, and a large cupola adorned the slate roof. Of Georgian architecture, it was a handsome building, despite the purpose it served. She knew it was rumored to have been a stop on the Underground Railroad, housing runaway slaves in the dungeon area.

At her knock, the heavy front door was swung open and a burly man with a pockmarked face stared at her, eyes narrowed in suspicion.

"I have some soup for one of your prisoners . . . a Captain McKenzie," she said nervously.

"You mean the Rebel?"

"Yes."

His small eyes squinted at her from behind heavy lids, traveling up and down her body. He flashed a dirty little grin. "'Fraid you're out of luck, Miss," he said, addressing his remarks to her breasts. "He's no longer here. About an hour ago they toted him off to prison, where he belongs."

Abby felt weak with disappointment. Now she would never have the chance to tell him that it was not she who had turned him over to the authorities.

"Where did they take him? . . . do you know?"

"Fort Delaware," he answered with a sneer.

* * *

A driving December wind rattled the tin roof, sleet pelted the kitchen window, and the fireplace refused to draw, forcing smoke down the chimney. After dropping yet another stitch, Abby tossed the sweater she was knitting into her yarn basket and trudged up the stairs to her bedroom.

She tossed and turned, her mind a muddle. She didn't like her mood; she felt increasingly helpless, completely unlike herself who was always in control of her emotions.

Impatiently, she climbed out of bed, wrapped herself in a wool blanket, and padded over to the window to check the amount of accumulating snow. Frost covered the window, turning it into a pane of delicate lace. She placed her hand against the star-shaped pattern, letting the warmth clean an opening through which she could see. The snow had stopped; bare trees cast long shadows across the moon-washed lawn covered with pristine white. The fields and orchards of Brookside lay before her as though wrapped in cotton batting. With a shuddering groan she pressed her forehead against the frosted window.

Although she couldn't see the mountains, she knew they were there. To the north the Kittatinny and Tuscarora giving way to beautiful valleys: Path Valley, Bear and Horse Valley, Amberson Valley, and Cove Gap, and to the south the rugged South Mountain chain. No matter where one was in the valley one could always see the mountains, like a protective shield around their little world. The richness of view inspired in Abby a remarkable love for the beautiful in nature, which she occasionally put to paper in the form of poetry.

A tide of joy washed over her. This was her legacy—this beautiful valley. Beneath the snow, ready to burst forth in spring, lay the lush grass. And standing sentinel over all, the mountains—their banks covered with trees of singular variety: black walnut, hickory, ash, elm, beech, chestnut, and linden.

This great Cumberland Valley she called home was broken into fertile farms by the beautiful limestone streams that crossed and recrossed its boundaries. Her ancestors had cleared this land, had plowed and planted, built and tended it. They had lived, and loved, and raised their families here.

Her hands balled into tight fists, her eyes brimming with tears. Why was she so melancholy tonight? Earlier in the day she had helped Ila clean the upstairs bedrooms, and the feeling of loss had again struck her like a knife. Her father, Tom, and, yes, even Ford.

There had been no fighting close by that fall and no call for couriers. The battles of Vicksburg and Gettysburg had exhausted both armies and they were both recuperating. What was ahead for her? She crossed the room with lagging steps to climb into the cold bed and peer out the window at the star-studded night.

CHAPTER

– 15 –

Journal, Fort Delaware, September 2, 1863

   Early in the morning of August twenty-ninth I was delivered to the prison compound at Fort Mifflin, Pennsylvania, where I was surprised to find thirty-three men from the 31st Georgia awaiting transport to the larger Union prison in Delaware. Several had been captured at Gettysburg, but the majority were apprehended at South Mountain during Lee's retreat.

   The first person I recognized was Aaron Fralich, who was captured just one day before his enlistment was up; then my old chum, John Gilbert, captured during the first days' fighting at Gettysburg, and then William Allison and Jack Wilhelm, all members of my company.

   Fort Delaware is the most dreaded of the Northern prisons and houses over fifteen thousand prisoners, all guarded by Negro troops, which I must say doesn't sit well with our boys.

   On the following day, we were informed that we might write to our families if we wished to, but that our letters would be examined by the Union authorities before they were sent south.

   I hurried to pen a letter to my mother and another to my faithful servant, Esau. Of course, knowing that it would not do for me to write anything that was detrimental to my enemy, I wrote only that I was a captive at Fort Delaware and doing well.

   Much of the fort is below sea-level, the water held back by earthen dikes, and the flimsy barracks in which the men live are dark and damp. There is no shade, no elevation, no breeze; it is only a low, flat, sultry, burning oven!

   The food, while palatable, is very scant. Breakfast consists of coffee and a small piece of corn-bread, usually hard as a rock. Our other meal is generally a tin cup of bean soup, and a small piece of meat, on which a little vinegar is poured to prevent scurvy.

The hospitals are full, smallpox the greatest villain, and all the nurses are men. I haven't seen a woman since I was incarcerated. But then who needs women?—I certainly will never trust one again. First, Cerise tricked me and then Abby, for whom I believed divorce and marriage possible. I'll admit my thoughts turn often to her, more than are good for me incarcerated as I am. The other night I even dreamed that we were making love, with embarrassing results.

The days are pleasant, the nights certainly not, as it grows colder and rains incessantly, and I am without blanket or coat. I have contracted dysentery and am quite sick.

Water is scarce, brackish, and polluted.

A most serious problem has developed regarding prisoner exchange. Under the cartel of July 1862 both sides agreed to exchange or parole all prisoners within ten days. Unfortunately, both sides have violated the cartel, and Grant has supposedly suspended further exchange of prisoners—technically on the ground of Confederate violations of the cartel, but actually because the Confederacy has more to gain by exchange than the Union.

* * *

Journal, Fort Delaware, November 20, 1863

I have been very sick and weak and have felt no desire to write in my journal, but now feel inclined to take pen to hand and record the happenings during the past few months, although it is unlikely that I will ever forget life in this hellhole.

How strange a thing it is to be hungry! Actually craving something to eat, and thinking about it from morning till night. For the past month our rations have been six, sometimes four, hard crackers and a piece of moldy bacon the size of a hen's egg. The cooks allege that the short rations are in retaliation for the scanty food supplied to their soldiers in Southern prisons.

I sit for hours dreaming of our former camp life and Esau's baked beans—beans prepared for all of the men in my company. Raw beans would be settled into an iron pot, covered with fat pork, sunk in a pit of coals, and kept baking all night. Sentries threw chunks on the fire, bayonets lifted out the kettle at dawn, and in the sunrise the beans and pork were found melted together—a rhapsodic memory to sustain us throughout the long day's march.

We look to the approach of winter with horror, knowing that our prison pens will offer scant protection from the blowing winds. Huddled together in our little bed of rags, shivering and cold, we suffer terribly during the night. Gilbert, the only one of my friends lucky enough to have a blanket, takes turns sharing it with me.

God has become an important part of our life here. We have succeeded in getting possession of a spot of ground in the prison-yard for the purpose of holding religious meetings, and on this spot for some time every evening the men come together and worship God. But what a contrast between these meetings and the ones I enjoyed at home. No ringing of bells, no happy family stepping along with light hearts to Christ Church with its eloquent sermons and swelling anthems. The men come to services covered with rags, mud, and vermin, suffering from disease and starvation. They sit close together on the ground, and it is a strange sight to see these men, side by side, enjoying this great privilege in so terrible a place. But they feel the need of Divine assistance even more in their deplorable condition than they would have felt if surrounded by the comforts of home, and they believe that God will hear their humble petitions here as well as anywhere else.

It is said that one of General Lee's favorite verses is:
"More things are wrought by prayer
Than this world dreams of,"
And so I pray every night that a prisoner exchange will come soon, else I fear I will perish in this dreadful place.

* * *

Journal, Fort Delaware, January 5, 1864

Two letters came in today's post. One filled me with good cheer, one with great sadness.

The first letter was from Sarah Kennedy. She wrote that Esau was pleased as punch that I had written to him. It was the first letter he had ever received and they helped him read it over and over again. She went on to apologize for my capture while in their home. It was Tom, not Abby, who reported my presence. I want to believe Sarah, it gives me a degree of comfort. What I had construed as yet another betrayal angered me deeply. I find myself thinking of Abby often. Of her eyes sparkling with purpose and life, of her desire to read and learn, of her understanding of Sarah's pain and her love for the little girl conceived in such tragic circumstance. My feelings disturb me. I vowed I would never allow a woman to hurt me again, yet my mind relives that moment by Falling Spring, and I yearn to hold her in my arms once more.

The other letter was from my mother. Cerise died in October of blood poisoning. Mother did not explain the circumstances and I thought her letter suspiciously evasive. She wrote to assure me that Michael is safe and will stay with her and Aunt Matilda in Savannah until I return.

In my sadness I find myself reliving the good times Cerise and I shared, not the bad. I did love her and I believe she had grown to love me. Awaiting Michael's birth was a time of happiness and anticipation for both of us.

I grieve for her and have not the heart to write more.

* * *

Journal, Fort Delaware, January 25, 1864

My thoughts tonight are on Michael. Before his mother's death I'll admit to a rather cavalier approach to this war; living or dying was not nearly as important as it is now. I do not want him to grow up without either parent, I want to live to hold him again. To feel his little hand clutching mine with trust.

I must keep my wits and find a way to get out of this hellhole of a prison.

The morning was quite pleasant, but toward evening the air changed and the night grew very cold, so cold that five of our men froze to death before morning.

The catching and eating of the huge rats that infest the camp has become a common thing. It is a curious sight; grown men, lurking, club in hand, near one of the many breathing holes which the long-tailed rodents have cut in the hard earth, patiently awaiting a chance to strike a blow for "fresh meat and rat soup"!

The rats are eaten by fully a score of the officers, and apparently with relish. The flesh of these rodents is quite white and when stewed they resemble young squirrels in looks. I have not yet mustered stomach enough to nibble one.

Some of the men are giving up all hope of ever being released, and their ravings, prayers, and curses add much to the horrors of the prison.

In musing over the past, my mind runs forward to the future. I hope I can be a proper father to little Michael. He should not have to pay for the mistakes Cerise made. How will society accept him with his mixed heritage? And what will be the outcome of this dreadful war and its effect on the plantation life I once knew?

As I look out at our once happy land, I try to analyze what led me into this terrible conflict. For us in the South we saw the war as a maneuver of the North to deprive us of the dearest right of every man, the right of each state to determine its own destiny. I believed myself a faithful soldier who did my duty as required of me.

It is true, ever since this war commenced, the South has been fighting against fearful odds; the North with all the manpower, arms and equipment needed to wage war and we, on the other hand, have nothing—only our "cause."

I am not by nature a religious man, but I believe we have incurred the displeasure of a just God and have been exceedingly wicked in the enslavement of the Negro, and that this enslavement is the cause of this war, and the reverses we have met of late. God grant that our young Confederacy may not be a vessel of wrath fitted out for destruction.

I have given up all hope of being exchanged. This may be the last page in my journal, as I am out of paper and have only the stub of a pencil.

Each day I search my mind for a way to escape.

* * *

On a warm May afternoon, Ford found himself and a group of his fellow prisoners herded to a nearby beach to bathe. He was filthy—his uniform stank and he wrinkled his nose at his own sour smell. With an enthusiastic yell he ran toward the water and jumped in, clothes and all. He let himself soak in the neck-high water until as much of his odor as possible washed away with the tide. Then he stripped and began to gingerly dunk his clothes up and down; the fabric so rotten any vigorous scrubbing would cause it to disintegrate. Finished with his laundry, he tucked his attire under one arm and dove beneath the water to secure a handful of sand. Vigorously he scoured himself with the gritty substance and let the welcome water wash his filth away.

God, but it felt good. He would never have guessed that simply being clean could produce such a feeling of euphoria, and he smiled at the irony of his situation. If only he could stay here and float in the gentle rise and fall of the tide all day. But that freedom was in another day, another time. The sentry on the shore was already beginning to move about, eyeing the prisoners with impatience. Ford glanced idly at a ramshackle barrel floating past him. Several wooden stays were missing, but it was upright in the water and moving with the current. If only he could float as unfettered as that barrel.

Suddenly, his heart leapt as an idea was born. Why not? Why not watch for his opportunity, slip his head under the barrel, then follow the tide, keeping as near the shore as necessary until he got beyond the reach of the guard? Woods hugged the shoreline. He could hide there till nightfall.

It had to be soon. The barrel was moving away from him and orders would soon be issued to come ashore. Gilbert was bathing close by and Ford caught his eye and nodded toward the floating container. Gilbert's brow wrinkled with bewilderment, and then he grinned and issued a thumb's up. He moved to position himself between Ford and the shore. Just then the guard turned to shout orders to several prisoners further downstream, and Ford dove beneath the water, clutching his small bundle of clothes in one hand.

He swam beneath the surface until he felt his lungs would burst, then with a surge of elation he saw the barrel directly above him and surfaced within its moldy interior. Now the trick was to keep his body as still as possible and float with the current. He maintained a tight clutch on his clothing and despite the cold water, beads of perspiration formed on his forehead. Punishment would be terrible if he were caught, but at last he was taking positive action to gain freedom.

He stayed in the river until his weakened body refused to cooperate, then waded ashore, still careful to keep his tracks at the water line. The Yankees kept a pack of bloodhounds; as soon as they discovered that he had escaped, the hounds would be put on his trail.

Naked, and with chattering teeth, he staggered along, uncertain how close to the stockade he was traveling. What was ahead of him? In what direction should he head? Then, with a sinking heart, he heard, not far ahead, the yelping of furious dogs as they were unchained and sent in pursuit.

He pulled on his wet clothing and began to run and within minutes came upon a small stream that emptied into the river. Gratefully he plunged in; the water would mask his trail. He picked his way along its rocky bottom, slipping and sliding, and cussing under his breath. The yelping was louder now and Ford's bad leg throbbed from water still icy from the spring runoff. He began to flounder; he had to get out of the stream before he collapsed and drowned. Then, from the corner of his eye he discerned a large tree, in full leaf, its roots clinging to the bank as it leaned precariously over the creek. He reached up and grabbed a knurled branch and inch by inch hoisted himself out of the water.

In desperation he climbed until he was high in a maze of branches and fluttering leaves. With a pounding heart he settled himself in the crook of a branch and leaned back against the thick trunk of the tree, looking down at the ground, still sun-flecked and wholly light. He would have to stay put till nightfall, but he gave a grunt of smug satisfaction. The bastards would never find him here!

Gradually, he brought his ragged breath under control and began to relax. He had never left the stream; surely the dogs would be unable to track him, and if he remained hidden in the tree for most of the day, the search would be abandoned.

Throughout the afternoon he sat under the great, hot dome of the sky, dozing, somehow managing not to fall out of the tree. Pain shot up his bad leg and his stomach ached with hunger, but he forced himself to stay on his leafy perch. Everything was silent now, the barking dogs and shouts of searchers no longer heard.

By dusk, clouds moved in and a cold mist began to fall. Ford shook with cold and exhaustion. The dysentery had returned, making his perch in the tree quite untenable. He cursed silently. Of all the places to get the runs! Slowly he lowered himself back into the shallow water and, after answering nature's call, looked up at the leaden sky. His aching stomach contracted like a fist. Without the stars to guide him he had no idea which direction to take. Grimly, he smacked his fist into the palm of his hand. This would never do—he could not stand here wallowing in his plight; he was an officer in the Confederate army and he needed to start acting like one.

First, he had to find some food. Searching diligently along the river bank he found nuts, berries, and wild mushrooms which he ate until his dizziness was abated. Temporarily sated, he sat down and began to work out a plan.

He would travel only at night and try to get to Sharpsburg, an area he was familiar with and where the Potomac was shallow enough to ford. That would get him into Virginia and safety. He moved his hand over blue-clad legs and gray tunic, their tattered condition a dead give-away that he had been incarcerated. Marylanders were divided in their loyalty and wearing any type of uniform was risky. How could he secure some clothes that would not advertise him as a soldier?

The rain stopped and a watery sun broke through the thin clouds and warmed away the chill. He must seek shelter before he was discovered—he was so close to freedom—he would not allow himself to be captured. His gaze swept the countryside around him, where freshly plowed fields ran almost to the water's edge. Not far away a farmer worked his horse-drawn plow, while in the far distance a boy and his dog led cows to pasture.

Abruptly, he halted in the road and sucked in his breath. In the early morning light a housewife appeared in the yard of the farmhouse with a basket under her arms and began to peg wet clothes to a line. Men's trousers and shirts flapped in the breeze. That was it! He would creep as close to the house as he could get, and when the woman finished her task and went inside, he would help himself to a set of clothing.

He crept closer. A dog barked and the hairs on Ford's arm stood on end. He froze, then realized that the barking seemed far away. He darted behind a smokehouse, keeping the woman in his line of vision. As he waited, she picked up her empty basket and disappeared into a summer kitchen.

Ford swallowed dryly, ran to the washline, grabbed a pair of trousers, a shirt, and a pair of underwear, then scurried back to the smokehouse. He unlatched the wooden door and crept inside. Dare he change his clothes here? Yes. It was undoubtedly the prudent thing to do. Quickly he removed his tattered uniform and donned the wet clothing of his unknown benefactor.

The pungent smell of smoked hams, sausage, and sides of beef permeated the tiny room. His stomach growled with desire. Unable to resist the temptation, he removed a length of sausage and stuffed it in his pocket. Next, he ripped his small cache of money from the lining of his tunic uniform and, with a smile of satisfaction, added it to the sausage. A piece of burlap lay against the wall and he used it to roll his uniform into a tight bundle before sidling out the door.

Ford forced himself to walk slowly along the farm lane. If he was noticed he hoped people would think him only a farmer on his way to town.

Back to the river's edge and out of sight of the farm he used a rock to scratch a hole in the earth where he buried the bag containing his clothing. Then he devoured the sausage and drank freely from the river. Scooping fresh water he doused his face and hands and for the first time in months felt almost human. Satisfied, he squatted on the ground against a tree and fought to keep himself awake.

"What should I do now?" he wondered aloud. "The last news I had was that the 31st was in western Maryland. If I must cross the state it will put me close to Pennsylvania. I could easily go north to Chambersburg and retrieve Esau. At the most it will only add a day and a half to my journey. Having Esau to nurse me through the worst bouts of dysentery will certainly help my frame of mind." He rubbed his belly. "And I could sure use a mess of his beans."

He grinned. Now who was he trying to fool? A vision of Abby, black cap of hair and stormy gray eyes, floated through his mind. It was more than Esau's beans he desired. And now he was free to claim her, if that was what he wanted.

Sharpsburg was at best a four-day trip across the state of Maryland, and in his weakened condition, probably more. Plus, he had to cross the Susquehanna River at some point and he didn't know how he could manage that. Travel in Maryland was always dangerous, but more so in Pennsylvania. Should he risk it?

Once more rain began to fall, adding to his misery. Sweat broke out on his face and he began to shake with fever. "Damned dysentery," he grumbled. "If I have to stop every few miles to shit I'll never get to Sharpsburg."

But sheer willpower forced him on, and by noontime of the second day he was looking across the broad expanse of the Susquehanna. It was rocky and shallow, but Ford doubted he had the stamina to swim across. A search of the shoreline revealed a skiff, but no oars. He sank to the ground in disappointment. Soon a little boy approached with paddles in hand, looking at Ford with curiosity. He appeared to be waiting.

"What are you waiting for?" Ford inquired.

"I'm waiting for my load."

"Will you take me over with your load?"

The boy looked at him suspiciously. "It'll cost you two dollars," he said.

"I haven't any money. Some guerilla raiders jumped me a while back and took all I had."

"Raiders? Must'a been Confederates. Yeah . . . I'll take you."

So, over the boy took him, and Ford felt his last great hurdle conquered.

Two more days and he was trudging up the main street of Sharpsburg, on the northern shore of the Potomac near Shepherdstown. He had passed through it several times on his marches north, and the streets were familiar. The sun rode high in the sky and heat rose in shimmering waves on the road ahead. Ford shivered with fever, exhaustion, and hunger; he hadn't eaten for over twenty-four hours. Unsteadily, he hobbled along the Hagerstown Road, limping badly, his stomach knotted with pain from the dysentery. Was it the sun or a fever that weakened him so? Still he pushed on—north to Pennsylvania.

Days later he rounded a bend in the road and saw Brookside just ahead of him. He staggered toward the meandering stream, gulping its cold water, dunking his sweat-soaked head in its cooling water. He didn't want to run into Brandon; he must plan a proper approach.

He sank to the ground in the shade of the tree, shaking water from his hair like a wet dog, squinting against the blazing sun. The grounds were overgrown, the roadway full of ruts and weeds. *It's more than they can handle*, he thought gloomily, *even with Esau's help. And now if I take him with me I'll take even that away from them.*

He drug himself to his feet and headed up the carriage path. Locust trees, dripping blossoms, filled the farm lane with fragrance, and for one delicious moment he thought himself at home, riding toward Retreat to meet with Lordy.

He shook his head and with gritted teeth reached the pillared porch girding the front of the house. Dead leaves lay in piles beneath curtained windows and an abandoned rake leaned against the wall. The porch was in need of paint, a board on one of the steps was loose, but smoke rose from the chimney, and a bright braided rug hung over the railing. His eyes sought for a sign of life and then the fever conquered him and he slumped to the ground.

CHAPTER
– 16 –

Strong arms carried Ford down a hall toward a bright light. *Was he dead? Or was this a dream?* The deep voice crooning to him sounded like Esau. He relaxed, comforted somehow, and secure.

A woman's voice penetrated the fog of fever and he struggled to open his eyes. Framed in brilliant sunlight pouring through a long window was the woman he had heard talking. Abby!

Esau wrung out a cloth and placed it on Ford's hot forehead while Abby bent over him with a warm smile and tucked a sheet around his shoulders.

"How did you get here? You about scared the life out of us," she said. "Have you been exchanged? Are you free?"

He could have said yes, but for some reason he uttered the truth. "I've escaped. Now I guess you feel it's your *duty* to send me back."

"No . . . you're safe here."

"Like I was before?"

Abby forced a smile, her hands clutched tightly in her lap. "I thought Sarah wrote you what happened."

"She did, but I worry whether I should believe her."

"You misunderstood what happened," she said. "We have a lot to talk about, but first I think we need to get some fluids into you and clean you up a bit. If it weren't for the color of your hair I wouldn't have recognized you." She rose to go. "I'll leave you in Esau's hands . . . we'll talk more this afternoon."

Esau moved to Ford's side. "My, my, Massa, you nothin' but skin and bones," he moaned. "Firs' thing we needs t' do is get some hot soup into you; after that I clean you up and shave all that hair offa you face."

Esau undressed Ford and began to bathe him. "I got t' fetch some turpentine and douse you haid. It be crawlin' with lice." He began to strop a razor. "When's the las' time you shave?"

"Not since I've been captured. But leave the beard; I've grown accustomed to it."

"Yessuh. After I kills all the bugs living in it."

Ford managed a wry laugh. "And elsewhere!"

Esau grinned back. "You shore nuf be a mess, Marse Ford, but at least you ain't daid."

Bathed, clad in clean underwear and pants and shirt belonging to Tom, his head, face, and privates tingling from Esau's ministrations of turpentine, Ford settled himself in a comfortable chair beside a window in the room he had occupied almost a year ago. It seemed a lifetime.

The window afforded an unlimited view of the small lane crossing the front of the house and beyond to the barn and an orchard. The window was open, sunlight flooded the little room, and the scent of lilacs hung in the air. He closed his eyes—after six months of prison life his senses craved their softness.

Abby came through the door with a tentative smile and pulled up a chair. They sat quietly for a few minutes, then she turned to face him. "First of all, Ford, your capture was the way Sarah wrote you. My brother reported your presence on our farm. . . . he felt it his duty as a Union soldier." Her eyes locked on his. "That's not to say I might not have done the same. Still, when I overheard you making plans with Sarah and Esau to escape I did nothing to stop you."

"Why?"

"I don't know." She sighed and pushed a strand of hair back from her cheek. "It's a cruel war. I've known families torn apart because of different loyalties, boys firing guns at best friends . . . and sometimes . . . lovers pitted against loved ones." Her gray eyes darkened. "I'm sure you know that. Try to understand my loyalty to the Union and I'll try to understand yours toward the Confederacy."

Ford was about to interrupt, but Abby held up her hand, the struggle to keep the conversation businesslike evident on her lovely face. "Let me finish. This is the third time the fates have brought us together, and I still look upon you as a representative of the South. I'm still angry and bitter for what happened to my family. Brookside suffers and we suffer. Slavery is wrong," her face flushed with indignation, "and the South must be punished; I'll do anything I can do to bring about its defeat." Her voice softened. "That said, against my better judgement I'm willing to help you get back to Virginia."

"Do you know where my division is?" Ford asked.

"The newspapers say that Early's II Corps was recently engaged in battle at Cold Harbor. Again!"

Ford nodded grimly. "Almost two years ago I was initiated into battle there. We won that time. Do the papers say who won this time?"

"As usual, both sides claim victory."

"You mentioned you would help me get back to Virginia. I want to return to my regiment as soon as possible."

"You intend to continue fighting then?"

"Yes, of course. Besides, I'm anxious to find out if my brother is safe. The last time I saw him was on the battlefield at Gettysburg." He grimaced. "That time and that battle seem a million miles away." Ford watched her carefully. "There's something troubling you, Abby, something I can't quite put my finger on."

"You haven't said anything about your *slave*," Abby said with a flashing challenge in her dark eyes. "Do you plan to take him with you?"

"I don't like your choice of words!"

"Esau is your slave is he not? Your property. As a Southerner you're fighting to keep him that way. You forget that this is a war for the abolition of slavery."

"Yes, it is that; but it's much, much more," Ford replied. "There are two issues, not just one. Slavery and States Rights. The former question is veiled in the latter; I wouldn't be fighting otherwise. To the Abolitionist, slavery is the only issue; to the Southerner, it is the right of each state to govern itself."

Abby watched him, a wary look on her pale face.

Ford continued. "Do I think slavery is right? No—it isn't right, but when I think of the misery and barbarism of the peasantry of my Scots ancestors and the sweat shop labor in your Northern factories and compare them with the well-cared-for people on my plantation, it does not seem so cruel. But bondage of another human being is wrong and I do intend to manumit Esau now, if he wants it."

Abby's brows raised in disbelief. "I'm relieved to hear you have some degree of conscience . . . if you mean it."

"Conscience? And what exactly is that? A misguided conscience is one thing; a conscience suddenly quickened by a sense of guilt is still another thing." Ford's eyes locked with hers. "Ah, Abby, you're so quick to condemn. Maybe with the end of the war there will come to all of us a feeling of forgiveness and reconciliation toward the sins of the South as well as the North."

Abby felt confused and unhappy as silence filled the tiny room and each sat locked in their own thoughts, each trying to understand the other. She could not allow herself to remember the tender moments beside Falling Spring Creek and the feel of his lips on hers; each still had their own mission to fulfill and obligations to their families. Besides, it was obvious that Ford did not fully believe her innocence in his arrest. Finally, she spoke. "You're in no condition to travel. Rest here for a few days until you're stronger."

Silence once more settled around them. The light in the small room mellowed as the sun passed overhead and Abby felt Ford watching her as she avoided his eyes and gazed through the window. Warblers in nearby trees sang a continuous song and baby rabbits sported in dying sunlight. "I'd like to paint you like that," he said softly, so as not to break the mood.

She looked at him in surprise. "You paint portraits?"

"Only of those I care about."

Abby moved to light an oil lamp to ward off the gloom of approaching evening, her emotions raw with longing as she watched Ford move about the room. This surely had to be what her books called "falling in love."

The hours ticked away as they sat and talked through the long afternoon. She told him about Amanda, now almost a year old, about the growing love between Ila and Esau, about Tom and Elizabeth and their plans to marry when Tom got his next furlough. She told him of the harsh winter just past, of the back-breaking work on the farm, of the books she had read. What she did not tell him was that the war was not going well for the South, that reports were that General Early's division had suffered terrible losses during the month of May in the Spotslvania and Wilderness campaigns.

Ford told her of life in prison, of his escape and his hope that his friend Gilbert had thought to secure the journal from his bunk; his hope that Gilbert would also be freed some day to return to the 31st. He told her about St. Simons and his love for the tiny island off Georgia's coast, and Abby could hear the pride in his voice as he talked of his plantation home.

As Abby listened to him talk, her eyes never left his face. Starvation had only served to make the planes of his narrow face stand out in sharper relief, and she beheld the way his thick copper hair fell across his forehead with an overwhelming urge to reach up and push it back. She listened to the wry comments that pulled up one corner of his thin lips, and laughed at his stories about humorous incidents that had lightened prison life.

Their eyes, when they met, spoke volumes, yet neither made a move toward the other. She felt the change in him; there was a softening in his manner, his eyes no longer wary.

And then he told her of Cerise's death.

She sat perfectly still; her shawl had fallen back and she stooped to pick it up. There was only the slightest tremble in her hand. The evening had grown chilly and Abby shivered. Ford jumped to his feet and moved to settle the soft blue wool against her neck. His warm hands lingered on her shoulders. Against her will she leaned her head back to rest against him. He bent and kissed the top of her head.

"Your hair smells like warm peaches," he said tenderly. His hands tightened on her shoulders. She thought she would die from the sensations coursing through her body. She had to stop this. She tilted her head up to make a tart remark, but as she did their eyes locked and the words would not come. He placed a gentle finger on her chin and lowered his lips to hers.

It started out as a soft innocent kiss, but his lips lingered and heat began to build. She couldn't stand it—she had to feel his arms about her, just once more. She stood up unsteadily and turned to meet the smoldering fire of his green eyes. With a groan he pulled her to him, his lips searching hers.

Abby had never kissed a man like this. Searing passion made her knees tremble and grow weak. He pulled her tight against his hard chest, grinding himself against her. White heat engulfed her.

He pulled away and began to move her toward the fainting couch in the corner. With a sob she pushed him away. "We mustn't," she whispered.

Ford cursed and she could see the muscles working in his jaw, his eyes wavering with indecision. Slowly, he took her by the elbow and forced her to look at him. "No, we mustn't," he admitted. "Not yet. I'm free now, but I must return to the war. I'm sorry, Abby, I never intended for this to happen. You are a lady . . . I'll not compromise your virtue."

Nearly a minute ticked by on the grandfather clock before she asked him what he meant. "I may be killed, I can make no commitments—don't know that I want to make any. Any other girl I could take to satisfy my need and move on, but not you."

"Then let's forget it happened," she said.

"I don't know that we can do that."

"We must. Oh, we must. Everything is against us. You're a Southerner. Our cultures and beliefs are different. Love between us is hopeless, doomed to failure."

Ford looked away and moved to the window. He stood with his back to her, his hands curled into fists. "Maybe not," she heard him say. "Maybe not."

That night Esau sat with his hands on his head, staring out at the stars, his thoughts on Ila. *How could he tell her? Tell her that from the moment he saw Marse Ford lying on that porch he knew he had to see him through this war. She didn't understand the Emancipation Proclamation, considered him free to stay in the North if he wanted. Would she understand? Would she wait for him? He could run away and take Ila with him; he doubted Marse Ford would pursue him. He stood and began to pace back and forth. From the day he was born he had been raised to serve; Ford was the center of his world, Ford trusted him, and until he met Ila he wanted nothing more. He wanted her now, but Marse Ford was ill from being in prison and needed him more.*

The choice between duty to his Master and his love for his woman made him sob with frustration. It was only temporary, he told himself. If the North won the war—and it sure enough looked like it would—he could return to Chambersburg and marry Ila after he got Ford safely home. That couldn't be much longer. He had listened carefully to the talk between Miz Abby and Miz Sarah and knew that Gettysburg had changed things for the South. His heart was full of worry. When the war ended and the North was the winner, what would happen to his people? Who would take care of them if Lincoln made all the slaves free?

His mammy always said, "things have a way of working out, God never gives us more than we can bear." He'd have to trust that. Trust that his Ila would still be there when his duty to the McKenzies could be laid aside and he could taste what it was to be free.

He shoved his big hands into his pockets, and with a heavy sigh went to ask Marse Ford when they were to leave. Then he would tell Ila.

Ford listened to Esau's determination to see him through the war, despite his love for Ila. He waited for him to finish, then placed his hand on the big shoulder and gripped it hard. "Esau, I've made a decision. I want to manumit you, now."

"Manumit. What that be?"

"Your release from slavery. You're free to go wherever you want."

Esau stood perfectly still, his face wrinkled in confusion.

"You have a choice," Ford said gently. "I will free you. You can do whatever you choose."

Esau smiled, white teeth gleaming in an ebony face. "Then I choose to follow you, Marse Ford. Till the war be ober an' you home safe."

The next day Abby worked hard to keep a safe distance from Ford. After supplying him with a horse and money to take passage on a ferry, she turned to Esau, curious as to how he would say goodby to his Master. With dismay she realized he had brought his knapsack from the house. She looked at him with knitted brows. "What are you doing, Esau?"

"I not be stayin' wif you, Miz Abby. I gots t' go with Marse Ford."

She turned furious eyes on Ford who was watching her carefully. "Esau, you don't have to stay with him, you know," she retorted sharply. "That man no longer owns you."

"We owns each other."

"What about Ila?"

"She be my woman—nothin' gonna change that. When the war be ober, I come back t' the farm and make her mine." Tears began to course down his black cheeks. "Try to make her believe, Miz Abby. Ask her t' forgive me and wait for me."

"I'll find it hard to explain when I don't understand it myself." Abby glared at Ford who stood beside the wagon, quietly listening to the exchange. "I thought you were going to free Esau. Did you talk him into this . . . to keep him in bondage to you, to leave Ila and all the love she has to offer him?"

"No. Esau has made his own decision. Don't try to denigrate loyalty, Abby."

"Loyalty . . . loyalty . . . how dare you speak of loyalty?"

She raised her tight jaw to him, jutted it out defiantly, her anger simmering. Whatever had possessed her to think she could submerge her bitterness toward this man and what he represented for a few passionate kisses?

Let them both go. She hoped to never see either one of them again.

* * *

May slid into June, a feverish time on the farm. Barley ripened, wheat grew golden, and young corn plants marched in straight rows across the brown fields. Strawberries were ripe and the first picking of peas and lettuce was ready.

In the north pasture the hay was ready for mowing and Brandon and Abby finished in the last light, well after the setting sun.

"Whew. Glad that's done," Brandon said.

"Whatever would I do without you, little man?" Abby smiled and reached over to tousle the top of his head.

He blushed and jerked away.

"I believe you have a birthday coming up," Abby said with a tender smile. "What would you like for your birthday supper?"

"Stuffed pig stomach," he answered without hesitation.

"But Brandon, that's a wintertime dish."

"Well, you ast me, didn't you. Don't we have none left?"

"Don't we have *any* left," she corrected.

"That's what I ast."

Abby sighed. Brandon's English was hopeless. She offered up a silent prayer that school would open once more in the fall. "I'll check with Ila. We may still have one put by."

"I get the crisp, chewy end," he announced with a grin. "An' maybe we could have some chocolate cornstarch pudding."

"We'll see."

"I get to lick the pan."

Abby laughed. "That's a promise. Now get on with you, young man."

She walked to the house with lagging steps while Brandon, bless his heart, unhitched the team and led them to the stable to feed and bed down for the night.

After a hasty supper, she wearily crept up the back stairs to her bedroom. Had she ever been this tired? She didn't think so; every muscle ached. She washed quickly, donned a clean nightgown, and collapsed into bed.

Tired as she was, though, full sleep would not come, and she lay between a hybrid of slumber and wake—where in chaotic dreams Jimmy appeared to have the red hair of the Confederate captain and Tom lay dead in Sarah's arms.

Abby woke to a rainy dawn with a feeling of relief. At least the horrible dreams were gone and, with the rain, they wouldn't be able to work the fields. She decided she'd go to Chambersburg instead, get a few supplies at Hoke's Dry Goods, visit the stationers to see if any new books had arrived and then visit for an hour or so with Elizabeth.

Within the hour she was on her way, walking briskly in a humid, drizzling rain, her head tilted sideways, letting the raindrops kiss her face. She wore a thin coat of waxed poplin and a bonnet rubbed with lanolin and, although it served well as a mackintosh, it was suffocatingly warm. Soon she was as damp with perspiration as she would have been were she exposed to the rain. Then suddenly the clouds broke open to reveal the sun. With a sigh of relief she removed the rainwear and balled it up to carry under her arm.

She began to hum.

The path was well trodden, paralleling the shallow bank of the Falling Spring Creek flowing briskly from the many underground limestone springs, and lined with numerous busy gristmills. The brightening sky was busy with wrens, scarlet tanagers, robins, and other resident birds swooping down from dripping trees to pluck fat insects from the damp earth. The path followed her beloved little creek as it twisted and turned like a worm on the end of a hook, flowing north toward the larger Conococheague. Since childhood the smell and sound of the tumbling creek had called to her heart.

For much of the morning she had been gloomy and long faced. Some of it she attributed to the hopelessness of her situation—head of the household—responsible for her young brother, her sister who would probably never marry, and an infant niece whom she had grown to love with all her heart. Tom would do his duty when the war was over, but she knew in her heart he had never wanted to be a farmer. He had always loved the feel and smell of new wood, dreamed of having his own carpentry business. They had all lost so much. Could she expect Tom to give up his dream, too?

She walked slowly, following the stream, the air clean and sweet as fresh laundry, past farms with giant bank barns and houses of blue-gray stone marbled with white, past fields where women and children and old men were forced to work the crops because every able-bodied man was off fighting the war. She wondered if school would open at all this fall; most of the boys were needed on their farms.

Yet, despite the unending work, she could not visualize living anywhere other than here, on this farm, in this valley sheltered by the distant smudge of mountains. Today the hillsides were covered with the white haze of catalpa trees in blossom, buttercups and daisies glowed gold in yet untilled fields, while lilacs bloomed in every farm yard. The ground was uneven here, the path strewn with pockets of last autumn's leaves. Peonies flourished as they clung to a sagging expanse of a wooden fence, their branches nodding under the weight of enormous blooms.

A frog, startled by her presence, plunked into the creek, and she laughed aloud as he issued a croaking protest. It felt good to laugh. Today was a holiday—she would not think of work, she would savor every minute of this rainy day.

Countryside yielded to a cluster of houses lining Market Street and she held her skirts high to avoid small pools of glinting water in streets, cut deep by narrow wagon wheels. Above the rooftops the steeple of the Reformed Church soared into the sky like a prayer rising to the heavens. Her heart beat faster as she heard the noise of the bustling town ahead and she picked up her pace, eager for the day ahead.

First, she would indulge herself with some goodies from Hoke's Dry Goods, then visit the bookstore before she sought out Elizabeth.

After chatting for a few minutes with Jacob Hoke, she bought thread, needles, and several yards of muslin for Sarah, a bag of black licorice for Brandon, a length of blue calico for Ila, and a bag of peppermints for herself, then walked outside to the busy street. It had begun to drizzle again, so she unfurled her umbrella and dashed down Front Street to Miller's Stationery Store.

Abby sniffed the delicious aroma of the small shop. Ink and paper vied with leather and tobacco, a smell like none other in the world. She hurried to the long shelves at the back of the shop where Mr. Miller displayed his magazines and novels, impatiently scanning the titles. Was there nothing new? Yes, here was one, *The Mill on the Floss* by George Eliot. It cost far more than she could afford to spend, but she bought it anyway.

After securing a new account book for the farm and the latest copy of *The Baltimore Sun* she left, eager to show her new book to Elizabeth and engage in a few hours of lighthearted girl talk.

Abby entered the Falling Spring Inn by the front door and headed directly to the dining room. The inn was quiet, the pungent smell of sauerkraut, onions, garlic, and smoked sausage heavy in the air. Elizabeth was clearing dishes from the lunch trade and after returning a hug, she pulled out a chair at one of the tables and urged Abby to sit down.

"I've only a few more tables to clear, then we can go to my room." She gave Abby a warm smile. "It's been so long since I've seen you. Can you stay? Can we have the whole afternoon together?"

"Yes, and yes! Here, let me help you and we can finish sooner. Have you heard from Tom, lately? We haven't had a letter for ages."

"One came in yesterday's post. I'll let you read it when we get to my room."

Later, settled in her rocker, Abby laid the letter aside. "Maybe this interminable war will soon be over. Tom says the fight has moved back into the Shenandoah Valley. Maybe Lee has given up any thought of invading the North."

"If only that were true. If only the war would end before any more great battles. If not, I won't see Tom until his enlistment is up, if then. What about Jimmy? Have you heard from him?"

"Yes. He's very faithful about writing. More faithful than I, I'm afraid."

"Abby . . . and you don't have to answer this if you don't want to, but I . . . I always assumed Jimmy would ask you to marry him once the war was over."

"That's the problem. Everyone has always assumed." Noting the troubled look on her friend's face, she hastened to add, "It's only natural, I guess. I did keep company with him before he joined up, and I know his family would like us to marry. After all," she added ironically, "it would merge the farms and make us one of the largest in the county." Sudden tears sprang to Abby's eyes, and she blinked furiously to keep them from falling.

Elizabeth sprang to her feet and hastened to place a gentle hand on Abby's shoulder. "What is it? What troubles you so?"

"I don't know. No, that's not true. I do know." Abby felt herself blush. "I've just never felt the passion for him, or any other boy for that matter, that I should. I feel for Jimmy what I feel for Brandon . . . for Tom . . . for you . . . or for any good friend. I could never put words to this until I realized what it was like to have your heart leap and your stomach flutter at the mere glance of a man. But I know now."

"Who?"

"Captain McKenzie."

Elizabeth's mouth fell open. "Captain McKenzie!"

"I know, I know. He's a Confederate—my sworn enemy."

"And he is married."

"Was . . . was married. His wife has died."

Elizabeth blinked with surprise. "Did he tell you that? Does he feel the same way about you?"

"Of course not, he doesn't know how I really feel and I'll never tell him," Abby said mournfully. "Not that I'll ever have the chance. He has gone back to his regiment in Virginia." Her hand moved to finger her neck. "Oh, Elizabeth, how could I let this happen to me? Everything about it is wrong. Everything! A Southerner, a slaveholder . . . I could never forgive him his loyalties and I vowed to seek vengeance for my father's death. But yes, I care for him. Oh, he made it clear that he would gladly bed me if I gave him any encouragement. But his eyes spoke of desire—not love."

"I just can't believe any of this. Whatever has possessed you? You've no future with this man." Elizabeth regarded Abby with cold speculation. "Captain McKenzie is very intriguing. I'm certain you're not the first to succumb to his enigmatic presence. It's an infatuation . . . something you've romanticized from all those books you read. Passion is fleeting."

"Has passion been fleeting for you? Do you simply feel comfortable with my brother, or do you feel a tingling in your belly when he looks at you?" Abby began to sob. "I know my feelings for Captain McKenzie are wrong, but don't you see, Elizabeth, now I know what love really can be."

"Give it time. Jimmy's a good man; he'd make a good home for you and Sarah. Wait for him to come home and see if absence hasn't made a difference in your feelings. He was a boy when he went off to war—he'll be a man when he comes back. Tom is not the same. I saw the change when I cared for him after he was wounded. War changes men, makes them grow up."

"Maybe you're right." Abby blew her nose and gave Elizabeth a watery smile. "This afternoon was supposed to be fun. Now, let's put all this serious talk aside and enjoy ourselves. Tell me what you've been doing since I last saw you."

The Big Ben in the hallway bonged four times before Abby bade Elizabeth goodby and began the long trek home.

The rain had stopped, the air fresh and clean. A glorious sunset streaked the sky before her. She walked slowly, savoring the beauty, swinging her string-bag of purchases, humming to herself.

In a way she wished she had not confessed her feelings about the captain to her friend. It was an impossible dilemma. Why revive the pain? Why not let the wound heal?

* * *

In the hen house Ila folded her apron to form a deep pocket and moved deftly from nest to nest gathering what eggs she could find. Her brow wrinkled in dismay. They had so few chickens left; scarcely enough to lay for their daily needs.

She carried the eggs to the cool springhouse where she had prepared a crock with water, coarse salt, and unslaked lime. Eggs would keep almost any length of time in lime-water, years even, if properly prepared. But too much lime would eat the shells right off the eggs. Carefully she lowered them into the water, one by one. A cracked shell would spoil the whole batch. She smiled to herself. That had never happened to her; she handled them gentle as a cradled babe.

When the eggs had all been submerged, Ila lifted the heavy crock to the corner of a broad ledge that ran the length of the spring. As she looked down at the reflection of her face in the crystal clear water, memories of Esau crowded in on her. She remembered the day he had helped her churn butter, here in the springhouse and they had leaned over this same spring, their heads close together, to laugh at their reflections.

A tear formed at the corner of her eye and fell unheeded down her cheek. She could remember every detail of his laughing face, the heavy brows, the flaring nostrils, the full lips that carried such passion when he kissed her. A hot wave swept into her belly at the memory. Their love was a raging fire that consumed her, even now in this cool, dark springhouse.

"It be more than just lovin' though," she muttered to herself. "He takes good care of the farm animals, helps Brandon with the heavy farming without being asked, gentles little Amanda in them big hands o' his, and shows his love for Marse Ford every day. Esau be a kind, lovin' man—he would make a good husband and father."

Would he come back for her? Would she go with him to the hated South if that were the only way she could have him? In her heart she knew the answer. Yes. It didn't do to make him think she was easy though, she had to make him work at getting her to go along with him. She sat down on the ledge with a sigh. What she wouldn't do to see him again. To hear his booming laughter, to hear his voice breathe words of desire, to look into his dark intelligent eyes and listen to his stories about his people and their ways. She groaned. If only he would come back and ask her to marry him again. She wouldn't be so sassy this time. Fiercely she poked her finger in the water, shattering her image and the uncertainty of the future.

CHAPTER
– 17 –

Three days passed before Ford, fighting a severe bout of diarrhea, reached the Potomac. Then, on a bright morning in June, he and Esau boarded a ferry for Virginia.

With Esau behind him in the saddle they rode through Virginia's Shenandoah Valley, the "Breadbasket of the Confederacy," in search of Early's II Corps. At Fredericksburg he happily located a scattered contingent of men, separated from their regiments for one reason or another, was given a uniform, and assimilated back into the ranks. On the following day they were formed into a temporary battalion and by evening reached the army, then in line of battle on the North Anna River. There they were informed that in the morning the battalion would be broken up and the men sent to their respective regiments.

Ford greeted the news with a surge of elation. At last he would be back with his own Georgia 31st.

Anxious to find his brother, he slipped out of camp as soon as it was dark, and after a good deal of hunting along the line, succeeded in finding Fitzpatrick's cavalry unit. The boys had just finished their supper, and were lying on the ground resting.

Ford's gaze anxiously searched the assemblage, coming to rest on one vaguely familiar form leaning against a tree, plumed hat pulled down over his face, long legs sprawled in front of him.

"Josh?" Ford's voice cracked with tension.

The figure jumped, the hat fell to the ground, and blue eyes stared in disbelief.

"Ford? My God, man, is that really you?" Josh jumped to his feet and ran across the ground separating them.

Ford grabbed him and they stood in a tight embrace rocking back and forth. Tears swam in Josh's eyes and Ford was not ashamed of his own.

Arms around each other, they walked to the campfire where Josh poured tins of coffee. He motioned to a stone wall a short distance from the fire. "Come, let's sit over there away from the boys, so we can talk."

They drank cup after cup and stayed up most of the night talking non-stop. The moon was high in the sky and still they talked on, bringing each other up to date on the happenings since Gettysburg, of plans for the future—Josh planned to marry Polly the minute he got home—and memories of the past. Finally, Josh began to fidget and made a great production of straightening his jacket. "Have you had any recent letters from Savannah?" he asked, his face pensive in the pale moonlight.

"Not since sometime in March. I know Cerise is dead—Mother wrote me."

"Did she tell you how?"

"Only that she died of blood poisoning. She didn't elaborate."

A spasm crossed Josh's face. "There's no easy way to tell you this, Ford, but you have a right to know. Cerise had an abortion."

Ford hurled himself to his feet, the news striking like hammer blows. "But I've been gone for over two years." His fists convulsed with suppressed rage. "That slut, that no good excuse for a woman . . . how could she do this to me again?"

Josh stood mutely, his face drawn and pinched.

Ford felt his heart drop and pause before it started a low, cold, thumping. A multitude of emotions ran across his mind like frightened deer. For a few minutes he couldn't speak, and Josh, sensing his turmoil, rushed on. "I'm sorry, Ford. I know at one point you loved her deeply. I wish things had turned out differently, that you had made peace with one another before you left for war, but that's the way life is." He cleared his throat. "She was buried in Savannah beside her parents."

"Where is Michael?"

"Mother has him with her." Josh jumped to his feet and began to pace.

A dull, empty ache began to replace Ford's anger and he sank to his knees, his eyes brimming. He still felt the pain. He had loved Cerise. Why couldn't she have been honest with him? He suspected that, had she asked for his help in the beginning, he would have married her anyhow. Despite his anger when they parted, she had promised to wait for him, to try to rebuild their marriage. And once more she had betrayed him.

"Was it that Indian again, do you know?"

"Mother said rumor had it that they had been seen together. There's no proof that the child was his, of course. She knew she was dying and she asked mother to promise that Michael would be cared for."

Ford nodded. *That poor little boy. What parents he had inherited—a whore for a mother and a married man for a father.* But he didn't say the words aloud. Instead he said, "He will be. He bears the McKenzie name and I grew to love him before I left." Ford's voice cracked. "He would hold my hand and look at me with such trust."

Josh placed a hand on Ford's shoulder and squeezed.

"If . . ."

"I need time alone, Josh. Time to sort my feelings through."

Josh gave him a faint smile. "Sure, big brother. Just know that I'm close by if you need to talk."

* * *

For months the Yankees, under command of General David Hunter, had been indulging in Hunter's favorite mode of warfare: pillaging and destroying property. Finally, Jubal Early's Rebels were ordered to the troubled area to stave off Hunter's aggression and throw a scare into the Union. If successful, a movement northward through the valley corridor, followed by a Potomac crossing into Maryland, could once again threaten Washington.

With three days' rations cooked, the march commenced at two A.M. on June 13. Days were warm, but nights were cool enough for a blanket; blankets which few of his men had. Each foot soldier was given a quarter pound of bacon and one pound of corn bread, marched two miles and rested ten minutes, sleeping on their arms at night. Still, travel in the wooded terrain stressed each man to the limit.

While in Charlottesville they received word that Hunter's men were about twenty miles from the important supply depot of Lynchburg. Abandoning everything except guns and filled cartridge boxes, the entire regiment boarded box and stock cars for the trip to Lynchburg. After a brief one-day skirmish Hunter retreated toward the western mountains of western Virginia.

Passing through Lexington, ten days later, the troops saw for themselves the destruction left behind by the Yankee vandals just a few days earlier. Anger clogged Ford's throat as he viewed the burned-out ruins of the Virginia Military Institute, where Stonewall Jackson had been a professor prior to the war.

Lexington was an engaging little town nestled in the mountains, with tree-lined streets and stately Southern homes. The kind women of the town had large tubs of buttermilk, bread, pies, cakes, and all kinds of baked meats, set out on tables in the street by the sidewalks. Young girls passed out the food with smiles of encouragement to the dirty, footsore infantrymen, and one in particular gave Ford a come-hither look. He was sorely tempted to take her up on her offer; it had been a long time since he'd had a woman. His encounters with Abby had left him unfulfilled and sharply aware of his needs. He toyed with the idea of striking camp for a day of rest in this little town with its enchanting women, but such respite was not to be if they wished to catch Hunter. His needs would have to wait.

At Staunton new clothing and shoes were issued to his ragged troops, and Ford and his men spent the next few days feasting off Yankee treats, the boys receiving new oil cloths and tent flies, whiskey and cigars. On the last night Ford, uncharacteristically, got quite drunk on confiscated whiskey and sought out the comfort of one of the camp followers. It was July 4, one year exactly since he had been wounded at Gettysburg.

Tuesday afternoon, after destroying a number of canal boats, they crossed the Potomac into Maryland at Shepherdstown. Ford smiled at the irony of it. He was getting to know this little town quite well.

Onward they marched, past Sharpsburg, past Boonsboro and Antietam Creek, into the town of Frederick, Maryland. Washington was dead ahead.

But so were the Yankees. The day was unbearably hot. Drought made the dust so thick that the rear ranks had to grope their way. The only water obtainable was from small streams and this, churned up by thousands of hoofs, was almost undrinkable.

That afternoon they entered battle against a considerable number of Federals firmly positioned on the eastern bank of the Monocacy River. A fierce two-hour charge broke the enemy lines, but the casualties on both sides were enormous. So profuse was the flow of blood from the killed and wounded of both these forces that it reddened the stream for more than one hundred yards below.

At daybreak the next day the march resumed. Ford pressed the men of his regiment as vigorously as possible in the stifling heat. When he and his staff rode past the sweating column he assured them that they would take Washington that day. They responded with their old Rebel yell, but the heat was draining the men. Long before noon, veterans who had endured some of the harder marches, were lying along the wayside. Ford slackened the pace but still they marched on; the Southern army was now closer to Washington than ever before. Church steeples and the dome of the U.S. Capitol building were visible in the summer haze, and he could hear the striking sounds of the city clocks. Ford's stomach contracted into a tight ball. Capture of Washington could bring an end to this war.

But could his men mount an offensive? They were completely exhausted. Skirmishers were thrown out and moved up to the vicinity of Yankee fortifications, which they soon found to be extremely strong. General Early, seeing the fatigue of his army, ordered them into bivouac for the night.

The next morning Ford walked to headquarters for his orders. In the soft summer dawn Early stood with an angry scowl on his face gazing at the far-spreading line of earthworks with cold speculation. They bristled with troops.

Finally he turned and fixed his officers with a level stare. "Our scouts tell us that overnight General Grant has strongly re-enforced the forts. The assault, even if successful, will entail such losses that we might not be able to escape." He stroked his beard, his black eyes sweeping the men before him. "Should we fail we will almost certainly lose the entire force. In either event, the destruction of a Confederate army in front of Washington might have a depressing effect on the South." Again his gaze swept the fortifications ahead. He cleared his throat. "I've reluctantly decided to retire back to Virginia."

"But we must at least try," Ford protested bitterly. "We can see the capital, it's within our grasp."

"Within our sight, not our grasp. Believe me, I've weighed the odds. They favor the enemy." Early's flashing black eyes forbade further argument. "Over the next few days we'll harass the devil out of the fortifications, so they fear our presence, but by the end of the week I plan to retreat to Virginia."

The general saw the disappointment etched on the faces of his officers, so he added, "Our day will come, gentlemen. If we are prudent now, we'll all be here to see it happen."

That night, as Esau prepared a meager supper of bacon and cornbread, Ford told him of the plan to return to Virginia.

"Chambersburg seem so close," Esau said with a sigh. "I thought the war t' be over this time an' I be gettin' back t' see if my Ila still wait fer me."

Ford's thoughts flew to Abby. He was free of his marriage now. Free to win back her favor, if that's what he wanted. He longed to see her again, just as Esau wanted to see Ila. They both had unfinished business in Chambersburg.

"I'm disappointed too. But as Old Jube said this morning, 'Our time will come.' Ila will wait for you."

"She be my woman," Esau said with a grin, nodding his wooly head. "I get her to come to our island, you wait an' see." He lifted the bacon from the sputtering fry pan and placed it on Ford's tin plate. "Maybe you talk that purty Miz Abby to come too," he added slyly.

"Maybe."

Later that morning the disappointing orders to cancel the attack on the capital were issued. For the next two days the troops demonstrated and put up a earnest show of intent to attack, but by the end of the third day they began their retreat.

Just before the column slipped away, General Early turned to Ford with a half smile. "Captain," he said, "we haven't taken Washington, but I believe we've scared the hell out of Abe Lincoln."

Since beginning this last expedition they had marched over eight hundred miles, on an average of twenty-seven miles per day. The issue of rations was irregular, with the common soldier in his outfit subsisting primarily on green corn, roasted in the ashes of a camp fire. Now, under the shade trees at Leesburg, Virginia, he ordered a full day of rest. It was only the second such day his foot-sore soldiers had enjoyed since leaving winter camp early in May.

Ford snuggled in the shade of an oak tree, removed his tunic and shirt and, clad only in a pair of ragged trousers, looked up into the shy face of a young musician from the 31st.

"Sir, I . . . that is . . . I was wondering . . ." The boy's voice faltered and he looked at the ground.

"Yes, son? Speak up. What do you want?"

"Well sir, I cain't rightly write, so my messmate was a hepin' me pen a letter to my mother. Only he was kilt back there at Snicker's Gap an' I need someone to finish it for me. Could you maybe he'p me with it?"

"Did you ask the band leader?"

The boy's face was scarlet. He was new to the company, couldn't be more than twelve or thirteen, if that. Too young to know that you don't approach an officer with a simple request to write a letter. *But since I'm out of uniform he probably doesn't know who I am*, Ford speculated. His heart softened as the boy licked dry lips, his eyes glued to the ground.

"Do you have the letter with you?" Ford asked.

"Yes, sir." He pulled a crumpled scrap of paper from his pocket.

Ford took the letter from his hand and began to read: "We are in sight of Washington City, and we believe we can take it with little effort, but as our boys might get scattered around seeing the sights, we might all be captured. We've been ordered to prepare to move and there is no telling where this letter will be finished."

Ford walked into his tent and returned with quill and ink. "What's your name, son?"

"Daniel. Daniel Baldwin."

"Well, sit down, Dan, and tell me what else you want to say to your mother. I'll write it out for you. You've missed today's post, but you can mail it tomorrow."

It took only minutes for the boy to dictate what he wanted said and to tell his mother how much he missed her and that he would be home soon. Daniel left the tent with a beaming face, and Ford felt a heaviness of despair he seldom acknowledged. The boy was so young—so terribly, terribly young.

The next morning wagons were packed and they prepared to move out. Esau got a good fire and water going in preparation for breakfast and listened to Ford's tale of the young Drummer Boy with a look of sadness, but, of course, he said nothing as he busied himself preparing a little hoe-cake and coffee with a small slice of bacon. They ate quickly. All was quiet, except for an occasional musket bark high in the mountains.

Esau began to strike the tent while Ford poured himself a last cup of coffee. As he sipped the dark, bitter brew in the shade of the oak tree young Daniel came running by, his drum slung over his shoulder, his cap at a rakish angle on his head. Ford hailed him.

"We're moving out. Did you get your letter posted?"

Daniel's eyes widened in surprise as he saw Ford in full uniform and comprehended his rank. The boy took three or four steps toward him just as a tremendous boom shattered the early morning quiet. A shell hit the limb of the oak tree under which they were standing, exploding fifteen feet overhead, sending a thick branch crashing to the ground. It struck Daniel on the back of his right shoulder and passed through, coming out at his breast, impaling him to the ground.

Ford, his breath coming raw in his throat, shouted Daniel's name and jumped to his feet. With a bleak, wintry feeling he lifted the boy's head in his arms. Daniel opened his eyes and looked at Ford with mute appeal. His fingers fumbled toward the pocket in his shirt.

"Your letter?" Ford asked.

Daniel nodded and closed his eyes.

Ford found himself simultaneously watching the life drain from what had been a young life, not yet lived, and watching his own reaction to what he was seeing. His hands were trembling. He had been a soldier long enough to be conditioned to death. He had carried the body of his best friend from the battlefield, seen bodies piled on top of one another in rifle pits, seen so many of his company slaughtered that he no longer tried to keep them sorted out in his memory. But he had never been involved in the death of someone so young, a boy whose loving thoughts for his mother Ford had shared only hours before. His face twisted in anguish. He had rationalized his military conditioning to avoid the dead, but he hadn't eliminated the ingrained knowledge that war was murder—pure and simple. He was sick of the senseless waste of young men whose lives had just begun. What was he fighting for that was this important?

He held up departure long enough to bury the young Drummer Boy on a hillside close to the river. The next day Ford mailed the letter, stained with blood and grime, to the boy's mother.

After a brief skirmish outside Winchester they resumed the line of march to Martinsburg, tearing up railroad tracks as they went. Ford was well aware that they were once more moving in the direction of Pennsylvania. Chambersburg and Abby were within a day's ride.

* * *

A week later, just before the rainy dawn of July 29, 1864, Esau delivered a message to Ford that General Early wanted him at once.

Ford arrived at the headquarter's tent to find Early, standing outside, engaged in deep conversation with two cavalry officers. He knew the one, "Tiger John" McCausland, a slender, handsome man with close-cropped, black hair, an impressive black handlebar mustache and bushy-browed black eyes. Ford guessed "Tiger John" to be only a few years older than himself, yet the man's swashbuckling, fierce exploits had recently earned him a promotion to brigadier general.

Early looked up at Ford's arrival and gave him a curt nod. "Captain McKenzie . . . this is General John McCausland and General Bradley Johnson. We're discussing a cavalry operation that will involve you." He turned away and resumed his conversation with the two generals.

Ford found himself watching Jubal Early, thinking how much he had changed since the Georgians' first engagement at Cold Harbor. Stooped by arthritis, his face had grown thin and haggard. Although unduly impetuous in earlier battles, he had developed into a sound commander. Much of what was bold and soldierly Ford credited to "Old Jube."

His reverie was broken when he heard the word "Chambersburg." He sucked in his breath and listened warily.

"You are to enter the town of Chambersburg and demand one hundred thousand in gold or five hundred thousand in greenbacks for the indemnification of Southerners whose property has been put to the torch by the Federals. If this indemnity is not forthcoming at once, reduce the town to ashes," Early said, his voice incisive and harsh.

Standing in the drizzle outside the tent, Ford clenched his fists. He let the rage swell. He well knew that the army demanded unquestioning obedience from its officers, but damned if he'd lend a hand to firing any town. The amount required was an impossible sum of money for Chambersburg to raise after being pillaged twice before during the war.

Ford broke into the conversation. "Why am I to be involved? I'm infantry, not cavalry."

Early turned to face Ford with a questioning look, as though surprised to see him there. "Because you know the area. . . . General McCausland and Johnson do not," he snapped. "We'll supply you with a good mount. You will, of course, leave your servant behind. The mission should not take more than a day or two."

"Why Chambersburg?"

"Because we can destroy an important rail head of the Cumberland Valley Railroad."

"Have you no stomach for this mission, Captain McKenzie?" General McCausland asked, his voice dripping contempt.

"I don't enjoy being involved in things I don't understand," Ford answered acidly. "I don't have the faintest idea why you need to take this action against innocent civilians. It's against Lee's specific code of conduct."

Early turned cold eyes on Ford. "You're a Georgian, are you not?"

"Yes, sir."

"Have you not heard of the wanton destruction of Darien just last year? Have you forgotten the scorched homes of Senator Hunter, of Colonel Boteler, and of Col. Edmund Lee, viciously burned by the Federals? Have you not seen the ruins of VMI? It's time to open the eyes of the people of the North to a war gone mad, by an act of retaliation for the destruction of private dwellings in western Virginia."

Ford had no answer. Abby's farm should be far enough from town to be out of harms way, but what about Elizabeth whom he had grown to like during her visits to Brookside? Her father's inn was in the center of town. He had to warn them. But how? Dared he send Esau on ahead to deliver the message? No! If Esau were picked up by Rebel pickets he would be treated as a runaway slave and shot on sight. How then?

"Yes, sir," he finally muttered. "I'll prepare to leave at once."

* * *

McCausland led his troops across the wide, deep Potomac at McCoy's Ferry Ford near Clear Spring, Maryland and turned north on the Mercersburg Pike. Ford rode at the head of the column, the route well remembered. They were traveling many of the same roads he had used when seeking out Jeb Stuart in '62 during his raid on

Chambersburg. *The first time he had seen Abby,* he thought with a pang.

About ten P.M. the cavalry halted on the outskirts of Mercersburg to feed their horses and wait for the stragglers to come up. Ford, exhausted and apprehensive, reported at headquarters to find Generals McCausland and Johnson huddled before a folding camp table examining a worn map. They barely looked up. Curtly, they informed Ford that the column would rest for several hours, then push on. They should be in Chambersburg by daylight.

Shortly after midnight he was back in the saddle. Close to three thousand men wound their weary way to Bridgeport and St. Thomas, then east on the Pittsburgh Pike towards Chambersburg. The route was familiar, although two years had passed since he chased Baines through this same valley. A lot of water had passed over the dam since then.

As dawn streaked the heavens the troops struck camp at the fairgrounds along the Pittsburgh Pike about a mile and a half west of Chambersburg. "Tiger John" McCausland, with a sardonic smile on his face, ordered several shells lobbed into the town to wake it up.

Leaving most of the raiding party in line of battle on the heights, Ford led McCausland and about four hundred men into the town. Ford's hands grew clammy as he clutched the pommel, swallowing dryly. Citizens should have been sleeping, but instead, lamps were flickering on in every window. He wondered if Abby had heard the exploding shells or if she was still asleep, unaware of the approaching danger.

McCausland broke the men into small squads. They dashed into Chambersburg by every street and alley and, finding the way clear, converged on the square.

"Tiger John" reined in beside Ford. "Where can we get breakfast and present our demands?" he asked.

"I'd suggest the Franklin Hotel over there on the corner of the Diamond. General Ewell used it as his headquarters when our troops staged around Chambersburg prior to the Battle of Gettysburg."

McCausland dismounted, pulling the end of his thick, handlebar mustache as his gaze swept the Diamond. Nearby, several old men watched them anxiously. "Have those men ring the courthouse bell to summon the town authorities," McCausland ordered. Then he swaggered to the hotel for his breakfast, his officers trailing behind.

Ford forced himself to eat, his eyes never leaving the front door of the hotel, willing someone to appear who could comply with the ransom. Unfortunately no one came. Furious, McCausland wiped a napkin across his mustache, threw it on the table, ordered General Johnson to arrest fifty or more professional citizens, put them under guard, and bring them to the Diamond at once to hear his demands.

The officers finished their breakfast in silence, every one certain of the fate that lay ahead for this fashionable hotel and the town of Chambersburg.

By this time the arrested citizens had been assembled before a dry goods store facing the Diamond and immediately in front of the Franklin Hotel. Ford recognized Judge Kimmel, who had handled his arrest last summer, and a doctor, whose name he couldn't remember, who had treated his leg. McCausland approached the men and read the document outlining General Early's demands and the amount of the ransom.

One of the citizens snorted in derision. "We won't pay you five cents. You've cleaned us out twice before, we haven't anything left and you damn well know it."

There was no mistaking the fire in "Tiger John's" eyes when he replied formally, "I will wait six hours for your compliance. When the six hours are up I will begin the destruction of this town." He meant every word of it.

Just then some scouts returned with a Union prisoner reporting that General William Averell was not far off, with a heavy force of cavalry.

Ford cleared his throat. "Sir, perhaps I . . ."

"You will ride east," McCausland interrupted curtly, "scout the area for those approaching Union troops, and report back to me."

Ford felt a tide of relief wash over him. East! It was the answer to his prayers. Brookside was just east of town.

He would stop and warn Abby.

CHAPTER
– 18 –

The sun sat high in the sky, the day hot and sultry with not a breath stirring. Abby straightened her back with a grimace, her pail brimming with the last blackcap raspberries of the season. She tilted her head to an unexpected sound, wiping stained, scratched hands across her limp skirt. A horse thundered up the lane, its hoofs sending up swirls of dust. Drat. Who could be coming to visit at such an untimely time of day? She must look a mess with berry juice smudging her hands and damp hair plastered to her forehead.

She squinted against the brilliant sun, trying to make out the blurred figure racing toward her. Anxiety stabbed her as she remembered the distant sound of cannon that had aroused her before dawn. Only days before she had carried a message to General Averell in Greencastle warning him that Confederates were in the area of nearby Mercersburg. Were Rebels once again threatening Chambersburg? Whoever was approaching was in an awful hurry.

Her heart gave a sudden lurch and she sucked in her breath as the sun glinted on copper hair. It was Ford.

She plunked her pail down so hard a dozen berries spilled out on the ground. I'm angry with him, she reminded herself. I've no business feeling as though I can't breathe every time he pops into my life.

A familiar whinny startled her and she turned her gaze from the figure jumping to the ground to look in disbelief at the big bay horse pawing the ground. It wasn't possible! Bay Hunter had been taken by the Confederates over two years ago. She had given him up for lost—or dead—a long time ago. It had to be another horse who looked just like him.

"Bay Hunter?" she whispered tentatively.

The horse's ears came forward, and he snuffed the air, tossing his head with interest. It was him! There was no mistaking the crooked white diamond on his forehead. She ran forward and flung her arms around his neck, burying her head in his thick mane. Bay Hunter tossed his head and nuzzled her arm.

"If I weren't in such a hurry to warn you I'd be mighty offended that you greet my horse with more affection than you do me," Ford grumbled in a tension-strained voice.

"This is our horse, this is Bay Hunter, taken by your raiders the night Papa was murdered. However did you get him?" She wrinkled her brow and looked at him keenly, suddenly aware of what he had said.

"Warn me?"

"Early this morning our General McCausland invaded Chambersburg and ordered your town to pay an enormous ransom or be put to the torch. The townspeople have been given six hours to come forth with the money."

Abby's stomach clenched. "Sarah and Amanda are in town," she gasped. "Ila took them in this morning to do our Saturday shopping."

Ford's face turned pale and he grabbed her arm. "We must hurry. There's no doubt in my mind that your town will be burned." He vaulted into the saddle. "Pull your skirts up," he ordered, his strong arm lifting her up behind him with such force she almost flew off the other side. Chagrined, she righted herself and grabbed Ford around his waist. He dug his spurs into the horse's side. Abby hung on for dear life as Bay Hunter lunged forward into a full gallop, north on Falling Spring Road.

Hot wind stung her face, dust swirling around them like a nest of hornets, as Ford gave her a terse account of McCausland's orders.

Abby listened in disbelief. Surely, the Confederates knew that the town could not raise a large sum of money that quickly. The town had been plundered twice before, leaving nothing of value behind. She felt a surge of hope. General Lee would never order an entire town burned—Ford was overreacting.

"And where did you get our horse?" she asked.

"From a group of confiscated horses. Since Ruffian was killed at Gettysburg I've taken whatever mount comes my way."

"When?"

"We've no time to talk now. I'll explain later."

Abby tightened her grip on Ford's waist as he swung Bay Hunter left, tearing down Market Street. Her mouth turned dry. Squads of soldiers were already breaking open the doors of stores and houses to steal their contents. Many of them staggered, their arms overflowing with all manner of personal belongings. She shook her head in disgust. From the yelling and profanity she could tell they staggered from more than the hindrance of their thievery. They were drunk.

Ford noticed it too. "The men have found the town's stock of whiskey," he muttered angrily, slowing Bay Hunter to a canter. "Where to?"

"Straight ahead. The Diamond in the center of town. We'll check Hoke's store first. It's on the corner in front of the courthouse."

Rebel cavalry was by this time dismounted, rolling barrels of turpentine and kerosene onto the street, fashioning torches from rags. Abby was truly frightened now.

Ford reined the horse at Hoke's hitching post and jumped to the ground. Abby didn't wait for his hand; in a tangle of skirts she was out of the saddle as if she had been ejected, running across the wooden porch, her heart pounding as she pushed the front door open and bolted inside.

Jacob Hoke stood just inside the door, surrounded by a mountain of books, bedding, clothing and pictures, engaged in earnest conversation with several officers in gray, one wearing the collar of the clergy. Abby gave a yelp of frustration as her gaze swept the store. Sarah and Ila were not here.

Mr. Hoke turned and waved his arm toward the back of the room. "Your kind sister and maid are upstairs helping Mrs. Hoke pack," he cried. "Tell them they must leave at once. This chaplain just told me the Rebels are determined to torch the town."

Abby sped across the floor and up the steps, Ford on her heels, the smell of smoke already invading the store.

She burst into the Hokes' bedroom and ran to gather her sister in her arms.

"Oh, Abby," Sarah sobbed. "I'm so scared. I prayed you'd come."

Ford accosted Mrs. Hoke. "Is this your home?"

"Yes, it is." Her gaze raked his gray uniform.

"Then, for God's sake, grab only what is the most valuable to you and give it to me. I'll take it to a place of safety. McCausland plans to fire everything."

Mrs. Hoke turned furious eyes on him. "If they are going to burn the whole town then there's no use to remove anything. It may as well burn here as somewhere else."

Outside the window a fire engine clanged furiously as a red glow sped across the sky. Ila dropped an armful of clothing on the floor and ran to Ford.

"Where's my Esau?"

"He's not with me."

Ila began to cry. "Oh, Lawd, we're all gonna burn to death. I just know it."

Her tears frightened Amanda, sitting on a mattress, playing with a ball of yarn. She began to wail. Ford snatched her up and herded everyone towards the door. "Help me get these women out of here," he snapped at Abby. "Move!"

Mrs. Hoke snatched several portraits from the wall and ran toward the stairs. Her husband and the clergyman had given up all attempts to remove their belongings and ran with the women to the front door. Ford followed. Flames were bursting from buildings all around.

Ford pushed everyone from the door. "Where's your carriage?" he barked at Sarah.

"Behind the Falling Spring Inn," she said, pointing down Market Street where leaping, crackling flames burst from buildings all around them.

He turned to Mr. Hoke. "Take your wife and head for the fields north of town. You should be safe there."

By now, Hoke's store, the courthouse, Franklin Hall, and the Franklin Hotel were in flames. Parties of soldiers heaved turpentine balls in all directions. A strong breeze communicated the flames to the surrounding buildings and, simultaneously, the right and left sides of the main street became one mass of flames. Within minutes the houses of both sides of the by-streets were in the same condition. Squads of men beat in the doors of houses, running inside to smash furniture with an axe, throw fluid or oil upon it and kindle a fire, with only a shouted warning to the people inside to get out.

And then one vast, lurid column of smoke and flame rose like a finger pointing to the sky.

Abby's eyes darted maniacally, trying to get her bearings in the gloom. Only one house was on fire north of the Diamond. "This way," she shrieked, running in that direction. The trees on either side of the dirt road met in an arch overhead, turning the long avenue into a dim tunnel filled with smoke. She pulled Ila behind her, and Sarah followed with Amanda clutched in her arms, all of them gasping for breath as they raced across the log footbridge spanning Falling Spring Creek and headed for the livery stable behind the inn.

Abby's eyes swept the empty yard.

"It be gone," Ila cried. "The buggy be gone."

Abby looked around for Ford, realizing for the first time that he was no longer with them. Was it possible that he had joined his comrades in this terrible act of destruction?

Just then smoke erupted from the inn and Elizabeth burst through the door, her face a mask of terror.

"The inn's on fire," she screamed.

Abby grabbed her by the arm. "Where's your father?"

"Gone. He headed north this morning with our whiskey. We never dreamed they'd actually burn the town. We thought they were only trying to scare us into paying the ransom."

Amid the screams of women and children, Abby did not hear the galloping horse until Ford jumped to the ground beside her.

Sarah grabbed Ford's arm. "Our carriage is gone!"

Ila was sobbing hysterically. "Oh, Lawd, Capt'in McKenzie. They're gonna burn us all up," she cried.

"No, they aren't," Ford answered. "But I was afraid of this. I stopped to get my horse; had to cover his eyes with this blanket till we got out of the Diamond." He uncinched the frightened animal and threw the saddle to the ground.

Abby realized what Ford was doing, and began to shake her head.

"Yes, Abby. The four of you can ride bareback. You must take the women and baby and get away. The entire town is on fire."

"I'm staying. People need help."

"Don't argue with me!" He began to propel her toward the horse.

She wiggled from his grasp, looking at Elizabeth with mute appeal. "Take everyone and leave. They're terrified. They'll never find their way out of this inferno alone."

"But, what about you?" Elizabeth cried, her voice high and hysterical as she looked toward the smoke billowing from the inn.

With an oath Ford hoisted the three women and baby onto the horse. He turned to Abby, and she returned his glare with defiant eyes. With a shake of his head he threw the reins to Elizabeth and raced toward the inn where smoke rolled from the windows.

Abby looked deep into Elizabeth's eyes. "I trust you to get them to safety. Ride in the creek, it'll keep you wet, and go to the cemetery behind our church."

"What if . . ."

"For heaven's sake, don't argue. Do it! I'll see if I can help Ford douse the flames." Without a backwards glance, Abby ran across the smoke-filled yard toward the inn.

Ford, coughing and gasping for breath, grabbed her before she could enter the smoking building. His eyebrows were singed and his hands trembled. "I've contained it to the dining room," he rasped. "There's no fire now, only smoke."

She struggled from his grasp, anger churning in her throat like bitter acid. "You're a band of monsters," she cried. "Monsters! All of you. Get away from me."

Boldly, she snatched up her skirts and sped toward King Street. Frightened people were fleeing in utter confusion, some running until they dropped to the ground exhausted. Cows and dogs and cats were burning to death, and the death cries of the poor dumb animals sounded like the groans of human beings. Abby shouted at the people to head for Cedar Grove, the town cemetery. It was only blocks away, just west of the Conococheague. Its trees should offer safety and shade from the scorching heat, which she judged must be well over one hundred degrees.

The scene was heartrending and appalling. The cracking and roaring of the flames as they leaped from house to house, the shrieks of terrified women, panicstricken children, and the pitiful appeals of the old and helpless, formed an indescribable scene of horror. Abby was panting, but she continued to run on as rapidly as she could, toward the Church of the Falling Spring, calling out to the milling throng to head for the safety of the creeks and cemeteries. Here only an occasional house was burning. Thank heavens the day was perfectly calm or the entire town would have been engulfed in flames.

As she hurried on she was hailed by a frantic black servant from the front porch of a home that seemed to have missed the torch.

"Help! Lawd have mercy, he'p us. Mrs. Hugs is gonna have her baby and they can't find Dr. Boyl."

Abby ran up on the porch. She hesitated. She knew Sophia Hug. Knew that her husband had recently been killed in the service of the Union. The poor girl was all alone and must be terrified. Should she stop and help or go in search of the doctor? How could she possibly find him in the chaos surrounding her? Where would he go? *His office is close to the cemetery*, she thought suddenly. *He may have gone there to help people suffering from burns.*

She nodded to the sobbing servant. "Go back inside and help her as much as you can. I'll try to find the doctor."

She turned and ran back toward King Street, struggling to breathe, flames roaring in her face, her heart pounding. Past the tannery, also in flames, she was forced to slow to a walk with a nasty stitch in her side. Wending her way through a black shroud of billowing smoke and squads of McCausland's cavalry, she finally found the doctor in Cedar Grove Cemetery and gave him the urgent message.

Now, she had to find her own family. She hurried back across the creek and followed its banks toward the church cemetery on the other side; the cemetery where her mother and father were buried and where she hoped Sarah and the baby had found sanctuary.

Peering through the smoke she saw a figure in the gloom. It was Susan Chambers, huddled in her rose garden, surrounded by furniture and bric-a-brac. She sat on her sofa, watching her home burn, tears running down her cheeks, her black shawl scorched from the roaring flames.

Abby stifled her sobs. "They won't see me cry," she moaned. "I won't let them see me cry."

Across from the church Ford was lifting an old woman into a buggy while flames kissed each other over his head. Abby's anger at him was spent as quickly as it had come, and she was relieved to see him. Suddenly, her leg began to feel warm. She looked down at her skirt with numbed horror as it began to smolder.

Ford saw her. He raced across the cemetery and began beating her skirt with his bare hands. "Climb into the creek," he commanded, propelling her toward the water.

He wadded in beside her and took her trembling hand in his own. "It's over, Abby. This hellish business has finally ended. Union troops are approaching from the east and McCausland's ordered us out of town the way we came." He pointed toward the west and Abby could see a line of at least a thousand Rebels on the heights, watching the destruction of her town and waiting for their retreating comrades.

Mutely Abby watched as the Rebel cavalry withdrew from town, most of them so drunk they were hardly capable of sitting on a horse.

"So much for your chivalrous Southern army," she said bitterly, anger once more welling to the surface as Ford helped her stagger from the creek.

Ford's eyes swept her damaged skirt. "Are you all right?"

"Yes."

"Then I'm needed elsewhere. We'll talk later tonight." With a tentative smile he hurried down the street.

So, he wasn't leaving with them? She dared to hope.

As the cavalry retreated, the people who had taken refuge in the cemeteries and fields around the town began to straggle back to the remains of their ruined homes.

It was like a scene from Hades. Children, separated from their parents, ran screaming through the streets. The sick and aged were being carried into the fields, the beautiful green meadows pitiful as groups of women and children, exposed to the rays of the burning sun, hovered over the few articles they had saved.

Merchandise of every description was strewn along the road, boots, clothing, window curtains, and even infants' shoes and little slips. The stench of burning cows, dogs, and cats hung like a pall in the air. Abby could bear no more. She turned and walked back to the creek, asking herself over and over if she could ever find forgiveness for this day of sacrifice. No . . . no . . . no! Never!

Flushed and breathing hard, her tears finally released, she sat down on a stump beside the Falling Spring. At first, Abby was aware of nothing but the overwhelming prevalence of black: black smoke billowing toward the heavens, each column black and straight, first one, and then another, and another, until the columns blended into a gray shroud; black cinders moving with the slow current of the creek; stark black branches of seared trees; black timbers of burned homes; black soot smudging her hands and clothing. And then she began to hear the sounds. The crackling and crash of falling timbers and walls, the groans of burning animals, the roar of the waterfall muted against pealing church bells. And then out of the darkness she heard a bird, perched high in a scorched tree, begin to cheep.

Gradually, her breath quieted and she felt a semblance of calm. Her town burned, but birds still flew, the Falling Spring tumbled on. Her eyes followed the tiny stream as it rushed past the ruins of homes and stores, tumbling down the drop of rocks to the placid Conococheague. *Peace in the midst of all this turmoil*, she thought, tears once more threatening.

More slowly now, she began to wend her way south on Front Street toward the Diamond. Buildings were smoldering everywhere. A dull, empty ache gnawed at Abby's soul. *The sight of a human dwelling being consumed by fire is a powerful, almost sacred thing,* she thought. *It eats at our sense of security, reminds us that all we have stored up can be wiped away in a matter of minutes.*

"I've been looking for you," a quiet voice said. Ford's hand touched her shoulder and squeezed it gently. She looked up into his soot-blackened face, fighting to calm her warring emotions.

"I'm sorry, Abby," he said. "I did all I could. Not all of our men obeyed McCausland's order, many helped people douse the flames and save their homes. I, myself, saved one entire block by disobeying a direct order."

"But many more lit their torches."

"Yes, I know."

Abby swallowed dryly. Every minute she expected to hear the pounding of horses' hooves and see the cavalry charging down the hill to resume their grisly task. But the minutes slipped by and they did not come. She looked at Ford, the pain in her heart swelling up again.

Ford watched her scan the distant hills. "They're gone. They won't be back. Your troops should arrive any minute to help."

"But it's too late. Our town is in ruins."

Ford pursed his thin lips and looked away. He did not answer her.

"If your army has left, then why are you still here?" she asked.

"I don't know if I can ever go back." His lips curved in a slow smile. "Besides, I want to see you safely home." Concern for her was clearly etched on his face. Her stomach gave that familiar lurch. Ford's actions today would surely be considered punishable insubordination, but she was just too drained to think about that.

"My family . . . I don't know if they're safe," she cried. Fear, held in abeyance during the past few hours, swept her like a tidal wave, causing her knees to buckle. Ford grabbed her and pulled her tightly to his chest. "Hang on, dear. We'll find them."

* * *

Later that night, Abby and Sarah moved quietly around the kitchen at Brookside, preparing a light meal, the first food any of them had touched since morning. Abby had persuaded Ila to go to bed, Brandon had eaten and gone upstairs long ago, and Amanda slept on a pallet beside the fireplace, an occasional hiccup breaking the quiet of her slumber.

Ford sat in a rocking chair, eyes shut and tunic wadded under his head as he napped in the airless heat, the windows closed to keep out the smoky air invading every room. Abby set a plate on the floor beside him and looked at his quiet face as if she did not know him, her heart touched in a sad, sweet way. Ford had aged.

Gently she laid her hand on his shoulder.

"What's on the plate?" he muttered without opening his eyes.

"I thought you were asleep."

He sat up and yawned. "Too tired to sleep. It's been at least forty-six hours since I last slept. What's on the plate?"

"Leftover chicken and warmed up beans." She sat the plate on his lap. "And some hot coffee."

"Smells wonderful."

She pulled up a chair beside him and watched him eat, feelings of love still warring with her hatred for the South. She felt herself begin to shake. The only feeling she'd been willing to accept was anger, and there was still a part of her that wanted to stay angry— but she was beginning to realize that hate is a sickness, an indulgence she enjoyed. It had to stop.

All she could be sure of now was that fate had once more brought Ford to her doorstep. And she wanted him. God, how she wanted him. It was hard to imagine that she had ever considered him an enemy. He looked . . . she searched for a word . . . defeated, shirt stained and torn, wisps of red hair long and unruly, narrow face pinched and pale from his chronic dysentery. A fresh scar snaked from under his right eye to disappear into the depths of his red beard. Ford had never been truly handsome in her eyes, but from that day, two years ago, when he had appeared at her door looking for Esau, she had loved him. It was as simple as that.

I must stop this, she thought. *There are too many problems facing us; I have an obligation to provide a home for Brandon and for Sarah and Amanda. The chance of Sarah finding a husband is very remote—there will be a drastic shortage of eligible young men when this war is finally over, and she does have an illegitimate child to raise.*

She chuckled ruefully. This whole thought process was mighty presumptuous of her. Ford had made it clear from the beginning that he mistrusted women and planned never to remarry. And he had his own child to raise, a widowed mother, a plantation that was probably in ruins, an island in the Southern sun that he loved.

His eyes were closed once more and she lifted the plate from his lap with trembling fingers. She should be thinking of this man with vengeance, but instead she thought about how she loved the clean angles of his cheek bones and the muscles of his shoulders and arms. She remembered the feel of his long fingers caressing her neck, how the hardness beneath his trousers felt pressed against her stomach, how soft his beard felt when it rubbed against her chin.

Sarah approached with a light blue shawl. She placed it across his shoulders and Abby saw a softness in her eyes. It touched Abby to see her that way.

"I'm taking Amanda upstairs," Sarah said. "The captain needs some rest. Stay with him."

She had barely disappeared up the steps when Ford sat up, his green eyes shining in the dark with a look Abby had never seen before.

"I'm sorry we had to meet again under these circumstances," he said quietly.

She did not reply, and he added, "But I'm not sorry to see you, only sorry for the reason."

"Good night, Ford." She started to get out of the chair, the anger she had thought put aside once more rising to the surface as she remembered her town lying in ruins.

"Don't go, Abby." He put his hand on her arm.

"What do you want? We have nothing to say to each other."

"Yes, we do. Please."

"I don't know what you want to say, Ford, but it's impossible for me to forget the past. You're an officer in the Confederate army—a Southerner killed my father, raped my sister, and today your army destroyed my town."

"I'm sorry," he said.

"Your being sorry doesn't change a thing." She began to cry, dabbing her eyes furiously with the corner of her apron.

"Please don't cry."

"I will if I want," she said ridiculously.

"I'm sorry," he said again, this time in a whisper, and she thought he was going to touch her. But he didn't. He leaned back in his chair and stared up at the ceiling.

"Look," he said, "I'm not trying to excuse what our troops did. But you must remember that we have seen a thousand ruined homes in Virginia—barns and houses burned and private property destroyed by Union troops. Many of the soldiers who set the torch today did so in bitter retaliation for their own home that lies in ashes."

"I still don't understand how your General Lee could order the destruction of an entire town. Nothing justifies that."

"General Early issued the order, Abby. Not General Lee. Lee knows nothing of this." Ford pulled at his lower lip, his eyes somber. "Did you know that General Lee's former nursemaid, a black woman, lives in Chambersburg? He stopped to see her when he passed through your town last summer . . . before the battle at Gettysburg. It was the only visit he made."

"I heard that."

He shifted in his chair. She could feel his eyes on her.

"Abby, look at me."

Reluctantly, she did.

"War is a game at which two contending parties play, like a game of chess. Retaliatory or cruel policy inaugurated by one is invariably followed by a similar action by the other."

A silence fell between them. Ford reached for her hand, and this time she did not pull away.

"Who can say on which side the right or wrong lies," his tone was deceptively quiet, almost lazy in its inflection.

"And slavery, Ford? Is that right or wrong?"

"The South didn't invent slavery. People have been held in bondage since biblical times. It was introduced to the North by the English and flourished here throughout the entire eighteenth century. Some of your townspeople own slaves." He ran a tired hand across his singed beard. "The North built its economy around factories . . . the South around agriculture. One is dependent on sweatshop labor, the other on slave labor." At the look on her face, he hastened to add, "I'm not saying slavery is right, because I know it's abused. Abraham Lincoln signed the Emancipation Proclamation, but it doesn't free the slaves in the Southern states that seceded. Ila is wrong about that . . . technically Esau is not free. The future of slavery in Georgia will be determined by the outcome of the war."

He saw the wounded look in Abby's eyes and cleared his throat. "Slavery never bothered me before because we took good care of our Negroes. They were fed and clothed, housed, and treated kindly."

Abby gave him a scorching look. "You say that as though they are little children. I'll never accept your view and you'll never accept mine."

"Then we seem to be at an impasse." His eyes locked with hers, desire blazing from their green depths. He groaned, "Abby, Abby, what have you done to me? I've tried to stop thinking about you. I can't."

He stood and pulled her toward him. He touched her cheek and she touched his, then he kissed the place his fingers had been, until he found her lips.

She detected the stale odor of smoke and a pungent hint of sweat. For some reason it excited her. She returned his kiss with an urgency that surprised and alarmed her.

Once more he was the one who stopped. "I must go, you know," he said.

"Go? Go where?"

His lips pulled up in a sardonic smile. "Back to my regiment. I can't be a deserter—I must see this war through."

So he was going back—perhaps to one day look down the muzzle of his gun at her brother. He made as though to take her in his arms once more, but she turned her back.

"Take care, dearest," he said softly. "I'll be back some day."

The door closed behind him.

CHAPTER
– 19 –

Winchester, Newton, Abraham's Creek, Fisher's Hill, Belle Grove—towns and battles, men and places, ran together in Ford's mind, like water tumbling over a dam.

He thumbed the page of his tattered calendar, drawing a circle around tomorrow's date, February 10, 1865. Soon they would break winter camp, and another spring would come as the anxious nation waited. More blood, more blood, and yet more blood as they headed for yet another battle, determined to continue the struggle. In the meantime he had been granted a leave of absence. Up until now furloughs had been severely restricted; however, early in the new year General Lee issued an order allowing one man in each company the advantage of a twenty-four-day furlough.

A bitter smile tugged at the corner of Ford's mouth. He desperately needed time away from the war, had not been on leave since the first year of his enlistment. Daily, the condition of the army became more desperate. Starvation, literal starvation, was doing its deadly work. Deep in his heart Ford knew they could not continue the fight much longer. He would stay until the bitter end, but what fate awaited him if Lee was pressed to surrender? He had to make plans for life after war, and the place to start was with Abby. He could no longer escape the fact that he was in love with her. He wanted her to share that life.

The next morning, eager to start the first day of his leave, he crawled from beneath his ragged blanket, shivering in the frigid air.

Esau already had a pot of coffee bubbling on the little camp stove and, seeing Ford awake, hurried to lay out fresh linens and shaving gear.

"Are you certain you want to go with me?" Ford asked. "We'll be traveling in enemy country, you know. It could be very dangerous."

Esau grinned, his white teeth gleaming in the half light. "I be sure. I be hurtin' to hold my woman in my arms, same as you be t' hold yours. Besides, who take care of you if'n I don' come?"

"The Lord's been doing a pretty fair job of it so far."

"De Lawd have his hands full keepin' you alive. I hasta take care of the rest of you."

Well, Ford thought, *the days of your ministering to my every need are fast coming to an end.* He regarded his servant with tenderness. He would miss him. Esau had served him as long as he could remember, tending not only to his physical needs, but acting as friend and confidant when the occasion demanded it. Only a fool would fail to see that things were not going well with the South. And if and when Lee surrendered it might mean imprisonment for the Southern soldier. Certainly there would be no accommodation from the Yankees for a slave—free or not. He gazed intently at his faithful servant. He knew what he had to do.

"You've earned your freedom, Esau. The war is all but over. I plan to leave you in Chambersburg with that woman of yours. I'll write your freedom papers when we get to the farm."

"That mighty good of you, Massa. I think on it. I promise myself t' see you t' the end, an' that ain't come yet."

Esau continued to fill Ford's knapsack, rolling a Union uniform taken from a captured wagon train, into a tight bundle and hiding it beneath a change of underwear and a tattered blanket.

"Miz Abby be mighty surprised when she see you dressed in blue," he said with a deep chuckle.

Ford laughed. "Indeed she will." Then his face sobered. "I'd be picked up in a second as a Rebel. Much as I hate it, it's the smart thing to do. I'll change clothes after we cross the Potomac. We'll part then and you follow about an hour behind me. Do you have that map I drew for you?"

"Yess'r, I gots it pinned t' the inside of my shirt."

Ford pushed his arms into a long blue woolen cape, this one taken from a dead Yankee major. The only coats any of his men had were blue, the fruits of plunder, the days of regulation uniforms long gone. Now they dressed in whatever came their way.

They went out to saddle up. He had obtained a mount for himself and a mule for Esau. The well-trained horses stood with drooping heads in the raw February wind, like statues, still as a churchyard at midnight. Ford heaved himself into the saddle and, before the sun peeked over the horizon, they were once more on their way.

At Boonsboro, Ford changed into the Union uniform, dug a hole along Antietam Creek to bury his Confederate uniform, marking it with a pile of stones. He repeated his instructions to Esau to lag behind. It would be suspicious if he and a black man were seen riding together. He just hoped Esau wasn't picked up by the Confederates. He had heard that many free black servants from the North had been confiscated by the Rebels and sent south as escaped slaves. Ford intended to pass himself off as a Union picket, separated from his company, attempting to rejoin them.

A sense of urgency overtook him and he sprang back into the saddle, eager to be off. Chambersburg was dead ahead. His entire future lay in the hands of the girl he planned to ask to marry him. But only if she would return to St. Simons with him when the war was over.

Sarah was the one to open the door to his knock. She stared at him open-mouthed for a minute, then with a cry of joy reached up to kiss his cheek. Good, at least one member of the household was glad to see him. His gaze traveled past her, searching for the one who was the reason for his being here.

If Sarah was surprised to see him, Abby was even more so. She came bustling into the hall to see who was at the door and stopped dead in her tracks. Her face turned pale.

"There's nothing to fear this time," he hastened to assure her.

Abby's gaze swept over his blue uniform. "Are you . . . did you? . . ." Her voice faltered.

"I'm on furlough. I wanted to see you." An icy blast of air pushed against the door. "May I come in?"

"Of course, forgive our rudeness," Sarah said, drawing him into the warm hall.

Ila came running into the hall at the sound of their voices, wiping her hands across her white apron. She looked anxiously at the closed door.

Ford smiled at her. "Esau is several hours behind me."

They were all standing in the hallway, unsure what to do next. Amanda, curious about all the fuss, came toddling from the kitchen. She stared at the tall stranger, then ran to hide behind her mother's skirts, peeking at him in blue-eyed wonder.

That seemed to break the tension. At Sarah's urging they moved into the familiar kitchen. Abby took his coat and motioned him into a rocker. She still had not spoken.

Sarah sat down beside him and settled Amanda on her lap. "Would you care for some hot coffee?" she asked.

"I'd love some." He rubbed his cold fingers. "I still haven't gotten used to your Northern winters."

Ila moved to the stove. "I gets it," she announced. She poured the steaming brew into a mug and shook the near empty pot. "I best make some more if Esau close by."

"Do that, and get us some ginger cakes," Abby said.

Amanda toddled across the room to look at him with a shy smile as she held out a tattered blue bunny with a missing ear for his admiration. At almost two years, Amanda was the picture of her mother with bright blue eyes and dimples denting her chubby cheeks. Only the color of her hair reflected her father—black as a raven's wing, tumbling about her face in a mass of curls.

"Kiss," she said, pushing the stuffed animal into Ford's hand.

With a sheepish grin he raised it to his lips and gave it a loud smack.

Amanda giggled with delight. "More, more."

"I'm afraid you've started something," Sarah chuckled, taking Amanda by the hand. "Later, honey. Ford came to see your Aunt Abby."

An uneasy silence settled on them. Brandon sat near the hearth, a schoolbook open, a pile of paper and pencils on the table nearby. He had looked up when Ford walked in, then quickly away, his eyes clouded with disapproval.

"What class are you in now?" Ford asked him, trying to break the heavy silence.

"Seventh." He scowled. "Where's Esau?"

"He's coming."

"Good. I like *him.*"

"And you don't like me! Well, I guess I can understand that."

Brandon looked him square in the eye. "You're still a Rebel, ain't you? . . . despite that blue uniform. What'd you do, steal it from one of our dead soldiers?"

"Brandon!" Abby admonished. "That's quite enough of that kind of talk. Captain McKenzie helped every one of us during the fire and we've invited him into our home. Now you be civil to him."

His young face flushed. He looked back at his books.

Abby walked over and put her hand on his shoulder. "I think it's time for bed, Brandon."

"But Esau . . ."

"You can see him in the morning." She gave Ford a hard look. "I assume Captain McKenzie plans to stay that long."

"As long as it takes," Ford replied with a wry smile.

*   *   *

Ila stood at the window of her little cabin, her eyes searching the pathway, straining to see the first sign of Esau. Her heart thumped against her ribs. She had heard his voice in the kitchen greeting his Master and hoped he would search her out as soon as he could. Then, in the milky moonlight she saw the burly figure pick its way through the trees, a miner's lamp swinging from his hands, his boots crunching on the frozen ground.

She threw the door open before he could knock, struggling to calm her heart and effect an attitude of disdain. "So, you've come to see me, has you? I suppose you think I be here waiting for you like you just ran for an armful of wood."

"I hoped that. I weren't sure."

"And are you here to stay? Or just 'till your Master crooks his little finger and tells you to come, like you was some kinda dog."

Esau pushed his way into the cozy room where a small fire emitted a warm glow that made her skin look like coffee with heavy cream. He sucked in his breath. He had forgotten how beautiful she was. "That depend on you," he answered gruffly as he removed his coat and draped it over a chair.

Ila looked surprised. "How that?"

"Come here, woman, an' give me a kiss, an' I tell you." His strong arms pulled her to him and his big hand caressed her cheek. "I've missed you," he whispered before he placed his lips on hers.

All of her resolve to stay angry dissolved as she melted against his broad chest. She ached with longing for this man, had thought of him every minute of every day since he left, would take him on any terms he wanted.

She finally pulled away. "We gotta get us some coffee before this leads to somethin'. You said you had somethin' to say. Say it."

"Sit down, then, an' listen." Ila had only one chair, so he took it while she perched on the edge of her cot. "Marse Ford talk to me on the way up here before we separated. At first I didn't want to pay him no mind, but I knows he talks the truth. He thinks the war be over soon. Rumors floatin' all over camp that the generals been talking about surrender. Marse Ford don't know what'll happen t' him then. He says he ain't been paid fer a long time, he gots no money atall an' his momma writes that McKenzie Groves be in ruins. He don't have money to pay me no wage if I's set free. He wants me t' stay here."

"What you want?"

"I want t' make you my wife. Here, or on my island, it don' matter which."

Ila got up and busied herself at the pot-bellied stove, adding a chunk of wood to the fire, pouring another cup of coffee, thinking of what he had just said. She understood his pain, understood his love for this man who had been the major influence in his life. She hadn't at first. It was only after several talks with Reverend Brown that she had found forgiveness for Esau's leaving her to care for his Master. She sighed and placed the coffee before her man with a shy smile.

He grabbed her hand.

"Ila?"

She bent over and kissed him. "I want to marry you, too. But somethin' bother me. Long time ago you said that you not really free. That Marse Ford be you friend not just you Master. I thought a lot 'bout that. I didn' understand and I be mad at you, but I think I know now. He needed you just like Miss Sarah needed me when her baby come. The Kennedys they be family to me too, just like your Marse Ford be to you."

Tears pooled in Esau's eyes and he nodded his head. "It be hard for me t' leave him."

"I know. An what 'bout that island you love so much, what 'bout you Mammy an' Pappy down in Savannah? What you gonna do 'bout them?"

"I don't know."

Ila felt a tug at her heart. *Why*, she wondered, *did the Lawd lay so many griefs on her people?* Her eyes were thoughtful as she worried a button on her dress. "I want more'n a husband and babies. I want us to be happy, an you not be happy if you hafta worry that you did the right thing."

Esau turned his gaze to the floor. He did not answer.

Ila nodded. "We all gotta trust the Lawd, trust what He ask. Ain't no other way to get through this. I think you should stay with Marse Ford till this whole thing over with. Then your heart won't hurt so much." Ila saw his eyes flash with disbelief and she hurried to finish what was so hard to say. "Afterwards go back to Georgia and see your family. Then come back and we'll get married. You can try working here on this farm for a year, then we'll go south for a year, stay with your family, maybe look for mine, see how the black folks are getting along now they're free. That suit both of us. After, we can figure out where we want to live."

Joy shone in Esau's eyes as he crushed her in his arms, nuzzling his wooly head against her sleek black hair. "How did I ever . . . ever find me such a woman?" he groaned.

"Why, I do believe you was stealin' chickens," she answered with a chuckle.

* * *

Coffee finished and cakes eaten, Ford and Abby moved across the hall to the parlor. Sarah, with a knowing smile at Ford, took Amanda upstairs to bed.

A log hissed as it settled in the grate, the clock ticked with a comforting sound, rockers creaked as they moved back and forth. Abby was silent, seemingly at a loss for words. Then she said, "Your army did not crush the spirit of Chambersburg, you know. Within weeks the town was swarming with workers constructing new houses and businesses, many of which will be larger and finer than the ones destroyed."

"How much of the town was burned?" Ford asked.

"Pretty much the entire downtown area. Over five hundred buildings including the courthouse." She smiled ruefully. "A building here and there still stands. Our Masonic building was saved when an officer, obviously a brother Mason, posted guards around the temple to make sure it was not harmed. And Louisa Brand wrapped herself in an American flag and stood with a loaded revolver at the front door of her home. Your Rebels bypassed her house."

In spite of himself Ford smiled.

Abby pursed her lips. "I'll admit not all Confederates were intent on robbing and burning. Some officers instructed their men to assist the civilians in retrieving as much of their household goods as possible. Some houses were spared for one reason or another."

"Did anyone die?"

"Only old Daniel Parker, a former slave. It's not known whether he was overcome with smoke or died of distress at the destruction of his home." Abby put her hand to her mouth to hide a smile. "Three of your Confederates were killed, though, during the burning. Two drunken soldiers were gunned down by Mr. Miller, the druggist, after they entered his shop to loot and burn it and accidently locked themselves inside. Both were consumed by the flames. And a Rebel captain, who got drunk and separated from his command, was shot by citizens after hiding in the basement of a burning home. But enough about that bitter time," Abby concluded. "What military action have you seen since then?"

Ford told her that the 31st Georgia was still in winter camp, although this winter they had seen considerable action in defense of Petersburg. The brave town, under siege for the past ten months, had not fallen, and the Union had now moved their line north of the Appomattox River. He did not tell her that he believed collapse of Lee's army was inevitable.

Abby listened intently, sharp with interest. Ford hesitated, uneasy, his eyes suddenly wary. He changed the subject. "What have you been doing all winter?"

Abby ignored his question and returned to the prior subject. "Are your fortifications around Richmond sufficient to stave off an attack by Sherman's forces, do you think?"

Ford's eyes narrowed. "Darn you, woman, are you leading me on, gaining my confidence so you can carry tales to your brother?"

"Of course not." She rose and busied herself with a poker at the fire. "Were you in trouble for helping us during the burning?" she finally asked.

"Not for long. I was arrested for insubordination, but within a day restored to rank. They needed me."

"How long do you have?" She reached up to tuck a strand of hair behind her ear. Ford noticed that the hand was trembling.

"Twenty-four days, minus travel time, but I hope to return sooner. The army is short of men, they really can't spare me."

"Why are you here, then?"

"I wanted to see you."

"You shouldn't say that, you know. We have nothing in common, you and I." She moved her tongue over her upper lip, a gesture Ford found excruciatingly sensuous. She swallowed and gazed at her lap.

"Abby, I know there are questions to be asked, issues to be resolved. You're still not able to separate your feelings of anger towards the South from me. I've resisted expressing my love for you because of my bitterness towards Cerise, and women in general. Neither one of us has been willing to trust or forgive. But surely we can change that." Her slender shoulders were rigid and her hands were clenched at her side.

"It's more than that, Ford," she said. "You've often spoken with a great deal of feeling for your island home, for the South and your way of life there. I could never live there and forgive the issue of slavery. I love Brookside. It's my home, my heritage." Her eyes pleaded for him to understand. "I've responsibilities here . . . Brandon, Sarah, Amanda . . . that I could never walk away from. Forgiveness aside, don't you see the chasm that exists between us?"

Ford smiled. "I'm afraid what we both want is for everything to be the way it used to be. But dearest, we can never go back."

Ford got up and stood looking down at her; the light of an oil lamp shone directly into her face, her hair glinted blue-black, her cheeks were flushed, her chin quivering ever so gently. She was in profile, her head turned away from him, and he was struck again by her unusual beauty. There was a great deal of strength in Abby, yet she was the most feminine woman he had ever met. He loved her. Enough to give up his heritage for hers? He wasn't sure of the answer to that. Surely there was compromise somewhere, some solution to their differences. He realized she didn't want to marry and raise her children in the South, strangers to their own culture, but he wouldn't be happy away from his. And if he made the sacrifice for her, she would be miserable because she had made him miserable.

He reached down and took her hand in his, raising it to his lips, kissing the palm, his lips gentle and warm.

"Don't you think we might figure out something for the future if we really try? I love you, Abby. I believe you love me."

She drew in a trembling breath and their eyes locked. There was no mistaking her answer. Carefully, he pulled her to her feet and gathered her into his arms. He kissed her eyes, her lips, her hair. He didn't want to frighten her, didn't want to lie to her. He didn't know what was ahead for them, but they loved each other, and he needed something to carry him through the end of this war.

"Abby . . . I love you so much . . . ," he whispered tenderly, holding her, feeling her body next to his, her scent inflaming him with a passion too long banked. All of his reasons for emotional caution evaporated in one long kiss. They belonged together and she was all he wanted. For this one moment in time, that was all that mattered.

He pulled her down before the fire.

Every night that week they spent before the fire, talking, learning about each other. They talked of marriage—then skittered away from the subject like frightened kittens, the future still hazy and uncertain. His leave was about up—he still had a war to fight.

* * *

He had only one more week of furlough before he would have to say good-by once more and rejoin his regiment.

Ford sat by the fire watching the golden light play across her cheekbones, her mouth pursed in thought, her eyes dark and troubled. *What are you thinking, Abigail Kennedy?* he wondered. *Will you leave Brookside and the Falling Spring because I want to live in the South, because I want Michael to inherit McKenzie Groves? Or will you marry your farm boy from Chambersburg for security and no change in the status quo.* But he did not ask these questions. She would only flare up in defense.

"Ford, what do you want of me?" Abby paused, her eyes uncertain.

"How do you feel about living in the South? About St. Simons Island becoming your home?"

She bit her lip and directed her gaze to the window framing the gently falling snow. "Ford, my emotions are so turbulent and mixed. I love the quiet winter days at Brookside, bare trees, the creek tumbling over rocks, snow pristine on its banks. I don't think I could ever live in the South. The change of seasons is like the phases of the moon; I need to experience the winter in order to appreciate the spring. Can you understand that? Brookside is a part of me."

"And St. Simons a part of me."

"Oh, Ford," she said. "Let's not . . ." She left it unfinished.

"Not get into that? That's what you were going to say. That's our problem. I want you to marry me. My people are part of me. And you want me to desert the army, to live in the North with you. But I can't do that. I have a little boy, who although not my flesh and blood, is my responsibility."

"And I have a niece who I consider my responsibility. Why can't we all just live together, here at Brookside?"

"Can you accept Michael as he is? People, here, will speculate about his heritage. His Indian features are very obvious."

"They speculate about Amanda, too," she smiled. "Our responsibilities seem to rest with two of society's outcasts." A minute passed before she continued, "I have to sort things out; find forgiveness for what the South has done to me . . . to us. Give me more time, please."

"Time is one luxury we don't have, dearest. You must make a decision soon."

* * *

Snow came gently to Brookside late one afternoon, dusting Falling Spring Creek with a soft feathery blanket. Abby knew the time had come. Ford could no longer delay his departure.

She saw him glance at the clock.

Three more hours and he would walk out of her life once more.

As she gazed at his dear face, eyes haunted by inner pain, she was finally able to fully forgive what she had unfairly held him responsible for. She remembered the compassion of this man, the way he held and talked to Amanda, the way he treated Esau. She would go to the ends of this earth if he asked her. But for some reason she didn't say that.

"I want to go with you," Abby said. "As far as town."

"But it's snowing. There's at least three inches on the ground."

"We'll take the sleigh. Esau can ride behind us with your horse."

"Abby . . ."

"We can have dinner at the inn—where we first met—and say goodby there. It was saved from the fire, you know. I'll spend the night with Elizabeth. Please, Ford. I don't want to spend this evening here, in this house, in this room, without you." She began to cry. "I don't want our goodbys said in this room where we found our love. I . . . I may never see you again."

"Never see me again? Abby, dearest, I'll always be with you. Like an echo each time you walk along the Falling Spring, each time you stare into flames flickering in the fireplace before which we first admitted our love. Love is like that. Regardless of what happens to us you'll never be alone as long as you have memories."

"I want more than memories—I want you." Abby's throat hurt, a huge weight had settled in her chest. Darn this man! She should never have allowed herself to love so deeply. He was a soldier, returning to a war not yet resolved. The South was her sworn enemy, even if Ford were not. Their love didn't change that.

"Oh, Abby, God how I love you," he moaned. A tear glinted in the edge of his eyes and when he kissed her she was startled by the extent of his passion. He was deeply emotional in a way she had never expected. Everything was bottled up inside, and had probably been for years. He kissed her again and she was breathless when she pulled away from him.

"Ford," she said hesitantly. "Will you tell your brother about me?" Her voice faltered. "Please. Tell him to write if anything . . . if anything happens to you."

"Of course. Now come, no more doom and gloom. Your idea to have dinner at the inn is a good one."

Dinner had been one of forced cheerfulness, but now the time had come. Ford retrieved her cloak and led her out into the quiet street. Candles, radiant in glass globes, shone from every window of the inn, spilling a cheery light into the night. Snow outlined the branches of bare trees, lying thick on the top rail of a fence behind which Esau waited, his hand holding the reins of Ford's horse.

Abby gazed at Ford. He was standing directly under a flickering lantern, its yellow flame throwing his strongly cut features into sharp relief. Snow accumulated on his hair and the shoulders of his overcoat, and fat white flakes of snow lay for fleeting seconds on his eyelashes. Their eyes met. Abby felt her heart drop and pause and then start its familiar low, slow, thumping. Instinctively, she knew there would never be a moment like this again. Just Ford, with snow on his eyelashes, on this street, in this elusive moment in time. First love only happened once.

She bowed her head, turning slightly away from him, clutching the ribbons of her bonnet with gloved hands pressed against her quivering chin.

Ford put his arm around her shoulder and pulled her towards him. He put a hand on her arm to comfort her, then withdrew her hands gently from under her chin, tilting it to run a finger along the ridge of her jawbone. His woolen coat smelled of wet snow, a lock of copper hair escaped his hat to lie across his forehead. She hugged her arms across her chest, saying nothing, savoring his masculinity, listening to the deep timbre of his voice, as it whispered her name.

"I'm not going to say goodby, dearest," he said gently. "Fate has brought us together too many times for it to be mere coincidence. We were meant to spend our lives together and somehow we will."

He brushed a kiss across her lips, not with passion this time, but with promise.

She could not reply. Sobs choked her throat and tears gathered in her eyes. She never knew love could hurt so much.

Ford smiled in understanding. He tucked her cloak tightly around her shoulders, kissed the tip of her nose, and, with boots crunching in the crusted snow, walked to Esau waiting in the shadows with his horse. He took the reins, doffed his hat, and turned south.

CHAPTER
– 20 –

Ford looked at the April sky. It was just before dawn, the moment when the heavens hadn't yet decided between night and day. To the west the sky was charcoal gray, to the east feathered with rose-edged clouds. Nearby, the thin, shrill notes of a willow whistle merged with the plaintive notes of a mourning dove to shatter the silence. He made his way slowly across plowed fields, rich red-brown, awaiting the seed for yet another season. The sky, lighter now, showed a line of plum trees white with blossoms against a shattered fence. Robins were already busy pulling worms from bullet-creased furrows in the red soil, the earth strewn with canteens, wasted bullets, and cartridge boxes. The terrible armaments of war.

Ford halted his horse, overlooking a small bluff above a narrow ribbon of river that separated Virginia farmland from the village of Appomattox Court House. He trained his field glasses in the direction of a modest farmhouse where he knew Lee and Grant were meeting to hammer out the terms of the Confederate surrender.

One of the many ironies of the war, Ford thought, *was that he had been told this farmhouse belonged to a man named McLean, a Virginian, who, when he found his farm overrun by soldiers at Bull Run during the first battle of the war, moved his family to Appomattox Court House to get away from the war.*

As Ford watched the silent, white-porticoed entrance, a door swung open and General Lee walked onto the porch. He stood motionless, looking off over the far hills, rubbing his hands together absently while his horse, Traveler, was being bridled. Lee swung into the saddle, then looked back at the porch where General Grant had appeared. The two generals saluted one another. Ford felt his heart would break.

Robert E. Lee and Ulysses S. Grant were a study in contrasts. Lee was the figure of legends, erect, gray, imposing, dressed today in his best uniform, with a sword belted at his side. Grant was rather scrubby, wearing mud-spattered boots and a rumpled enlisted man's coat with his lieutenant general's stars tacked to the shoulders. He wore no sword.

Yet the contrast goes far beyond the matter of personal appearance, Ford thought. Two separate versions of America were represented by these men.

From the day of its beginning America became a land of unending change. Fighting to remain alive, it had laid hands on the curious combination of modern machinery and slave labor.

To Ford, Robert E. Lee personified the dignity of the South, bound to the past with a rigid code of conduct, gentlemanly manners and a sense of learning and order.

Ulysses S. Grant symbolized the North. Here a man's worth was reckoned, not on the past, but on the future. It was rough and uncultivated. Yet it had its own dignity and its own standards; a people who decided that they would no longer be bound by the restriction of the past.

Through his field glasses Ford watched General Lee as he cantered down the Pike toward the bluff where the remnant of his army waited. The men of the 31st Georgia closed in, and Lee reined Traveler. Tears misted Ford's eyes as he stared at the legendary figure. He could hear him distinctly, hear him say: "Go home and make as good citizens as you have soldiers."

Ford thought briefly of what was ahead, knowing instinctively that he could never resume his old way of life. The fight had been made to preserve the Southern "cause" and it had been lost, and everything that had been dreamed and tried and fought for had died on this day.

The awful moment came. On a chill gray morning just before ten A.M. on the 12th of April, 1865, Ford was ordered to form his lines for the "laying down of arms" ceremony. The honor of leading the Confederate army on its final march had been given to Major General John Gordon.

On the slopes of the Appomattox River, Ford got the 31st Georgia ready, breaking camp for one last time. Esau took down their little shelter-tent, folding it carefully, pushing what few personal items Ford still owned into a tattered knapsack.

Ford moved his men into gray columns of march—tall, thin, spare men with long hair and beards, clad in ragged, dirty gray uniforms and broad-brimmed slouch hats. Silently they began to march, with their old swinging step and swaying battle flags, into a triangular area just east of the courthouse.

Brigadier General Joshua L. Chamberlain, former commander of the 20th Maine, waited behind the blue ranks to receive the formal stacking of arms. As the Confederates got closer, Ford's eyebrows shot up in surprise. He had expected to hear sneers and gloating catcalls from the Yankees facing him, but instead a bugle sounded and Ford heard the sounds of Chamberlain's men shifting arms as they issued the marching salute. Ahead of Ford, General Gordon, who had been riding with heavy spirit and downcast face, also heard the shifting arms. He drew himself erect in the saddle, wheeled his mount toward Chamberlain, and returned the compliment with a salute, dropping the point of his sword to the toes of his boot; then, facing his men, gave word for each brigade to pass—honor answering honor.

Not a cheer, nor word, nor whisper of victory broke the awed stillness as men held their breaths and prepared for the formalities. Ford's voice cracked and he clamped and unclamped his teeth trying to maintain control of his feelings as he issued his final orders. The men halted, facing the Yankees across a narrow road as Ford carefully "dressed" his line. He took pains for the good appearance of his men, worn and half starved as they were, then he wheeled and sat solemnly watching as his loyal soldiers relinquished their weapons. They fixed bayonets, stacked their arms, removed cartridge boxes and lay them down. At last, reluctantly, faces agonized and humiliated, they tenderly folded their flag—two red bars with eleven stars on a field of blue—heart-holding colors, battle-worn, torn and blood-stained, and placed it atop the stand of arms.

This heart-wrenching sight was worse than any funeral Ford had ever been to, that mound of weapons topped by torn and tattered colors, the coffin of their hopes. Ford's throat hurt with suppressed sobs. Visions massed as he looked into the eyes of his fellow officers. Here were the men of Antietam, the Bloody Lane, the Sunken Road, the Cornfield, Burnside-Bridge; the men whom Stonewall Jackson had commanded at Fredericksburg; the men who swept away the Eleventh Corps at Chancellorsville; the men who left six thousand of their companions around the bases of Culp's and Cemetery Hills at Gettysburg; the men who had survived the Wilderness, Spotsylvania, and the slaughter pen of Cold Harbor! Men whom neither suffering, nor the fact of death, could bend from their resolve—worn, famished, but erect, with eyes looking level at the blue-clad ranks before them.

And then Ford's composure, held in rigid control during the ceremonies, broke. He leaned his forehead against the neck of his horse and cried.

It was over.

* * *

Rather than humiliate the defeated army, the terms of surrender issued by Grant were drafted in a manner to reconcile the divided nation. Confederate officers would be permitted to retain side arms, their horses, and their personal belongings. There would be no imprisonment. The Rebels were to be issued parole and could return to their homes unmolested.

Ford felt an exhilarating rush of relief. He was free. Free to go whichever direction he chose. But he knew he must go south first, to Georgia and his home. He had to see his mother, see what was left of his plantation on St. Simons, see a little boy named Michael McKenzie.

And so, the day after the final laying down of arms, the men of the 31st Georgia said goodby to one another and left Appomattox Court House, for a dubious future in the devastated South.

Ford, Josh, and Esau set out for Georgia, a trip of over five hundred miles. The roads were crowded with thousands of men beginning the tedious journey, most by foot, uncertain of what they would find when they reached their homes.

After four days on the road Ford suggested they set up camp along the banks of the James River. It was Good Friday and he wanted to attend Easter services at the small Episcopal Church he had seen in a nearby village. He wondered what church Abby attended. He had never thought to ask.

On Saturday they were sitting at the campfire enjoying a mess of Esau's beans when a rider stopped to tell them that Abraham Lincoln had been shot the night before while attending a play at Ford's Theater in Washington. The president had died that morning.

After the initial shock wore off, Ford poured himself a mug of coffee and walked to look across the stretch of lazy river. How ironic life was. To be assassinated on Good Friday, after four bitter years of war, only five days after Lee surrendered to Grant. Ford felt sadness but not sorrow. In his mind he would always believe that Lincoln was the man responsible for the war, the man who had disrupted his life and changed it forever.

As April turned into May—a time of bud, and bloom, and birdsong—Ford guided his brother and servant across Virginia toward the coast, begging food and a place to camp as they went. Hillsides, where only months ago men with muskets slaughtered one another across stone walls, were now covered with the soft pink haze of apple trees in blossom.

In Wilmington, North Carolina, he sought out the home of an old friend of his father's, a retired colonel from VMI, hoping for several nights' lodging and rest before resuming their trek down the coast. It was a lucky choice. The colonel insisted on giving each of them a set of clothing and booking passage on the steamer *Windrush* bound for Savannah. Ford would be home within the week.

   He stood at the rail of the sailing ship, feet braced, face to the stinging salt breeze, searching for the barrier islands and salt flats that lay between him and home. His mind sought a plan for the future ahead. Would it include Abby? Was there any solution to their problems? And if so, could he put aside his lingering prejudices and once more trust a woman with his heart?

   As the *Windrush* docked, the setting sun, dull red off the Savannah River, bathed the ballast stone walls of deserted cotton warehouses in salmon shadow. Ford and Josh, with Esau in tow, hurried along the waterfront. Fingers of mist curled off the harbor, gas lamps cast a friendly glow, catwalks were shielded by palmettos and oaks, and sea gulls wobbled along the cobblestone streets. All brought back memories of the many trips he and his father had made into this port with their sea-island cotton, to store it in these very warehouses until a factor could arrange for its sale. At that time it had seemed a happy way of life that would never change. Now many of the offices along Factor's Walk were deserted, the warehouses empty.

   Ford and Josh clambered up steps fashioned from the ballast of ocean-going vessels, turned left, past Factor's Walk onto Bay Street, then hurried past the U.S. Custom House with its massive granite columns. Ford was amazed to find the Custom House still intact, in fact, none of the buildings showed the ravages of war. He wondered why. Sherman's devastating march from Atlanta to the sea seemed not to have touched Savannah.

   Ford's steps quickened. His mother and Michael, together with Esau's parents, had been staying with his widowed Aunt Matilda since their evacuation from St. Simons. Eagerly he traversed the short distance over glistening cobbles to Bull Street, a wide sandy thoroughfare that bisected the city from the river on the north to South Broad Street at the far limits; then he, Josh, and Esau entered lovely Johnson Square, the oldest square in the city. The streets were lined with gracious pastel houses fronted by high stoops and shuttered windows. Only a short distance ahead, on Abercorn Street, his mother and son waited. He practically ran through the small park.

   "How much farther, Marse Ford?" Esau asked.

   "As I remember it, only a few blocks. It's been years since we were here for Uncle Paul's funeral, but I believe their house is just beyond Reynolds Square."

   Esau sniffed the tropical air, heavy with the fragrance of flowers and salt air. "Smells like home," he said with a broad grin.

   Ford agreed. Clumps of pink and white azaleas with petals as big as sand dollars billowed beneath live oaks, and Spanish moss and purple wisteria tumbled over elegantly wrought-iron gateways and fences. The houses rose tall and elegant as ladies in ball gowns. It was the South at her best—it was home.

"I remember Savannah now," Josh commented, "although I was a young lad when we visited here. A beautiful city, full of little parks."

Ford was breathing hard as they hurried along. "The people here call them squares. I remember Aunt Matilda telling me there are exactly twenty-one squares . . . planed by General Oglethorpe when he laid out Savannah in 1733."

With quickening steps the trio left Reynolds Square and turned onto Abercorn Street.

Aunt Matilda's home sat behind a fence of wrought-iron as delicate as lace. An arch over the gate proclaimed the name "McKenzie" and Ford sucked in his breath. Aunt Matilda's house was graceful as a ship in full sail: white-washed brick constructed high off the ground, a winding double-stairway adorned with wrought-iron railings, tall, arched windows set off by ornate ironwork balconies. Two colonnaded piazzas open to refreshing ocean breezes ran the length of the east side, and the small yard was a riot of azaleas and camellias.

With a joyous whoop Josh bounded up the front steps and banged on the knocker.

Matilda answered his knock. She was a bouncy, plump woman with gray hair fashioned into a chignon, dressed in a long, black mourning dress of heavy brocade. She looked at them with a puzzled frown, then recognition lit her lively blue eyes and with a cry she threw out her arms and gathered Ford to her ample bosom. She was giving Josh the same welcome when Ford's mother hurried into the hallway.

Annabel McKenzie was small in stature, weighing barely one hundred pounds. She walked with shoulders perfectly squared, her back unbowed, her head held high though time and tragedy had turned her once red hair into a pure white cloud. She also wore mourning.

"Ford, Josh," she cried. "Oh, thank the good Lord you're home." She began to cry.

Josh rushed to hug his mother, swinging her off her feet with a joyful laugh. "Safe, and all in one piece, and hungry as two bears in a cave," he said with a hearty laugh.

Aunt Matilda clapped her plump hands together. "You're just in time. Dinner is about ready."

As Ford hugged his mother his gaze swept the foyer. "Where's Michael?" he asked anxiously.

"Upstairs in the playroom. We've been trying to keep him occupied; the poor little fellow is so excited that his daddy was coming home he is almost sick."

"I'll go get him," Matilda offered. As she turned, she noticed Esau, standing outside the open door, grinning from ear to ear. "Your mammy is dying to see you, Esau," she said with a smile. "She's in the kitchen. Go tell her to set two more places at the table. And tell your pappy to go to the wine cellar and get us the best bottle of wine he can find."

"Yesum," he said, sprinting down the steps.

After giving Ford another hug, Matilda hurried up the stairs to fetch Michael. Annabel led them to the parlor, her face still streaked with tears. "Josh," she said with a shaky laugh, "I hardly know you. You've grown into a man."

Josh laughed. "We're hardly the two naive boys you saw march off to serve the South four years ago. But you haven't changed a bit; you're still as beautiful as I remembered."

His mother turned to look at Ford, her eyes sparkling. "Wait until you see Michael. He was a baby when you left." She hesitated. "But take it slow with him, Ford. He's bound to be shy, he really doesn't know you."

"Nor I him."

Annabel tilted her head and smiled. "Michael is an adorable child, intelligent and happy, with beautiful manners. Cerise taught him well."

A hush fell over the room. Ford cleared his throat. "She . . . Cerise . . . is buried here in Savannah?"

"At Bonaventure. Beside her father."

"I'll want to visit her grave before I leave for St. Simons." He smiled gently. "I'll take Michael with me."

Just then, Michael dashed into the room, his face red with excitement. He skittered to an abrupt halt, looking from his grandmother to the two men sitting on the couch then back to his grandmother, his dark eyes suddenly uncertain. He sidled over to her chair and stuck his thumb in his mouth.

She put an arm around his waist and hugged him to her. "Your father is the one with the dark red hair and the beard," she whispered in his ear.

Michael shot an anxious glance in his direction and Ford managed a weak smile. He was as uncertain as the child. He had known that Michael would not remember him, yet he had been looking forward to this moment since setting sail for Savannah.

Ford rose from the couch and held out his arms. Michael stayed put.

His grandmother gave him a slight push. "It's alright, dear. Your father only wants to say hello to you. Remember how happy you were when you heard he was coming home?" Michael did not budge. "Go now, give him a hug—Grandma is right here."

Cautiously, the child inched towards Ford. He was a stocky, well-built, four year old with fine black hair and dark eyes. His high cheekbones and reddish skin spoke of his Indian blood, but there was a lot of Cerise in him too. His eyes were dark brown, almost black, but they had Cerise's long eyelashes. His nose was straight and true, his lips full and slightly pouting as his mother's had been, and as he tendered a shy smile a dimple creased his cheek. Ford felt incurably sad.

"Well now, little man," he said, reaching out his big hand to grasp the little fist, "I think it's time we got acquainted, don't you?"

Michael nodded solemnly.

"Why don't you take me upstairs and show me your room? I'll bet you have lots of toys."

"I have a wooden train . . . an' a ball . . . an' a puzzle Grandma just bought me."

"A wooden train? I had one of those when I was a little boy. It might even be the same one. Why don't we go upstairs and see?"

"Are you really my daddy?"

Ford felt a tug at his heart. "Yes, son. I am." He rose and took Michael's warm little hand. As they headed out the door and up the spiral staircase, Michael began to bounce beside him and chatter gaily, everything once more right in his world.

That evening, after good food, much laughter, and glad harking back to the past, Michael was taken up to bed and everyone retired once more to the parlor.

An oriental rug carpeted the room's gleaming heart-of-pine floors. Wallpaper, a muted pattern of pastel flowers against a blue background, complimented the silk-upholstered Biedermeier sofa. Yet the rug, the sofa, the needlepoint chair, the oil paintings—all paled before the striking beauty of the room's elegant crystal chandelier, sparkling with fire against the dying rays of the sun slanting through rounded windows.

Josh, Matilda, and Annabel settled into comfortable chairs, while Ford strode to a set of french doors opening onto the piazza and threw them open to catch the freshening breeze.

"Savannah's such a gentle city," he said. "The war seems to have passed it by."

"To some extent it did," Matilda said. "Our city fathers, practical businessmen that they are, recognized that our paltry army of ten thousand could never hold off a Union army of over sixty thousand men, so they decided not to actively fight. They knew devastation was about to befall them, had heard what happened to Atlanta and Charleston."

Annabel nodded in agreement. "Savannah was thought to be the climax of Sherman's march to the sea. So we turned the city over without a shot being fired, with a promise from General Sherman that they would not burn it." She chuckled. "He occupied Savannah only a short time, then marched to Columbia, South Carolina, and burned that poor city to the ground."

Ford frowned.

"We did cause him some mischief," Matilda hastened to add. "Our men flooded the rice fields between the city and the sea and that temporarily blocked the Union's access to their supply ships."

She turned to Josh with a slight smile. "Now, enough about the war and all its problems. What are your plans, Josh? Will you marry your Polly?"

"If she'll still have me," he laughed. "It's been some time since I heard from her, what with the war ending and the mails being all messed up."

"Then you probably haven't heard that her brother was killed at Farmville, just days before the surrender."

"No, I didn't know." His face turned pale. "Oh, God, how terrible. He was only sixteen." He jumped to his feet. "I must go to Alma, as soon as possible, to comfort Polly."

"Go tomorrow," Ford interjected. "You can come to St. Simons after you see her."

"That's hardly fair to you."

"Nonsense. Whatever awaits us there can't be changed now." Ford looked at his mother, afraid to ask the question, afraid to hear the answer. "What have you heard about home, Mamma?"

She didn't answer for a minute, worrying the ring on her finger, clasping and unclasping her thin hands, but once begun, the words came out in an agonized rush, tumbling over one another in their haste to be said.

"Miles Hazaard . . . you remember him, don't you? . . . went back to the island the minute Lee's surrender was announced. He says none of the plantation owners have returned yet, the fields are overgrown by scrub and wild holly, those homes not in ruins are occupied by the former slaves. He didn't have the time to visit McKenzie Groves, so he couldn't tell me of its condition. The lighthouse is gone, though, destroyed by the Rebels before they left the island so it couldn't be used by Northern ships as a navigational aid. Retreat Plantation is still standing, he saw that, but the Gould's beautiful home at St. Clair was burned to the ground."

Annabel lifted a lace handkerchief to her eyes and dabbed at tears forming there. "I . . . I'm afraid I haven't told you the worst. One of the reasons Mr. Hazaard had for going to the island was to visit the family graveyard at Christ Church. He found the church sacked and in ruins, the cemetery violated. Human excrement covered overturned tombstones—including your father's. He has written a formal complaint to the Federal government, but I doubt it will do any good."

Josh swore, a spasm of disgust crossing his face. "Not Christ Church! Not Papa's grave! The filthy scum . . . excuse me, Mother . . . they had no right. Our Southern troops never touched a Northern church. Who was the commander in charge?"

"Brigadier General Rufus Saxton."

"The military governor of South Carolina?"

"Yes. He was in charge of the First Carolina Regiment Volunteers. Ah . . . a black regiment."

Ford banged his fist on the arm of the sofa with such force one of Matilda's antimacassars bounced to the floor. "I'll leave for St. Simons first thing in the morning," he said, surging to his feet, grinding out the words between clenched teeth.

"But you must spend some time with your little boy," his mother cried. "Michael will be devastated if he learns you left again. Please, Ford. He's had so many unexplained departures in his young life."

Josh placed a hand on Ford's shoulder. "Mother's right. There's nothing we can do about it now. A few more days won't make any difference. I know you're angry, but spend a little time with the boy."

Ford stooped to pick up the lace antimacassar and re-placed it carefully on the arm of the sofa, his emotions in a turmoil. Mother was right of course, mother always saw through to the heart of the matter.

He nodded. It had been very thoughtless of him—Michael should be his first priority.

The next afternoon, after stopping at a street vender to buy flowers, Ford and his mother took Michael to the cemetery. Bonaventure reminded Ford of a primeval forest, its avenues bordered by magnificent oaks, guarded by moss-covered statues, and an overgrowth of shrubbery. In just a few minutes they came to a small family plot shaded by a large oak. Three graves lay inside a low curbstone. One of the graves was obviously newer than the others.

Michael dumped the flowers on the ground, explained to Ford that his mother was "sleeping," and ran off to explore a nearby tomb enclosed by a wrought-iron fence.

Annabel shook her head and, gathering her full skirts, settled herself on a stone bench where she could keep an eye on him. "He's a handful, he is," she said.

"I can see he's all boy. He has his mother's exuberance." Ford rearranged the flowers they had brought before he sank down beside her to stare at the granite monument, bearing the simple inscription "Cerise Descartes McKenzie." Sod, not yet healed, defined the narrow grave. Ford sat with bowed head, hurt and anger warring with nostalgia for a love once shared. His arm felt the comforting warmth of his mother as his body slumped against her. He closed his eyes for a minute, drawing comfort from her presence. As far back as Ford could remember, his mother had been the steadying influence in his life. Unlike his often boisterous, fiery tempered father he had never seen his mother stirred from her austere calm. Her voice was always soft, her manner unhurried despite the exhausting demands of a planter's wife. She made certain the Negroes, "her people," had secure, tabby cabins with their own garden, and she treated them in times of sickness and birth and death with stately gentleness. To Ford, she symbolized the Southern lady.

They sat quietly, each alone with their thoughts. Out in the bay a foghorn sounded, warblers in a nearby cyprus sang songs as continuous as a waterfall, muted sounds of children broke the heavy silence.

His mother finally spoke. "Cerise thought you dead, Ford. We talked before she died. She made a foolish choice before you were married, but the girl did love you. She was faithful to her marriage vows until she believed you gone, then she sought out Grayhorse to procure financial protection for Michael. She was lonely and vulnerable and the affair resumed, but when she found you were alive she went to him to end the affair. She wanted you back. That's why, when she discovered she was pregnant, she had the abortion."

"Another bad choice," Ford said bitterly.

"Yes, it was. We, all of us, at some time in our lives make unwise decisions in the name of love."

"I fail to see how you can call what she did to me love."

"I don't condone her actions, but I think I understand and I have forgiven her." She took his hand. "You must do the same—let go of your hate, son. It will only destroy you in the end. Forgive Cerise for her weakness and get on with your life."

Ford sighed and heaved himself to his feet. "I can't, Mother. I'm sorry, but I can't. Not yet."

"Then let's turn our faces to the future, not the past."

"Until I know the extent of damage to McKenzie Groves I can't plan for you and Michael to return home."

"Yes, well . . . Matilda has made it clear that she would like for Michael and me to continue to live with her. With no children of her own and your uncle dead, she gets lonely in that big house."

Ford blinked in surprise. "But I always imagined all of us together. Back on St. Simons."

"You must move forward on your own. Josh told me last night that he plans to marry Polly without delay. Her father has offered him a place in his hardware store, so I imagine they will live in Alma. Regardless of the condition of the house at St. Simons I'm afraid the plantation days are gone . . . along with most of our money. I think it best I stay in Savannah."

"What about Michael?"

She gave him a pensive look. "That's up to you, dear. He is welcome to stay with me. I made Cerise a promise that he would be cared for, and he will be."

Ford's thoughts flew to Abby. How did all of this affect them? He hadn't told his mother about her, still uncertain if Abby was to be a part of his future. Doubts assailed him—could he commit to another marriage? Would Abby and her Northern community accept Michael? Should he forget all that had happened between them and resume his life on St. Simons Island?

Ford gazed at the dark-haired child running toward him clutching a mangled dandelion in his chubby fist.

"Look, Daddy," he cried. "My flower for Mommy."

Ford lifted him onto his lap. "That's a fine gift . . . , son. What do you say we dig a little hole beside the stone with her name on it and plant the flower?"

Michael squirmed off his lap and ran to the monument. He squatted in the grass, pointing to the spot he wanted. "Here, Daddy . . . right here." Ford dug a small hole with his fingers, and, with Michael's help, placed the limp dandelion in the depression and covered it with dirt.

With a big smile of accomplishment, the little boy turned his dirt-stained face up to Ford's. The dimple in his cheek deepened, eyes flecked with gold sparkled with happiness and trust.

Ford pulled him to his chest. He knew at least one answer. Whatever his future—north or south, with or without Abby— Michael would be a part of it.

CHAPTER
– 21 –

By sunrise the next day, Ford and Esau were on the last leg of their journey home. The small mail boat steamed away from Savannah's dock, past Skidaway Island, past Beaulieu where they had carefully trained him to become a killer, past Ossabou, St. Catherines, and Sapelo Islands, through turbulent Dobay Sound and into the snaking inlet of the Darien River.

Almost home! His throat clogged with joy as the ship rounded Generals Island, headed towards the port of Darien where he hoped to rent a smaller craft to transport them out to St. Simons.

The captain snugged up to the Darien wharf, once a thriving seaport for steamboats and sailing ships, now a charred, desolate ruin. His mother had warned him about the sorry state of the town, but it had done little to prepare him for the sight that greeted his eyes. His knuckles grasping the rail turned white and a muscle twitched in his jaw as his gaze raked the burned warehouses, shops, and taverns lining the waterfront. "Damn," he muttered. "Damn . . . damn . . . damn!" If this was a portrait of Darien, what would he find at St. Simons?

Beside him, Esau lowered his head. He knew the shameful story as well as Ford.

Darien, abandoned, war-torn and defenseless, had received its final violation when Union forces returned late in '63 and reduced it to ashes. The senseless action, committed by black troops of the 54th Massachusetts and the South Carolina Volunteers stationed at St. Simons was doubly ironic because early in the century this courageous little town had twice petitioned the state of Georgia to bar the introduction of slavery. Now it had been destroyed by blacks. Why? Hate—anger— retribution? Or simply the desperation of slaves seeking revenge for their race?

Ford made no move to disembark. Captain Latimore threaded his way across the mail-boat's deck with a quizzical look. "What do you want to do?" he asked.

"There'll be no skiff for hire, here," Ford growled.

The captain, a lifetime on the water reflected on his leathery face, spat a stream of tobacco juice over the rail and nodded. "Better you stay aboard till Brunswick. An ex-slave, name of Jerusalem, still runs a supply boat to the island." He emphasized the word "ex" as he glowered at Esau. "Guess he'll be willing to take you an' your man across. Fer a hefty fee, that is."

"I imagine," Ford said ruefully. "Their labor doesn't come free anymore." He shaded his eyes against the midday sun and stared eastward, across the endless salt marsh to where the crisping water of the Altamaha reached the sea. A gust of sweet, clean, salt air kissed the bow of the boat and Ford felt the subtle pressure of Esau's warm arm on the rail as it rested beside him. He turned to look the skipper in the eye. "That's where home is. I'll pay any price to get there."

"Your choice. I'm warning you though . . . ain't gonna find nothin' but ashes and niggers."

Two hours later a thirty-foot dugout, hollowed from a single cyprus tree, with five men at the oars, drew away from Brunswick harbor with Ford and Esau aboard. It was by no means as swift and elegant as the eight-oared long boats in which Ford had traveled from mainland to island before the war, but it was going where he wanted to go, and he sat in the middle surrounded by sacks of salt, sugar, and barrels of flour. Esau, his face radiant with good cheer, took an oar. Ford recognized two of the other blacks. Tom had pulled oar on Butler boats, and Liverpool had been a house servant at Retreat.

Long oars and strong arms moved them out into the Sound. A strong southwest wind carried the sound of a distant steamer whistle across the five salt creeks that separated St. Simons from the mainland. As the boat followed the channel through quiet wheat-colored marsh grass, the men sang a spirited shout song:

> Tis well an' good I come here tonight
> come here tonight
> come here tonight
> well an' good I come here tonight
> For to do my Master's will

Ford had heard it many times, but this time he recognized that they were singing of their ultimate Master, not of their former owners.

The boat pulled past neighboring Jekyll Island, around the southern tip of St. Simons, and entered the shallow waters of the Frederica

River at Gascoigne Bluff. Esau waded ashore and twisted a frayed line to a cleat on the abandoned dock while Ford paid Jerusalem his outrageous fee.

"Come back tomorrow afternoon, about the same time," Ford ordered. "We'll know then if we're staying."

"Cos' yuh double."

"I'm good for it. Just be sure you come."

Jerusalem didn't answer. Instead he set his men to unloading the boat with shouted commands of his own.

Ford and Esau stood silently, surveying the empty dock. Gone was the once busy lumber mill, the whine of saws, the work songs of the slaves. Only the strident notes of unseen birds and the clattering call of a marsh hen broke the heavy silence.

"Don' know 'bout you, Marse Ford, but I be mighty glad to be home," Esau commented, his eyes glinting with pleasure.

Ford's mouth twisted in a wry smile. "I'm afraid we'll find this home a far cry from the one we left."

"It still be home."

Ford squared his broad shoulders and began to wend his way through the tangled crepe myrtle that crowded the rotting dock. "Right you are, old friend," he flung over his shoulder, "let's get moving while we still have light. Maybe things aren't as bad as Mother painted them."

With long strides he led them along a sandy path, still discernable in the tangled underbrush, bordered by giant clumps of pink and white azaleas in the height of bloom. A stand of giant live oaks formed a canopy over their heads, dappled shadows played at his feet, and beards of spanish moss brushed his face. Esau was right; it was good to be home. He paused for a moment to lay his hand against one of the magnificent trees, fingering the gnarled bark, his eyes following the lacy trail of resurrection fern that climbed wide-flung branches dipping to the ground. At least the trees were still here—to Ford the very essence of his island. Nothing broke the silence except the distant cacophony of gulls and waterbirds in the lapping surf and the tiny rustling of small things moving in the mud of the waving marsh grass.

They followed a better defined oyster-shell lane winding a sinuous course through the James Hamilton plantation, a world of marsh and woodland. The once stately home was still standing, but it looked far from stately now. Empty tabby buildings and untended fields told a melancholy tale of defeat and desertion. Ford hurried past, eager for some sign of life. The names of the plantations echoed like a litany in his mind: Blackbanks, West Point, Retreat, Lawrence, Hampton, Kelvin Grove, Cannon's Point. Surely a few of their owners had returned to the island to reclaim their land. But as he and Esau trod the sandy lane leading to Frederica Road, sidestepping annoying sand-spurs and Russian thistle, they passed only two solitary Negroes, and with growing despair Ford's mind played back the story his mother had told.

Early in the war the Confederacy had realized the value of the island, a strategic spit of land offering a defense of St. Simons Sound and Brunswick harbor. The Georgia authorities commandeered island slaves and began to fortify Retreat Plantation which overlooked the entrance to the sound. Five batteries were constructed on the very beach where Ford and Lordy King had played as boys. They were built of earth with an overlayment of palmetto logs that would not splinter if hit by shells. Iron rails and heavy iron shutters completed the fortification, guns were mounted, and St. Simons prepared for invasion.

In November, five months after the war began, Federal gunboats won a decisive naval battle at Hilton Head, South Carolina. It was then that Ford's mother, along with other Georgia planters, grew apprehensive and began to close up their homes and move their slaves inland. Then in February of '62 General Robert E. Lee ordered the destruction of the lighthouse whose beacon had long warned vessels of the dangerous offshore bar.

It did not take the Union long to act. Commander Gordon, aboard the USS *Mohican,* commandeered an exploratory survey of the waters about the island. Not only were the batteries at Retreat unmanned and unarmed, but Brunswick and Darien were likewise deserted. Federal troops were quickly moved into the abandoned fortifications.

And then, Ford's mother had tearfully related, another event took place which sealed St. Simons' fate.

Blacks, classified as contraband, set adrift by the consequences of Union occupation and seeking refuge from slavery, had become an increasing problem for the Union army. St. Simons seemed an ideal spot to establish a "Contraband" colony. Retreat Plantation's abandoned slave quarters, with its attendant hospital, was ideal. Control of the island was given to General Saxton, and within a year, contrabands experiencing their first taste of freedom, numbered over five hundred.

These contrabands were armed and together with other black troops manning the fortifications were able to deter Confederate raiders attempting to regain control of St. Simons. The island had stayed in contraband control until the end of the war.

By now, Ford and Esau had reached the center of the island and were walking along historic Military Road. A canopy of live oaks on either side of the road met overhead, and deep shadows played along the path. Kelvin Grove was just around the next curve and Ford's pace quickened. If only his old friend and neighbor, James Postell, were there to greet him. He remembered the hours they had spent together, James encouraging Ford to learn to commit pictures to canvas, while he, an expert in seashells, birds, and butterflies, painted word pictures of the unseen life of the mysterious marsh.

"De Postell place still standin'," Esau said as they approached the weathered two-story frame and tabby dwelling, surrounded on three sides by a wide piazza and topped with a long widow's walk, abandoned now, dreaming in its shroud of silvery moss and the mild sun.

"But it's plain to see James and Annie are no longer here," Ford said, eyeing a group of blacks who lounged on the litter- strewn porch.

"Nor the lady they call 'Ole Miss.' Neber thought that proud ole lady leave her house to sech as these. I sees Abraham, an' John, an' Big Jim. They be Hampton nigras. Never was much good."

"I believe you're right. I wonder if the house at Hampton was burned. That might account for them taking possession here."

Esau's face was hard and grim. Broken wagon wheels and litter were strewn across the lawn, shutters had been removed and used to construct makeshift corn cribs and every pane of glass was broken. "No need fer them to lib in the big house," he said. "Slave quarters still standin'. The Postells be fine peoples and they gonna be mighty sad to see their home like that. I gots half a notion to go tell 'em to clean up the place before Ole Miss come home an' gib em a good tongue lashin'."

Ford's lips quirked in amusement. He wondered how long it would take Esau to realize just how much things had changed for his people. "Come," he said, "we'd better move on if we want to get home before dark." He turned his back on the sorry sight and pushed his way through waving sea oats, smelling the salt on the wind, his ears straining for the sound of sea breaking on beach. It was not much further. Just beyond that hammock of oak and cedar.

And then he saw it.

He stopped so suddenly Esau crashed into him and they both stared in disbelief at the scene before them.

No! his mind screamed. No! It could not be. Not this solitary chimney rising from a pile of charred rubble. He stared, unable to absorb the finality of what he saw. His mother had left him with some small hope that all might not be gone. But there was nothing salvageable here.

"Oh, Massa!" Esau sobbed. A tear trickled down his dusty cheek. "I be so sorry."

Ford began to move forward, his fists clenched, his throat clogged with emotion. The foundation walls had been taken over by a tangle of vines, but although the once tidy lawn had reverted back to nature, the air was fragrant with great trees of camellias, oleander, and cape jasmine. A clump of his mother's Little Chickasaw roses clung forlornly to the crumbling tabby foundation. Something rolled under his foot; he gazed at the charred remains of a wooden top his grandfather had whittled for him as a child.

And once more the tears came.

An overgrown lane behind the ruins of his home led to a row of pink tabby cabins still standing, one of them a praise house built by his father to encourage religious services among his people. It was here that he and Esau stretched out on crude wooden benches to get some rest.

But sleep would not come and after a fitful hour he rose and walked into the mild, silvery night. The tide was out and the sandbar lay free of water. He followed it to the very edge of the sea. Moonlight slept on the Atlantic, the scent of the ocean dense and sweet, rinsing away the bleakness of the day. He sank to the wet sand and looked out at the black ocean. Memories came flooding back until he felt he was drowning in them. Memories of picnics on the beach, of spacious homes with simple lines that conformed to the island and the times. Memories of the South as she had been. Memories of Cerise leaning against the railing of the widows-walk, her body lush and teasing, his own filled with lust and anticipation.

Funny how one always spoke of the South as "she." He guessed it reflected the soft femininity of their women, a dignity of manner and dress, grace and culture. But the elegant life of a Southern planter was gone. When the waters of the Civil War subsided, Ford knew he would know a different South than that of his father and grandfather.

He felt, rather than heard, movement behind him and turned to see the silent figure of Esau outlined in the moonlight.

Ford pointed his hand towards a spot beside him and Esau lowered his big body to the sand. Only the washing tide broke the silence as each gained comfort from the other, neither finding it necessary to put that feeling into words. It was Esau who spoke first.

"I knows you mournin' the loss of you home, Massa. I be sad, too. But it be only a house built of sticks. The lan' still be here. Nobody done take that away. An' the trees you always love . . . they still be here. They's more important things in this ole life, waitin' for you to take hol' of. 'Sides, you kin rebuild the house, if that be what you want."

"What with? Dreams and memories. It takes lumber . . . building materials . . . man-power . . . money. I've none of those."

"You Grandpappy had mostly dreams when he came here."

He had a lot more than dreams, Ford thought grimly. *He had the sweat and blood of hundreds of Negro slaves.* But Ford didn't put these thoughts into words.

"McKenzie Groves was more than mere sticks, Esau," he said instead. "It was a generation of love and family."

"That love neber go away. It still there. You right, Massa, when you talk of love an' family. That what important. An' the good Lawd gib that to you. Your Papa teach me that God take care of us. That God, he still there. He be with us eber day of that terrible war an' he be out there right now, feelin' your hurt."

Ford swallowed hard. All day he had been cursing God. He had never been overly religious; in fact, during his years at college he had spent hours of intellectual debate with his classmates over the very existence of God. He had prayed, out of fear, in the heat of battle, but always afterward he felt chagrined at his vulnerability. Whom had he prayed to if he didn't truly believe that someone was out there listening?

Esau held out his black, work-worn hand to offer comfort and Ford clasped it. A shiver of surprise ran through him. He had felt Esau's hand many times throughout his life, but never like this. He clung to it as though it were a lifeline and then suddenly he realized it was like this to put your life in God's hand. He couldn't explain it— didn't want to try. All the years of intellectualizing had not brought him the peace he felt take root in him now.

It took courage for a slave to hold out his hand to his Master. Did Ford have the same courage? He squeezed the warm hand still clutching his and smiled into the darkness.

"Thank you, Esau," he said humbly.

They sat quietly, not speaking, only the soft pounding at the shoreline breaking the silence.

"You know, don't you," Ford finally said, "that under the proclamation of the president of the United States your people are free and that according to General Sherman's order all former slaves are entitled to settle forty-acre tracts of tillable land anywhere on the South Atlantic coast. That means you can take forty acres of McKenzie Plantation as your own, grow cotton, rice, or sugar cane for yourself. You can be independent."

Esau shook his wooly head. "That not what I want. My Ila be up there in the North an' I promise her that when the war be ober and I gets you safe to your island I gonna come back an' we gonna be married. No 'jumping over the broom' like my mammy an' pappy did, but married by a regular preacher man. My Ila don' want no part of the South."

"But your home is in the South."

"My home be with Ila." He hesitated. "You an' your daddy be good to his people, but not every Master be like that. Ila was born on a plantation. Her folks suffered terrible beatings and ran away. They was captured by slavehunters an' theys probably daid. She not able to forgive the South fer the life she had as a chile. 'Sides Miz Abby say she'll gib me a job on the farm. Your pappy always pay me for my chickens an' the baskets I weave an' I have a tidy sum buried behind my cabin. Maybe me an' Ila buy us a little house in Chambersburg."

"You never told me any of this."

"Weren't my place."

They sat listening to the measured lap of the sea, each lost in his own thoughts as the changeless, yet ever changing, sea crept toward them.

"How can I ever leave this place?" Ford moaned.

"'Caus God, he put you' face on the front o' your haid so's you look forward, not backward."

Ford thought about that profound statement as they lapsed once more into silence. The water was silken, endless white-lace surf breaking against the sandbar and he thought about the sad outline of Cerise's grave and his mother's words of forgiveness for Cerise's actions. He had allowed himself to believe evil of all women because of the hurt caused by one. His contempt for women had stemmed from the easy conquests of girls of easy virtue in his youth, a few lonely housewives, and camp prostitutes. But, he realized now, they were the exception, not the rule. Cerise had been weak, had let her emotions rule her actions. His mother was right—he must forgive and pluck the bitterness from his soul.

A sense of peace filled him and he gave a deep sigh of release. Then he turned to Esau with a grin.

"I think we know the answer to our future, don't we?"

"What dat be?"

"The love of the two women who wait for us."

"I like dat. You think they still waitin'?"

"I know they are. Didn't you just tell me that God would take care of our every need?"

Esau's white teeth gleamed in the darkness. "Dat be some powerful need, Marse Ford."

Ford laughed. How right he was!

"You take dat fine li'l' boy with you?" Esau asked.

"Of course."

Esau smiled. "Miz Abby make him a fine mama. She gots lots a love to gib to him."

The mention of her name brought a knot to Ford's stomach. He and Abby had a lot of problems, but love was not one of them. Then his face grew sober and he turned to look hard into the eyes of this man he trusted so deeply and knew so little . . . Esau . . . a true African with the calm, philosophic power of his race to accept the most radical changes in life without comment or complaint.

"De tide be turnin'," Esau said, jumping to his feet. "We needs to get offa' de bar."

They walked slowly, side by side, until they reached a mound of dunes at the edge of the beach. "You go back to the cabin and get some sleep," Ford said. "I want to sit here and see one more St. Simons sunrise." He chuckled. "And think about putting my face on forward."

"You think you and Miz Abby eber come back here?"

"Maybe . . . maybe someday. Maybe someday the wounds caused by this war, and the reasons for it, will heal. Maybe someday your sons and mine will rebuild the old house together."

Esau sighed. "Neber gonna be like it was though, is it?"

"No—never again."

As Ford waited for the sunrise a shrimp boat glided silently past, saffron lanterns casting a silver sheen on the light chop of the ocean. The horizon was changing now, still black where sea met sky. As the eye traveled upward it began to lighten, charcoal gray at first, then tinged with pink and streaks of crimson as the golden globe of sun appeared on the horizon.

He stared, trying to imprint the colors on his memory. His fingers ached for paint brush and canvas. The horizon became more distinct now. Where scarlet touched the dark sea the pale orange sky cast a warm glow on the pewter water.

Ford's thoughts drifted to his mother. She could live a comfortable life in Savannah. He knew his father had sold all of their field hands early in the war and, with typical Scottish frugality, invested wisely. What money she had left should last her the rest of her life.

Ford felt his pulse quicken as a golden crescent of sun peeked over the tangerine horizon. Gulls, black in silhouette, wheeled in search of their morning breakfast, the north star gleamed brightly in the otherwise starless sky, and the tide moved ever closer across the beach.

Soothing, comforting. Sunrise on St. Simons.

Despite man's ability to destroy material things, the earth remained unchanged. Its inhabitants moved about, always in a state of change, marked by passing time that did not seem to change the sea and the sky.

He had spent the past four years on the torn and bloody battle-fields, yet it seemed only yesterday that he had sat on this same beach with legs outstretched, feeling the relentless sea kiss his toes.

It was daylight now. Wispy clouds glowed pink in the watery sky. The tide was fully in, his footprints on the hard-packed sand washed away. Ford rose and spanked the sand from his damp trousers, suddenly eager for the new day. Someday he would share a St. Simons sunrise with Abby, when or how he did not know, but surely someday. A smile pulled at his lips as he thought of Abby, all doubts suddenly as erased as his footprints in the sand.

As Esau had so ably put it, his land would always be here. Who knew what the future held? He only knew that his immediate future lay with the headstrong woman he loved with every fiber of his being. And he would always carry a love for St. Simons deep in his heart. Anyone who ever saw the moonlight gleaming through the towering oaks or watched the sun set across the endless, silent marsh would never forget her. All through the war the thought of returning home to the island had been uppermost in his mind, yet he realized now that home was people, not places.

Ford began to lope across the hard sand. He and Esau would return to Savannah just as soon as they could book passage, pick up little Michael and his belongings and catch the first steamer bound for Philadelphia. With any luck they should be in Chambersburg by early summer.

* * *

Abby gathered her skirts and settled on a blanket in her favorite spot beside Falling Spring Creek. The little stream ran full from a recent July thunderstorm and the cobalt blue sky billowed with fleecy white clouds. It was a glorious day.

She opened a slim book of poetry and began to read, but her thoughts would not stay on the printed page. With a sigh, she laid the book aside, trailing her hand in the icy water of the brook, her senses alert to the scents and sounds of Brookside: the soothing passage of water over rocks, the hum of bees and buzz of insects, birds chirping, and the smell of new mown grass.

The war had been over for months and Ford had not returned. Except for a hastily penned note posted at Appomattox Court House saying that he was headed south to see his mother and son, she had not heard from him. Had the pull of his island home proved stronger than their love? Yet she still waited for him, hoped he would come.

She closed her eyes, listening to the echoes from the past.

Ford had kissed her for the first time on this very spot, and Abby's mind was a kaleidoscope of memories—of firelight playing on the deep panes of his face, of his soft Southern drawl as he talked of home, of snow lying thick on his eyelashes as he said goodby one last time.

A mother duck paddled down the creek with a brood of ducklings, colts tested spindly legs on greening pastures, young rabbits frolicked in the meadow sun. Tom and Elizabeth were on their honeymoon, Brandon was smitten with a young girl from his Sunday school class, and Sarah had been seeing a young amputee returned from the war. Life was moving on—everyone's but hers.

In the pasture next to the creek Bay Hunter whinnied, running to rest his head on the paddock fence. He whinnied again and Abby turned her head to look toward the source of his interest.

A man was walking down the lane toward her and, with a lurch of her heart, she saw the sun glinting on copper hair. He began to run now, his arms outstretched, her name on his lips. She stumbled to her feet as strong arms crushed her against a starched white shirt. Their lips met, their kiss full of promise.

He released her and she tilted her head to look into his eyes.

"Yes?" he whispered.

"Yes," she answered simply.

THE END